The S

HANS ANDERSEN

Forty-two Stories

HANS ANDERSEN

Forty-two Stories

Translated from
the Danish
by
M. R. JAMES

Illustrated by
ROBIN JACQUES

FABER AND FABER
3 Queen Square
London

First published in 1930
First published in this edition 1968
by Faber and Faber Limited
Reprinted 1971
Printed in Great Britain by
Latimer Trend & Co Ltd Whitstable
All rights reserved

ISBN 0 571 08620 9 (Faber Paper Covered Edition)
ISBN 0 571 01475 5 (Hard Bound Edition)

To

P. W. D. BARRINGTON

Contents

Contents

Preface

Yet another translation of *Hans Andersen*! Nearly forty years ago Mr. Nisbet Bain enumerated ten English versions and added an eleventh of his own, and how many more have appeared since 1893? I have not attempted to ascertain. Why am I adding to the pile? For the simple reason that I am very fond of the originals, and do not think that justice has been done to them by any of the versions I have come across. There are two in particular which appear to hold the field, those of Dr. Dulcken and Mrs. Paull (the relation of one to the other, by the way, would be a curious subject of investigation for the unemployed) and both of these seem to me unfaithful and un-English. Dr. Dulcken was imperfectly acquainted with the English language, and Mrs. Paull with either the Danish, or possibly, the German (for I have long had a suspicion that neither translation was made direct from the Danish). I have accordingly tried to produce a translation from Danish into what I hope is decent English, of some of the most typical of Andersen's stories.

Andersen reckoned his stories as numbering one hundred and fifty-six (among which *What the Moon Saw* is not included). These are contained in five volumes, issued by the Gyldendalske Boghandel at Copenhagen in many reprints, with the original illustrations. This set of books comprises two collections, the first of which—volumes I and II—came out in 1862, the second—volumes III to V —in 1874, the year before Andersen's death. Each collection is provided with an epilogue in which he tells of the occasions and origins of the several stories. The contents of these collections had all appeared before from time to time in small instalments of a few stories apiece, the first of which was published in 1835. The five volumes preserve the chronological order. It has seemed worth while to specify the text I have used, because my reader, if he refers to

Preface

Dulcken or Paull, may perhaps be puzzled at finding those writers adding or omitting sentences from time to time. Their versions were in fact made in Andersen's lifetime, before the issue of the authorized edition, and we may take it that Andersen himself removed or added the clauses in question, which indeed are of no particular importance.

My selection of stories has not been based on any principle but that of choosing the ones I liked best. I have taken a larger number from the first of the five volumes than from any other. It is undeniable that as Andersen went on his stories became less generally interesting. Fewer of them have any link with the older folk-lore; more of them are sketches from ordinary life with no touch of the supernatural; there is, I am afraid, more of the mawkishness which was Andersen's besetting danger, and less—almost none—of the humour of his own special brand. Exceptions, to be sure, there are: the *Beetle*, which is one of the funniest of all the stories, is in the fourth volume. In the fifth, however, I could find but one story which I cared to translate, and that is a highly compressed historical novel. I shall of course be blamed for omissions, as all makers of anthologies must be blamed. Some quite famous stories are left out. From one, *The Marsh King's Daughter*, which has excellent points, I was deterred by its length and the confusedness of its plot. Others, such as the *Story from the Sandhills*, seemed to approach the novel rather than the story. Again, those which, like the *Ice Maiden*, were inspired by Andersen's foreign travels, lack the native flavour.

It will probably be new and interesting to readers to learn what Andersen himself says about the stories contained in this volume. The epilogue mentioned above, is naturally, the source.

The very first story he wrote was a draft of the *Travelling Companion*, which he published in 1829 with some poems, and which I have never seen. "This," says Andersen, "I heard told when a child."

Passing over small details, we read that in 1835 the following stories were published in a little volume: *The Tinder Box*, *Little Claus and Big Claus*, *The Princess on the Pea*, *Little Ida's Flowers*. The first three are fairy-tales he had heard in childhood, the fourth, which I have omitted, he invented.

In 1836 came *Tommelise* (*Thumbelina*) and *The Travelling Com-*

panion, with another. The former is his own invention, the other a very famous folk-tale. In 1837 came *The Little Mermaid* and *The Emperor's New Clothes.* Of the latter he says, "it is of Spanish origin: the whole of the amusing notion we owe to Prince Don Manuel (b. 1277, d. 1347)", and he adds that the idea was also used by Cervantes in a play. *The Dauntless Tin Soldier* he made up. *The Wild Swans* is based on a Danish folk-tale. *The Garden of Eden* "is one of the many stories I heard told when a child, and one that specially appealed to me, so that I wished it were longer: the four winds of the world must have been able to tell much more; the Garden of Eden might have been shown much more clearly. So I now made an essay in this direction." *The Flying Trunk* has its motif from the Thousand and One Nights. *The Storks* is based on popular beliefs and children's rhymes about storks.

The idea of *The Elf of the Rose* is taken from an Italian popular ballad: *The Pig Boy* has some features of an old Danish folk-tale, "told me when a child".

Almost all the tales subsequent to this, he says, are his own composition. He tells us in most cases where they were written: *The Shadow,* for instance, was begun at Naples, where we may imagine the opening scene to be laid. He tells, too, of suggestions which led to the writing of others, and of incidents which he used in them. *The Old House* has two such, the gift of the tin soldier and the little girl dancing to a hymn tune. The burdock forest in *The Happy Family* he saw at Glorup in Funen.

Soup from a Sausage-Peg was, naturally, written round a proverbial phrase. The incident of the old woman in *Something* he heard in Schleswig. *The Girl Who Trod on the Loaf* has a folk-tale for its text.

His account of the origin of *The Beetle* is interesting. "In a number of *Household Words,* Charles Dickens had put together a good many Arabic proverbs and sayings, and among them he called attention to this, 'When the Emperor's horse was shod with gold, the dung beetle held out his leg too'. 'We recommend Hans Christian Andersen (said Dickens in a note) to write a story about this.' I liked the notion, but no story came. Not till nine years later, when I was on a visit . . . and chanced to read Dickens's words again, did the story suddenly blossom out."

Two of the stories which he considered were the best told are

What the Old Man Does is Always Right and *The Snow Man.* The former is a folktale, the latter he wrote at Christmas time.

The last story I have included, *Chicken Greta's Family*, is the only one of its kind that I have admitted. The three marriages of Marie Grubbe are historical, and so is Holberg's meeting with her in Falster.

The foregoing survey leads me to discourse at rather more length upon Andersen's indebtedness to the old folklore of his country. We see that he began by retelling stories that he had heard as a child, though he very soon broke away from this and invented a genre of his own. The number of old stories retold is in fact very small. The list may as well be given in full. The complete storiعs are *The Tinder Box, Little Claus and Big Claus, The Princess on the Pea, The Travelling Companion, The Wild Swans, Klods Hans* (Stupid Hans), *What the Old Man Does is Always Right.*

Those in which an old story is used, but modified or supplemented, are *The Garden of Eden, The Pig Boy, The Girl who Trod on the Loaf.*

Those in which popular beliefs or anecdotes are most conspicuously drawn upon are, *The Storks, Elder Tree Mother, The Elf Hill, The Story of a Mother, The Marsh King's Daughter, The Pool of the Bell, Anne Lisbeth, Something.* Of course, in many of the other stories there are allusions to folklore, but they are slighter. It may be remarked in passing that such beings as the Snow Queen, the Marsh King, and the Ice Maiden seem to be of Andersen's own creation. Yet in his autobiography we find that his father spoke of the Ice Maiden.

Now I have found it interesting to compare Andersen's retelling of the old stories and his use of the old beliefs with the raw material. For that material I have had recourse principally to the amazingly full collections of Danish folktales, local legends and superstitions made by Evald Tang Kristensen between the year 1868 and the beginning of the present century. Words fail me to characterize the patience and diligence of this admirable man, and I cannot rightly estimate the debt which all lovers of ancient lore owe him. The least that can be said of him is that he holds one of the highest places among the successors of the Brothers Grimm.

We do not find—at least, I have not found—in Kristensen's volumes the originals of all Andersen's folktales; but we get a good deal of help from him. I fancy that a glance at the folk-lore of Andersen, in itself, and as illustrated by Kristensen may not be out of place here, but it can be only a glance.

I have not wholly neglected other sources, Thiele, Grundtvig, etc., but Kristensen stands easily first.

For *The Tinder Box* (which has relations with Aladdin) I find an amusing illustration in Kristensen. His story is essentially that of the Pedlar of Swaffham, but contains a relevant incident.

It happened one day at Hamburg that there was a man going to and fro on the bridge as if he was looking for something. A harbour man came by and noticed him and after a while went up to him and asked what he was looking for. Why, he had dreamt that here on the bridge he would find his fortune, and he had been here all day long and no fortune could he see. "Oh, things that like aren't worth worrying about," said the other, "why, some time back I dreamt that down in Jutland there was a part called Salling and in a parish there by the name of Roslev, there was a dale called Lodal, and in it was buried a pot full of money; but of course I'm not going to rove about after any such foolishness. I should have enough on my hands if I did." But the other man bethought him, "There now, I've found my fortune anyway, that I dreamt of," and he trudged off through south Jutland and north Jutland asking where Roslev was. He had a job to make out Lodal, for their way of saying the name was different, but in the end he found Lodal, and there he dug and was lucky enough to hit on the pot. Only (and here we rejoin *The Tinder Box*) on the top of the treasure there sat a dragon, as they mostly do. At first he was very much startled at the sight of it, but then he thought it was no use letting himself be frightened off, so he pulled off his coat and spread it out beside the pot and then took up the beast very carefully and laid it down on the coat. Then he pulled the pot out of the hole and put the dragon back as gently as before in its old place. When he had done that, the dragon said to him, "If you hadn't picked me up so gentle and laid me down so soft, you should have paid dear for your trouble".

We remember the blue checked apron of the witch and how she gave it to the soldier and what he did with it. The moral is that we should take care to be polite to the guardians of treasure.

Little Claus and Big Claus is the common property of all nations, and Andersen has kept very close to the course of the story. *The*

Princess on the Pea I have not found in Kristensen; we know it better, perhaps, as the Sybarite and the Crumpled Roseleaf.

The Travelling Companion is not only one of Andersen's most beautiful achievements in story-telling, but is in itself one of the most noble and famous of all folktales. The basis of the Book of Tobit, used in George Peele's *Old Wives' Tales*, and very clumsily foisted into the chap-book story of Jack the Giant Killer, it has a whole volume of learning devoted to it in the Folklore Society's publications, under the name of the *Grateful Dead*. I have ventured to append to Andersen's telling of it two others from Kristensen, both of which seem to me to have excellent points.

The Wild Swans Andersen heard told in his childhood, but I have not found an exact Danish parallel, though plenty exist in Germany and elsewhere. Andersen has changed the ending. Usually the dumb princess is accused by the queen mother of having eaten her children. Here the archbishop suspects her, with some show of reason, of being in league with the Lamias, whom Andersen perhaps adapted from the Ghouls of the Arabian Nights. He did not much alter the stories of *Klods Hans* and *What the Old Man Did is Always Right*.

The case of the *Garden of Eden* is a complete puzzle to me. We have seen what Andersen says of it—that he heard it when a child—but in what form? Three-quarters of it is plainly of his own devising, and it does not remind me of any folktale; true, we do occasionally find the cave of the winds, and there is a familiar story of the man and his wife who declared that if they had been Adam and Eve they would not have sinned, and who were speedily disabused of that idea; but these hardly suffice to make up Andersen's story.

From the popular form of *The Pig Boy* he only took a fragment; the end of it, as he says, could not be politely told as it stood. There are many versions of it in Kristensen.

Kristensen also has six versions, at least, of *The Girl who Trod on the Loaf*. Here is the first.

A miserably poor couple had a daughter who went to service, had a good place and was very well treated. A child was born at her home, and she got leave to go and see her people, and her mistress gave her half of a large loaf to take with her, seeing they were so badly off. On the way she came to a place where the road was very muddy, and she didn't want to get in a mess; so she put the bread down in the mud and stepped on it. But at once the loaf sank down into the ground and she sank with it up to her middle. There was no way to get her up, and they were obliged to send for the priest, and he conjured her right down. Other versions give the name and place, and one says that the girl's finger was long seen sticking up out of the ground.

We come now to the tales about storks: how they bring the babies, how it is wrong to make game of them, how they talk to one another, how wise they are. Indeed, they are very impressive figures, and whether you watch them on the nest or as they follow the plough, you inevitably think of them as people. So did the ancients. Aelian in his book about animals quotes Alexander of Myndus as telling how the storks in their old age repair to the Fortunate Islands and are changed into men as a reward for their filial kindness, and Aelian adds that he finds it difficult not to believe this, for what profit could Alexander expect from inventing the story? A question to be answered. Later on comes information in a *soi-disant* letter of one Fermes to the Emperor Hadrian, describing the marvels of the East. "There are also men with thighs twelve feet long and the rest of their body likewise twelve feet high. Their arms are white to the shoulders, their calves black, their feet red, their heads round, their noses long. These men at certain seasons of the year are changed into storks, and breed up their young among us every year." Leaping over the centuries, we find two stories in Kristensen, current in our own time.

There was a man mowing, and a stork was keeping close by him, as they will. The man thought he was too close and might peck him, so he drew his pocket-knife and threw it at the stork. It picked up the knife and flew off. Soon after that the man began to feel so queer, he thought he must go travelling, and he travelled about everywhere, and went to so many countries, it was something cruel. At last he got down to Egypt, and there he went into an inn. The landlord asked him what he was travelling about for, but he couldn't give him any good reason, only it was like this: He'd once thrown a knife at a stork, and that weighed on him. Then the landlord got up and went out and fetched his knife and gave it him; and furthermore, said he, "If it hadn't been that I'd hatched out so many young on your father's barn, you'd have come off worse; but

as it is you shall have your knife, and now you can go home quiet."
But he laid it on him that he must never do hurt to a stork again.
So the man went off home again.

A sailor once got to a foreign country where he met a man who
hailed him and said he was much obliged to him; and when the
sailor said he didn't know where they had become acquainted, the
foreigner told him he had brought up thirteen children at his home.
The sailor was very much puzzled, but the other man explained
that for some months of the year he was a man and for some a
stork. And that's the case with all storks; they are men for some
months every year, and that's the reason why nobody will kill them.

Another very fascinating story, full of the native mythology, is
The Elf Hill. It would be tedious to give chapter and verse for all
the details; *The Elf Hill* being propped up on four red posts, the
elf maidens being hollow like troughs, and so on, but one may
spend a few words on the night-raven. What is a night-raven? In
natural history and real life one must suppose it is a *nycticorax*, but
that appears to be a night-heron, which never caused anxiety to
anybody, whereas the poet of the libretto of the music in *Macbeth*
says, "At the night-raven's dismal voice, When others tremble, we
rejoice," and yet more convincingly Benedict in *Much Ado* ob-
serves, "I pray his bad voice bode no mischief. I had as lief have
heard the night-raven, come what plague could have come after
it." Whence we gather that the sound was preternatural and omin-
ous. Had Shakespeare been asked, I think he would have told us
that a night-raven was no ordinary bird. Certainly it is not in Denmark. This is what we learn of it from Kristensen.

A night-raven is a person that has been buried where three boundaries meet, and has done a wrong. There are certain veins or
passages underground that they have to work along before they
can get out. When they do come up they go faring all about. A girl
had been out milking one evening and she heard the night-raven,
and said (something rude) to it. But it came after her, and she had
to hurry to get within doors and shut the door, and in the morning
the door was all over blood.

Another man tells how when he was a boy, late one summer
night he heard a strange bird flying from the westward overhead
with a loud cry, and asked what it was. "Don't you meddle with
that," said a man, "that's the night-raven." "I wasn't meddling

with it, I only asked." Later on he heard the old people say that everyone that put an end to themselves had to be buried where three boundaries met, and they can dig themselves out at the rate of a grain of sand a year, and after many years have gone by they come up and take their flight towards the Holy Sepulchre; but they can only fly a certain distance a year. So perhaps it might be several hundred years before they could get there.

As for the grave-pig, the hell-horse, and the death-lamb, they are all animals that have been buried in the foundations of churches or older sacred places, and their only function is to appear as harbingers of death. Consequently the stories of their manifestations, which are many, are rather monotonous.

In the tale called *Something* the episode of Old Margaret setting fire to her house to save the people on the ice from the coming storm was told to Andersen in Schleswig. It may quite well be true, but it is an ancient story; several forms of it are in Kristensen, e.g., "Some young people were off one evening to a dance on the other side of the fjord, and there was a bridge over, but it had given way. They knew nothing of that, but an old woman who lived hard by the bridge, had noticed it. As they came one after another and tried to cross in the dark, they fell in and were drowned, and the old woman took it so to heart that they should go on losing their lives that way, that she set her house on fire. The men that came next, meaning to cross, stopped at the house to put the fire out, and so, she got a chance to warn them."

There are other stories which might be illustrated in the same way, but probably enough has been said.

I hope it is not necessary to praise Andersen at this time of day. I much prefer to let him speak for himself; I have tried to make him do so a little more simply, a little less clumsily, than my predecessors (to my thinking) have allowed him to do. Whether I shall be found to have interpreted him correctly in every point is another and a painful question. I have done my best, but I have no claim to be considered a finished Danish scholar. My attempt is in the nature of a tribute to a beloved author, an admirable people and a most delightful country.

The Tinder Box

Asoldier came marching away along the highroad. One! two! One! two! He had his knapsack on his back and a sword at his side, for he had been in the wars, and now he was off home. Well, he met an old witch on the highroad. She *was* ugly! Her lower lip hung right down on her chest. Said she, "Good evening, Soldier! What a fine sword, and what a big knapsack you've got! You *are* a proper soldier. Now you shall get as much money as you care to have."

"Much obliged to you, old Witch," said the soldier.

"Do you see that tree?" said the witch, pointing to the tree that stood just by them. "It's quite hollow inside. You climb up to the top of it, and you'll see a hole that you can let yourself slide down and get right to the bottom of the tree. I'll tie a rope round your waist so as I can hoist you up again when you call to me."

"Well, what am I to do at the bottom of the tree?" asked the soldier.

"Get money," said the witch. "You must know that when you get down to the bottom of the tree you'll be in a long passage. It's quite light, there are more than a hundred lamps burning. There you'll see three doors: you can open them, the keys are in them. If you go into the first room, there you'll see in the middle of the floor a big chest, and on it there sits a dog. He's got a pair of eyes as big as a couple of teacups, but you needn't mind that. I'll give you my blue check apron. You can spread it out on the floor, and then go straight up and pick up the dog and put him on the apron. Open the chest and take as many pence as you like. They're all copper; but if you'd rather have silver, you must go into the next room. There sits a dog who's got a pair of eyes as big as millwheels, but you needn't mind about that: put him on my apron and take the money. But, if on the other hand, you'd like gold, you can get that too, and as much of it as you can carry, if you go into the third room. Only the dog that sits on the chest there has two eyes, each of 'em as big as the Round Tower. He's a dog and a half, I can tell you. But you needn't mind that. Just put him on my apron, he'll do nothing to you, and take as much gold out of the chest as you like."

"That's not so bad," said the soldier, "but what am I to give you, old Witch? For of course you'll be wanting something too, I suppose?"

"No," said the witch, "I don't want a single penny. You need only bring me an old tinder box which my granny left behind by mistake the last time she was down there."

"Right! let's have the rope round me," said the soldier.

"Here you are!" said the witch, "and here's my blue check apron."

So the soldier climbed up the tree and let himself plump down into the hole, and there he was, as the witch had said, down in the big passage where all the hundreds of lamps were burning.

Then he opened the first door. Lor! there sat the dog with eyes as big as teacups, and stared at him.

"You're a nice sort of chap!" said the soldier, and put him on the apron and took as many copper pence as he could carry in his pocket, shut the chest, put the dog on the top again and went into the second room. Gracious! there sat the dog with eyes as big as millwheels.

"You shouldn't look at me so hard!" said the soldier. "You might injure your eyesight!" Then he put the dog on the witch's apron; but when he saw the heaps of silver money in the chest, he threw away all the copper money he had got and filled his pocket and his knapsack with nothing but silver. Then he went into the third room. No, now, that was awful! The dog there really had two eyes as big as the Round Tower, and they went round and round in his head like wheels.

"Good evening!" said the soldier, and saluted, for such a dog he never had seen before. But after looking at him for a bit he thought perhaps that would do, and lifted him down on to the floor and opened the chest. Mercy on me, what a lot of gold there was! Enough to pay for all Copenhagen and the cakewomen's sugar pigs, and all the tin soldiers and whips and rocking-horses there were in the whole world. There was money there right enough! So the soldier threw away all the silver shillings he had filled his pockets and his knapsack with, and took gold instead; till all his pockets and his knapsack and his cap and his boots got filled up so that he could hardly walk. Now he *had* got some money! He put the dog back on the chest, slammed the door and then shouted up through the tree:

"Pull me up now, old Witch!"

"Have you got the tinder box?" asked the witch.

"That's true!" said the soldier. "I'd clean forgotten it." So he went and got it. The witch pulled him up and there he was back again on the highroad with his pockets and boots and knapsack and cap full of money.

"What do you want with the tinder box?" asked the soldier.

"That's got nothing to do with you!" said the witch. "You've got your money all right. Just give me the tinder box."

"Fiddlesticks!" said the soldier. "You tell me straight off what you mean to do with it, or I'll out with my sword and cut your head off."

"No!" said the witch.

So the soldier cut her head off. There she lay! But he tied up all his money in her apron and put it on his shoulder in a bundle, shoved the tinder box into his pocket and went straight to the town.

It was a splendid town, and into the finest hotel he went, and ordered the very best rooms and the dishes he liked best, for he was rich, now that he had all that money.

The servant who had to clean his boots certainly thought they were very funny old boots for such a rich gentleman to have; but he hadn't bought any new ones yet. Next day he got boots to walk in and clothes of the smartest. The soldier was now become a fine gentleman, and they told him about all the splendid things that were in their town, and about their King, and what a pretty princess his daughter was.

"Where can one get a sight of her?" the soldier asked.

"Oh, she can't be seen at all," they all said. "She lives in a big copper castle with lots of walls and towers round it. Nobody but the King dares go in and out to her, for it's been foretold that she'll be married to a quite common soldier, and the King can't have that!"

"Well, I'd like enough to see her," thought the soldier; but he couldn't anyhow get leave to do so.

Well, he lived a very merry life, went to the play, drove in the royal gardens, and gave a lot of money to the poor, and that was a nice thing to do; he knew well enough from old times how horrid it was not to have a penny-piece. He was well off now, and had smart clothes and made a number of friends, who all said he was a

good sort and a real gentleman, which pleased the soldier very much. But as every day he laid out money and got none at all back, the end of it was that he had no more than twopence left, and so he had to shift out of the nice rooms where he had lodged, up into a tiny little garret right under the roof, and clean his boots for himself and mend them with a darning needle; and none of his friends came to see him, because there were so many stairs to climb.

The Tinder Box

One evening it was quite dark, and he couldn't even buy himself a candle. But just then he remembered that there was a little stump of one in the tinder box he had got from the hollow tree where the witch had helped him down. He got out the tinder box and the stump of candle, and just as he struck it and the spark flew out of the flint, the door sprang open, and the dog that had eyes as big as teacups, whom he had seen down under the tree, stood before him and said: "What are my lord's orders?" "What's this?" said the soldier, "why, this is a jolly tinder box. Can I get whatever I want like this? Get me some money," said he to the dog, and pop! he was back again with a big bag full of coppers in his mouth. Now the soldier saw what a lovely tinder box this was. If he struck once, the dog came that sat on the chest with the copper money, if he struck twice the one that had the silver came, and if he struck three times the one that had the gold. The soldier moved back now into the nice rooms, got into the smart clothes, and at once all his friends recognized him, and were very fond of him indeed.

Well, once upon a time he thought to himself: "It's a rum thing, so it is, that one can't get a sight of the Princess. They all say she's very pretty, but what's the use of that if she's got to stay all the time inside that big copper castle with all the towers? Can't I anyhow get a sight of her? Where's that tinder box?" So he struck a light, and pop! here comes the dog with the eyes as big as teacups. "I know it's the middle of the night," said the soldier, "all the same, I should dearly like to see the Princess, if it was only for a minute." The dog was off through the door at once, and before the soldier had time to think, here he was again with the Princess: she was sitting on the dog's back, asleep, and she was so pretty, anybody could see she was a real Princess. The soldier couldn't help it, he had to kiss her, for he was a genuine soldier. Then the dog ran back again with the Princess. But when it was morning, and the King and Queen were pouring out their tea, the Princess said she had had such a funny dream that night about a dog and a soldier! She had ridden on the dog, and the soldier had kissed her.

"Upon my word, that's a nice story!" said the Queen.

One of the old Court ladies had to watch at the Princess's bedside the next night, to see if it really was a dream, or what else it might be.

The soldier longed dreadfully to see the beautiful Princess again:

so the dog came in the night and took her and raced off as hard as he could. But the old lady-in-waiting put on water boots and ran after him just as fast, and when she saw them disappear into a big house she thought: "Now I know where it is," and she drew a large cross on the door with a bit of chalk. Then she went home and got into bed, and the dog came back too, with the Princess. But when he saw there was a cross drawn on the door where the soldier lived, he too took a bit of chalk and put crosses on all the doors in the whole town; and that was clever of him, for now the lady-in-waiting couldn't find the right door, since there was a cross on every one of them.

Early in the morning the King and Queen and the old lady-in-waiting and all the officials came out to see where it was that the Princess had been. "Here it is!" said the King, when he saw the first door with a cross on it. "No, it's here, my darling husband," said the Queen who spied the next door with a cross on it.

"But here's one, and there's one!" said everybody. Wherever they looked there were crosses on the doors, so they could see it was no use searching.

The Queen, however, was a very clever woman who knew more than how to drive in a coach. She took her large gold scissors and clipped a big piece of silk into bits, and then made a pretty little bag; this she filled with fine buckwheat flour, tied it to the Princess's back, and when that was done, she cut a little hole in the bag so that the flour could run out all along the way where the Princess went.

At night the dog came again and took the Princess on his back and ran off with her to the soldier, who was very fond of her and would dearly have liked to be a prince, so as to have her for his wife.

The dog never noticed the flour running out all the way from the castle to the soldier's window, where he used to run up the wall with the Princess. So in the morning the King and Queen could see plain enough where their daughter had disappeared to, and they took the soldier and put him in the lock-up.

There he sat. Ugh! how dark and dismal it was; and then they said to him: "To-morrow you're to be hung." It wasn't amusing to be told that; and he'd left his tinder box behind at the hotel. Next morning he could see, through the iron bars of the little window, the people hurrying out of the town to see him hung. He heard the drums and saw the soldiers march off. Everybody was on the move; among them a shoemaker's boy with a leather apron and slippers, going at such a galloping pace that one of his slippers flew off right against the wall where the soldier sat peering out between the iron bars.

"Hi! you shoemaker's boy, you needn't be in such a hurry," said the soldier to him; "nothing'll happen before I come there, but if you don't mind running to the place I lived at and fetching me my tinder box, you shall have fourpence; only you must put your best foot foremost." The shoemaker's boy wanted the fourpence, so he darted off to get the tinder box, and gave it to the soldier, and— now we shall hear what happened!

Outside the town a great gallows had been built, and around it stood the soldiers and many hundred thousands of people. The King and Queen sat on a splendid throne straight opposite the Judge and the whole Privy Council.

The soldier was already on the ladder, but just as they were going to put the rope round his neck, he said that as a criminal was always allowed, before he underwent his punishment, to have one innocent wish granted him, he would dearly like to smoke one pipe of tobacco: it would be the last pipe he smoked in this world. The King wouldn't say no to this, so the soldier took out his tinder box and struck a light. One! two! three! and there were all the dogs; the one with eyes as big as teacups, the one with eyes like millwheels, and the one with eyes as big as the Round Tower.

"Help me now, so as I shan't be hung," said the soldier; and the dogs dashed at the judges, and all the council; took one by the legs and another by the nose and threw them yards and yards up in the air, so that they tumbled down and were broken all to bits.

"I won't!" said the King; but the biggest dog took him and the Queen too, and threw them after all the rest. Then the soldiers took fright, and all the people called out: "Dear good soldier, you shall be our King and have the lovely Princess." So they put the soldier into the King's coach, and all three dogs danced in front and shouted "hurrah!" and the boys whistled on their fingers, and the soldiers presented arms. The Princess was brought out of the copper castle and made Queen, and very much pleased she was. The wedding lasted eight days, and the dogs sat at table and made great eyes.

Little Claus and Big Claus

There were two men in a town, who both had the same name, both were called Claus; but one of them owned four horses, and the other only one. Now, in order to be able to tell one from the other, people called the one who had four horses Big Claus, and the one who had only one horse, Little Claus. Now we must hear how these two got on, for it makes a regular story.

All the week through, Little Claus had to plough for Big Claus, and lend him his one horse; and in return Big Claus used to help him with all his four horses, but only once a week, and that was on the Sunday. Hurrah! how Little Claus did crack his whip over all the five horses, that were as good as his own for that one day. The sun shone bright, and all the bells in the church tower rang for church, and the people were dressed out and going past with their hymn books under their arms to hear the clergyman preach; and they looked at Little Claus ploughing away with five horses , and he was so pleased, he cracked his whip again and called out, "Hup, all my horses!"

"You mustn't say that," said Big Claus, "it's only the one horse that's yours."

But again, when somebody else went by going to church, Little Claus forgot that he wasn't to say that, and he called out, "Hup, all my horses!"

"Now then, I'll ask you kindly to leave off," said Big Claus. "For if you say that once more I shall knock your horse on the head, so that it'll die on the spot, and that'll be the end of it."

"To be sure, I won't say it any more," said Little Claus. But when some people went by and nodded him good morning, he was delighted; and he thought it looked so fine, his having five horses to plough his field with, that he cracked his whip and called out, "Hup, all my horses!"

"I'll hup your horses," said Big Claus, and he took the tether-peg mallet and hit Little Claus's only horse on the forehead, so that it tumbled down quite dead.

"Oh! now I haven't got any horse at all!" said Little Claus, and began to cry. Later on he flayed the horse, took the hide and let it dry well in the open air, and then stuffed it into a bag which he put on his back, and went off to the town to sell his horse-hide.

He had a long way to go, which took him through a large dark forest, and there a terrible bad storm came on and he quite lost himself, and before he could find the right road, it was evening, and too late to get either to the town or home again before night fell.

Hard by the road there stood a big farmhouse. The shutters outside were closed in front of the windows, but still the light shone out at the top of them. "I expect I can get leave to stay there for the night," thought Little Claus, and he went and knocked at the door.

The farmer's wife opened the door, but when she heard what he wanted, she told him to go along: her husband wasn't at home and she wouldn't take in any strangers.

"Oh, well then, I must lie out of doors," said Little Claus, and the farmer's wife shut the door in his face.

Close by there stood a large haystack, and between it and the house a little shed had been built, with a flat roof of thatch.

"I can lie up there," said Little Claus when he saw the roof. "It makes a beautiful bed. I don't suppose the stork will fly down and peck my legs"; for there was a live stork up on the roof, where it had its nest.

So Little Claus climbed up on the shed, and there he lay down, and rolled about in order to lie comfortably. The wooden shutters in front of the windows did not reach up to the top of them; so he could look right into the room. There was a big table laid out with wine and a roast joint, and such a splendid fish! The farmer's wife and the parish clerk were sitting at table, and nobody else; and she helped him to wine, and he helped himself to fish: a thing he was very fond of.

"If only one could get some of that!" said Little Claus, and poked his head right close to the window. Gracious! what a beautiful cake he could see in there! Really it was a feast.

Just then he heard someone coming, riding along the highroad towards the house. It was the woman's husband coming home.

He was an excellent man, but he had this very odd ailment, that he could never bear to see a parish clerk; if he caught sight of a parish clerk he went quite mad with rage, and this was why the clerk had come in to say how-do-you-do to the woman, because he knew her husband wasn't at home; and so the kind woman had got out all the best victuals she had for him. But now when they heard the husband coming they were terribly frightened, and the woman begged the clerk to creep into a great empty chest that stood in the corner; and so he did, for he knew well enough that the poor husband couldn't bear to see parish clerks. The woman made haste to hide all the good victuals and the wine in her oven, for if her husband had caught sight of them he would have been certain to ask what it all meant.

"Ah dear!" sighed Little Claus on the top of the shed, when he saw all the victuals taken away. "Is there somebody up there?" asked the farmer, and looked up at Little Claus. "What are you lying up there for? Better come indoors along of me."

Then Little Claus told him how he had lost his way, and asked if he might stay there for the night.

"Yes, to be sure," said the farmer, "but first we must have a bit to eat."

The wife greeted them very friendly, both of them, and spread a long table and gave them a large dish of porridge. The farmer was hungry and ate with a fine appetite, but Little Claus couldn't help thinking about the beautiful roast joint and fish and cake, which he knew were there in the oven. He had laid his sack with the horse's hide in it under the table beside his feet; we remember, of course, that that was what he had come away from home with, to sell it in the town. He had no taste for the porridge, and so he trod on his bag, and the dry hide in the sack squeaked quite loud.

"Hush," said Little Claus to his sack; but at the same moment he trod on it again, and it squeaked much louder than before.

"Why, what have you got in your bag?" asked the farmer. "Oh, that's a wizard," said Little Claus. "He's saying that we mustn't eat porridge, for he's conjured the whole oven full of roast meat and fish and cake."

"What's that?" said the farmer, and in a trice opened the oven and saw in it all the good victuals which his wife had hidden there, but which—as he thought—the wizard in the bag had conjured into it. His wife durstn't say anything, but put the food on the table at once, and so they had their fill of the fish and the joint and the cake. Directly after, Little Claus trod on his bag again and made the hide speak.

"What's he saying now?" asked the farmer. "He's saying", said Little Claus, "that he's also conjured us up three bottles of wine, and they are in the oven too." Then the wife had to bring out the wine she had hidden, and the farmer drank and got quite mérry. Such a wizard as Little Claus had in the bag he would dearly like to have.

"Can he call up the devil, too?" asked the farmer. "I'd like to see him, for I'm in spirits now."

"Yes," said Little Claus, "my wizard can do anything I require. Can't you?" he asked, and he trod on the bag and it squeaked. "D'you hear? he says 'Yes'. But the devil is very ugly to look at, and I wouldn't trouble about seeing him."

"Oh, I'm not a bit afraid. What do you suppose he looks like?"

"Why, he'll show himself for all the world like a parish clerk."

"Ugh!" said the farmer, "that is horrid; you must know that I can't abide to see parish clerks. But it don't matter; so long as I know it's the devil, I can put up with it better. I've got some courage in me, only he mustn't come too near me."

"Now I'll ask my wizard," said Little Claus. He trod on the bag and held his ear to it.

"What does he say?"

He says, "You can go over there and open the chest that stands in the corner, and you'll see the devil, where he's hiding, but you must hold the lid so that he can't slip out." "You come and help me hold it," said the farmer, and went over to the chest where his wife had hidden the real parish clerk, who was sitting there in a great fright.

The farmer lifted the lid a little and peeped in under it. "Ugh!" he screamed, and jumped back. "Yes, I did see him, and he's for all the world like our clerk. No, now, that was a dreadful sight!"

They had to have a drink on the strength of it, and still they sat and drank till late on at night.

"You must sell me that wizard," said the farmer. "Ask what you like for him. Why, I'd give you a whole bushel of money straight off."

"No, I can't do that," said Little Claus; "just think what profit I can make out of that wizard."

"Oh dear! I do so want to have him," said the farmer, and kept on begging.

"Well," said Little Claus at last, "as you've been so kind as to give me a night's lodging, I don't mind. You shall have the wizard for a bushel of money; but I must have full measure."

"So you shall," said the farmer, "but you must take that chest there away with you. I won't have it an hour longer in the house. Who's to know if he isn't sitting in it still?" Little Claus gave the farmer his sack with the dry hide in it, and got a whole bushel of money, full measure, in exchange. The farmer gave him a big wheel-barrow into the bargain to wheel off his money and the box.

"Good-bye," said Little Claus, and wheeled the barrow off with his money and the big chest in which the clerk was still sitting. On the other side of the forest there was a broad deep river, running so swift that it was hardly possible to swim against the stream. A fine new bridge had been built over it, and Little Claus stopped half-way across it and said, quite loud, so that the clerk in the chest could hear:

"Come, what do I want with this silly chest; it's as heavy as if it was full of stones! I'm quite tired of wheeling it. I'll heave it out into the river: if it floats down to me at home, that's all right, and if it doesn't, why, I don't mind." With that he took hold of it with one hand and lifted it a little as if he was going to throw it down into the water.

"No! Stop!" cried the clerk inside the chest. "Do let me get out!"

"O—oh," said Little Claus, pretending to be frightened. "He's in there still! I must get him into the river this minute and drown him." "O no, O no!" cried the clerk, "I'll give you a whole bushel of money if you'll only stop."

"Why, that's a different affair," said Little Claus, and he opened the chest. The clerk crept out quickly and pushed the empty chest over into the river, and went off to his house, where Little Claus got a whole bushel of money. He'd got one already from the far-mer, so now he had his wheelbarrow quite full of money.

"Look here, I've got a very fine price for that horse," said he to himself when he got home to his own room and emptied all the money out in a great heap in the middle of the floor. "Big Claus won't like it a bit when he gets to know how rich I've become by the means of my one horse; but I can't tell him right out, all the same."

With that he sent a boy over to Big Claus to borrow a bushel measure.

"What ever does he want with that?" thought Big Claus, and he smeared some tar on the bottom of it, so that some of what was being measured should stick to it. And so it did, for when he got the measure back there were three new silver groats sticking there.

"What's the meaning of this?" said Big Claus. He ran straight across to the Little one. "Where did you get all that money from?" "Oh, that was for my horse's hide, I sold it yesterday." "Upon my word, that was a good price," said Big Claus. He ran off home, took an axe, knocked all his four horses on the head, got the hides off them, and drove to the town with them. "Hides! Hides! Who'll buy hides?" he went shouting through the streets.

All the shoemakers and tanners came running up and asked what he wanted for them.

"A bushel of money, apiece," said Big Claus.

"Are you mad?" they all said. "Do you think we've got money in bushels?"

"Hides! Hides! Who'll buy hides?" he shouted again, and to everyone who asked what the hides cost, he answered: "A bushel of money!" "He wants to make fools of us," they all said; and then all the shoemakers got out their straps and the tanners their leather aprons and began to thrash Big Claus.

"Hides! Hides!" they sneered at him. "Yes, we'll give you a hide with nice red stripes on it. Out of the town with him," they cried, and Big Claus had to make off as quick as ever he could, he'd never been so thrashed in his life. "Very well," said he when he got home, "Little Claus shall be paid out for this. I'll kill him for it."

But now, at Little Claus's house it so happened that his old grandmother had died; true enough she had been very cross and nasty to him, but all the same he was very much grieved, and took the old woman and laid her in his own warm bed to see if she might possibly come to life again. She should lie there all night, and he would sit over in the corner on a stool and sleep there, as he had often done before. And as he sat there in the night the door opened and Big Claus came in with an axe. He knew well enough where

Little Claus's bed stood, and went straight to it and hit the dead grandmother on the head, thinking it was Little Claus.

"There now," said he, "you won't make a fool of me again!" and off he went home.

"Now that's a real bad man," said Little Claus, "he meant to kill me; it's lucky for old mother that she was dead already, else he'd have had the life out of her." Then he dressed the old grandmother in her Sunday clothes, borrowed a horse of his neighbour, harnessed it to his cart and set the old grandmother up in the back seat so as she couldn't fall out when he drove; and then they rattled off through the forest. When the sun rose they were just by a big inn, and there Little Claus pulled up and went in to get something to eat.

The landlord had ever so much money, and he was a good sort of man, but very hot tempered, as if he was full of pepper and snuff.

"Good morning," said he to Little Claus, "you've got your best clothes on early to-day."

"Yes," said Little Claus, "I'm off to town with my old grandmother. She's sitting out there in the cart; I can't get her to come indoors. Would you mind taking her a glass of mead? But you must speak to her pretty loud, for she's hard of hearing."

"Yes, that I will," said the landlord, and he poured out a large glass of mead and went out with it to the dead grandmother, who was set up in the cart.

"Here's a glass of mead from your son," said the landlord; but the dead woman didn't say a word: she sat quite still.

"Can't you hear?" shouted the landlord, as loud as he could. "Here's a glass of mead from your son!"

Once more he shouted it out, and once again after that, but as she didn't stir at all from her seat, he lost his temper and threw the glass straight in her face. The mead ran down her nose and she tumbled over, backwards into the cart, for she was only propped up, and not tied fast.

"Now, now!" shouted Little Claus, rushing out of the inn and seizing hold of the landlord by the collar. "You've been and killed my grandmother! Just look! There's a great hole in her forehead!"

"Oh, dear, what a sad business!" cried the landlord, wringing his hands, "it all comes of me being so hot tempered. My dear friend Little Claus, I'll give you a whole bushel of money and have your

34

grandmother buried as if she was my own, if only you'll hold your tongue; else they'll cut my head off, and that is so unpleasant!"

So Little Claus got a whole bushel of money, and the landlord buried his old grandmother as if she'd been his own.

Now when Little Claus got home again with all the money, he sent his boy over at once to Big Claus to ask if he would kindly lend him a bushel measure. "What's the meaning of this?" said Big Claus. "Haven't I killed him? I must look into this myself." So he went across to Little Claus with the bushel.

"Why, where did you get all that money from?" he asked, and opened his eyes wide when he saw all that had come in.

"It was my grandmother you killed, not me," said Little Claus. "I've just sold her, and got a bushel of money for her."

"My word, that's a good price," said Big Claus; and he hurried off home, took an axe and killed his own old grandmother at once, put her in his cart, drove to town to where the doctor lived, and asked if he wanted to buy a dead person.

"Who is it, and where did you get it from?" asked the doctor. "It's my grandmother," said Big Claus "I've killed her to get a bushel of money."

"God be good to us," said the doctor, "that's a madman's talk! For goodness' sake don't say such things. You might lose your head." And then he told him straight out what a fearfully wicked thing it was that he had done, and what a bad man he was, and how he deserved to be punished, and Big Claus got so frightened that he darted out of the doctor's shop and into the cart, whipped up the horses and hurried home. But the doctor and everyone else thought he must be mad, so they let him drive off whither he would.

"You shall be paid out for this," said Big Claus as he drove along the highroad. "Yes, you shall be paid out for this, Little Claus." And as soon as ever he got home, he took the biggest sack he could find, went across to Little Claus and said: "Now you've fooled me again! First I killed my horses, and then my old grandmother! It's all your fault, but never again shall you make a fool of me." With that he seized Little Claus by the waist, stuffed him into his sack, threw it over his shoulder and called out to him: "Now I'm off to drown you!"

There was a long bit to go before he came to the river, and Little Claus was not over light to carry. The road went close by the church where the organ was playing and the people singing very beautifully. So Big Claus put down his sack with Little Claus in it beside the church door, and thought to himself it might be quite a good thing to go in and listen to a hymn before he went any further. Little Claus couldn't get away, and everybody was in church; so in he went. "Oh dear! Oh dear!" sighed Little Claus inside the sack. He turned about and about, but he couldn't manage to get the string untied. At that moment there came by an old drover with snow-white hair and a great walking stick in his hand. Before him was a whole drove of cows and steers, and they ran against the sack where Little Claus was, so that it tumbled over.

"Oh dear!" sighed Little Claus, "I'm quite young, and I've got to go to heaven already!"

"And poor old me," said the drover, "I'm quite old and I can't get there yet!"

"Open the sack," cried Little Claus, "creep in instead of me, and you'll get to heaven straight off!"

"Yes, that I will, and glad to do it," said the drover. He untied the sack for Little Claus, who jumped out at once. "You'll take care of the cattle, won't you?" said the old man, creeping into the sack, which Little Claus tied up, and then went on his way with all the cows and steers.

Soon after, Big Claus came out of the church, loaded the sack on his shoulders again, and thought, rightly enough, it had become quite light, for the old drover weighed not more than half as much as Little Claus. "How light he has become to carry! That's just because I've been and listened to a hymn!" So on he went to the river, which was deep and broad, threw the sack and the old drover out into the water and shouted after him (for of course he thought it was Little Claus): "There now! You shan't make a fool of me any more."

Then he set off home: but when he got to where the roads crossed he met Little Claus coming along with all his cattle. "What's this?" said Big Claus. "Haven't I drowned you?"

"Yes," said Little Claus, "you threw me into the water all right not half an hour ago!"

"But where have you got all those lovely cattle from?" asked Big Claus.

"Why, they're sea cattle," said Little Claus. "I'll tell you the whole story, and very much obliged to you I am for drowning me. I'm on the top now, properly rich I am, I can tell you. I was terribly frightened when I was lying in the sack, and the wind whistled about my ears when you threw me down off the bridge into the cold water. I sank straight to the bottom, but I didn't bump myself, for down there the finest of soft grass grows, and on to that I fell, and the sack came open at once, and the most lovely girl in pure white clothes and with a green wreath on her wet hair, took my hand and said: 'Is that you, Little Claus? Here's some cattle for you to begin with, and four miles further up the road there's another whole drove waiting, which I'll make you a present of!' Then I made out that the river was a broad highway for the sea people. They were walking along down at the bottom and driving straight up from the sea, right inland to where the river comes to an end. It was so pleasant there with flowers, and the freshest of grass! And the fishes that swam in the water, they darted past my ears like the birds in the air up here. Dear! what fine folk there were, and what a lot of cattle going about along ditches and fences!"

"But why have you come up so quick to us again?" asked Big Claus. "I wouldn't have done that if it was so nice down there." "Why," said Little Claus, "that was just my cleverness! You recollect I told you the sea girl said that four miles along the road (and by the road she meant the river, for she can't get along any other way) there was a whole drove more of cattle for me; but I know how the river goes in bends, first this way and then that way, it's a regular roundabout. No, you can make it shorter by coming up on land if you can, and driving across country to the river again. I shall save almost a couple of miles and get to my sea cattle all the sooner."

"Oh, you are a lucky man!" said Big Claus. "Do you think I should get some sea cattle too if I got down to the bottom of the river?"

"Why, I should think so," said Little Claus. "But I can't carry you to the river in the sack, you're too heavy for me. If you'll walk there yourself and get into the bag, I'll throw you in with the greatest of pleasure."

"I'll be much obliged to you," said Big Claus, "but if I don't get any sea cattle when I get down there, I shall give you a thrashing, you may depend upon that."

"Oh no, don't be so unkind!" So they went across to the river. When the cattle, which were thirsty, saw the water, they ran as fast as they could to get down there and drink.

"Look what a hurry they're in," said Little Claus, "they're longing to get to the bottom again."

"Yes, but you've got to help me first," said Big Claus, "else you'll get a thrashing!" So he crept into a big sack that had lain on the back of one of the steers. "Just put a stone in it, or I'm afraid I shan't sink," said Big Claus.

"It'll sink all right," said Little Claus; but all the same he put a big stone in the sack, tied the string tight and gave it a push. Splash! There lay Big Claus in the river and sank to the bottom straight.

"I'm *afraid* he won't find those cattle," said Little Claus; and drove off home with what he had.

The Princess on the Pea

Once upon a time there was a Prince, and he wanted to get himself a Princess; but she must be a proper Princess. So he travelled all the world over to find one, but everywhere there was some obstacle. There were Princesses enough, but whether they were real proper princesses he could not be quite certain; there was always something not perfectly correct. So he came back home and was very much cast down, for he did so want to get a real princess.

One evening there was a terrible storm; it lightened and thun-

dered and the rain poured down; it was quite fearful. There came
a knock at the town gate and the old King went off to open it.

It was a Princess that was standing outside: but gracious! what a
figure she was with the rain and bad weather! The water ran all
down her hair and her clothes and in at the toes of her shoes and
out at the heels; and she said she was a real Princess.

"Ah, we'll find that out right enough," thought the old Queen
to herself, but she didn't say anything; she went into the bedroom,
took all the clothes off the bed and laid one dried pea on the bottom
of the bed. Then she took twenty mattresses and laid them on top
of the pea, and then twenty eiderdowns on top of the mattresses,
and there the Princess was to sleep that night.

39

In the morning they asked her how she had slept, "Oh, dreadfully badly," said the Princess; "I hardly closed my eyes the whole night! Goodness knows what there was in the bed! There was something hard I lay on that has made me black and blue all over! It's quite dreadful."

Then they could see that this was a proper Princess, since she had felt the pea through the twenty mattresses and the twenty eiderdowns. Nobody could possibly have such a tender skin but a real Princess.

So the Prince took her to wife, for now he knew that he had got a proper Princess; and the pea was put in the treasure chamber, where it is still to be seen, unless somebody has taken it away.

Now there is a proper story for you.

Thumbelina

O nce upon a time there was a woman who very much wanted to have a little tiny child, but didn't know where she could get one from; so she went to an old witch and said to her: "I do so want to have a little child; will you kindly tell me where I can get one?"

"Oh, we can manage that," said the witch, "there's a barleycorn for you! it isn't the kind that grows in the farmers' fields or that the chickens have to eat; just put it in a flower-pot, and you shall see what you shall see."

"Much obliged," said the woman, and gave the witch twelve

pence, and went home and planted the barleycorn; and very soon a fine large flower came up which looked just like a tulip, but the petals were closed up tight as if it were still a bud.

"That's a charming flower," said the woman, and gave it a kiss on its pretty red and yellow petals. But just as she kissed it the flower gave a loud crack and opened. You could see it was a real tulip, only right in the middle of it, on the green stool that is there, sat a tiny little girl, as delicate and pretty as could be. She was only a thumb-joint long, so she was called Thumbelina. She was given a splendid lacquered walnut shell for a cradle, blue violet leaves for mattresses, and a rose-leaf for a counterpane. There she slept at night, but in the daytime she played about on the table, where the woman had put a plate, round which she put a whole wreath of flowers with their stalks in the water; and on the water floated a large tulip-leaf on which Thumbelina could sit and sail from one side of the plate to the other. She had two white horse-hairs to row with. It was really beautiful to see her; she could sing too—oh, so delicately and prettily as no one had ever heard.

One night, as she lay in her pretty bed, a horrid Toad came hopping in at the window, which had a broken pane. The Toad was ugly and big and wet, and hopped right down on to the table where Thumbelina lay asleep under her rose-leaf.

"That would make a lovely wife for my son," said the Toad; so she took hold of the walnut-shell where Thumbelina slept and hopped off with her through the window and down into the garden. Through it flowed a big broad stream, but just at the edge it was marshy and muddy, and there the Toad lived with her son. Ugh! he was ugly and horrid too, just like his mother. "Koäx, koäx, brekke-ke-kex," was all he could say when he saw the pretty little girl in the walnut-shell. "Don't talk so loud, you'll wake her," said the old Toad, "and she might run away from us now, for she's as light as a swansdown feather. We'll put her out in the river on one of the broad water-lily leaves. It'll be like an island for her, she's so little and light. She can run about there while we get the drawing-room under the mud ready for you two to make your home in."

There were a great many water-lilies growing out in the stream, with broad green leaves that looked as if they were floating on the water; and the leaf that was furthest out was also the biggest of all. To this leaf the old Toad swam out and put the walnut-shell with

Thumbelina on it. The poor little wretch woke up very early in the morning, and when she saw where she was, she began to cry—oh, so bitterly!—for there was water all round the big leaf and she couldn't possibly get to land.

The old Toad stayed down in the mud and set about decorating her room with rushes and yellow water-lily buds, so as to make it nice and neat for her new daughter-in-law; and then she swam out with her ugly son to the leaf where Thumbelina stood; they were going to fetch her pretty bed and put it up in the bridal chamber before she came there herself. The old Toad curtsied low in the water before her and said: "I present my son to you. He is going to be your husband, and you will have a delightful life with him down in the mud."

"Koäx, koäx, brekke-ke-kex," was all the son could say.

So they took the beautiful little bed and swam off with it while Thumbelina sat all alone on the green leaf crying, for she didn't want to live with the horrid Toad or have her ugly son for a husband. The little fishes, swimming beneath in the water, had seen the Toad and heard what she said, so they put their heads up; they wanted to see the little girl. But as soon as they saw her, they thought her so pretty that it grieved them very much to think that she had to go down to the ugly Toad. No, that could never be. So they swarmed together down in the water, all round the green stalk that held the leaf she was on, and gnawed it through with their teeth; so the leaf went floating down the stream, and bore Thumbelina far, far away, where the Toad could not go. Thumbelina sailed past many places, and the little birds in the bushes saw her and sang, "What a pretty little maid!" The leaf floated further and further away with her, and thus it was that Thumbelina went on her travels.

A beautiful little white butterfly kept flying round her, and at last settled on the leaf, for it took a fancy to Thumbelina, and she was very happy, for now the Toad could not get at her, and everything was beautiful where she was sailing: the sun shone on the water and made it glitter like gold. She took her sash and tied one end of it to the butterfly, and the other end she fastened to the leaf, and it went along much faster with her, for of course she was standing on the leaf. Just then a large Cockchafer came flying by and caught sight of her, and in an instant he had grasped her slender body in his claws, and flew up into a tree with her. But the green leaf went floating downstream and the butterfly with it, for he was tied to the leaf and could not get loose.

Goodness! how frightened poor Thumbelina was when the Cockchafer flew up into the tree with her. But she was most of all grieved for the pretty white butterfly which she had tied to the leaf, for unless it got loose it would be starved to death. However, the Cockchafer cared nothing about that. He alighted with her on the largest green leaf on the tree, and gave her honey out of the flowers to eat, and told her she was very pretty, though she wasn't in the least like a Cockchafer. Later on all the other Cockchafers that lived in the tree came and paid calls. They looked at Thumbelina, and the young lady Cockchafers brushed their feelers and said: "Why, she's only got two legs! a wretched sight!" "She's got no feelers," they said. "She's quite thin in the waist. Dreadful! She looks just like a human being! How ugly she is!" said all the lady Cockchafers; yet Thumbelina was as pretty as could be, and so thought the Cockchafer who had carried her off; but when all the rest said she was horrid, he came to think so too at last, and wouldn't have anything to do with her, she could go wherever she chose. They flew down from the tree with her and put her on a daisy, and there she sat and cried because she was so ugly that the Cockchafers wouldn't keep her—and yet she was the prettiest thing you could imagine, and delicate and bright like the loveliest rose-leaf. All the summer through poor Thumbelina lived quite alone in the big wood. She plaited herself a bed of green stalks and hung it up under a large dock leaf so as to be out of the rain. She picked the honey out of the flowers and ate it, and she drank the dew which lay every morning on the leaves. There she spent the summer and the autumn; but then came winter, the long cold winter. All the birds that had sung so prettily to her, flew their way; the trees and flowers withered, and the big dock-leaf under which she had lived rolled up and turned to nothing but a yellow dry stalk, and she was terribly cold, for her clothes were in rags, and she herself was so little and delicate. Poor Thumbelina! She was like to be frozen to death! Then it began to snow, and every snowflake that fell on her was just as when anybody throws a whole shovelful on any of us— for we are big, and Thumbelina was only an inch high. So she wrapped herself up in a dead leaf, but there was no warmth in it, and she shivered with the cold.

Just outside the wood where she was now, lay a large cornfield, but the corn had long been off it, and only the bare dry stubble stuck out of the frozen ground. This was like a whole forest for her to get through, and oh! how she did shiver with cold! At last she came to a Fieldmouse's door, which was a little hole down among the stubble. There the Fieldmouse lived snug and happy, with a whole room full of corn, a lovely kitchen and dining-room. Poor Thumbelina went up to the door just like any little beggar girl, and asked for a little bit of barleycorn, for she hadn't had anything whatever to eat for two days. "Poor little thing," said the Field-mouse, who was at heart a kind old fieldmouse, "you come into my warm room and have dinner with me." And as she had taken a liking to Thumbelina she said: "You can stay the winter with me and welcome, only you'll have to keep my room nice and clean and tell me stories, for I'm very fond of them." And Thumbelina did as the kind old Fieldmouse asked, and had a very pleasant time of it.

"We shall soon be having a visitor," said the Fieldmouse. "My neighbour calls on me every weekday; he's even better housed than I am; his rooms are big, and he goes about in such a beautiful black velvet coat! Ah, if only you could get him for a husband! You would be well set up. But he can't see. Mind and tell him the very prettiest stories you know!" But Thumbelina didn't care much about this—she didn't want to marry the neighbour, for he was a Mole. He came and paid a call in his black velvet coat. He was very well off and very learned, the Fieldmouse said: "His mansion was more than twenty times the size of hers, and he was very well in-formed"; but he didn't like the sun and the pretty flowers, and abused them, for he had never seen them. Thumbelina had to sing, and she sang both "Cockchafer, Cockchafer fly away home" and also "The monk walked in the meadow", and the Mole fell in love with her for her pretty voice; but said nothing about it, for he was a very cautious man.

He had recently dug a big passage through the earth from his house to theirs, and gave the Fieldmouse and Thumbelina leave to walk there whenever they liked; but he begged them not to be frightened at the dead bird that lay in the passage—a whole bird with beak and feathers which had certainly been dead only a little time, at the beginning of the winter, and was now buried just where he had made his passage.

The Mole took a bit of touchwood in his mouth (for that shines like fire in the dark) and went in front and lighted them along through the long dark passage, and when they got to where the dead bird lay, the Mole pushed his broad back against the ceiling and lifted the earth so that there was a big hole which let in the light: in the middle of this floor lay a dead swallow with its pretty wings close against its sides and its legs and head down in among its feathers: the poor bird had certainly died of cold. Thumbelina was very sorry for it; she was fond of all the little birds that had sung and twittered so prettily to her all the summer long; but the Mole kicked it with his short leg and said: "He won't be squeaking any more! It must be wretched to be born a little bird! Thank God, none of my children will be like that. A bird has nothing but its twit, twit, and is bound to starve to death in winter."

"Yes, you may well say so as a reasonable man," said the Field-mouse; "what has the bird to show for all its twit, twit, when winter comes? Why, it has to starve and freeze, and yet they're so proud about it!"

Thumbelina said nothing, but when the others turned their backs on the bird, she stooped down and parted the feathers that covered its head, and kissed its dead eyes. "Perhaps this was the one that sang to me so prettily in the summer," she thought; "what a lot of pleasure it gave me, the dear little bird."

The Mole now stopped up the hole through which the daylight shone in, and saw the ladies home. But that night Thumbelina couldn't sleep at all, so she got out of bed and plaited a nice large coverlet of hay, and carried it down and spread it about the dead bird, and then she laid some soft cotton wool she had found in the Fieldmouse's room, on the bird's sides, so that it might lie warmly on the cold ground. "Farewell, you pretty little bird," said she; "farewell, and thank you for your lovely singing in the summer, when all the trees were green and the sun shone so hot on us." She laid her head against the bird's heart, and got quite a fright all at once, for it seemed as if something was knocking inside! It was the bird's heart. The bird was not dead; it was only in a swoon, and now that it was warmed, it came to life again.

In autumn, you know, all the swallows fly away to the warm countries, but if there is one that lags behind it gets frozen so that it tumbles down quite dead and lies where it fell, and the cold snow covers it over.

Thumbelina really shivered, so frightened was she: for the bird was enormously big compared with her who was only an inch high: but she took courage and laid the cotton wool closer about the poor swallow, and folded a peppermint leaf, that she had for her own counterpane, and put it over the bird's head. Next night she stole down to it again, and this time it was quite alive, but so weak that it could only open its eyes for a second, and look at Thumbelina who stood there with a bit of touchwood in her hand, for other light she had none.

"Thank you, you pretty little child," the sick swallow said to her, "I've been beautifully warmed. Soon I shall get back my strength and be able to fly about again in the warm sun outside."

"Oh," said Thumbelina, "but it's dreadfully cold outside, snowing and freezing! You must stay in your warm bed, I'll nurse you, be sure!" Then she brought the swallow some water in the leaf of a plant, and it drank, and told her how it had hurt its wing on a thorn bush, and so couldn't fly as well as the other swallows when they set out to fly, far, far away to the warm countries. At last it had fallen to the ground, but it couldn't remember any more and didn't know in the least how it had got to where it was.

All the winter it stayed down there, and Thumbelina was very kind to it, and got very fond of it, but neither the Mole nor the Fieldmouse heard anything whatever about it; they disliked the poor wretched swallow.

As soon as spring came and the sun's warmth got into the ground, the swallow said good-bye to Thumbelina, who opened the hole which the Mole had made above. The sun shone in delightfully, and the swallow asked if Thumbelina would not come with it: she could sit on its back and they would fly away into the green wood. But Thumbelina knew that it would grieve the old Fieldmouse, if she left her like that. "No, I can't," said Thumbelina. "Good-bye, good-bye, you kind pretty maid," said the swallow, and flew out into the sunshine. Thumbelina stood looking after it, and the water stood in her eyes, for she was very fond of the poor swallow.

"Twit, twit," sang the bird, and flew off into the greenwood.

Thumbelina was very unhappy; she got no chance to go out into the warm sunshine, because the corn that had been sown in the field over the Fieldmouse's house was grown tall, and made a thick forest for the poor little maid, no more than an inch high.

"This summer you must make your trousseau," the Fieldmouse told her; for their neighbour, the tiresome Mole in the black velvet coat, had proposed to her. "You shall have both woollen and linen —something to sit in and to lie on when you are the Mole's wife." So Thumbelina had to spin on the distaff, and the Fieldmouse hired four spiders to spin and weave day and night. Every evening the Mole called in, and they always talked about how when summer was over the sun wouldn't be near as hot: just now it was scorching the ground as hard as a stone: ah yes, when the summer was over Thumbelina should be married. But she wasn't at all pleased; she didn't like the tiresome Mole one bit. Every morning when the sun rose and every evening when it set she stole out to the doorway, and there, when the wind parted the heads of corn, so that she could see the blue sky, she thought how bright and pretty it was outside, and longed to get another sight of the dear swallow: but he never came, he must certainly be flying far away in the beautiful green wood. By the time autumn came, Thumbelina had all her trousseau ready.

"In four weeks' time you shall be married," the Fieldmouse told her, but Thumbelina cried and said she wouldn't marry the tiresome Mole. "Rubbish," said the Fieldmouse, "don't be pigheaded or I'll bite you with my white teeth. It's a splendid husband you're getting. The queen herself hasn't the like of his black velvet coat; and a full kitchen and cellar he has, too! Just you thank your Maker for him."

So the wedding was to be; already the Mole had come to fetch Thumbelina, and with him she must go deep down underground, and never come out into the warm sun, for he couldn't stand it. The poor child was bitterly grieved, for now she must bid farewell to the beautiful sunshine which she had at least had the chance of seeing from the Fieldmouse's door.

"Farewell! Farewell! bright sun," she said, stretching her arms upwards and stepping a little way outside the Fieldmouse's house, for now the corn was reaped, and only the dry stubble left. "Farewell! Farewell!" she said again, and threw her arms about a little red flower that grew there. "Give my love to the dear swallow for me if ever you see him."

Twit! Twit! sounded at that moment above her head. She looked up and there was the swallow just flying by. He was overjoyed when he caught sight of Thumbelina, and she told him how she hated to have the ugly Mole for a husband, and how she must live right down underground where the sun never shone. She couldn't help crying.

"Cold winter is coming," said the swallow. "I am going to fly far away to the warm countries, will you come with me? You can sit on my back, only tie yourself tight with your sash, and we'll fly far away from the ugly Mole and his dark home, far over the mountains to the warm countries where the sun shines fairer than here, and there is always summer and lovely flowers. Do fly away with me, you sweet little Thumbelina, who saved my life when I lay frozen in that dark cellar underground."

"Yes, I will come with you," said Thumbelina. So she got up on the bird's back, put her feet upon his outspread wings, tied her belt fast to one of his strongest feathers, and off flew the swallow high in the air over forest and lake, high above the great mountains where the snow always lies, and where Thumbelina might have frozen in the cold air but that she crept in among the bird's warm feathers, and only put her little head out to see all the beauty beneath her.

At last they got to the warm countries. There the sun shone far brighter than here, the sky seemed twice as high, and on hedges and ditches grew the loveliest clusters of grapes, green and purple. In the woods grew oranges and lemons, there was a scent of myrtle and mint, and in the roads pretty children ran about and played with great gay butterflies. But the swallow flew still further, and the country grew more and more delightful. Under splendid trees, beside a blue lake, stood a shining palace of white marble, built in ancient days, with creepers twining about its tall pillars. At its top were a number of swallows' nests, one of which was the home of the swallow who was carrying Thumbelina.

"Here is my house," said the swallow, "but won't you look out for yourself one of the finest of the flowers that grow down below? And I'll put you there, and you shall find everything as happy as your heart can wish."

"That will be lovely," said she, and clapped her little hands.

A great white marble column lay there, which had fallen down and broken into three pieces: between them grew large beautiful white flowers. The swallow flew down with Thumbelina and set her on one of the broad leaves. But what a surprise for her! A little man was sitting in the middle of the flower, as white and transparent as if he were made of glass, with the prettiest gold crown on his head and the loveliest bright wings on his shoulders, and he was no bigger than Thumbelina. He was the angel of the flower. In each of them there lived such another little man or woman, but this one was the king of them all.

"Goodness, how beautiful he is," Thumbelina whispered to the swallow. The little prince was quite alarmed by the swallow, which was a giant bird to him, tiny and delicate as he was, but when he saw Thumbelina he was delighted, for she was by far the prettiest girl he had ever seen. He took his gold crown off his head and laid it upon hers, asked what her name was, and whether she would be his wife, for then she would become queen of all the flowers. Here indeed was a husband—very different from the Toad's son or the Mole with his black velvet coat. So she said "Yes" to the handsome prince; and out of every flower there came a lady or a lord, so pretty that it was a pleasure to see them. Everyone brought Thumbelina a present, but the best of all was a pair of beautiful wings taken from a big white fly. They were fastened to Thumbelina's back, and then she could fly from flower to flower. There were great rejoicings, and the swallow sat on his nest up there and sang to them as well as ever he could; but at heart he was sad, for he was very fond of Thumbelina and would have liked never to be parted from her. "You shan't be called Thumbelina," the angel of the flower said to her; "it's an ugly name, and you are very pretty; we will call you Maia."

"Good-bye, good-bye," said the swallow, when he flew back, away from the warm countries; far, far, back to Denmark. There he had a little nest above the window, where the man who can tell stories lives; and to him he sang, "Twit, twit", and that's the way we came by the whole story.

The Travelling Companion

Poor John was in sad trouble, for his father was very ill and could not recover. No one besides the two of them was in the little room. The lamp on the table was on the point of going out, and it was quite late on in the evening.

"You have been a good son, John," said the sick father, "God will be sure to help you on in the world!" And he gazed on him with solemn kind eyes, drew a very deep breath and died; it seemed just as if he were asleep. But John burst into tears; he had no one left now in all the world, neither father, mother, sister or brother. Poor John! He fell on his knees by the bedside and kissed his dead father's hand; many salt tears he shed, but at last his eyes closed and he went to sleep, with his head on the hard bedstead.

Then he dreamt a wonderful dream; he saw the sun and moon bowing to him, and he saw his father well and hearty once more, and heard him laugh as he always laughed when he was really happy. A beautiful girl with a golden crown on her long pretty hair stretched out her hand to John, and his father said, "Do you see what a bride you have won; she is the fairest in all the world?" Then he woke up, and all that pretty sight was gone; his father lay dead and cold in the bed, and there was no one at all with them. Poor John!

The week after, the dead man was buried. John walked close behind the coffin. He would never again see the good father who had been so fond of him. He listened to them casting the earth down upon the coffin, and he saw the last little corner of it, but, with the next shovelful of earth that was cast on it, that was hidden too. And then it seemed as if his heart would break asunder, so sharp was his sorrow. Round about him the people were singing a hymn, and the sound of it was very sweet; tears came into John's eyes; he wept, and that eased his sorrow. The sun shed a beautiful light on the green trees as if it would say, "You mustn't be so cast down, John, you see how beautiful and blue the sky is: your father is up there now, praying to the good God that it may be always well with you".

"I will always be good," said John, "and then I too shall go up to heaven to my father, and what a joy that will be, when we see one another again! What a lot there will be for me to tell him, and what a number of things he will have to show me, and teach me about all the beautiful things in heaven, just as he used to teach me here on earth. Oh, what a joy it will all be." John imagined all this to himself so clearly that he smiled while the tears were still running down over his cheeks. The little birds sat in the chestnut trees above him and twittered, "Kiwit, kiwit", they were as happy as possible, although they were attending the funeral; but then they knew well enough that the dead man was now up in heaven, and had wings far finer and bigger than theirs, and was happy because he had been good here on earth; and so they were happy. John watched them fly away from the green trees out into the wide world, and at that he felt a longing to fly away too. But first he hewed out a large cross of wood to set on his father's grave, and that evening when he brought it to the place he found the grave decked out with sand and flowers. It had been done by strangers, because they were so fond of the dear father who now lay there dead.

Early next morning John packed up his little bundle, and in his belt he put away all his inheritance. It was just fifty-six dollars and a few silver pennies; with that he meant to go out into the world, but first he went to the churchyard to his father's grave, and repeated the Lord's Prayer and said, "Good-bye, dear father, I will always be a good man, and then you will be able to pray to the good God that it may be well with me".

Out in the fields through which he walked, all the flowers were standing fresh and fair in the warm sunshine and they nodded in the breeze as if they would say, "Welcome to the green country; isn't it pleasant here?" But John turned round yet once again to look at the old church where he had been christened as a little child, and where he had been every Sunday to service with his old father and had sung his hymn, and there he saw high up in one of the openings in the tower the church Brownie standing in his little red peaked cap; he was shading his eyes with his bent arm, for the sun dazzled him. John waved a farewell to him, and the little Brownie waved his red cap and laid his hand on his heart and kissed his fingers over and over again to show how well he wished John, and hoped he would have a good journey.

John kept on thinking of all the charming things he would come to see in the splendid wide world; and on he went, further and further, never before had he been so far. He knew nothing of the villages he passed through or of the people he met, he was far away now, among strangers.

The first night he had to lie down to sleep in a haystack in the fields; no other bed could he get. But to his thinking it was just delightful; the King himself could have no prettier sleeping place. The open country and the river, the haystack and the blue sky over it made the pleasantest of bedrooms. The green grass with the little red and white flowers was the carpet, and the elder trees and the wild rosebushes stood for posies, and for a bath he had the whole river with its clear fresh water where the reeds waved, and wished him good night and good morning. The moon was a proper big night light, hung high up under the blue ceiling, and wouldn't set fire to the curtains. John could sleep there as tranquilly as possible, and that is what he did. He did not wake up again till the sun rose and all the little birds round about sang: "Good morning, good morning! Aren't you up yet?"

The bells were ringing for service; it was Sunday. The people were on their way to listen to the parson, and John went too. He sang a hymn and hearkened to God's word, and it seemed to him as if he were in his own church at home, where he had been christened and had sung hymns with his father.

Out in the churchyard were many many graves, and on some of them the grass was growing tall and rank. At that John thought of his father's grave, and how it too might come to look like these, now that he could no longer weed it and tidy it. So he sat himself down and pulled up the long grass, set up the wooden crosses that had fallen down, and laid the wreaths that the wind had blown off the graves back in their places; for he thought: "Perhaps someone will do the like for my father's grave now that I can't do it any more myself."

Outside the churchyard gate an old beggar stood leaning on his crutch. John gave him the silver pennies he had and went forward, cheerful and happy, out into the wide world.

Towards evening the weather turned very bad and John hurried on to get under shelter, but very soon it came to be dark night. At last he came in sight of a little church standing quite alone on a rising. Luckily the door stood ajar and he slipped in; he would stop there till the storm was over.

"I'll sit down here in a corner," said he, "I'm very tired and can manage with a bit of a rest," and so he sat down, clasped his hands, and said his evening prayer, and before he knew it he was asleep and dreaming while it thundered and lightened outside.

When he woke up again it was far on in the night, but the storm had passed over, and the moon was shining in on him through the windows. In the middle of the church floor there stood an open coffin with a dead man in it who had not yet been buried. John was not at all frightened, for he had a clear conscience, and knew well enough that the dead do no one any harm. It is bad men who are alive who do the mischief. Two bad live men of this sort were standing there, close by the dead man who had been put in the church before being laid in the grave; they meant to do him a mischief and not let him lie in his coffin, but throw him out in front of the church door: poor dead man!

"Why do you want to do that?" asked John. "It's wrong and wicked; let him sleep in Jesus' name."

"Oh, ah!" said the two villainous men, "he's made fools of us: he owed us money and couldn't pay, and now he's gone dead into the bargain, and we shan't get a penny, so we're going to take it out of him properly, and he shall lie like a dog outside the church door."

"I've got but fifty dollars," said John, "it's all my property, but I'll give it you and be glad to do it if you'll promise me faithfully to leave the poor dead man in peace. I shall get on all right without the money; I've got good sound arms and legs, and God will be helping me always."

"All right," said the two ruffians, "if you'll pay his debts of course we won't do anything to him, you may take your oath on that." So they took the money John gave them, shouted with laughter at his simpleness and went their way. But John laid the body reverently in the coffin, crossed its hands on its breast, bade it good-bye and went on contentedly through the deep wood.

All round him, wherever the moonlight could pierce between the trees, he saw the prettiest little elves playing about most delightfully. They didn't take fright at him; they knew that he was a good innocent being; it's only the bad people who cannot catch a glimpse of the elves. Some of them were no bigger than a finger, and had their long yellow hair fastened up with golden combs. They would be running in pairs on the big dewdrops that lay on the leaves and the long grass. Sometimes the dewdrop would fall down, and then they tumbled over among the tall green blades and there was a great laughter and commotion among the rest of the tiny creatures. It was monstrous funny. They would sing, and John recognized as plain as possible all the pretty tunes he had learnt as a little child. Big spotted spiders with silver crowns on their heads were kept spinning long hanging bridges from one bush to another, and palaces, which looked like glittering glass in the moonlight when the fine dew settled on them. And so it went on until the sun rose, when the little elves crept into the flower buds and the breeze caught their bridges and palaces, and they flew away through the air in great webs of gossamer.

Now John had just got out of the wood when from behind him a deep voice called out, "Hallo, comrade, where are you making for?" "Out into the wide world," said John, "I've neither father nor mother, and I'm only a poor lad, but God will help me, I know." "I'm for the wide world too," said the stranger, "shall we bear each other company?" "All right," said John, and they went on together. It wasn't long before they took to each other very much, for they were both good fellows. But John was soon aware that the stranger was much cleverer than he; he had been almost all the world over, and could tell all about everything we can imagine.

The sun was already high when they sat themselves down under a big tree to eat their breakfast, and just as they did so there came along an old woman. Oh how old she was! She was quite doubled up, and went leaning on a crutch stick, and on her back she had a bundle of sticks for firing which she had picked up in the wood. Her apron was pinned up, and John saw sticking out from it three long rods made of bracken and willow twigs. Just as she had got to where they were, her foot slipped, down she fell, and she gave a loud scream, for she had broken her leg, poor old thing.

John was anxious to carry her home at once to where she lived, but the strange man opened his knapsack and took out a bottle; and he said that in it he had an ointment which could make her leg properly well, so that she could get home by herself as well as if she had never broken her leg, but in return he wanted her first to give him the three rods she had in her apron.

"That's a good price," said the old woman, and she wagged her head in a very odd fashion. She didn't care about parting with her rods, but it wasn't much fun either to lie there with a broken leg, so she gave him the rods, and the minute he had rubbed the ointment on the leg, the old mother got up and walked off much quicker than before. That was what the ointment could do. But then it wasn't an ointment that you could buy at the chemist's.

"What do you want with the rods?" John asked his companion. "Why, they're three pretty nosegays," said he, "I've a fancy for them. I'm an odd sort of fellow."

So on they went for a good bit. "Goodness me, how overcast it is getting!" said John and pointed in front. "Those are tremendous thick clouds." "No," said his comrade, "those are not clouds; they are the mountains, the splendid great mountains where one gets right up beyond the clouds in the fresh air. That is noble, I can tell you; to-morrow we shall be sure enough right out in the world."

But they weren't so near as they seemed; it needed a whole day's walk before they got to the mountains where the great forests grew straight up towards heaven, and where there were rocks as big as a whole town. It would sure enough be a heavy job to get up to the top, and for that very reason John and his comrade went into an inn to get a good rest and gather strength for the morrow's march.

Down in the big taproom in the inn there was a large company come together, for a man with a puppet show was there: he had just put up his little theatre, and people were seated round in front to see the play, but in the very front of all a fat old butcher had taken a seat—the best seat there was. His big bulldog (and ugh! how fierce he looked) sat by his side and stared with all his eyes like the rest of the company.

Now the play began, and a pretty play it was, with a King and Queen who sat on a velvet throne with gold crowns on their heads and long trains to their robes, as was right and proper. The most charming wooden puppets with glass eyes and big moustaches stood at all the doors and opened and shut them to let folk into the room. It was really a delightful play and not in the least sad, but just as the Queen got up and walked across the floor—God knows what the big bulldog was thinking of—but as the fat butcher wasn't holding him, he made one bound right on to the stage, seized the Queen by her slender waist, and crick-crack it went: it was quite frightful.

The poor man who was performing the whole of the play was dreadfully frightened and upset about his Queen, for she was the prettiest by far of all the dolls he had, and now the horrid bulldog had bitten her head off. But afterwards, when the people were gone, the strange man—I mean the man who had come with John—said he could put her to rights well enough; and he got out his bottle and rubbed the doll with the ointment he had used to cure the poor old woman when she had broken her leg. The moment the doll was rubbed it became quite sound again, and what was more, it could move all its limbs itself; there was no need to pull the string. The doll was just like a living human being except that it couldn't talk. The man who owned the little theatre was delighted. There was no necessity for him to hold the doll any longer; it could dance by itself, and there were none of the others that could do that.

When at last night came, and all the people in the inn were gone to bed, someone was heard sighing—sighing so deep and going on so long that everybody got up to see who it could be. The man who had played the comedy went to his little theatre, for it was in there that the someone was sighing. All the wooden dolls were lying there mixed up together, the King and all the bodyguard, and it was they who were sighing so miserably, staring with their big glass eyes: for they wanted dreadfully to be rubbed with the ointment like the Queen, so that they too might be able to move of themselves. The Queen threw herself right down on her knees and held up her beautiful golden crown. "Take it," she begged, "only do anoint my husband and my court people." At that the poor man who owned the play and all the dolls could not keep from crying; he was really grieved for them. He promised the Travelling Companion at once to give him all the money he got for his play next evening if he would only anoint four or five of his best dolls. But the Companion said that all he would ask for was the big sword the man wore at his side; and when he had got that he rubbed six of the dolls, which began to dance that moment; and so delightfully did they dance that all the girls, the living, human girls who were looking on, began to dance too. The ostler and kitchenmaid, the cook and the chambermaid, all danced, and so did all the visitors, and the shovel and tongs into the bargain; but they both tumbled down

just as they were making their first hop! Ah, they had a merry night of it, I can tell you.

Next morning John and his comrade left them all, and started off towards the high mountains and through the great pine forests. So high did they climb that the church towers far below them looked at last like little red berries down there in the midst of the green, and they could see far and wide for many and many a mile over country where they had never been. So much of the beauty of the beautiful world John had never before seen at one time; and the sun shone so hot in the fresh blue sky, and he heard huntsmen sounding their horns in among the hills—such a lovely blessed sound—that the water stood in his eyes from pure pleasure, and he could not help saying: "O kind Lord! I could kiss you for being so good to us and giving us all the beauty there is in the world!"

His Companion stood there too, with clasped hands, looking out over the woods and villages in the hot sunshine. Just then a marvellously beautiful sound rang out above them, and they looked upwards. A great white swan was hovering in the sky; beautiful it was, and it sang as they had never before heard a bird sing; but gradually it became weaker and weaker, its head drooped, and slowly it sank down till it lay at their feet dead, the splendid bird.

"Two such fine wings," said the Companion, "so big and so white as these are, are worth money. I'll take them with me. It's a good thing I've got a sword, you can see that now?" And he cut both wings off the dead swan with a single stroke, for he meant to keep them.

And so now they travelled on for many and many a mile across the mountains, till at last they saw before them a great city with more than a hundred towers that shone like silver in the sun. In the centre of this town was a stately marble palace roofed with red gold, and there lived the King.

John and his Companion would not go into the city at once, but stayed in an inn just outside it to make themselves tidy, for they wanted to look smart when they appeared in the streets. The landlord told them that the King was a good sort of man who never did nothing to nobody, neither the one nor yet the other: but his daughter, why there! God help us, she was a bad Princess. Beauty she had and to spare, nobody was ever so pretty and attractive as what she was, but where was the use of that? She was a right down wicked witch, and so it came about that so many fine young princes had lost their lives. She'd given everybody leave to come courting her; any person could come, no matter whether he was a prince or a beggar, that was all one to her, and all he'd got to do was to guess three things as she asked him; if he could do that she would marry him and he'd be King over the whole country when her father died, but if he couldn't guess the three things, why she had him hung or else beheaded; so wicked and cruel was this lovely Princess. Her father, the old King, was terribly upset about it, but he couldn't prevent her being so nasty, for he had said once he never would have anything whatever to do with her lovers, she might do just as she pleased. Every time a Prince came to guess and to win the Princess, he couldn't make anything of it, and so he was hung or had his head chopped off: well, they'd warned him beforehand; he might have left it alone. The old King was so troubled at all the sorrow and misery, that once every year he spent a whole day on his knees with all his soldiers, praying that the Princess might turn good, but she wouldn't. The old women who drank brandy coloured it quite black before they drank it; that was their way of mourning, and more than that they couldn't do.

"What a hateful Princess," said John, "she ought to be whipped, that would do her good. If I was the old King she should get her red stripes right enough."

Just then they heard the people outside shouting: "Hurrah!" The Princess passed by, and she was really so lovely that everybody forgot how horrid she was, and so they shouted: "Hurrah!" Twelve fair maidens, all in white silk dresses and each with a gold tulip in her hand, rode on coal-black horses beside her. The Princess herself had a milk-white horse, caparisoned with diamonds and rubies; her riding habit was of pure gold, and the whip she had in her hand looked like a ray of sunlight. The gold crown on her head was like little stars from up in heaven, and her cloak was made of thousands of butterflies' wings sewn together, and yet she was far more beautiful than all her clothes.

When John caught sight of her, he went as red in the face as a drop of blood, and could hardly say a word; the Princess looked exactly like the lovely girl with a gold crown he had dreamt of the night his father died. He thought her most beautiful, and couldn't help loving her. It certainly wasn't true, he said, that she could be an evil witch who had people hung or beheaded when they couldn't guess what she asked them. "Well, everyone is free to court her, even the poorest beggar; and on my word I will go up to the Palace; I can't help it." They all said he must not do that; it would certainly go with him as with the rest, and the Travelling Companion too advised him not to go, but John said it would be all right, brushed his shoes and his clothes, washed his face and hands, combed his nice fair hair and went all alone into the town and up to the palace.

"Come in," said the old King when John knocked at the door. John opened it, and the old King in his dressing-gown and embroidered slippers came to meet him. He had the gold crown on his head, the sceptre in one hand and the gold orb in the other. "Half a minute," said he, and tucked the orb under his arm in order to give John his hand. But the moment he heard that here was a suitor, he began to cry so that both sceptre and orb fell on the floor and he had to dry his eyes with his dressing-gown. Poor old King!

"Do let it alone," he said, "it'll go with you just like all the rest. You shall just see for yourself," and he took John out into the Princess's garden. It was a horrible sight. On every tree there hung three or four king's sons who had courted the Princess, but couldn't guess the things she asked them. Every time the wind blew, all the bones rattled so that the little birds were frightened and never would come into the garden. All the flowers were tied up to human bones, and in the flower-pots there were dead men's skulls grinning. That was a nice garden for a Princess.

"There, you see," said the old King, "it will go with you just like all the others you see here, so do let it alone; you really do make me quite wretched, I feel these things so much."

John kissed the kind old King's hand and said it would be all right, he was so fond of the lovely Princess.

Just then, here came the Princess herself with all her ladies riding into the palace court, so they went out to meet her, and said good morning. She was beautiful, in all conscience; she shook hands with John and he grew more in love with her than before; he was certain she could not be a dreadful wicked witch as everybody said she was. They went up into the hall, and the little pages offered them sweetmeats and gingernuts, but the old King was so wretched he couldn't eat anything, and besides the gingernuts were too hard for him.

So now it was settled that John should come back to the palace next morning, and then the judges and all the council should be assembled and hear how he got on with his guessing. If he succeeded, he was to come twice more; but so far there had never been anybody who had guessed the first time, and so they had to lose their lives.

John was not the least troubled about what would happen to him, he was merely happy, he only thought about the lovely Princess, and believed most surely that the good God would help him all right; but how, he didn't know in the least, nor did he care to think. He danced all along the street when he went back to the inn where the Travelling Companion was waiting for him.

John never tired of telling how prettily the Princess had behaved to him and how lovely she was; he longed already for the next day when he should go there to the palace and try his luck at guessing.

But the Travelling Companion shook his head and was quite depressed. "I'm so fond of you," he said, "and we might have been together for a long time yet; and now I'm to lose you already. My poor, dear John, I could cry—but I won't spoil your pleasure on this last evening perhaps, that we shall be together; we'll be merry, so we will; to-morrow when you are gone I shall have time to cry."

Everybody in town had got to know at once that a new suitor to the Princess had come, and there was great lamentation in consequence. The theatre was closed, and all the cake women tied black crape round their sugar pigs; the King and the clergy were on their knees in the church, and there was the deepest of sorrow, because of course John could not fare better than all the rest of the suitors.

Late in the evening the Travelling Companion made a big bowl of punch, and said to John that now they would make merry and drink the health of the Princess. But no sooner had John drunk a couple of glasses than he turned so sleepy that he couldn't keep his eyes open, he must have a nap. The Travelling Companion lifted him off his chair very gently and laid him on his bed, and when it was dark night he took the two great wings that he had cut from the swan and tied them fast to his shoulders; the biggest of the rods he got from the old woman who fell down and broke her leg, he put in his pocket, he opened the window and flew over the town right away to the palace and there he sat himself in a corner up under the window which opened into the Princess's bedroom.

The whole town was perfectly still. When the clock struck a quarter to twelve, the window opened, and the Princess flew out in a great white cloak, and with long black wings, away over the town, and out to a great hill. But the Travelling Companion made himself invisible so that she couldn't see him, and flew after her, and he whipped the Princess with his rod so that the blood actually came at every blow. Ugh, what a flight that was through the air! The wind caught her cloak, and it spread out all round like a great sail, and the moon shone through it. "How it hails, how it hails," said the Princess at every stroke she got of the rod—and much good might it do her. At last she got out to the hill, and knocked. There was a rumbling as of thunder when the hill opened, and the Princess went in, and the Travelling Companion after her, for nobody could see him, he was invisible. They went through a great long passage where the walls glistened in a marvellous fashion; there were thousands of glowing spiders that ran up and down along the wall and gave a light like fire. Then they came to a large hall built of silver and gold: flowers as big as sunflowers, red and blue, shone from the walls, but nobody could pick them, for the stalks were poisonous snakes and the flowers were fire that shot out of their mouths. The whole ceiling was set with shining glow-worms and sky-blue bats that flapped their thin wings; it was a most extraordinary sight. In the middle of the floor was a throne supported by four skeletons of horses which had harness of red fire-spiders. The throne itself was of milk-white glass, and the cushions to sit on were of little black mice all biting each others' tails. Over it was a canopy of rose-red cobweb set with the prettiest little green flies, shining like jewels. On the throne sat an old Troll with a crown on his hideous head and a sceptre in his hand. He kissed the Princess on her forehead and made her sit by his side on the splendid throne; and now the music struck up. Great black grasshoppers played their Jew's harps, and the owl beat on its stomach, for it hadn't got a drum. That was a funny concert: tiny little goblins with will-o'-the-wisps in their caps danced round the hall. Nobody could see the Travelling Companion; he had placed himself right behind the throne and heard and saw everything. The courtiers who now came in were as fine and stately as could be; but anyone who could see properly noticed at once what they were. They were nothing but broomsticks with cabbage heads on them —into which the Troll had bewitched life, and given them embroidered clothes. But that didn't matter after all, for they were only used for show.

When the dancing had gone on some time, the Princess told the Troll that she had got a new suitor, and asked what she should think of to ask him about next morning when he came to the palace.

"Listen," said the Troll, "now I'll tell you something. You must choose something very easy, for then he won't hit on it. Think of one of your shoes; he won't guess that. Then have his head cut off, but don't forget when you come out here to me to-morrow night to bring me his eyes, for I want to eat them."

The Princess made a very deep curtsey and said she would not forget the eyes. Then the Troll opened the hill and she flew home again, but the Travelling Companion followed her and thrashed her so hard with the rod that she moaned and sighed at the fierce hail storm and made all the haste she could to get in at her bedroom window.

But the Travelling Companion flew back to the inn where John was still asleep, took off his wings and laid himself too down on the bed; for he had every right to be tired.

It was quite early in the morning when John awoke. The Travelling Companion got up too and told him that he had had a very strange dream about the Princess and one of her shoes; and therefore he earnestly begged him to ask if the Princess had not thought of one of her shoes. That, of course, was what he had heard from the Troll in the hill; but he didn't want to tell John anything about that, but only begged him to ask whether she had thought of one of her shoes.

"I may as well ask about one thing as another," said John, "perhaps what you have dreamt about may be quite right, for I believe always that God will be sure and help me. Still, I'll bid you goodbye, for if I do guess wrong, I shall never get a sight of you again."

So they kissed each other, and John went into the town and up to the palace. The whole hall was quite full of people; the judges were in their armchairs and had eiderdown cushions for their heads because they had so much to think about! The old King stood up drying his eyes with a white pocket handkerchief; then the Princess entered. She was even more lovely than the day before, and she greeted them all most kindly, but to John she gave her hand and said: "Good morning to you."

Now John had to guess what she had thought of. Goodness, how kindly she looked at him—but the moment she heard the single word *shoe* she turned as white as a sheet in the face and shivered all over her body; but that didn't do her any good, for he had guessed right. Bless his heart, how delighted the old King was! He turned right head over heels, and everybody clapped their hands at him and at John, who had guessed right the first time.

The Travelling Companion beamed with pleasure when he learned how well all had gone. But John clasped his hands and thanked the good God, who would surely help him again the other two times.

There was to be a second guessing no later than next day.

The evening passed just like the one before. When John was asleep the Travelling Companion flew out after the Princess to the hill and thrashed her even harder than the first time, for now he had taken two rods. No one got a sight of him, and he heard everything. The Princess was to think of her glove, and this he told to John as if it had been a dream.

So John was able again to guess right, and there was the greatest rejoicing at the Palace. The whole court turned head over heels as they had seen the King do the first time; but the Princess lay on the sofa and would not utter a single word. Now the question was if John could guess right the third time. If that went well he would, of course, win the lovely Princess and inherit the whole countryside when the old King died; if he guessed wrong, he would lose his life, and the Troll would eat his pretty blue eyes.

The evening before, John went to bed early, said his evening prayer and went quite peacefully to sleep. But the Travelling Companion fastened his wings to his back, bound his sword to his side and took all his three rods with him and flew off to the palace.

It was a pitch dark night; it blew so that the tiles flew off the house roofs and the trees in the garden where the skeletons hung bent like reeds under the blast; it lightened every minute, and the thunder rumbled as if it were but a single peal that lasted the whole night.

Suddenly the window opened and the Princess flew out. She was as pale as a corpse, but she laughed at the awful storm; she thought it was not fierce enough; her white cloak whirled abroad in the air like a great sail, but the Travelling Companion flogged her so hard with his three rods that the blood dripped down on to the earth and at last could she scarcely fly any further. Finally she reached the hill.

"It is hailing and blowing," said she, "never have I been out in such a storm."

"Well, one can have too much of a good thing," said the Troll. Then she told him that John had again guessed right the second time. If he did the same on the morrow, he would have won, and she could never again come out to the Troll to the hill, and never could do such witchcraft as before; and so she was greatly troubled.

"He shan't be able to guess," said the Troll, "I shall hit on something he's never thought of, never fear, or else he must be a bigger wizard than me. But now let's enjoy ourselves," and with that he took the Princess by both hands and they danced round with all the little goblins and will-o'-the-wisps that were in the room. The red spiders ran merrily up and down along the walls, and it seemed as if the fire flowers shed sparks. The owl beat the drum, the crickets whistled, and the black grasshoppers blew the Jew's harp. It was a merry ball.

When they had danced long enough the Princess had to get home otherwise she might be missed at the Palace. The Troll said he would come with her, and so they would at any rate still be together for so long.

So they flew off through the awful storm, and the Travelling Companion wore out his three rods on their backs; never had the Troll been out in such a hailstorm. Outside the palace he said good-bye to the Princess and in the same instant whispered in her ear, "Think of my head". But the Travelling Companion heard it all the same, and at the moment when the Princess slipped in through the window into her bedroom, and the Troll was turning to go back, he caught him by his long black beard and with his sword hewed off his hideous Troll's head at the shoulders, so that the Troll himself never once caught sight of him. The body he threw out into the lake to the fishes, but the head he only dipped into the water and then tied it up in his silk pocket handkerchief, took it home to the inn, and lay down to sleep.

Next morning he gave John the handkerchief, but told him he must not untie it before the Princess asked what it was she had thought of.

There were so many people in the great hall of the Palace that they stood on one another like radishes tied in a bundle. The council sat in their chairs with their soft pillows, and the old King had a new suit on, and the golden crown and the sceptre had been polished so that it all looked splendid. But the Princess was quite pale and had on a coal black dress as if she were going to a funeral.

"What have I thought of?" said she to John, and at once he untied the handkerchief, and was quite startled when he saw the hideous Troll's head. A shudder ran through everyone, for it was frightful to look upon, but the Princess sat like a stone image and could not utter a single word. At last she rose and gave her hand to John, for, of course, he had guessed right. She looked on neither one nor another, but with a deep deep sigh she said, "Now you are my lord, to-night we will hold our bridal."

"That's the sort for me," said the old King; "so we will!" All the people shouted "Hurrah", the guards' band played in the street, the bells rang, and the cake women took the black crape off their sugar pigs, for now there was rejoicing. Three whole roasted oxen, stuffed with ducks and chickens, were set out in the middle of the market-place; anyone could cut himself a slice. The fountains ran with the most delicious wine, and anyone who bought a penny roll at the baker's had six large buns given him into the bargain, buns, mark you, with raisins in them.

At night the whole town was illuminated and the soldiers fired off cannons, and the boys peashooters, and there was eating and drinking, singing and springing, up at the palace; all the noble lords and the lovely ladies danced together, and from far away you could hear them when they sang:

> Here are so many pretty maidens
> That all want a turn.
> They are asking for the drum and fife march;
> Pretty maiden, take a turn,
> Dance about and stamp about
> Till your shoe soles tumble out.

But the Princess was still a witch and cared not at all for John. This the Travelling Companion was aware of, and therefore he gave John three feathers from the swan's wings, and a little bottle with some drops in it, and told him that he must have a large tub full of water put by the bride's bed, and when the Princess was going to get into bed, he must give her a little push so that she should fall into the water; then he must duck her thrice—having first put the feathers and the drops into the bath—and then she would be rid of her witchcraft and would come to be very fond of him.

John did all that the Travelling Companion had advised him. The Princess screamed aloud when he plunged her beneath the water, and wriggled in his hands in the form of a great coal-black swan with fiery eyes. When she came up from the water a second time, the swan was white, save for a black ring round its neck. John prayed earnestly to God and made the water run over the bird the third time, and in that instant it was changed to a real lovely Princess. She was even prettier than before, and she thanked him with tears in her beautiful eyes for having freed her from the spell that was on her.

Next morning the old King came with all his court, and there were congratulations that lasted till late on in the day; last of all came the Travelling Companion. He had his stick in his hand and his knapsack on his back. John kissed him over and over again and said he must never go away, but must stay with him; he had been the cause of all his good fortune; but the Travelling Companion shook his head and said—how kindly and lovingly—"No, now my time is up, I have but paid my debt. Do you remember the dead man whom those evil men would have injured? You gave all you had that he might rest in his grave. I am that dead man." And that same instant he was gone.

The bridal lasted a whole month. John and the Princess were as fond of each other as could be, and the old King lived for many happy days and let their little children ride a cock horse on his knee and play with his sceptre. But John was king over the whole realm.

The Green Boy and the Three Witches

There was a Prince who went out one day to hunt, and as he rode out in the wood he lost his way, and evening came on almost before he knew. He got off his horse and led it after him through the trees. At last he became aware of a light, and he made for that. It turned out to be a poor little cottage where there were an old man and an old woman. He asked them if they could either show him his way or house him for the night. Yes, that they could, both the one and the other; but he had much better stay the night there, if he could put up with the simple fare, and in the morning they would help him to get out of the forest. So the woman got him supper, and the old people gave up their own bed and lay, for that night, on some straw by the stove. Next morning the old man said they would go together to church, for it was Sunday, and then come home and have some kail for dinner and after that he could set off.

And so it was settled; but when the Prince got to the churchyard, he saw an open grave, and he went off and looked down into it.

"Why isn't that grave filled in?" he said; "it looks to me like an old grave."

"Why," says the man, "that's because we have a law here in these parts that when a poor man dies and leaves a debt behind him, the earth mustn't be cast on him until the debt is paid; and besides, the body must be taken up once a year and whipped, until that's done."

"That's an ugly sort of law," said the Prince. "Can't it be altered? Can't this here grave be filled in?"

"No," said the man, "for there's no one who'll pay his debt."

"Well I should like to have a word with the people who have any claim on him."

It so happened that they were at church, and he got hold of them and asked how much the debt was. "If you got the half of it, mightn't the earth be cast on him and a proper funeral done, like anywhere else?" "Yes," they said, "they would be satisfied with that." So the Prince paid, and the priest cast the earth on the body, and the grave was filled in, and everything was settled and done with that same day.

Then he went home with the old man, and had bacon and kail to his dinner. After that he put him on the right way out of the forest; and there was a path that went along by the edge of the wood, and he kept along that.

There he met a boy in green. "Where are you off to, my boy?" says the Prince. "I'm coming with you; for I know you've set your mind on finding the most beautiful Princess in the world, and I can guide you to her."

Well, to be sure, the Prince would like to find her, so off they set at once, the boy running and the Prince riding. On towards evening they came to a castle. "And there," says the boy, "you'd better stay the night." "And what's to become of you?" says the Prince. "I can easily get a lodging, for I have an uncle here in the village." The boy took his horse and led it into the stable, foddered it, and laid himself down in an empty stall on some straw. When it was midnight, or a little past, he went out to a hill a little outside the village; and knocked on it. The Hillman came out and asked, "What do you want, my lad?" "You've got a cloak, and when anyone puts it on they become invisible; I want it." "You can't have that, my lad, for I can't do without it."

"Yes I will have it, and if I don't get it I shall break up your hill into little bits."

"You're a very fierce boy. Will you threaten a man out of what he can't do without? Well, there it is then."

So home he went and lay down in his empty stall. In the morning, down comes the Prince, to look to his horse. "If you've fed him, my boy, we'll set off now." Yes he had, and they started to go as they did the day before. They went on all day till late on at night, and then they came to another castle.

"We'd best stay here, for we can't get lodgings anywhere else," says the boy; and he took the horse and looked after it. "What's to become of you?" says the Prince. "I've got an uncle here, too, I can stay here for certain."

He lay down in an empty stall, and when it was a little past midnight, he went out of the village to a hill where another Hillman lived.

"What do you want, my boy?"

"I don't want anything of you but a club. It can't be seen, and when you hold it out, whatever it touches, sticks to it. That club you've got, and that I will have."

"You won't get it, for I can't do without it."

"Yes, have it I will, or I'll break your hill into little bits."

"What a horrid boy you are; will you threaten a man out of what he can't spare? Well, there it is then."

So he went back to the castle and lay down in the empty stall near the horse. In the morning the Prince came and asked if the horse had been fed, for if so, they would make a start. Yes, sure enough it had, and everything was ready.

Towards the middle of the afternoon they came once more to a castle. "We'd better sleep here to-night," says the boy. "It's too early," said the Prince; "we can ride a bit further yet."

"No, we must stay here," says the boy, "for here is the Princess you're looking for. Now you can just go in and see if you can get speech of her; but you mustn't pledge yourself to anything with her, before letting me know." "But what's to become of you all this time?" "You needn't trouble about me," said the boy. "I've got an uncle here in the village, and I can stay with him as long as there's any need."

So the boy led his horse into the stable and saw to it. In the morning the Prince came down to him and said, "Yes, I've seen her now, and I fancy her well enough if only I can get her; but that's not an easy matter, to be sure." "Oh yes, that'll go well enough, but you must see about proposing to her if you get an opportunity."

When they had finished dinner, he proposed to her. But she answered that that could not be unless he could accomplish three things she would set him to do. "The first thing shall be, that you shall bring me my gold ring which I have here on my finger to-morrow when dinner is over; and yet I'm to keep the ring myself." So he went down to the boy, and he said: "No, I shall never get her, for now she's set it down that I'm to do three things for her, and the first thing is, that I'm to bring her her gold ring to-morrow at dinner time, and yet she's to keep it herself; I can't do that, for she can certainly hide it so that I can't find it."

"I shall get it right enough," said the boy; "but take care that you don't have too much to do with her at first without letting me know; for she's in league with three witches, and it's not a very easy job to deal with them."

In the evening, the boy took his cloak and his club—so that he became invisible—and went into the Princess's room to hear what the other witches would talk about. When she was just going to get into bed she said: "Ah, by the way, where shall I hide my ring, so that I can be sure he won't find it? I'll put it in my drawer and leave the key under my pillow."

When she was safe in bed, the witches came. "You've got a suitor," said they, "and you've said 'yes' to him; you're not faithful to us."

"Well, it's only on conditions," said she. "He's got to do three things for me, and I can make them so hard that it'll be impossible for him."

So she told them the first thing she had asked for, and where she had hidden the key. "No, that won't do," they said; "let us others have the ring, we'll hide it fast enough." So the witches took the ring and went off with it, and the boy after them. When they got to the seashore they got aboard a little boat and sailed out a stage. Then one of them said: "Take soundings." They sounded, and made it five fathoms of water. "Just throw the ring out!" And as one of them threw the ring the boy thrust his club at it and drew it up to him. They sailed back to land and the boy went home and lay down in his stall. Next morning the Prince came, very dismal.

"Here's the ring for you," says the boy.

"You *are* a good boy. I'll remember you for that." When dinner was over, the Princess said: "Might I ask for my ring?"

"Yes, if you please, here it is, provided it's the right one." "Yes!" She made the other ladies look at it, and it was plain enough that it was the right one, for the Princess's name was on it. So now he must have the second task set him.

"Now, to-morrow, when we've finished dinner, you shall bring me my necklace; and yet I'll keep it myself."

He went off, down to the boy, and told him. "That I can't do; it's wholly impossible for me."

"Oh yes we can, sure enough; I shall get it all right," says the boy.

71

When it was evening he went again to the Princess's bedroom, with his cloak and his club, which made him invisible. As she was going to bed she said: "Ah yes, now I'll hide it in my box and put the key under my pillow."

All of a sudden, here came the three witches again. "Well, how did it go?" said they. "Yes, how did it go indeed?" says she, a little peevish. "I should do best to ask you that." "What do you mean?" said they.

"Why! You're in league with him; so he came with my ring right enough."

"What's the meaning of that?" said they. "Is he a tall man?" "Why, I don't know—a tall one? He's the same height as men usually are."

They couldn't understand it. "But what have you set him to do now?"

She told them, and said where she'd hidden the necklace. "We can't trust to that," they said; "let us have it and keep it. We'll sail out so far with it that he can't wade out to it."

So they went down and got aboard a ship, but the boy was with them, you may be sure. When they had got a tremendous long stage out, one of them said, "Take soundings." When they had sounded, they made it ten fathoms of water. "Well, we must go further out yet. If he could wade out to five fathoms depth, and find the ring, he can surely wade out to ten." So they sailed out till they got to five and twenty fathoms of water, and threw the necklace out there. But the boy thrust his club at it and pulled it in to him. They sailed back to land, and he went and lay down in the stall.

Next morning the Prince came and asked how it had gone with him. "Why, it had gone very well, and here is the necklace." "You really are a wonderful boy; if I hadn't got you, what would have become of me? But things aren't right with me, for my money's going. I hadn't provided myself for such a long journey. Can you help me about that?"

"Yes, I can get money from my uncle for certain, but you must manage to keep yourself till to-morrow."

When they had finished dinner, the Princess wanted her gold chain. "Here it is," says he, "provided it is the right one." "Yes," she thought it was; and she made the other ladies look at it. "It is the one, for the Princess's name is on it." So she must set him the third thing. "Now then, to-morrow when we've finished dinner, you must give me the head of the person that's painted here, on a silver dish." And with that, she handed him a portrait.

So down he went to the boy, and said: "Well, the worst is left to do." "Why, what's that then?"

With that he took the picture out of his pocket. "Look here." "Ugh! a—ah! did you do that yourself?" "No, it's a portrait, and that head I've got to bring her on a silver dish. I've never seen such a horrible face in all my days, but how ever can I get it for her?"

"Yes, that phiz I know well enough," says the boy. "That's the old witch's head, that is; the thing's not worth crying about." "But the silver dish, too! I can't borrow a silver dish at the court." "That can be managed too," says the boy.

When it was evening he went out to the Hillman and knocked.

"What do you want now, my boy?" says the Hillman.

"I only want you to lend me a big silver dish you've got."

"No, you can't have that; I won't lend out things like that." "Well, but I'll give it you back, and if I don't get it, I'll break up you and your hill into bits."

"You're a dreadful fierce boy, threatening a man like that, but— well, there, you can have it."

So home he went with it, and set off to the Princess with his cloak and his club.

They hadn't gone to bed yet, but at last the Princess went to bed, and he went with her into the room and stowed himself under the stove while she was getting ready. Immediately after, came all the three witches.

"Well, how went it to-day?" said they.

"Yes, how went it? You know well enough, seeing he's one of your company. He brought the chain all right."

"Why! what a fearful creature he is," said they; "he must be a giant."

"No, he's no bigger than people usually are," said she. "Well, we can't understand that. The first time we sailed out to five fathoms, and the second time to five and twenty fathoms. You ought not to have said 'yes' to him."

"No," she was sorry she had, herself. But seeing he was as high in rank as she was, she couldn't bring herself to give him his dismissal straight off. But that was why she had set him things to do which she thought he couldn't possibly manage. "And no more he could have, if you hadn't helped him."

Well, but they hadn't.

"And now I've set him to do something which will show plain enough whether he's with you or against you. What he's got to do is to bring me your old mother's head on a silver dish."

"O ho! O ho!" said they. "Let's get off, let's get off. What a horrid dreadful thing for you to hit upon." They clawed off out of the house as quick as ever they could, but when they'd got a little way out of the town, the two younger ones ran away from the old one. She couldn't keep up with them, and they were afraid *he* would catch them too. So the boy stayed alone with the old one till he got a chance to snip the head off her; and the body he threw into a ditch, but the head he took home with him, and lay down himself in the empty stall till day.

Then the Prince came and asked him how things had gone. "They went well; here's the face." He could tell that it was the right one, though he had never seen it before. "But how am I to bring it in?" "This time I'll come with you and put myself under the table while you're at dinner, and then when she asks for it, you've only to reach your hand down and take it from me," says the boy.

Well, when dinner was over, she says, "Come now, have you done the third thing, and can you produce that head?" "Yes, here it is."

"Ugh! a—ah! Take it away; put it out of my sight," she screamed, and made as if she was really ill. "Why, then I'm bound to you," said she, "and we must see about arranging for the wedding."

In the afternoon, the Prince came out and had a talk with the boy about all this. "Yes, well, you can just let them go and make ready, but you mustn't be with her just at the first, for though the old witch is out of the way, there are still the two of them left." "Oh, by the by," says the Prince; "did you get me any money?" "No, I forgot about that, I was so busy last night; but you shall have some to-morrow."

In the evening he went out to the hill and knocked. Out came the Hillman: "What do you want, my boy?"

"Here's your silver dish, and thanks for the loan of it, but you've got a leather purse which the money never runs out of; I want that, and that I must have."

"No, you won't get that, for I can't do without it," says the Hill-man. "Yes, you can do without it, perfectly well, but I can't, and if I don't get it, I shall break up your hill now."

"You are the worst boy I've ever had to do with in all my days; but there it is for you." So he went home and lay down in the stall.

In the morning he gave the purse to the Prince. "You needn't be afraid to spend money now; it'll last you out, for however much you take, there's always enough left."

So they got all the wedding affairs ready, and on the day when the marriage was to be, the boy said to the Prince when he came and told him of it: "Yes, now you can let them marry you to her, but when you have to go to the bride chamber, you must take care to lay yourself on the outside, so that she lies next to the wall, and for my sake take care you don't fall asleep, but let her go to sleep as soon as she can. The minute you notice she's asleep, you must get up and go into another room, for then the witches will come, but I shall come with you right enough, and meet them, and go out after them."

So that's what happened. As soon as he saw her asleep, he got up and went through the other door, and then the witches came. She woke up, and they began to talk to her.

"So you've been married to-day?" said they.

"Yes, we have, but talk low, for he's asleep."

They felt about after him, but there was no one but her in the bed. "Well, he must be in this room, for he came in here, and got into bed too."

They felt after him, all round, but couldn't find him.

"Ah, stop, hush!" says one; "here he is under the stove." But there, he was gone again. They could feel him, but they couldn't see him. Once again they found him in the room, but yet they couldn't get hold of him. All at once they said, "We won't have anything to do with him. We've lost our mother by his means; we won't stay here." And they rushed out of the door, and the boy after them. When they got outside the town, they went along talk-ing about him; such a person they never had known the like of. About that time, the boy stole up and gave one of them a good whack with his club across the shin. "Ow!" says she to the other, "what did you kick me for, like that?" "I never kicked you," says she. Then the boy gave the other just as good a whack over the shin. "You said I kicked you, I promise you you kicked me proper that time. Phew! Fie! how it did hurt."

They kept on like that, until at last they began to fight, and they tumbled over, both of them, and lay there kicking about a long time. Then the boy ran up and snipped the heads off them as they lay there, and threw their bodies down to the rest of the mess where the old woman lay in the ditch, and there was an end of all three. Meanwhile, the Prince had gone back to his Princess and slept quietly till morning; and in the morning he came down and asked how things had gone.

"Oh, I had very good luck. The three of them won't do you any more harm now, they're all out of the way."

"Well, now we shall have to pay a visit at home to my parents in a few days' time," said the Prince. "You'll come too?"

Yes, he would. And the two of them, the Prince and Princess, set off riding, but the boy ran. They stayed at each of the places where they had been on the way out, and at last they came to the dyke by the wood, where the boy had come to him.

"Well, my boy, here it was that we two came into company," said the Prince.

"Yes, so it was."

"And now you shall come home with me to my palace and be received as my own son for as long as you live."

"No, I will not," said he; "but all the same I thank the Prince over and over again."

"Yes, indeed you must, for you have done me so great service that this is the very least I can do for you." "No, I cannot, for here I must part from you. The truth is, I am the spirit of that man whom you cared for to have the earth cast on his body; and that is why I came to guide you on your dangerous journey, and now I bid you farewell."

And with that, they saw no more of the boy. The Prince and his wife rode home to his father's palace, and a little while after they had come, the old King died, and so the Prince was proclaimed King of the country, and so excellent a King and Queen there have hardly ever been found in the world.

The White Silk Boy

There was a farm called Larkendal, and there lived an old couple who had fallen into poverty. Well, they had a son, and when he had been confirmed they could not afford to keep him at home any longer. So his father told him that it was time for him to travel out into the world and try his luck. But they had nothing to give him to take away with him but a pair of big mittens which his mother tied to him; it was cold weather, and she didn't want him to get his hands frostbitten. So off he set, to go to look for a place. The last thing his mother told him was, never to pass by a church without going into it.

At the first church he came to, he saw a lot of people gathered in the churchyard and quarrelling with all their might. He was inquisitive, as boys like that always are, and he went up to them to listen to what was going on. It was the people of the parish, and each of them had his plot in the churchyard; but a poor man had just died who had no plot, and nobody would have him in theirs for ess than three marks, and the three marks nobody would pay for him: that was what they were quarrelling about. Well, one of the men came up to this here poor boy and asked him what he would take for his mittens. "You might give me three marks for them," said he. The other man was willing to give that, and they made a bargain of it. Then the poor boy went off and paid the three marks to have the poor man buried, and when that was all properly done, he set off again along the high road.

When he had been walking a little time and it was now near evening, he happened to look behind him and there was a boy coming running after him in white silk clothes and with a white silk cap on his head. So he began to run too, for he didn't like the idea of getting in company with a person like that whom he didn't know, but the faster he ran, the faster this bit of a boy ran too, and at last he came up with him. And this boy said, "What made you run away from me like that?" "Why, I thought I could find room for to-night easier alone than if there were two of us."

"Where are you going, then?" says he.

"Oh, wherever I can get a lodging for God's sake," says the poor boy, "for I've nothing to pay for it with."

"Well, I won't do that," says the White Silk Boy. "I shall lodge in the inn, and so shall you; I'll pay for both of us all right. But shall we make it a bargain, and agree to go shares in whatever we can earn here in the world?"

"That might do," said he, and so they came to the inn, and the Silk Boy made him come in, though he wasn't much for it. He ordered in wine and meat and cakes and it looked as if they were to live like any lord. "It *looks* well enough," the poor boy thought to himself, "but if this should be a bit of a rascal and won't pay for me, what am I going to do then? But anyhow they can't get more off the fox than the skin."

At night time they were to be in one bed: and when late on in the night the poor boy woke up, the other was gone. "Ah," he thought, "this looks well! Not a penny have I to give them for all that bill, I'd best run off away from the whole business." So he made up his mind to jump out of the window; but just as he had got it open and was going to get out, here comes the Silk Boy running and pushing him in at the window again. "You meant to make a fool of me, I see, and run away from me," said he. So they got into bed again and slept till day. When the reckoning came, all went well, for the Silk Boy paid for both of them.

Next day they came in the neighbourhood of a market town, and the Silk Boy said, "Can you guess what I'll manage when we get there?" No, that wasn't easy. But the lad repented of the bargain he had struck, for he was afraid the other one was a bad lot.

They went to a very large inn, and the Silk Boy said, "You can stop here. I must go out into the town for a bit. You can order something to eat, you mustn't sit and starve, and I'll pay all right when I come back." So off he went, but the other one durst not order anything. He was that hungry that his belly cried out in his body. But meanwhile the Silk Boy had been busy enough. He had been out in the town and bought a coach with four black horses, and he had been to a goldsmith and got four silver shoes put on each and every horse, and he had bought a proper fine suit of clothes for the poor boy. So he came driving into the inn yard and made such a knocking as shook the whole place. Then the lad was dressed up in the fine clothes, and then they got them something to eat, and for the time being that was the best of all, for he was that hungry that he whined with it. The Silk Boy scolded him a bit for being so mistrustful. "It's not according to our agreement," he said, and the other promised to behave better in the future.

In the morning when they had had their breakfast, they were to go out driving; and away they drove past a big palace, and there sat one of the owner's daughters up on the second floor, and she had the casement windows open and sat and sewed. So they drove past, so fast that one of the horses hind shoes flew off, and fell into her lap. In she ran to her father with it and called out, "Those must be some pretty rich folk that drove by; they've got silver shoes on their horses, for one flew up into my lap." "Well, you look out when they come back," said he, "so that they can have their shoe."

Well, she stood at the window and stared and looked for them. They hadn't driven but a short way along the road when they turned round; but when the Silk Boy got near the palace he cracked his whip fit to shake the whole place, and they flew by like a shooting star; so she got no chance to speak to them and give back the shoe.

It was settled now, that the poor lad should give himself out to be the master, and the Silk Boy was to be his coachman and servant. He went out with his horses and drove to the goldsmith to get him to take off the four silver shoes and put four gold shoes to each horse instead.

Next day they were to go out driving again. The girl was sitting up there at the window sewing, as on the day before, and a gold shoe flew off one of the horses on to her lap, as they went by at a great pace. So she ran in to her father and called out: "Those must be terrible rich people that came past here! Yesterday they had silver shoes, and to-day they've got gold shoes to their horses." "So!" said he; "well, we must look out for them when they come back, so that they can have it."

When they had been out driving a bit, and had turned the coach, the Silk Boy said: "Now, when we come near the palace, they'll be standing outside and will be for giving you the shoe; but you mustn't take it; you must say you don't reckon of such things at all, and the young lady is welcome to keep it. Then they will ask you in to dine with them, and that you must accept. I shall be coming in too, and I shall be put at the lower end of the table, but you needn't mind about that. Then they'll want to know where you come from, but you must say you come from a castle out in the country here. Then the man will offer you his daughter's hand, and you must accept her, and welcome."

Well, as soon as the Silk Boy had given him these instructions, they drove past the palace. There stood the owner and his daughter, outside the door. They clapped their hands and beckoned to them to pull up, so they did; and the daughter came to offer the gentleman the shoe that his horse had dropped. Oh no, he didn't mind about that, she might keep it, and welcome. "Well, would he please to come in and take dinner with them?" "Yes, that he would." And so in he went, and was set up at the high table, but the Silk Boy was put at the lower table, for he was only the coachman. Then they wanted him to tell them where he came from, and he said, according as the other had told him, that he came from a big castle out here in the country. Then the gentleman made him the offer; wouldn't he perhaps take a fancy to his daughter? Yes, he would. And they agreed on it, and as she was just as ready, everything was settled and signed. The wedding clothes were bought, and the wedding arranged, and everything went off in great style.

When it was all over, the poor lad was to go home to his castle with his wife. He didn't know where he was going to take her, for one thing was quite certain, that he hadn't got any castle—but he left everything to the White Silk Boy. The closed carriage, with the four horses, drove up to the door, and her father and mother were to come with them and see the husband's home, and the Silk Boy sat up on a dickey behind, but he looked after the driving all the same. When they had driven a short way, they came to a paddock where there was a big flock of sheep. Now, the White Boy had given the bridegroom his instructions beforehand, so when they asked whose sheep those were, he said: "Oh, they're mine." "Now, I never knew the like of that," said his wife. "My father has many sheep, and has had many sheep, but never have I seen such good sheep and so many sheep as there are here."

So they drove on a little, and they came past another paddock, that was full of bullocks. "Whose might the bullocks be?" said she.

"Oh, they're mine," said the poor lad. "Now, I never knew the like of that," said she; "no, really now, I never could have believed you were so well off. For my father has many bullocks, and has had many bullocks, but never have I seen such good bullocks nor so many bullocks nor such big bullocks as there are here."

So they drove on a bit, till they came to another paddock that was full of cows and nothing else. "Whose might the cows be?" said she. "Oh, they're mine," said the lad. "Well, the farther I go the more I am surprised," said she. "My father has many cows, and has had many cows, but never have I seen such good cows, nor such big cows nor so many cows as there are here." So they drove a little further, and they came to another paddock that was ful of horses. "Who might be the owner of these horses?" said she. "Oh, that's me," said the lad. "No! now really, I never knew the like," said she. "My father has many horses, and has had many horses, but such good horses and such big horses and so many horses, as there are here, I never did see."

A little after, they came to the fifth paddock, and that was full of pigs and nothing else. "What! Are these really yours, too, these pigs?" said she. "Yes, to be sure they are." "Oh no, now really, never did I see the like," said she. "My father has many pigs, and has had many pigs, but so many pigs and such good pigs and such large pigs, I really and truly never did see."

When they had driven a little farther, they could just see a big castle, a long way off. So she asked him whose castle that was. It was his, he said. Now really, she never had known the like. Her father had a big castle, and she had seen a number of them, but never had she seen one so big as this here one.

Meanwhile, evening had come on, and they were driving through a wood. It so happened, that the lad looked out of the window, and the Silk Boy was gone! What was he to do, now? He didn't know the way, and he did know that the whole of what he had been sitting and stuffing up his wife with, was lies from beginning to end. A regular bad lot, this boy was, who was leaving him in the lurch at the end of it all. Anyhow, he made up his mind that he would run away from the lot of them. He threw open the carriage door and was just jumping out, when at the very minute his servant came running, and slammed the door to again, and said: "What sort of a trick is this? Do you mean to make a fool of me again?"

So then they drove on a bit, and the coachman asked what it was he could see up there. That was the big house they were to go to, said the servant. It was dark, to be sure, but when they got close up to it, they could see there was a moat round it, and a drawbridge, too. Everything was in readiness to receive them when they drove into the castle, and the parents were in the greatest of delight, that they had got their daughter married into such a nice place. So they must go for a look round, and of course the lad must show his wife over the castle; but he was as much of a stranger there as she was, and the Silk Boy was gone out to unharness his horses. But after all, he came, and he knew it all and could show them all about. Every room they went into was full of gold and silver, and there was store of all manner of things, and it was like that all through the place. And the parents, they were near losing their mouths and noses at the sight of all the grandeur there was.

Now, when a day had passed by after their coming there, the servant had disappeared again. The lad went and hunted for him all round about, and at last he found him, round behind the castle in a straw-stack. "Why will you make me so sad, stopping away like this?" said he. "Ah! now I must be leaving you," said the other. "Oh no, no! Why should you do that? Do stay with me; there's enough for us both to live on."

No, he couldn't do so, he said. "But now we ought to divide up what we've got, together; that's what we agreed to do." Yes, the lad was ready to do that, but what should they do about his wife? "You'd better take the house and all that, while I keep her; it isn't mine anyhow."

"Well, now I'll tell you how it all hangs together. It was I that you paid three marks for, to have me buried in the churchyard, and so I wanted to do you a good turn and repay you. The first time I went off from you—that was at night in the inn—I was out at the castle here, to kill a troll who had taken possession of it; but I had no luck that time, you woke too quick, and I was obliged to meet you at the window. When we drove out here, by the road, I was off again, and this time I got the better of the troll and got everything ready to receive the gentry who I said were coming. But it was something of a shock for me, when you wanted to try and steal off again. I have no need of anything that is here on earth, and so you may have it all yourself. I don't wish for any of it at all, and so I must bid you farewell." Thereupon, they took a solemn leave of each other, and the poor lad went on living with his wife there at the mansion, in great state and happiness, till their dying day.

The Little Mermaid

Far out in the sea the water is as blue as the petals of the loveliest of cornflowers, and as clear as the clearest glass; but it is very deep, deeper than any anchor-cable can reach, and many church towers would have to be put one on the top of another to reach from the bottom out of the water. Down there live the sea people.

Now you must not think for a moment that there is only a bare white sandy bottom there; no, no: there the most extraordinary trees and plants grow, which have stems and leaves so supple that they stir at the slightest movement of the water, as if they were alive. All the fish, big and little, flit among the branches, like the birds in the air up here. In the deepest place of all lies the sea King's palace. The walls are of coral, and the tall pointed windows of the clearest possible amber, but the roof is of mussel-shells that open and shut themselves as the water moves. It all looks beautiful, for in every one of them lie shining pearls, a single one of which would be the principal ornament in a Queen's crown.

The sea King down there had been a widower for many years, but his old mother kept house for him. She was a clever woman, but proud of her rank, for which reason she went about with twelve oysters on her tail, while the rest of the nobility might only carry six. For the rest she deserved high praise, especially because she was so fond of the little sea Princesses, her grandchildren. There were six of them, beautiful children, but the youngest was the prettiest of them all. Her skin was as bright and pure as a rose-leaf, her eyes were as blue as the deepest lake; but like all the rest, she had no feet —her body ended in a fish's tail. All the live-long day they might play down in the palace in the great halls where live flowers grew out of the walls. The big windows of amber stood open, and the fishes swam in through them, just as with us swallows fly in when we open the windows; but the fishes used to swim right up to the little Princesses and feed out of their hands and allow themselves to be stroked.

Outside the palace there was a large garden with fiery red and dark blue trees, whose fruit shone like gold, and their flowers were like a flaming fire, because they were always moving their stems and leaves. The ground was of the finest sand, but blue like the flame of sulphur. Over the whole expanse down there lay a wonderful blue sheen. You could more easily imagine that you were far up in the air and could see the sky above you and below you, than that you were at the bottom of the sea. In a dead calm you could see the sun: it looked like a purple flower out of whose cup all the light was streaming.

Each of the young Princesses had her little plot in the garden, where she could dig and plant as she liked. One would make her flower-bed in the shape of a whale, another preferred to have hers like a little mermaid, but the youngest made hers quite round, like the sun, and would only have flowers that shone red like it. She was an odd child, quiet and thoughtful, and whereas the other sisters would deck out their gardens with the quaintest things, that they had got from sunken ships, she would only have—besides the rose-red flowers that were like the sun far up in the sky—a pretty statue of marble. It was of a handsome boy, carved out of bright white stone, which had come down to the sea bottom from a wreck. Beside the statue she planted a rose-red weeping willow, which grew splendidly and hung its fresh branches over it, right down to the blue sand bottom, on which the shadows showed violet, and moved with the branches; it looked as if the top and the roots of the tree were playing at kissing each other.

She had no greater delight than in dreaming about the world of men up above. The old grandmother had to tell her all she knew about ships and horses and men and animals. It seemed to her particularly delightful that up there on earth the flowers smelt sweet (which they did not at the sea bottom), and that the woods were green and the fish which one saw among the branches could sing so loud and prettily that it was a joy to hear them. It was the little birds that the grandmother called fish, otherwise they could not have understood, for they had never seen a bird.

"When you're full fifteen years old," said the grandmother, "you shall have leave to come up out of the sea and sit on the rocks in the moonlight, and see the big ships that come sailing by; and forests and houses you shall see."

During the year that was passing one of the sisters was fifteen years old; but the rest—why, each was a year younger than the next, and so the youngest had a clear five years to wait before she could come up from the sea bottom and see how things go with us. But the first promised the next one to tell her what she had seen and had thought beautiful on the first day, for their grandmother didn't tell them enough: there were very many things they wanted to know about.

None of them was so full of longing as the youngest, the very one who had the longest time to wait, and was so quiet and thoughtful. Many a night she stood at the open window and gazed up through the dark blue waters where the fish went waving their fins and tails. She could see the moon and the stars; of course they were very pale, but, seen through the water, they looked much larger than they do to our eyes. If something like a black cloud passed along beneath them, she knew that it was either a whale swimming above her, or even a ship with a number of people in it. Certainly they never thought that beneath them there was a lovely little mermaid stretching her hands up towards the keel.

And now the eldest Princess was fifteen years old and could rise up above the surface of the sea.

When she came back she had a hundred things to tell; but the most beautiful thing, she said, was to lie on a sandbank in the moonlight in the calm sea, and to see close by the shore the big town where the lights twinkled like hundreds of stars, and to hear the sound of music and the noise and stir of carts and people, and see all the church towers and steeples and hear the bells ringing; and just because she couldn't go up there, she longed after all that, most of all.

Oh, how the youngest sister did listen! And when, later on in the evening, she stood at the open window and gazed up through the dark blue water, she thought about the big town and all the noise and stir, and then she fancied she could hear the church bells ringing down to her.

The year after, the second sister had leave to rise up through the water and swim where she liked; she ducked up just as the sun was going down, and the sight of that she thought the most beautiful of all. The whole heaven, she said, had looked like gold, and the clouds—oh! the beauty of them she could not describe: red and violet, they sailed past above her, but far swifter than they there flew, like a large white ribbon, a skein of wild swans away over the water, to where the sun was. She swam towards it, but it sank, and the rosy glow died from the clouds and the face of the sea.

Next year the third sister went up; she was the boldest of them all; and so she swam up a broad river that ran into the sea. Beautiful green hills she saw, with rows of vines upon them. Palaces and mansions peeped out from among stately woods. She heard all the birds singing, and the sun shone so hot that she had to dive beneath the water to cool her burning face. In a little inlet she came upon a whole crowd of young human children; they were quite naked, and ran about and splashed in the water. She wanted to play with them, but they ran away in a fright, and then came a little black creature (it was a dog, but she had never seen a dog before) and it barked at her so dreadfully that she was terrified and took refuge in the open sea; but never could she forget the splendid woods and the green hills and the pretty children who could swim in the water, though they had no fish-tails.

The fourth sister was not so daring. She stayed out in the lonely sea, and told them that that was the most beautiful of all. You could see many many miles all round, and the sky arched over you like a great bell of glass. Ships she had seen, but far away they looked like gulls. The merry dolphins had turned somersaults, and the big whales had squirted up water out of their nostrils, so that it looked like hundreds of fountains all around her.

Now came the turn of the fifth sister. Her birthday, it happened, was in winter, and so she saw what the others had not seen on their first visit. The sea was all green to look at, and round about there floated large icebergs, everyone looking like a pearl, she said, and yet they were far bigger than the church towers that men built. They showed themselves in the strangest shapes and were like diamonds. She had seated herself on one of the largest, and all the ships made a wide circle in fear, away from the place where she was sitting and letting the wind set her long hair flying; but on towards evening the sky was covered with clouds, it lightened and thundered, while the black sea lifted the masses of ice high up, and made them glitter in the fierce lightning. Aboard of all the ships they took in sail, and there was anxiety and fear, but she sat calmly on her floating iceberg and watched the blue flashes strike zig-zagging into the shining sea.

The first time any of the sisters came to the top of the water, each one of them was always entranced by all the new pretty sights she saw, but now that, as grown girls, they had leave to go up whenever they liked, it became quite ordinary to them, and they longed to be at home again; and after a month had passed they said that after all it was far prettier down at the bottom, and there one was so comfortable at home.

On many an evening the five sisters would link arms together and rise in a row above the water. They had lovely voices, more beautiful than any human being's, and when a storm was coming on, and they thought some ships might be lost, they would swim before the ships and sing most beautifully of how pretty it was at the bottom of the sea, and bade the seafarers not to be afraid of coming down there.

But they could not understand their words; they thought it was the storm. Nor did they see any beautiful things down there either, for when the ship sank they were drowned, and only as dead corpses did they ever reach the sea King's palace.

When of an evening the sisters rose like this, arm in arm, up through the sea, their little sister was left behind quite alone, looking after them, and it seemed as if she must have wept, but a mermaid has no tears, and that makes her suffer all the more.

"Oh! if only I was fifteen," she said, "I know I shall become really fond of that world up there and of the people who have their homes there!"

At last she was fifteen years old.

"There now! We've got you off our hands," said the grand-mother, the old widow Queen. "Come here, and let me dress you out like your other sisters"; and she put a wreath of white lilies on her hair, only every petal in the flower was a half-pearl, and the old lady made eight large oysters take tight hold of the Princess's tail, to indicate her high rank.

"But it hurts so," said the little mermaid.

"Yes, one must suffer a little for smartness' sake," said the old lady.

Oh dear! She would gladly have shaken off all this finery and put away the heavy wreath. The red flowers in her garden became her much better; but she dare not change it. "Good-bye," she said, and rose bright and light as a bubble, up through the water. The sun had just gone down when she lifted her head above the sea, but all the clouds were still glowing like gold and roses, and in the midst of the pale red heaven the evening star shone clear and beautiful. The air was soft and cool, and the sea dead calm. There lay a great ship with three masts; only a single sail was set, for no wind was stirring, and round about on the rigging and on the yard, sailors were sitting. There was music and singing, and as evening grew darker hundreds of variegated lamps were lit. They looked as if the flags of all nations were waving in the air. The little mermaid swam straight up to the cabin window, and every time a wave lifted her, she could see through at the windows, clear as mirrors, numbers of gaily dressed people; but the handsomest of them all was the young Prince with the big black eyes: he was certainly not much over six-teen, and this was his birthday, and that was why there were all these fine doings. The sailors danced on the deck, and when the young Prince came out there, more than a hundred rockets shot up into the sky. They shone as bright as day, and the little mermaid was quite frightened and dived down beneath the water, but soon she put up her head again, and then it seemed as if all the stars in the sky were falling down on her. She had never seen fireworks like that. Great suns whizzed round, splendid fire-fish darted into the blue heaven, and everything was reflected back from the bright calm sea. On the ship itself there was so much light that you could see every least rope, let alone the people. Oh! how handsome the young Prince was; he shook hands with the crew and smiled and

The Little Mermaid

laughed, while the music rang out into the beautiful night. It grew late, but the little mermaid could not take her eyes off the ship and the beautiful Prince. The coloured lamps were put out, no more rockets flew up into the sky, no more guns were let off, but deep down in the sea there was a murmur and a rumbling. Meanwhile she sat on the water and swung up and down, so that she could see into the cabin; but the ship now took a swifter pace, one sail after another was spread, the waves rose higher, great clouds came up in the distance, there was lightning. Oh, there would be a terrible storm; and the seamen took in sail. The great ship ploughed with the speed of a bird over the wild sea, the water piled itself into huge black mountains, as if to top the masts, but the ship dived down like a swan between the tall billows, and rose again over the heaving waters. To the little mermaid it seemed just a pleasant jaunt, but not so to the sailors. The ship creaked and cracked, the stout planks bent with the mighty blows that the sea dealt. The mast snapped in the midst as if it had been a reed, and the ship heeled over on her side, while the water rushed into her hull. Now the little mermaid saw they were in peril; she herself had to beware of the beams and broken pieces of the ship that were driven about in the sea. At one instant it was so pitch-dark that she could see nothing whatever; then, when it lightened, it was so bright that she could see everyone on board. Everyone was leaping off as best he could. The young Prince above all she looked for, and she saw him, when the ship parted, sink down into the deep. For a moment she was full of joy that now he was coming down to her; but then she remembered that men could not live in the water, and that he could never come alive to her father's palace. No, die he must not! So she swam in among the beams and planks that drove about in the water, quite forgetting that they might have crushed her—dived deep beneath the water, and rose high among the billows, and so came at last to the young Prince, who could hardly keep himself afloat any longer in the stormy sea. His arms and legs were beginning to tire, his beautiful eyes were closing; but he would perforce have died had not the little mermaid come to him. She held his head above the water, and let the waves drive her with him whither they would.

At dawn the tempest was over; of the ship there was not a bit to be seen. The sun rose red and bright out of the water, and it seemed

89

as if thereat life came into the Prince's cheeks; but his eyes were still closed. The mermaid kissed his fair high forehead and stroked back his wet hair. She thought he resembled the marble statue down in her little garden. She kissed him again and wished that he might live after all.

And now she saw in front of her the dry land, high blue hills on whose top the white snow shone as if swans were lying there. Down by the shore were lovely green woods, and in front of them lay a church or an abbey (she knew not what), but at least a building. Lemon and apple trees grew in the garden, and before the gate were tall palms. At this spot the sea made a little bay; it was dead calm, but very deep right up to the rocks where the fine white sand was washed up. Hither she swam with the fair Prince and laid him on the sand, but took care that his head should rest uppermost in the warm sunshine.

Now the bells rang out from the great white building, and a number of young maidens came out through the gardens. The little mermaid swam further out, behind some high boulders which stuck up out of the water, laid some sea-foam over her hair and her bosom, so that no one could see her little face, and there she watched to see who would come to the poor Prince. It was not long before a young girl came that way, and seemed to be quite terrified, but only for a moment. Then she fetched more people, and the mermaid saw the Prince revive, and smile on all those about him. But on her, out there, he did not smile; he had, of course, no notion that she had rescued him. She felt very sad, and when he was carried into the great building, she dived sorrowfully down into the water, and betook herself home to her father's palace.

She had always been quiet and thoughtful, but now she became much more so. The sisters asked her what she had seen the first time she went up, but she did not tell them anything about it.

Every evening and morning did she go up to the place where she had left the Prince. She saw how the fruits in the garden grew ripe and were picked; she saw how the snow melted on the high mountains; but the Prince she never saw, so she always turned homeward sadder than before. It was her one comfort to sit in her little garden and throw her arms about the fair marble statue which was like the Prince; but she took no care of her flowers, and they spread as in a wild wood over all the paths, and wove their long stems and leaves in among the branches of the trees, so that it was quite dark there.

At last she could contain herself no longer, but told one of her sisters, and at once all the others got to know it, but nobody else except them and just one or two other mermaids, who didn't tell anyone but their dearest friends. One of these could tell who the Prince was: she too had seen the fete on the ship, and knew where he came from and where his kingdom lay.

"Come, little sister," said the other Princesses, and with their arms about each other's shoulders they rose in a long line out of the sea in front of the spot where they knew the Prince's palace was.

It was built of a kind of pale yellow shining stone, with great marble steps that you could go down straight into the sea. Stately gilded domes rose above the roof, and between the pillars that surrounded the whole building stood statues of marble which seemed alive. Through the clear glass of the tall windows you could see into the noble halls, where costly silk curtains and tapestries were hung, and all the walls were decked with great paintings that it was delightful to gaze at. In the middle of the largest hall a great fountain splashed; its jet soared high up towards the glass dome in the roof, through which the sun shone on the water and on the beautiful plants that grew in the wide basin.

Now she knew where he lived, and thither she came on many an evening and night upon the water. She swam much closer to the land than any of the others had dared to do; she even went right up the narrow canal beneath the stately balcony of marble, which cast a shadow far over the water. Here she would sit and gaze at the young Prince, who believed himself to be quite alone in the bright moonlight.

Many an evening she saw him sail, to the sound of music, in his splendid boat, where the flags waved; she peeped out from among the green weed, and if the breeze caught her long silver white veil, and anyone saw it, they thought it was a swan flapping its wings.

Many a night when the fishermen lay out at sea with torches, she heard them telling all manner of good about the young Prince, and it made her glad that she had saved his life when he was being tossed half dead upon the waves, and she thought of how close his head had lain on her bosom, and how lovingly she had kissed him then; he knew nothing whatever about it, and could not so much as dream about her.

She became fonder and fonder of human people, and more and more did she long to be able to go up amongst them. Their world, she thought, was far larger than hers: for they could fly far over the sea in ships, climb high up above the clouds on the lofty mountains; and the lands they owned stretched over forests and fields farther than she could see. There was a great deal she wanted to know, but her sisters could not answer all her questions, so she asked the old grandmother: she knew well the upper world, as she very properly called the countries above the sea.

"If the human people aren't drowned," the little mermaid inquired, "can they go on living always? Don't they die as we do down here in the sea?"

"Yes," said the old lady, "they have to die, too, and besides, their lifetime is shorter than ours. We can live for three hundred years, but when we cease to be here, we only turn to foam on the water, and have not even a grave down here among our dear ones. We have no mortal souls, we never live again; we are like the green weed: once it is cut down it never grows green again. Human kind, on the other hand, have a soul that lives always after the body has turned into earth. It rises up through the clear air, up to all the shining stars; just as we rise out of the sea and look at the human people's country, so do they rise up to unknown beautiful places, which we never attain."

"Why did we have no immortal souls given us?" said the little mermaid, very sadly. "I would give all my hundreds of years that I have to live to be a human being for only one day, and then get a share in the heavenly world."

"You mustn't go thinking about that," said the old lady, "we have a much happier and better lot than the people up there."

"So then I've got to die and float like foam on the sea, and not hear the noise of the waves and see the lovely flowers and the red sun! Can't I do anything at all to gain an everlasting soul?"

"No," said the old lady, "only if a human being held you so dear that you were to him more than father or mother, and if with all his thoughts and affections he clung to you and made the priest lay his right hand in yours with the promise to be faithful to you here and for ever, then his soul would flow over into your body, and you too would have a share in the destiny of men. He would give you a soul and still keep his own. But that can never happen. The very thing that is counted beautiful here in the sea, I mean your fish's tail, they think horrid up there on the earth; they have no notion of what's proper: up there people must needs have two clumsy props which they call legs, if they're to look nice."

The little mermaid sighed and looked sadly at her fish's tail. "Let's be cheerful," said the old lady. "We'll jump and dance about for the three hundred years we have to live. It's long enough in all conscience; after that one can sleep it out all the pleasanter in one's grave. To-night we're to have a court ball."

Truly, it was a magnificent affair, such as you never see on earth. The walls and ceilings of the great ballroom were of glass, thick but clear. Many hundreds of large mussel-shells, rose-red and grass-green, were set in rows on either side, with a blue flame burning in them that lighted up the whole hall and shone out through the walls, so that the sea outside was all lit up. You could see all the innumerable fish, big and little, swimming round the glass walls. The scales of some of them shone purple-red, on others they shone like silver and gold. In the middle of the hall there flowed a broad rapid stream, and on it mermen and mermaids danced to their own beautiful singing. Such charming voices no one on earth possesses. The little mermaid sang the most beautifully of them all, and they clapped their hands at her, and for a moment she felt joy at her heart, for she knew that she had the loveliest voice of anyone on earth or sea. But soon she began to think again about the world above her. She could not forget the handsome Prince, and her own sorrow that she did not, like him, possess an immortal soul. So she stole out of her father's palace, and while everything there was song and merriment she sat sadly in her little garden. There she heard the beating waves sounding down through the water, and she thought, sure, he is sailing up there, he whom I love more than father or mother, he to whom my thoughts cling and in whose hand I would lay the destiny of my life. I would risk everything to win him and an immortal soul. While my sisters are dancing in my father's palace, I will go to the old Sea Witch. I've always been dreadfully afraid of her, but it may be she can advise me and help me.

So the little mermaid went off out of her garden, towards the roaring maelstrom behind which the witch lived. She had never been that way before. No flowers grew there, and no sea grass: only the bare grey sandy bottom stretched out round the maelstrom, where the water whirled round like a roaring millwheel and swept everything it caught hold of down with it into the deep. Right through those tearing whirls she must go to enter the Sea Witch's domain, and here for a long way the only path ran over hot bubbling mire which the Witch called her peat moss. Behind it lay her house, in the middle of a hideous wood. All the trees and bushes of it were polypi, half animal and half plant, which looked like hundred-headed snakes growing out of the ground. All their branches were long slimy arms with fingers like pliant worms, and joint after joint they kept in motion from the root till the outermost tip. Everything in the sea that they could grasp they twined themselves about, and never let it go again. The little mermaid was in terrible fear as she stopped outside the wood. Her heart beat with terror, and she almost turned back, but then she thought of the Prince and of the human soul, and so she took courage. She bound her long flowing hair close about her head, so that the polypi should not catch her by it; she joined her two hands together on her breast, and darted along as a fish darts through the water, in among the terrible polypi, which stretched out their pliant arms and fingers after her. She saw that every one of these held something it had caught, and hundreds of little arms held it like strong bands of iron. Men who had been lost at sea and had sunk deep down there, looked out, white skeletons, from among the arms of the polypi. Rudders of ships and chests they held fast; skeletons of land beasts, and even a little mermaid, which they had caught and killed. That, to her, was almost the most frightful thing of all.

Now she came to a great slimy clearing in the wood, where large fat water-snakes wallowed, showing their ugly whitey-yellow coils. In the centre of the clearing was a house built of the white bones of men: there the Sea Witch sat, making a toad feed out of her mouth, as we make a little canary bird eat sugar.

The hideous fat water-snakes she called her little chicks, and let them coil about over her great spongy bosom.

"I know well enough what you want," said the Sea Witch, "and a silly thing, too; all the same, you shall have your way, for it'll bring you to a bad end, my pretty Princess. You want to be rid of your fish tail and have two props to walk on instead, like humans, so that the young Prince may fall in love with you, and you may get

Robin Jacques

him and an immortal soul." With that the Witch laughed so loud and so hideously that the toad and the snakes tumbled down on to the ground and wallowed about there. "You've come just in the nick of time," said the Witch; "to-morrow after sunrise I couldn't help you till another year came round. I shall make a drink for you, and with it you must swim to the land before the sun rises, put yourself on the beach there, and drink it up; then your tail will part and open into what men call pretty legs. But it'll hurt, it'll be like a sharp sword going through you. Everybody that sees you will say you are the prettiest human child they ever saw. You'll keep your swimming gait, and no dancer will be able to float along like you. But every step you take will be as if you were treading on a sharp knife, so that you would think your blood must gush out. If you can bear all that, I will do what you wish."

"Yes," said the little mermaid, with a faltering voice; and she thought of the Prince and of winning an immortal soul. "But remember," said the Witch, "when you've once taken a human shape, you can never become a mermaid again, you can never go down through the water to your sisters or to your father's palace; and if you don't win the love of the Prince, so that for you he forgets father and mother, and clings to you with all his thoughts, and makes the priest lay your hands in one another's, so that you become man and wife, then you won't get your immortal soul. On the first morning after he is married to anyone else, your heart will break and you will become foam on the water."

"It is my wish," said the little mermaid, pale as a corpse.

"But I must be paid, too," said the witch, "and it's not a small matter that I require. You have the loveliest voice of anyone down here at the bottom of the sea, and with it no doubt you think you'll be able to charm him; but that voice you must give me. I must have the best thing you possess as the price of my precious drink. I shall have to give you my own blood in it, that the drink may be as sharp as a two-edged sword.

"But if you take away my voice," said the little mermaid, "what have I left?"

"Your beautiful form," said the witch, "and your floating gait, and your speaking eyes: with them you can easily delude a human heart. What, have you lost courage? Put out your little tongue, and I'll cut it off for the price, and you shall have the potent drink."

"So be it," said the little mermaid, and the witch put her cauldron on the fire to boil the magic drink. "Cleanliness is a good thing," said she, and scoured out the cauldron with some snakes which she tied in a knot. Then she scratched herself in the breast and let the black blood drip into the pot. The steam took the most dreadful shapes, enough to fill one with fear and horror. Every moment the witch cast something afresh into the cauldron, and when it was really boiling, the sound was like that of a crocodile weeping. At last the drink was ready, and it looked like the clearest of water.

"There you are," said the witch, and cut off the tongue of the little mermaid. Now she was dumb, she could neither sing nor speak.

"If the polypi should catch you when you are going back through my wood," said the Witch, "just throw one drop of that drink on them, and their arms and fingers will break into a thousand bits." But there was no need for the little mermaid to do that; the polypi shrank back in fear before her when they saw the shining drink which glittered in her hand as if it had been a twinkling star. So she passed quickly through the wood, and the marsh, and the roaring maelstrom.

She could see her father's palace. The torches were quenched in the great ballroom. No doubt everyone in there was asleep, but she dared not go to them now that she was dumb and was going to leave them for ever. It seemed as if her heart must burst asunder with sorrow. She stole into the garden and took one flower from each of her sister's flower-beds, and blew on her fingers a thousand kisses towards the palace, and rose up through the dark blue sea.

The sun was not yet up when she saw the Prince's palace, and clambered up the stately marble steps. The moon was shining beautifully bright. The little mermaid swallowed the sharp burning drink, and it was as though a two-edged sword was piercing her delicate body: she swooned with the pain, and lay as one dead. When the sun shone out over the sea, she awoke and felt a torturing pang, but right in front of her stood the beautiful young Prince. He fixed his coal-black eyes on her, so that she cast her own eyes down, and saw that her fish's tail was gone and that she now had the prettiest small white legs that any young girl could have. But she was quite naked, so she wrapped herself in her masses of long hair. The Prince asked who she was and how she had come there, and she gazed at him sweetly and yet sadly with her dark blue eyes, for she could not speak. Then he took her by the hand and led her into the palace. Every step she took was, as the witch had warned her, as if she was treading on pointed swords and sharp knives, yet she bore it gladly. Led by the Prince's hand, she walked light as a bubble, and he and everyone else marvelled at her graceful floating gait.

Costly robes of silk and muslin were put upon her, and she was the fairest of all in the palace; but she was dumb and could neither speak nor sing. Beautiful slave girls clad in silks and gold came forward and sang to the Prince and his royal parents. One sang more sweetly than all the rest, and the Prince applauded her and smiled on her. Then the little mermaid was sad, for she knew that she herself had sung far more sweetly; and she thought: Oh! if he could but know that to be near him I have given my voice away for ever!

Then the slave girls danced graceful floating dances to the noblest of music, and now the little mermaid raised her pretty white arms and rose on tip-toe and floated over the floor, and danced as none had ever yet danced. At every movement her beauty grew yet more on the sight, and her eyes spoke more deeply to the heart than the song of the slave girls.

Everyone was enraptured by it, and more than all, the Prince, who called her his little foundling; and she danced again and again, though every time her foot touched the ground it was as though she was treading on sharp knives. The Prince said that now she should always be near him, and she was allowed to sleep outside his door on a cushion of silk.

He had a boy's dress made for her, so that she might ride with him on horseback. They rode through the sweet-smelling woods, where the green boughs brushed her shoulders, and the little birds sang in the cover of the young leaves. With the Prince she clambered up the high mountains, and though her delicate feet were cut so that everyone could see, she only laughed, and followed him till they could see the clouds beneath them like a flock of birds flying towards the distant lands.

At home at the Prince's palace, when at night all the others were asleep, she would go out to the broad marble stairs, and it cooled her burning feet to stand in the cold sea water, and then she thought about those who were down in the deeps below.

The Little Mermaid

One night her sisters came up arm in arm, singing mournfully as they swam on the water, and she beckoned to them, and they recognized her, and told her how sad she had made them all. After that they visited her every night; and one night she saw far out in the sea, the old grandmother, who had not been to the top of the water for many a year; and the Sea King, with his crown on his head. They stretched their arms towards her, but they dared not trust themselves so near the land as the sisters.

Day by day she grew dearer to the Prince: he loved her as one might love a dear good child, but he never had a thought of making her his Queen: and his wife she must be, or else she could never win an immortal soul, but on his wedding morning she would turn into foam on the sea.

"Are not you fonder of me than of all the rest?" the little mermaid's eyes seemed to say when he took her in his arms and kissed her fair brow. "Yes, you are dearest of all to me," said the Prince, "for you have the best heart of them all. You are dearest to me, and you are like a young maiden whom I saw once and certainly shall never meet again. I was on a ship that was wrecked, and the waves drove me to land near a holy temple where a number of young maidens ministered. The youngest of them found me on the bank and saved my life. I saw her only twice. She was the only one I could love in all the world, but you are like her, you almost stamp her likeness on my soul. She belongs to that holy temple, and therefore my good fortune has sent you to me, and we never will part." "Ah, he doesn't know that I saved his life," thought the little mermaid. "I bore him over the sea, away to the grove where the temple stands; I sat behind him in the foam and watched to see if anyone would come, and saw the pretty maiden whom he loves more than me"; and the mermaid heaved a deep sigh. Weep she could not: " 'The maiden belongs to the holy temple,' he said; she will never come out into the world: they will never meet again. I am with him, I see him every day. I will tend him and love him and give up my life to him."

But now the Prince was to be married, people said, and to take the beautiful daughter of the neighbouring king; and it was for that that he was fitting out such a splendid ship. "They say, of course, that the Prince is going to travel to see the country of the king next door, but it really is to see his daughter. He's to have a

99

great suite with him." But the little mermaid shook her head and laughed: she knew the Prince's mind better than anyone else. "I must travel," he had said to her, "I must see the pretty Princess; my father and mother require that, but they will not force me to bring her home as my bride. I cannot love her. She is not like the fair maiden of the temple, as you are. If ever I chose a bride it would be you first, my dumb foundling with the speaking eyes." And he kissed her red lips and played with her long hair and laid his head on her heart, so that it dreamed of man's destiny and an undying soul.

"You're not afraid of the sea, are you, my dumb child?" said he as they stood on the splendid ship that was to bear them to the country of the neighbouring King. And he told her of storms and calm, of strange fishes in the deep, and of what divers had seen down there, and she smiled at his description, for, of course, she knew more than anybody else about the bottom of the sea. In the moonlit night, when all but the steersman were asleep, she sat on the gunwale of the ship and gazed down through the clear water and fancied she saw her father's palace. On the summit of it stood the old grandmother, with a crown of silver on her head, gazing up through the swift current at the ship's keel. Then her sisters came up upon the water, and looked mournfully at her and wrung their white hands. She beckoned to them and smiled, and wanted to tell them that all was going well and happily with her; but then the ship's boy came towards her, and the sisters dived down: so he thought the white arms he had seen were foam on the sea.

Next morning the ship sailed into the harbour of the neighbouring King's fine city. All the church bells rang out, and from the tall towers there came blaring of trumpets, while the soldiers paraded with waving flags and glittering bayonets. Every day there was a fete, balls and parties followed on one another; but as yet the Princess was not there. She was being brought up far away in a sacred temple, they said, and there was learning all royal accomplishments. At last she arrived.

The little mermaid waited, eager to see her beauty, and she had to confess that a more graceful form she had never seen. The skin was so delicate and pure, and behind the long dark eyelashes a pair of dark-blue beautiful eyes smiled out.

"It is you!" said the Prince, "you, who saved me when I lay like a corpse on the shore!" and he clasped his blushing bride in his arms. "Oh, I am more than happy!" he said to the little mermaid; "my dearest wish, the thing I never dared hope for, has been granted me. You will rejoice in my happiness, for you are fonder of me than all the rest"; and the little mermaid kissed his hand, and thought she felt her heart breaking. His wedding morning would bring death to her, and would change her into foam upon the sea.

All the church bells were ringing; the heralds rode about and proclaimed the betrothal. On every altar fragrant oil was burning in precious silver lamps; the priests swung their censers, and the bride and bridegroom joined hands and received the blessing of the Bishop. The little mermaid, clad in silk and gold, stood holding the bride's train; but her ears heard not the festal music, her eyes saw not the holy rite; she thought, on the eve of her death, of all that she had lost in the world.

That very evening the bride and the bridegroom embarked on the ship, and the cannons were fired and the flags waved, and amidship was raised a royal tent of gold and purple with the loveliest of curtains, and there the married pair were to sleep in that calm cool night.

The sails bellied in the wind, and the ship glided easily and with little motion, away over the bright sea.

When it grew dark, variegated lamps were lit and the crew danced merry dances on the deck. The little mermaid could not but think of the first time she rose up out of the sea and saw that same splendour and merriment; and she too whirled about in the dance, swerving as the swallow swerves when it is chased; and everyone was in ecstasies of wonder at her: never before had she danced so wonderfully. Sharp knives seemed to be cutting her delicate feet, but she hardly felt it: the wounds in her heart were sharper. She knew that was the last night she would see him for whom she had forsaken her race and her home, and given up her lovely voice, and daily had suffered unending pain unknown to him. This was the last night that she would breathe the same air as he, or see the deep ocean and the starlit heavens. An eternal night without thought, without dream, awaited her who neither had a soul nor could win one.

But all was joy and merriment aboard the ship till long past midnight. She laughed and danced with the thought of death in her heart. The Prince kissed his beautiful bride, and she played with his black hair, and arm in arm they went to rest in the splendid tent.

It was still and quiet now on the ship: only the helmsman stood at the tiller. The little mermaid laid her white arms on the bulwark and gazed eastward for the red of dawn: the first ray of the sun, she knew, would kill her. Then she saw her sisters rise out of the sea; they were pale as she, their beautiful long hair no longer fluttered in the breeze: it had been cut off.

"We have given it to the witch to make her help us, that you may not die to-night. She has given us a knife. Here it is! Do you see how sharp it is? Before the sun rises you must plunge it into the Prince's heart, and when his warm blood gushes out upon your feet, they will grow together into a fish tail and you will become a mermaid again, and will be able to come down to us in the water and live out your three hundred years before you turn into the dead salt sea foam. Make haste! He or you must die before the sun rises. Our old grandmother has been mourning till her white hair has fallen off as ours fell before the witch's shears. Kill the Prince and come back! Make haste: do you not see the red band in the heavens? In a few minutes the sun will climb into the sky, and then you must die"; and with a strange heavy sigh they sank beneath the waves.

The little mermaid drew aside the purple curtain of the tent and saw the beautiful bride sleeping with her head on the Prince's breast, and she stopped and kissed him on his fair brow, and looked at the sky where the red of the dawn was shining brighter and brighter, looked at the sharp knife, and fixed her eyes again on the Prince, who in his sleep was murmuring the name of his bride. She alone was in his thoughts, and the knife quivered in the mermaid's hand—but then—she cast it far out into the waves, and where it fell they shone red, and it seemed as if drops of blood spurted up out of the water. Once more she gazed with a half-dying glance on the Prince, and then threw herself from the ship into the sea, and felt that her body was dissolving into foam.

Now the sun ascended out of the sea, and his rays fell mild and warm upon the death-cold foam, and the little mermaid felt no touch of death. She saw the bright sun, and above her floated hundreds of lovely transparent forms. Through them she could see the white sails of the ship and the rosy clouds in the sky. Their voices were as music, but so ethereal that no human ear could hear it, just as no earthly eye could see them: wingless, they floated by their own lightness through the air. The little mermaid saw that she too had a body like theirs, which was rising further and further up out of the foam.

"To whom am I coming?" said she, and her voice rang like that of the other beings, so ethereally that no earthly music can re-echo its sound.

"To the daughters of the air," the others answered; "the mermaid has no immortal soul, and can never gain one unless she wins the love of a mortal; it is on a power outside her that her eternal being depends. The daughters of the air have no everlasting soul either, but they can by good deeds shape one for themselves. We are flying to the hot countries, where the stagnant air of pestilence kills men: there we waft coolness, we spread the perfume of the flowers through the air and send men new life and healing. When for three hundred years we have striven to do the good we can, we receive an immortal soul and have a share in the everlasting happiness of mankind. You, poor little mermaid, have striven for that too with all your heart; you have suffered and endured and raised yourself into the world of the spirits of the air, and you also, by good deeds, can shape for yourself an immortal soul in the space of three hundred years."

And the little mermaid raised her bright arms towards God's sun, and for the first time she felt the gift of tears.

On the ship there was stir and life again. She saw the Prince with his fair bride seeking for her: in deep sorrow they gazed down into the bubbling foam as if they knew she had cast herself into the waves. Unseen, she kissed the bride's forehead, and on him she smiled and then soared upward with the other children of the air to a rose-red cloud sailing in the heavens. "So, when three hundred years are over, we shall float into the heavenly kingdom, and we may reach it yet sooner," whispered one of them. "Unseen we float into the homes of men, where children are, and for every day on which we find a good child that makes its parents happy and earns their love, God shortens our time of trial. The child does not know it when we are flying through the room; and when we smile on it in happiness, a year is taken from the three hundred. But if we see a perverse and evil child, we have to weep in sorrow, and every tear we shed adds a day to our time of trial."

The Emperor's New Clothes

Many years ago there lived an Emperor who was so monstrous fond of fine new clothes that he spent all his money on being really smart. He didn't care about his army, he didn't care for going to the play, or driving out in the park, unless it was to show his new clothes. He had a coat for every hour in the day; and just as people say about a king, that "he's holding a council", so in this country they always said, "The Emperor is in his dressing room". In the great city where he lived, life was very pleasant, lots of strangers came there every day; and one day there arrived two swindlers. They gave out that they were weavers, and said they knew how to make the loveliest stuff that could possibly be imagined. Not only were the colours and patterns extraordinarily pretty, but the clothes that were made of the stuff had this marvellous property: that they were invisible to anyone who was either unfit for his situation or else was intolerably stupid. "Very excellent clothes those must be," thought the Emperor; "if I wore them I could tell which are the men in my realm who aren't fit for the posts they hold. I could tell clever people from stupid ones: to be sure that stuff must be made for me directly." Accordingly he gave the two swindlers a large sum in advance, so that they might begin their work. They set up two looms and pretended to be working, but they hadn't a vestige of anything on the looms. In hot haste they demanded the finest of silk and the best of gold, which they stuffed into their own pockets; and they worked away at the bare looms till any hour of the night.

"I *should* like to know how they are getting on with the stuff," thought the Emperor. But to tell the truth he had a little misgiving when he reflected that anyone who was stupid or unsuited to his post couldn't see the stuff. Of course, he was confident that he needn't be afraid for himself: all the same he decided to send someone else first to see how things were. Everybody in the whole city knew what a marvellous power was in the stuff, and everybody was agog to see how incompetent and how stupid his neighbour was.

"I'll send my good old minister down to the weavers," thought the Emperor; "he can quite well see how the stuff is shaping: he's an intelligent man, and no one is better fitted for his post than he."

So the worthy old minister went into the hall where the two swindlers were sitting working at the bare loom. "Heaven help us," thought the old minister, staring with all his eyes; "I can't see a thing"; but he didn't say so.

Both the swindlers begged him to be pleased to step nearer, and asked if here was not a pretty pattern, and beautiful colours; and they pointed to the bare looms, and the poor old minister kept staring at it, but he couldn't see anything, because there was nothing to be seen. "Gracious goodness!" thought he; "can I be stupid? I never thought so, and nobody must get to know it. Can I be unfit for my office? No, no! It won't do for me to say I can't see the stuff." "Well, have you nothing to say about it?" said the one who was weaving.

"Oh, it's charming! Most delightful!" said the old minister, looking through his spectacles. "The pattern! The colour! Yes, indeed, I must tell the Emperor I am infinitely pleased with it."

"We are glad indeed to hear it," said both the weavers, and proceeded to describe the colours, naming them, and the uncommon pattern. The old minister listened carefully so as to be able to repeat it when he went back to the Emperor; and so he did. The swindlers now demanded more money and more silk and gold to be used in the weaving. They pocketed it all; not a thread was put up, but they went on, as before, weaving at the bare loom.

Very soon, the Emperor sent another honest official over to see how the weaving progressed and whether the stuff would be ready soon. He fared just like the minister. He looked and looked, but as there was nothing there but the empty loom, nothing could be seen.

"Well, isn't that a fine piece of stuff?" said both the swindlers, exhibiting and explaining the lovely patterns that weren't there at all. "Stupid, I am not," thought the man; "it must be my nice post that I'm not fit for? That would be a good joke! But I mustn't let people notice anything." Whereupon he praised the stuff which he couldn't see, and assured them of his pleasure in the pretty colours and the exquisite pattern. "Yes, it is positively sweet," he told the Emperor. Everybody in the city was talking of the splendid stuff.

At last the Emperor decided to see it, while it was still on the loom, with a large suite of select people—among them the two worthy officials who had been there before. He went over to the two clever swindlers, who were now weaving with all their might; only without a vestige of a thread.

"Now, is not that magnificent?" said both the worthy officials "Will Your Majesty deign to note the beauty of the pattern and the colours?"; and they pointed to the bare loom, for they supposed that all the rest could certainly see the stuff. "What's the meaning of this?" thought the Emperor. "I can't see a thing! This is terrible! Am I stupid? Am I not fit to be Emperor? That would be the most frightful thing that could befall me." "Oh, it's very pretty, it has my all-highest approval!" said he, nodding complacently and gazing on the empty loom: of course, he wouldn't say he could see nothing. The whole of the suite he had with him looked and looked, but got no more out of that than the rest. However, they said, as the Emperor had said: "Oh, it's very pretty!" And they advised him to put on this splendid new stuff for the first time, on the occasion of a great procession which was to take place shortly. "Magnificent! Exquisite! Excellent!" went from mouth to mouth; the whole company was in the highest state of gratification. The Emperor gave each of the swindlers a knight's cross to hang in his buttonhole and the title of "Gentleman in Weaving".

The whole night, previous to the morning on which the procession was to take place, the swindlers sat up, and had upwards of sixteen candles lit; people could see they were hard put to it to get the Emperor's new clothes finished. They pretended to be taking the stuff off the loom; they clipped with scissors in the air, they sewed with a needle without thread—and finally they said: "Look now! The clothes are finished." The Emperor with the noblest of his personal attendants came thither himself. Each of the swindlers raised an arm in the air as if holding something up, and said: "See, here are the hose, this is the coat, this is the mantle, and so on. It is as light as a spider's web, you would think you had nothing whatever on; but that is, of course, the beauty of it." "Yes," said all the attendants; but they couldn't see anything, for there was nothing to be seen.

The Emperor's New Clothes

"Will Your Imperial Majesty be graciously pleased to take off your clothes?" said the swindlers. "We can then put the new ones upon you here, before the large mirror." The Emperor took off all his clothes, and the swindlers behaved as if they were handing him each piece of the new suit which was supposed to have been made; and they put their hands about his waist and pretended to tie some thing securely. It was the train. The Emperor turned and twisted himself in front of the glass.

"Heaven! How well it fits? How beautifully it sets," said everyone. "The pattern! The colours! It is indeed a noble costume!"

"They are waiting, outside, with the canopy which is to be borne over Your Majesty in the procession," said the chief master of the ceremonies. "Very well, I am ready," said the Emperor; "doesn't it set well?" Once more he turned about in front of the glass that it might seem as if he was really examining his finery. The lords in waiting, who were to carry the train, fumbled with their hands in the direction of the floor as if they were picking the train up. They walked on, holding the air—they didn't want to let it be noticed that they could see nothing at all.

So the Emperor walked in the procession under the beautiful canopy, and everybody in the streets and at the windows said: "Lord! How splendid the Emperor's new clothes are. What a lovely train he has to his coat! What a beautiful fit it is!" Nobody wanted to be detected seeing nothing: that would mean that he was no good at his job, or that he was very stupid. None of the Emperor's costumes had ever been such a success.

"But he hasn't got anything on!" said a little child. "Lor! Just hark at the innocent," said its father. And one whispered to the other what the child had said: "That little child there says he hasn't got anything on."

"Why, he hasn't got anything on!" the whole crowd was shouting at last; and the Emperor's flesh crept, for it seemed to him they were right. "But all the same," he thought to himself, "I must go through with the procession." So he held himself more proudly than before, and the lords in waiting walked on bearing the train— the train that wasn't there at all.

The Dauntless Tin Soldier

There were once five-and-twenty tin soldiers who were all brothers, for they were all born of one old tin spoon; they all shouldered arms and stood eyes front; red and blue was their beautiful uniform. The very first thing they heard in this world when the lid was taken off the box they lay in, were the words "Tin soldiers!" It was a little boy who shouted it, and clapped his hands: he had been given them because it was his birthday; and now he set them up on the table. Each soldier was exactly like his neighbour; there was only one who was a little different. He had one leg. He had been the last to be cast, and there was not enough tin left. Still, he stood just as steady on his one leg as the rest on their two, and he it is to whom we have to pay attention.

On the table where they were set up stood a great many other toys, but the one which caught the eye most was a lovely paper castle. Through the little windows you could see right into the rooms. In front of it little trees stood round a tiny looking-glass, which was meant to look like a lake. Swans made of wax swam on it and looked at their reflections. The whole thing was very pretty, but prettiest of all was a little lady who stood in the open door of the castle: she too was cut out of paper, but she had a skirt of the finest possible muslin, and a little painted blue stripe crossing her shoulder like a scarf: in the middle of it was a bright spangle as big as the whole of her face. The little lady had her arms stretched out, for she was a dancer, and one of her legs was lifted so high that the tin soldier could not see it, and thought that she had only one leg like him.

"That would be the wife for me," he thought, "but she's very genteel. She lives in a castle, and I have only a box, and there's five-and-twenty of us to go in it—it's no place for her. Still, I must try to get introduced."

Then he laid himself down at his full length behind a snuff-box which was on the table. From there he could look straight at the elegant little lady, who continued to stand on one leg without losing her balance.

In the evening, all the other Tin Soldiers were put into their box, and the people of the house went to bed. Then the toys began to play: they played at paying calls, at fighting battles, and getting up balls. The Tin Soldiers rattled in their box, for they wanted to join in, but they couldn't get the lid off. The nutcracker turned head over heels, the slate pencil made a great to-do on the slate. Such a fuss there was that the canary woke up and began to talk—in verse, too! The only two who did not leave their places were the Tin Soldier and the little dancer; she stood stock-still on tiptoe, with her arms spread out; and he was just as steady on his one leg. He did not take his eyes off her for a second.

Then the clock struck twelve, and "crack", up sprang the lid of the snuff-box. But there was no snuff in it, no, but a little black troll—it was just a trick.

"Tin Soldier," said the troll, "will you keep your eyes to yourself?"

But the Tin Soldier pretended not to hear.

"All right, wait till to-morrow," said the troll.

Well, when to-morrow came and the children got up, the Tin Soldier was put on the window-sill, and whether it was the troll's doing or the draught, all at once the window flew open and the soldier fell down on his head from the third story. It was a fearful fall. His leg pointed straight up, and there he stayed on his cap, with his bayonet stuck between two paving-stones.

The nurserymaid and the little boy ran down at once to look for him, but though they as nearly as possible trod on him, they could not see him. If the Tin Soldier had only shouted "Here I am", they would have found him easily enough, but he thought it was not proper to call out loud, seeing he was in uniform.

Next it began to rain. The drops came faster, one after another; it became a regular downpour. When it was over, two street-boys came along.

"Look here," said one of them, "there's a Tin Soldier. He shall go for a voyage."

So they made a boat out of newspaper, put the Tin Soldier in it and off he sailed, down the gutter; the two boys ran along with him and clapped their hands. Mercy on us! What billows raged in that gutter, and what a stream was there! There had, indeed, been a torrent of rain. The paper boat tossed up and down and sometimes whirled round and round so that the Tin Soldier became dizzy; but he was as steady as ever, turned not a hair, looked straight in front of him, and kept shouldering arms.

All at once the boat darted under a broad culvert. It was as dark there as if he had been still in his box.

"Where can I be going to now?" thought he. "Aye, this is the troll's doing. Ah, dear, if that little lady was here in the boat, it might be twice as dark for all I cared!" Just then came up a big water-rat who lived under the culvert.

"Got a pass? Out with your pass!"

But the Tin Soldier said nothing, and held his rifle tighter than ever. The boat rushed on, and the rat after it.

Ugh! How it gnashed its teeth and called out to the chips and straws: "Stop him! Stop him! He hasn't paid the toll! He hasn't shown his pass!"

But the stream ran stronger and stronger. Already the Tin Soldier could see daylight, ahead where the culvert ended; but at the same time he heard a rushing sound that was enough to appal the bravest heart. Think of it! At the end of the culvert the gutter ran straight into a huge canal. For him it was as dreadful as for us to go down a great waterfall in a boat.

By this time he was so near it that he could not stop: on went the boat, and the poor Tin Soldier held himself as stiff as he could—no one should say of him that he winked an eye. The boat turned round three or four times, and filled with water to the gunwale: it was bound to sink. The Tin Soldier was up to his neck in water. Deeper and deeper sank the boat. Softer and softer grew the paper. The water closed over the Soldier's head, and he thought of the pretty little dancer whom he should never see again, and in his ears rang the words:

> *Onward, onward, warrior,*
> *Death waits for thee!*

Then the paper parted in sunder, and the Tin Soldier fell through —and in the same instant was swallowed by a fish.

Goodness, how dark it was in there!—darker even than in the culvert, and besides, the space was so cramped. But the Tin Soldier was steady as ever and lay all his length with shouldered arms.

The fish darted hither and thither and executed the most alarming movements. Finally it became quite quiet, then a ray of light seemed to break through. The light shone out full, and somebody called out: "A Tin Soldier!" The fact was, the fish had been caught brought to market, sold and taken into the kitchen, where a maid

cut it open with a big knife. She took the Soldier by the body in her finger and thumb and carried him into the parlour, where everybody wanted to see the remarkable man who had travelled about in the inside of a fish. But the Tin Soldier was not in the least above himself.

They set him up on the table, and there—well! it is funny how things do come about in the world—the Tin Soldier was in the self-same room he had been in before: he saw the very same children, and the toys were on the table—the lovely castle with the pretty little dancer, who was still standing on one leg, with the other lifted high up. She too was steadfast. The Tin Soldier was touched, and could have wept tears of tin, but it would not have been becoming. He looked at her and she looked at him, but neither of them said a word.

At that moment one of the little boys picked up the Soldier and threw him right into the stove. He had no explanation to give: of course, it was the troll in the snuff-box who was responsible.

The Tin Soldier stood there, all lit up, and felt a heat that was overpowering, but whether it came from the real fire, or from love, he did not know. The colours had all come off him: nobody could say whether that had happened on his journey or was the result of sorrow. He looked at the little lady, and she looked at him; and he felt he was melting, but still he stood steady with shouldered arms. Then a door opened, the wind caught the dancer, and she flew like a sylph into the stove to the Tin Soldier, blazed up into a flame and was gone. The Tin Soldier melted down into a lump, and when next day the maid took out the ashes, she found him in the shape of a little tin heart. Of the dancer, only the spangle was left, and that was burnt as black as a coal.

The Eleven Wild Swans

F ar away from here, in the lands the swallows fly to when we are having winter, there lived a King who had eleven sons and one daughter, Elisa. The eleven brothers, princes they were, went to school with stars on their breasts and swords at their sides. They wrote on gold slates with diamond pencils, and could read backwards as easily as forwards; anybody could see straight off that they were prices. Their sister Elisa sat at home on a little stool made of looking-glass, and had a picture book that had cost half the kingdom to buy.

Ah, those children had a fine time of it, to be sure; but it wasn't to be like that for ever.

Their father, who was King of the whole country, married a bad Queen, and she was not at all nice to the poor children—the very first day they noticed it. There were great doings all over the palace, and the children played at visitors; but instead of their having all the cakes and baked apples that were left, she only gave them sand in a teacup and told them they could pretend it was something real.

The week after, she boarded the little sister Elisa out in the country, with some labourers, and it wasn't long before she got the King to believe such things about the poor princes, that he cared not a rap about them any more.

"Fly away out into the world, and fend for yourselves," said the wicked Queen; "fly as big birds without any voice." But she couldn't do all the harm she would have dearly liked to do, and they turned into eleven beautiful wild swans. With a strange cry they flew out of the palace windows, far away over the fields and woods.

It was still quite early morning when they passed the place where their sister Elisa lay asleep in the labourer's room. There they hovered over the roof and turned their long necks hither and thither and flapped their wings, but nobody heard or saw it; they had to go on, far upward towards the clouds, far out into the wide world. They flew into a great dark forest that stretched right down to the sea-shore.

Poor little Elisa, in the labourer's cottage, played with a green leaf—the only toy she had, and she pricked a hole in the leaf and peeped up through it towards the sun, and it seemed as if she was looking at the bright eyes of her brothers; and every time the warm rays shone on her cheek, she thought of all the kisses they had given her.

One day passed just like another; when the breeze blew through the great rose bushes outside the house, it whispered to the roses: "Who can be prettier than you?" But the roses shook their heads and said: "Why, Elisa!" And when the old woman sat in the door-way, of a Sunday, and read her hymn book, the breeze would turn the leaves and say to the book: "Who can be better than you?" "Why, Elisa!" said the hymn book; and what the roses and the hymn book said was no more than the truth.

When she was fifteen years old, she was sent for to go home—and when the Queen saw how pretty she was she became full of anger and hatred for her. She would have dearly liked to turn her into a wild swan like her brothers, but that she dared not do at once, for the King wanted to see his daughter.

Early in the morning the Queen went into the bathroom, which was built of marble and decked out with soft skins and lovely rugs, and she took three toads and kissed them and said to the first: "Hop on to Elisa's head when she gets into the bath, that she may become as stupid as you. Sit yourself on her forehead," said she to the second, "that she may become as ugly as you, so that her father shall not know her. Lie on her heart," she whispered to the third; "let her have an evil mind, and let her suffer anguish from it." Then she put the toads into the clear water, which forthwith took on a greenish tint, and called Elisa and undressed her and made her go down into the water; and as she dived into it, the first toad clambered into her hair, and the second on to her forehead, and the third on to her heart; but Elisa seemed not to notice it. At the moment when she stood up, there were three red poppies floating on the water. Had the beasts not been poisonous and not been kissed by the witch, they would have been changed into red roses. Still, flowers they did become, merely from resting on her head and her heart. She was too good and innocent for any witchcraft to have power over her.

When the wicked Queen saw that, she rubbed Elisa all over with walnut juice, so that she was all dark-brown, and she smeared her pretty face with a nasty ointment, and let her lovely hair get all in a tangle. It was impossible to recognize that pretty Elisa; and so when her father saw her he was dreadfully shocked and said that was never his daughter; and indeed nobody knew her but the watch-dog and the swallows, and they were poor dumb creatures that couldn't do anything.

Poor Elisa! She cried and she thought of her eleven brothers, all gone! Sorrowfully she stole out of the palace and walked all day over field and moor, into the great forest. She had no notion where she wanted to go, but she was in such trouble, and yearned so for her brothers, who, she was sure, had been driven out into the wide world like herself, and she was set on trying to find them.

Only a short while had she been in the forest before the night fell. She had wandered far from any road or path, so she laid herself down on the soft moss, said her evening prayer, and rested her head against a stump. All was quiet, the air was very soft, and round about in the grass and moss there shone, like a green fire, hundreds of glow-worms. When she gently stirred a twig with her hand, the shining creatures fell down beside her like shooting stars.

All night long she dreamt of her brothers. They were playing together again as children, writing with the diamond pencils on the gold slates, and looking at the lovely picture book that had cost half the kingdom. But on the slates they didn't write as they used to do—noughts and crosses—no, but the bravest of deeds that they had done and all that they had lived through and seen; and in the picture book everything was alive: the birds sang, and the people came out of the book and talked to Elisa and her brothers, but when she turned the page, they jumped back again at once, so as not to cause confusion in the pictures.

When she woke up the sun was already high. She could not actually see it, for the tall trees spread their branches thick and close; but the rays played through them like a glittering cloth of gold. There was a fragrance from the fresh greenwood, and the birds were almost ready to perch on her shoulders. She heard a splashing of water. There were a number of springs, all falling into a pool that had the most beautiful sandy bottom. True, the bushes grew thick about it, but in one place the deer had made a wide opening, and there Eliza went to the water, which was so clear that if the breeze had not so stirred the branches and bushes that they moved she would have thought they were painted on the bottom of the pool, so sharply was every leaf reflected there, alike those that the sun shone through and those that were in the deepest shadow.

As soon as she saw her own face she was quite horrified, so brown and ugly it was; but when she wetted her little hand and rubbed her eyes and forehead the white skin gleamed out once more. So she laid aside all her clothes and slipped out into the cool water. A fairer King's daughter than she there was not in all the world.

When she had dressed herself again, and plaited her long hair, she went to the spouting spring and drank from the hollow of her hand, and so wandered further into the forest without knowing whither she went. She thought about her brothers, and she thought about the good God who certainly would not forsake her. It was He who made the wild apples grow to feed the hungry; it was He who guided her to a tree of them, its boughs bending under the fruit, and there she made her midday meal and set props under the branches, and then went on into the darkest part of the forest.

It was so still there that she could hear her own footsteps, nay, every little withered leaf that bent beneath her feet; not a bird was to be seen, not a sunbeam could pierce between the many close-set branches. The tall trunks stood so close together that when she looked straight before her, it seemed as though there was one great fence of timber, trunk after trunk, closing her in all round; yes, indeed, there was a solitude here, the like of which she had never known.

The night was very dark; not a single little glow-worm shone out of the moss, and with a troubled mind she lay down to sleep; and then she thought that the branches above her parted and Our Lord looked down on her with loving eyes, and little angels peeped out above His head and beneath His arms.

When she woke in the morning she was not sure whether she had dreamt it or whether it really had happened.

She walked on but a few steps, and then she met an old woman with a basket of berries, some of which she gave her. Elisa asked her if she had not seen eleven princes riding through the forest.

"No," said the old woman; "but yesterday I saw eleven swans, with gold crowns on their heads, swimming down the river close by here." And she guided Elisa some way further to a high bank, at the bottom of which was a winding stream. The trees on its banks stretched their long leafy branches across it towards each other, and where their natural growth did not let them meet they had torn their roots loose from the earth and leant over the water and twined their boughs together.

Elisa said good-bye to the old woman, and walked along the stream to the place where it flowed out, on the broad open sea-shore. All the beautiful sea lay spread out before the young girl, and not a sail showed itself, not a boat was to be seen: how could she get further? She gazed at the numberless pebbles on the beach. The water had worn every one of them round. Glass, iron, stone, everything that lay washed up there had taken its shape from the water, and yet the water was far softer than her own delicate hand. "It keeps rolling on, untiring, and that is how it shapes the hard things smooth, and I will be as untiring as it is. I thank you for your lesson, you clear rolling billows. One day, my heart tells me, you will bear me to my brothers."

On the seaweed that had been washed up lay eleven swans' feathers. She gathered them into a bunch; there were drops of water on them: whether dew or tears, who could tell? It was lonely down there on the shore, but she did not feel it, for the sea gave her infinite changes to look at, more within a few hours' space than a fresh-water lake would show in a whole year. If a big black cloud came over, it was as if the sea would say: "I too can look black." Then the wind blew and the waves showed their white sides; but if the clouds shone red, and the wind fell to sleep, then the sea was like a rose-leaf. Sometimes it was green, sometimes white; but however still it slept there was always a gentle movement along the beach: the water heaved, softly as the breast of a sleeping child.

Just as the sun was about to set, Elisa saw eleven wild swans, with golden crowns on their heads, flying towards the land; they floated one behind another, looking like a long white ribbon. Elisa clambered up the bank and hid behind a bush. The swans alighted close to her, and flapped their great white wings.

The moment the sun was beneath the waves the swans' skins fell off and there stood eleven fair princes, Elisa's brothers. She uttered a loud cry, for though they were greatly altered she knew that it was they—was sure it must be they—and she sprang into their arms, and called them by their names. And happy were they when they saw and recognized their little sister, now so tall and so beautiful. They laughed and wept, and very quickly they came to know about each other, and how ill their stepmother had dealt with them all.

"We brothers", said the eldest, "fly about in the shape of wild swans so long as the sun is in the sky; when it is set we take our human shape: so at sunset we must always take care to have a resting place for our feet, for if we were flying then, up among the clouds, we should fall in man's form down into the deep. We do not live here a fair land like this lies on the other side of the water, but the way to it is long. We have to cross the wide sea, and there is no island on our course where we could spend the night. There is only a little lonely rock that stands up, half-way out: it's only large enough for us to stand side by side and rest on it; if the sea is high, the water leaps up high above us, yet we thank God for it. There we spend the night in our human form; but for it we could never visit our dear fatherland, for our flight takes up two of the longest days in the year. Only once a year is it permitted to us to visit our father's home. Eleven days we can stay here: we fly over this great forest, and from there we can look at the castle where we were born and where our father lives, and see the bell-tower of the church where our mother is buried. Here we feel the very trees and bushes are an heirloom; here the wild horses gallop over the plains as we saw them in our childhood. Here the charcoal-burner sings the old songs we danced to as children. Here is our father's land, here we grew up, and here we have found you, you dear little sister. We have still two days to stay here, and then we must away over the sea, to a land that is beautiful, but is not our own. How can we take you with us? We have neither ship nor boat."

"How can I contrive to free you?" said their sister. And they went on talking together almost all night, with only an hour or two of sleep.

Elisa was wakened by the sound of swans' wings rustling above her. The brothers were changed once more, and flew about in wide circles, and at last flew away; but one of them, the youngest, stayed behind. The swan laid his head on her bosom and she fondled his white wings: they spent the whole day together. Towards evening the others came back, and when the sun was down they stood there in their proper forms.

"To-morrow we fly away from here, and dare not come back for nearly a whole year; but we cannot leave you like this. Have you the courage to come with us? My arm is strong enough to carry you through the forest, and must we not together have strong enough wings to fly with you over the sea?"

"Yes, take me with you," said Elisa.

They spent the whole night in weaving a net out of the pliant willow bark and the stout reeds, and it was large and strong. On it Elisa lay down, and when the sun came up and the brothers changed into wild swans they gripped the net in their beaks and flew high up towards the clouds, with their dear sister, who was still asleep. The sunbeams fell hotly on her face, so one of the swans flew above her head, that his broad wings might shade her.

They were far from land when Elisa awoke. She thought she was still dreaming, so strange it seemed to her to be borne over the sea, high through the air. At her side lay a branch with beautiful ripe berries on it, and a bundle of sweet-tasting roots. Her youngest brother had gathered them and laid them by her; and she smiled gratefully at him, for she knew it was he who was flying straight over her head and shading her with his wings.

They were so high up that the first ship they saw beneath them looked like a white gull lying on the water. A great cloud came behind them, like a mighty mountain, and on it Elisa saw the shadows of herself and of the eleven swans, flying there as huge as giants; it was like a drawing, prettier than any she had seen before; but as the sun climbed higher and the cloud was left farther behind, the moving shadow-picture disappeared. All day they flew on like a rushing dart through the air, yet their pace was slower than at other times, now that they had their sister to carry. Bad weather, too, came on, and evening grew near. With terror Elisa saw the sun sinking, and yet the lonely rock in the sea was not in sight. She thought the swans were plying their wings more strongly. Ah! It was her fault that they could not go swiftly enough; when the sun was down they would turn into men and fall into the sea and be drowned! From the very bottom of her heart she sent up a prayer to Our Lord; but still she could see no rock. The black cloud drew nearer, the heavy gusts of wind portended a storm. The clouds gathered into a single huge menacing billow which sped onward, looking like a mass of lead. One flash of lightning followed hard on another.

The sun was now at the very rim of the sea. Elisa's heart beat quickly then; the swans plunged downward so quickly that she thought she must fall, but then they floated again. The sun was half beneath the water. Then first she sighted the little rock beneath her, looking no larger than a seal's head sticking up above the water. How swiftly the sun sank! It was no bigger than a star. Then her foot touched the firm ground and the sun went out like the last spark on a bit of burning paper. She saw her brothers standing about her, arm in arm, but there was no room for any more than them and herself. The sea beat against the rock and burst over them like a shower of rain: the heavens shone with a blaze that kept flaring out, and the thunder rolled, peal on peal, but the sister and the brothers held each other's hands and sang a hymn, and it brought them comfort and courage.

At dawn the air was clear and still, and so soon as the sun was up the swans flew off with Elisa from the islet. The sea was still rough, and when they were high up in the air it looked as if the white foam on the dark green sea were millions of swans floating on the water.

When the sun rose higher, Elisa saw ahead of her, half-swimming in the air, a range of mountains with shining masses of ice on their slopes, and in the midst of it there lay, stretched out, a palace—a good mile long—with one mighty colonnade rising over another. Low down before it waved groves of palms and wonderful blossoms, large as mill-wheels. She asked if that were the land she was bound for, but the swans shook their heads: for that which she was looking at was the lovely ever-changing cloud-palace of the fairy Morgana, and into it they dared bring no mortal. Elisa gazed upon it. Suddenly, mountains, groves and palace all fell to pieces, and in their place rose a score of noble churches, each like the next, all with lofty towers and pointed windows. She fancied she could hear the organ sounding, but it was the sea she heard. And now she was quite near the churches, but they changed into a fleet of ships sailing onward beneath her. She looked down, and it was but the sea wrack that was spreading over the water. Yes, it was an endless series of changes that she had to look at; but now she saw the real land she was bound for. There rose the beautiful blue mountains, with forests of cedar and towns and castles. Long ere the sun had set she was seated on the slope before a large cave, whose mouth was grown over with delicate green creeping plants that seemed like broidered carpets. "Now we shall see what you dream of here to-night," said the youngest brother, as he led her to her sleeping chamber.

"If I could but dream how to free you!" said she; and the thought filled her mind most vividly, and earnestly did she pray to God for His help—nay, even in her sleep she went on praying; and then it seemed to her that she flew high up into the air, to the cloud-palace of the fairy Morgana; and the fairy came to meet her, all beautiful and shining, but all the same, very like the old woman who had given her berries in the forest and told her of the swans with the golden crowns.

"Your brothers can be freed," said she, "but have you courage and endurance? True it is that the sea is softer than your delicate hands, and yet can change the shape of the hard stones. But it does not feel the pain that your fingers will feel: it has no heart, and does not suffer the fear and trouble that you must go through. Do you see this stinging-nettle that I hold in my hand? Many of this kind grow about the cave where you are sleeping, but only they and those that grow out of churchyard graves are fit for your purpose; mark you that! These you must pick, though they will burn your skin into blisters. You must break them up with your feet, and you will get flax from them, and with it you must weave and hem eleven shirts with long sleeves. Cast these over the eleven wild swans, and the spell will be broken. But remember this well: that from the moment you begin this work, and until it is wholly ended, even though a year should pass in the meantime, you must not speak. The first word you utter will pierce the heart of your brothers like a deadly dagger: on your tongue hangs their life. Take good heed of these things." And at the same moment she touched her hand with the nettle: it was like a scorching flame. Elisa awoke with the touch. It was bright day, and close by where she had slept lay a nettle like that which she had seen in her dream. She fell on her knees and gave thanks to God, and went out of the cave to begin her work. With her delicate hands she grasped the horrible nettles, which were like fire to touch, and burnt great blisters on her hands and arms, but she suffered that gladly, if she might but free her dear brothers. She crushed every nettle with her bare feet and wound up the green flax from it.

When the sun was down the brothers came, and were terrified at finding her so silent. They thought it must be a fresh spell cast by that wicked stepmother; but when they saw her hands they understood what she was doing for their sake, and the youngest brother wept, and where his tears fell she felt no more pain, and the burning blisters vanished.

All night she spent on her work, for she could have no rest till she had freed the beloved brothers. All the next day, while the swans were away, she sat in solitude; but the time had never flown so quickly. One shirt was finished, and she set to work on the second.

Just then a hunting horn rang out among the hills. She was stricken with fear; the sound came nearer. She heard the baying of hounds; in terror she took refuge in the cave, and tied the nettles she had gathered and hackled into a bundle, and seated herself on it.

A great hound came leaping from among the bushes—another just after it, and yet another. They bayed aloud and ran forward and then back again. Before many minutes had passed the whole band of hunters were outside the cave, and the handsomest of them all was the King of the country. He advanced towards Elisa. Never had he beheld a fairer maid.

"How came you here, you beautiful child?" said he. Elisa shook her head, she dared not speak, the saving of her brothers, nay, their life was at stake: and she hid her hand, beneath her apron, that the King might not see what she was suffering.

"Come with me," said he, "you must not stop here. If you are as good as you are beautiful I will dress you in silks and velvets, and put a golden crown on your head, and you shall have your home in the finest of my palaces." And with that he lifted her up on his horse. She wept and wrung her hands, but the King said: "I only desire your happiness; one day you will thank me." And so off he rode among the mountains, holding her before him on his horse, and the huntsmen followed.

At sunset the fair city with its churches and domes lay before them; and the King led her into the palace where great fountains plashed in the lofty marble halls, and walls and roof glowed with paintings; but she had no eyes for that; she wept and sorrowed. Listlessly she allowed the women to dress her in royal apparel, twine pearls in her hair, and put delicate gloves upon her blistered hands.

When at last she stood arrayed in all her splendour, she was so dazzlingly beautiful that all the court bowed deep and low before her, and the King chose her for his bride. Yet the Archbishop shook his head and muttered that this pretty wood-maiden was surely a witch who had dazzled their eyes, and corrupted the heart of the King.

But the King would not listen to that. He bade the music ring out, and the costliest dishes be served, and the fairest girls dance about her, and she walked through fragrant gardens into splendid halls: but not a smile came to her lips or into her eyes. Sorrow stood there, the perpetual heir and possessor. But now the King opened a little chamber, hard by the place where she was to sleep. It was decked with costly green hangings, and was just like the cave she had been in. On the floor lay the bundle of flax she had spun from the nettles, and from the ceiling hung the shirt that had already been woven. All this, one of the huntsmen had brought with him as a curiosity.

"Here you can dream yourself back in your old home," said the King; "here is the work you were busying yourself with. Now in the midst of all your splendour it will amuse you to remember that old time."

When Elisa saw this, which lay so near her heart, a smile played about her mouth, and the colour came back into her cheeks at the thought of the saving of her brothers, and she kissed the King's hand and he pressed her to his heart, and bade all the church bells proclaim the wedding festival. The lovely dumb girl from the forest was to be Queen of all the land.

The Archbishop whispered slanderous words into the ear of the King, but they did not make their way to his heart. The bridal was to be. The Archbishop himself had to set the crown on her head, and he spitefully pressed down the narrow ring upon her brow so that it hurt her, yet a heavier ring lay about her heart; sorrow for her brothers; she hardly felt the bodily pain. Her mouth was dumb, for a single word would end her brothers' life, but in her eyes there lay a deep affection for the handsome King who did everything to make her happy. With her whole heart, she grew more loving towards him day by day. Oh, if she could but confide in him and tell him of her suffering! but dumb she must remain, in dumbness must she finish her task. So at night she would steal from his side and go into the little room apart, that was decked out like the cave, and weave one shirt after another. But when she began on the seventh she had no flax left.

In the churchyard, she knew, grew the nettles she must use: but she had to gather them herself. How was she to get there?

"Oh, what is the pain in my fingers to the suffering in my heart," she thought; "I must risk it! Our Lord will not let me fall out of His hands." With a pain at her heart as if it were a crime she was plotting, she stole down to the garden, in the bright moonlight night, and went along the long avenues out into the empty streets, away to the churchyard. There she saw seated on one of the largest of the gravestones, a ring of Lamias, horrible witches. They put off their rags as if they meant to bathe, and then dug down with their long thin fingers into the newly made graves, pulled out the corpses and ate their flesh. Elisa had to pass close by them, and they fastened their dreadful eyes on her, but she prayed her prayer, and gathered the burning nettles and carried them back to the palace.

Only one person had seen her—the Archbishop. He was awake while everyone else was asleep. Now, then, he had found the truth of what he suspected! All was not as it should be with the Queen. She was a witch, and that was how she had corrupted the King and the whole people.

In the confessional he told the King what he had seen and what he feared, and as the cruel words came from his tongue, the carven images of the saints shook their heads, as if to say: "It is not so; Elisa is innocent." But the Archbishop interpreted it otherwise; he said they were bearing witness against her, shaking their heads at her guilt. Two heavy tears rolled down the King's cheek! He went home with misgiving in his heart, and he feigned to be asleep at night, but no sleep came to his eyes: he saw how Elisa got up, and each night she did so again, and every time he followed her quietly he saw that she disappeared into her tiny chamber. Day by day his mien grew sadder. Elisa saw it, but did not understand the cause, yet it troubled her; and what did she not suffer at heart for her brothers! On the royal velvets and purple her salt tears ran down, and lay there like glistening diamonds; while everyone who saw her rich attire wished they were Queen.

Meanwhile she was nearly at the end of her task; only one shirt was still wanting. But flax she had none, and not a single nettle.

Once again then—only this time—must she go to the churchyard and pluck some handfuls. She thought with horror of the lonely journey and the frightful Lamias: but her will was as steadfast as her trust in God.

Elisa went, but the King and the Archbishop followed. They saw her disappear through the iron gates into the churchyard, and when they neared it, there sat the Lamias upon the gravestones, as Elisa had seen them: and the King turned away, for among them, he thought, was she whose head had that very evening rested on his bosom.

"The people must judge her," said he. And the people did judge her: "She shall be burned in the red fire." From the splendid royal halls she was taken away to a dark damp vault where the wind whistled through the barred window. In place of velvet and silk they gave her the bundle of nettles she had gathered—she might lay her head on that. The coarse heavy shirts she had woven should be her mattress and coverlets: but nothing dearer to her could they have given her. She began again upon her work and prayed to her God. Outside, the street-boys sang mocking ballads about her, and no soul comforted her with a kind word.

Towards evening came the sound of a swan's wing; it was the youngest of the brothers: he had found his sister; and she sobbed aloud with joy, though she knew that the night now coming on was perhaps the last she had to live. But now, too, the work was all but finished, and her brothers were there.

The Archbishop came to pass the last hours with her: he had promised the King that he would. But she shook her head and with look and gesture prayed him to go. That night she must finish her task, or else all would have been in vain—everything—the pain, the tears, the sleepless nights. The Archbishop went away with slander-ous words against her, but poor Elisa knew she was guiltless, and went on with her work.

The little mice ran over the floor and dragged the nettles to her feet to help her ever so little: and the thrush perched on the window bar and sang the whole night as gaily as he could, that she might not lose heart.

It was still little more than dawn, an hour before the sun would be up, when the eleven brothers were at the palace gate, demanding to be brought to the King. But it could not be, was the answer: it was still night, the King was asleep and could not be roused. They besought, they threatened, the guard came, nay, the King himself came out and asked what it all meant. At that instant the sun rose, and there were no brothers to be seen, but over the palace eleven wild swans were flying.

The whole population came streaming out of the city gates to see the witch burnt. A wretched horse drew the tumbril in which she sat: they had put on her a kirtle of coarse sackcloth; her beautiful long hair hung loose about her fair head, her cheeks were deathly pale, her lips moved a little, while her fingers twined the green flax.

Even on her way to death she did not leave off the work she had begun. Ten of the shirts lay at her feet, and she was working at the eleventh.

The crowd jeered at her. "Look at the witch mumbling there. No hymn book in her hands, no. She's still messing at her foul job. Tear it from her into a thousand shreds." They all crowded in upon her and tried to tear it to bits. But there came eleven swans flying and perched round about her on the tumbril and flapped their great wings. The mob retreated, in terror.

"It's a sign from heaven. Surely she is innocent," many of them whispered; but they dared not say it aloud.

Then the executioner seized her by the hand, but hastily she threw the shirts over the swans, and there stood eleven beautiful princes! But the youngest had one swan's wing instead of an arm, for a sleeve was lacking to his shirt; she had not quite finished it.

"Now I may speak," she said, "I am innocent." And the people who beheld what had come to pass, bowed down before her as before a saint. But she sank lifeless into the arms of her brothers, so hardly had the suffering, the fear and the pain weighed upon her.

"Yes, she is innocent," said the eldest brother. And he began to tell all that had befallen: and, while he spoke, there spread abroad a perfume as of millions of roses, for every faggot in the pyre had taken root and put forth branches: a fragrant bush stood there, tall and bright with red roses. At its summit was a flower, white and shining, that glistened like a star. The King plucked it and laid it on Elisa's breast, and she awoke with peace and gladness in her heart.

And all the church bells rang out of their own accord, and the birds came in great flocks, and such a bridal train went back to the palace, as no King yet had ever seen.

The Garden of Eden

There was once a King's son. Nobody ever had so many or such pretty books as he: everything that ever happened in the world was there for him to read. About every nation and every country he could get information. But of where the Garden of Eden was to be found there was not a word; and that was exactly the thing he thought about most.

His grandmother had told him when he was still quite little, just going to begin attending school, that every flower in the Garden of Eden was the sweetest of cakes, and the pistils the finest of wine. On one flower was written History, on another Geography or Tables: you need only eat a cake and you knew your lesson. The more you ate the more Geography or History or Tables you took in.

He believed it at the time, but as he got to be a bigger boy and learned more and became so much cleverer, he understood that there must be quite a different sort of beauty in the Garden of Eden.

"Oh, why did Eve pluck from the Tree of Knowledge? Why did Adam eat of the forbidden fruit? If it had been I, it would not have happened; sin would never have come into the world." So he said then, and still he said it, when he was seventeen years old. The Garden of Eden took up the whole of his thoughts.

One day he went out into the forest: alone, for that pleased him best.

Evening came on, the clouds drew together, there was such a storm of rain, as if the whole sky were one single sluice out of which the water was rushing: it was as dark as it would be in the deepest well at night. Sometimes he slipped on the wet grass, sometimes he fell down over bare stones that jutted out of the rocky surface. Everything was drenched: there was not a dry thread on the unhappy Prince. He had to clamber over great blocks of stone where the water oozed out of the deep moss. He was ready to faint, when he heard a strange rushing sound, and saw in front of him a large cave, lit up within. In the middle of it blazed a fire at which you could have roasted a deer, and indeed that was what was happening. A magnificent stag with tall antlers was stuck on a spit and was turning slowly round between two rough-hewn pine-trunks. An elderly woman, tall and strong, like a man in disguise, was sitting by the fire throwing log after log into it.

"Just you come a bit nearer," said she. "Sit down by the fire and get your clothes dry." "There's an awful draught here," said the Prince, as he sat down on the floor. "It'll be worse yet when my sons come home," said the woman. "This is the cave of the winds you're in, and my sons are the four winds of the world. Can you understand that?"

"Where are your sons?" asked the Prince.

"Why, it's no use answering when people ask stupid questions," said the woman. "My sons are on their own: they're playing bowls with the clouds in the big room upstairs," and she pointed up in the air.

"Oh, ah!" said the Prince. "Well, you talk rather sharp and you're not so gentle as the ladies I generally see about me." "Ah, they've nothing else to do; I've got to be sharp if I'm to keep my sons in order. But I can do it, though they've stiff necks of their own. Do you see those four sacks hanging on the wall? They're as frightened of them as you used to be of the birch-rod behind the looking-glass. I can double the boys up, I can tell you, and into the bag they go! We make no bones about it. There they stay and don't come out to play till I think proper. But here we have one of them."

It was the North Wind, who came in with a freezing blast. Big hailstones fell and hopped on the floor and snowflakes came floating all round. He was dressed in bearskin breeches and coat, and a seal-skin hat was pulled down over his ears: long icicles hung on his beard, and one hailstone after another slid down from his coat collar. "Don't go near the fire at once," said the Prince, "you might easily get frostbite in your face and hands if you do!"

"Frostbite!" said the North Wind, and laughed out loud. "Frost-bite! Why, that's what I like best! And what sort of a shrimp may you be? How do you come into the cave of the winds?" "He's my guest," said the old lady, "and if you're not satisfied with that explanation, you can go into the bag. Now you know my decision."

Well, that had its effect, and the North Wind told them where he had come from and where he had been for nigh upon a whole month. "I come from the Polar sea," he said; "I've been on Bering Island with the Russian whalers. I sat and slept at the helm when they set sail from the North Cape, and every now and then, when I woke up a little, the petrel flew about my legs. That's a funny bird; it gives one quick flap of its wings, and then keeps them spread out without moving them, and gets way enough."

"Don't make such a long story of it," said the mother of the winds. "And so you got to Bering Island, did you?"

"It's beautiful! There's a floor to dance on as flat as a plate. Half-thawed snow and moss, sharp rocks and skeletons of whales and white bears lying about. They looked like the arm- and leg-bones of giants, with a mouldy green on them. You'd think the sun had never shone on them. I blew at the mist a little, so as to get a sight of the shelter; it was a house built of wreck-wood and covered with whale-hides, the fleshy side was outward, red and green all over: on the roof a live white bear sat growling. I went to the beach and looked at the bird's nests and the unfledged young, screaming and gaping. I blew down into their thousand windpipes and taught them to keep their mouths still. Down below the whales were wallowing like live guts or great worms with pigs' heads and teeth an ell long."

"You tell your tale well, my boy!" said his mother; "my mouth waters to listen to you."

"Then the hunt began. The harpoon was planted in the heart of the whale and made the steaming jet of blood spurt up like a fountain over the ice. Then I too thought of my own game. I blew hard and made my sailing ships, the icebergs as tall as cliffs, freeze the boats right in. Whew! how they did squeak and scream! But I screamed louder. The dead whales, the chests and the tackle, they had to turn them out on the ice. I shook snowflakes over them and left them drifting southward in the frozen-in craft, with their prey, to taste salt water. They'll never come back to Bering Island."

"So you've done mischief!" said the mother of the winds. "How much good I've done let the others tell," said he. "But here we have my brother from the west. I like him best of the lot. He has a smack of the sea and a blessed coolness about him."

"Is that the little Zephyr?" asked the Prince.

"Yes, certainly it's the Zephyr," said the old lady, "but he isn't very little now. In old days he was a pretty boy, but that's past and over."

He looked like a wild man, but he had a slouch hat to prevent his being hurt: in his hand he held a mahogany club, cut in the mahogany forests of America. He couldn't do with a smaller one.

"Where do you come from?" asked his mother.

"From the wildernesses of the forest," he said, "where the thorny lianas make a fence from one tree to the next, where the water snake lies in the wet growth and human beings seem not to be wanted."

"How did you employ yourself there?" "I looked at the deep river, where it was dashing down from the rocks and turning into spray to carry the rainbow. I saw the wild buffalo try to swim the river, but the stream hurried him down with it, drifting with a flock of wild ducks which flew up in the air when they came to the waterfall; but the buffalo had to go down it. I liked that, and I blew such a gale that the oldest trees sailed off and turned to chips." "And didn't you get anything else done?" the old lady asked. "I turned somersaults over the savannahs, I patted the wild horses and shook down coco-nuts. Yes, yes, I've plenty of stories to tell, but one mustn't tell everything one knows. You know that well enough, old lady!" And with that he kissed his mother so hard she nearly went over backwards! He was a regular wild boy.

Next came the South Wind with a turban and a floating Bedouin's cloak.

"Precious cold in here," said he, throwing logs on the fire. "One can easily tell that North Wind got here first."

"It's hot enough here to roast a white bear," said North Wind. "White bear yourself!" said South Wind.

"Do you want to be stuffed in the bag?" asked the old lady; "sit yourself down on the stone there and tell where you've been."

"In Africa, Mother," he answered. "I was with the Hottentots, lion hunting in Kaffir land. What grass does grow on the plains there, green as an olive! The gnu capered about and the ostrich ran races with me, but I am quicker on my legs. I got to the desert, the yellow sand that looks like the sea-bottom. There I met a caravan: they'd killed their last camel to get some water to drink, but it was only a little they got. The sun was burning them overhead and the sand roasting them underfoot. The desert stretched away without a bound. Then I rolled in the loose fine sand and whirled it up into great pillars—that was a dance! You should have seen how the dromedary stood still and the merchant pulled his kaftan over his head. He threw himself down before me as if before Allah, his God. They are buried now. There's a pyramid of sand piled over them all, but when I blow it away, the sun will bleach the white bones, and the travellers will see there have been men there before them: else you wouldn't believe it in the desert."

"So then you've done nothing but mischief!" said his mother. "March into the bag!" And before he knew it she had South Wind by the body and into the bag, which wallowed round about the floor till she sat on it, and it had to be quiet.

"A lively lot of boys you've got!" said the Prince, "They surely are," she said. "Oh, I can tame 'em. Here we have the fourth."

It was East Wind, dressed like a Chinaman.

"Oh, you come from that quarter, do you?" said his mother. "I thought you'd been to the Garden of Eden."

"I'm going to fly there first thing in the morning," said East Wind. "To-morrow, it'll be a hundred years since I was there. I've come now from China, where I danced round the porcelain towers and made all the bells ring. In the street below the officials were being beaten: bamboo sticks were being used up on their shoulders, and they were men of the first to the ninth class. They kept crying, 'Many thanks, my fatherly benefactor'; but they didn't really mean it. And I rang the bells and sang: 'Tsing, Tsang, Tsu'."

"You're a mischievous boy," said the old lady; "it's a good thing you're going to the Garden of Eden to-morrow; it always improves your manners a bit. Mind you take a good drink of the well of wisdom and bring a little bottle full for me."

"I will," said East Wind. "But what have you stuck my brother from the South into the bag for? Out with him, he must tell me about the Phoenix bird. The Princess in the Garden of Eden always wants to hear about that bird when I pay her a visit every hundred years. Open the bag, do, and you'll be my darling mother, and I'll make you a present of two pockets full of tea, quite green and fresh, that I picked on the spot." "Well then, for the tea's sake, and because you are my pet boy, I will open the bag." So she did, and South Wind crawled out, but looked very sheepish because the strange Prince had seen it. "There's a palm leaf for you, for the Princess," said South Wind; "that leaf was given me by the old Phoenix bird, the only one there was in the world; he's scratched on it with his beak the account of his whole life, the hundred years he lived: now she can read it for herself. I saw how the Phoenix bird himself set fire to his nest and sat there and was burned up like a Hindu's wife. How the dry branches did crackle, and what a smoke and perfume there was! At last it all flamed up in a blaze, and the old Phoenix bird burned to ashes. But his egg lay red hot in the fire, and then burst with a loud report, and the young one flew out; and now he is Regent over all the birds and the only Phoenix in the world. He's bitten a hole in the palm leaf I gave you, and that is his greeting to the Princess."

"Now let's have something to eat," said the mother of the winds; so they all sat down to eat the roasted stag, and the Prince sat by East Wind; and so they soon became good friends.

"Now do just tell me", said the Prince, "what sort of a Princess is that who is so much talked about here, and where is the Garden of Eden?"

"Ho, ho!" said East Wind, "if you want to go there, why, fly there with me to-morrow. Only I must tell you this, there hasn't been a mortal there since Adam and Eve. You know about them from your Bible History."

"Of course," said the Prince.

"When they were driven out, the Garden of Eden sank down into the earth, but it kept its warm sunshine and its soft air, and all its beauty. The Queen of the Fairies lives there, and there lies the Island of Happiness, where death never comes, and it is delightful to be. You put yourself on my back to-morrow and I'll take you with me: I think it can be done. But now you mustn't talk any more, for I want to go to sleep."

So they all of them went to sleep.

Early in the morning the Prince woke up, and was not a little startled at finding he was already high up above the clouds. He was sitting on East Wind's back, who was holding him very trustily. They were so high up in the sky that woods and fields, rivers and lakes, looked as they would on a large coloured map of the country.

"Good morning," said East Wind. "You might as well have slept a bit longer, for there isn't much to look at in this flat country beneath us, unless you care to count the churches: they show up like blocks of chalk down there on the green board." It was the fields and meadows that he called the green board.

"It was very uncivil of me not to say good-bye to your mother and your brothers," said the Prince. "Oh, when one's asleep one stands excused," said East Wind; and thereupon they flew on yet faster: you could hear the going in the tops of the woods, when they flew over them, every bough and leaf rustled: you could hear it on the sea and on the lakes, for where they flew the waves rolled higher and the great ships bowed deep in the water like swimming swans.

Towards evening, when it grew dark, it was very amusing to see the big towns. Lights burned below them, now here, now there: it was just as when one has burnt a bit of paper and sees all the little sparks, which are children coming out of school. The Prince clapped his hands, but East Wind begged him to stop that and hold tight instead, or he might easily fall down and be left hanging on a church steeple.

Swift flew the eagle in the dark forest, but swifter flew East Wind. The Cossack on his little horse coursed over the Steppes, but far swifter was the pace the Prince went.

"Now you can see the Himalayas," said East Wind, "they're the highest mountains in Asia: we shall soon get to the Garden of Eden now." And then they wheeled further to the southward, and soon there came a perfume of spices and flowers. The fig and the pomegranate grew wild, and on the wild vines were red and blue clusters. Here they both alighted and stretched themselves on the soft grass where the flowers nodded to the wind as if to say: "Welcome back again."

"Are we in the Garden of Eden now?" asked the Prince. "No, of course not," replied East Wind, "but we shall soon be there now. Do you see that wall of rocks and that big cave where the creepers hang down like great green curtains? That's what we have to go through. Wrap yourself up in your cloak: the sun is burning hot here, but a step further on and it's icy cold. A bird that flits past the cave has one wing out here in the warm summer, and the other inside in the cold of winter." "So that's the way to the Garden of Eden, is it?" asked the Prince. Then they entered the cave. Hoo, how icy cold it was! But that didn't last long. East Wind spread out his wings and they shone like the brightest flame. Why, what a cave it was! The great masses of stone from which water dripped hung above them in the strangest shapes: here it was so narrow that they had to crawl on their hands and knees, here it stretched above them seemingly as high as the open air. Elsewhere were places like funeral chapels, with silent organ pipes and banners turned to stone.

"We seem to be going by the path of Death to the Garden of Eden," said the Prince, but East Wind answered not a word, only pointed ahead, and there the most beautiful blue light flashed out to meet them. The masses of stone overhead became more and more like a mist, which finally was as light as a white cloud in the moonlight. And now they were in the most delightful soft air, cool as on a mountain-top, fragrant as among the roses of a valley.

There flowed a stream, clear as the air itself, and the fishes in it were like silver and gold. Eels of purple-red hue that flashed like blue sparks at every bend of their bodies, played about in the water below, and the broad water-lily leaves had the colours of the rainbow, while the flower itself glowed with burning yellow-red, nourished by the water, as oil keeps a lamp ever burning. A bridge of marble, firm but so artfully and finely carved as if it were of filigree and beads of glass, led over the stream to the Island of Happiness, where the Garden of Eden blossomed.

East Wind took the Prince in his arms and bore him across, and there the flowers and leaves sang him the sweetest songs of his childhood, but so overwhelmingly lovely were they as no human voice can sing the like here.

Were those palm trees or gigantic water plants that grew there? Trees so full of sap and so large the Prince had never yet seen. The strangest creeping plants hung down in long wreaths like those you find painted in gold and colours in the margins of the old service books, or twining themselves about the initial letters. There were the quaintest blendings of birds, flowers and tendrils. Close by in the grass stood a flock of peacocks with their radiant tails spread out. Yes, it really was so! Yet no, when the Prince touched them he found they were not animals but plants; they were the great dock leaves which here shone like the beautiful tail of the peacock. The lion and the tiger darted like lithe cats through the green thicket that smelt like the blossom of the olive, and the lion and the tiger were tame; the wild wood-pigeon shining like the fairest of pearls fluttered the lion's mane with its wings, and the antelope, that elsewhere is so timid, stood still and nodded its head, as if it too would like to join in the play.

Now came forth the Fairy of Eden: her dress shone like the sun, and her face was kind as that of a happy mother rejoicing over her child. Young and fair was she, and beautiful girls, each with a shining star in her hair, followed her.

East Wind gave her the written leaf from the Phoenix, and her eyes sparkled with pleasure: she took the Prince's hand and led him into the palace where the walls were of the colour of the most splendid tulip-petals when held against the sunlight. The very roof was one great shining flower, and the more one gazed up into it the deeper seemed its cup. The Prince walked over to a window and looked through one of the panes, and there he beheld the Tree of Knowledge with the serpent and Adam and Eve standing close by. "Were they not driven out?" he asked. The Fairy smiled and showed him that on every pane time had burnt in its picture, but not so as one is used to see it; no, there was life in it, the leaves of the trees moved, the people came and went as they do in a looking-glass. He looked through another pane, and there was Jacob's dream, where the ladder reached into heaven and the angels with their broad wings hovered up and down. Everything that has happened in the world lived and moved in these panes of glass; such skilful painting only time could have imprinted.

The Fairy smiled and led him into a hall, great and high, whose walls seemed to be of transparent imagery, each face more lovely than the last. Here were millions of happy ones, who laughed and sang so that their voices flowed together into a single melody. Those at the top were so tiny that they seemed smaller than the least rosebud that is drawn like a dot on the paper. And in the midst of the hall stood a mighty tree with hanging boughs. Lovely golden apples, large and small, hung like oranges among the green leaves. This was the Tree of Knowledge of whose fruit Adam and Eve had eaten. From every leaf dripped a bright-red dewdrop: it seemed as if the tree were weeping tears of blood.

"Now let us take the boat," said the Fairy, "there we shall enjoy the coolness of the heaving water. The boat swings, yet does not leave its place, but all the countries of the world glide along before our eyes." And it was marvellous to see how the whole shore moved. There were the high Swiss Alps, the clouds and the dark pine forests: the sound of the horn came deep and melancholy, and the yodel of the shepherd rose sweet from the valley. Again, the banyan trees bowed their long hanging branches over the boat. Coal-black swans swam in the water, and the strangest beasts and flowers showed themselves on the brink. It was New Holland, the fifth continent of the world, that glided by, showing its blue mountains far away. One heard the song of the priests and watched the wild men dance to the sound of drums and pipes of bone. The Pyramids of Egypt, piercing the clouds, fallen pillars and Sphinxes half-buried in the sand, slid by. The northern lights blazed above the craters of the North—a show of fireworks such as none could equal. The Prince was at the height of happiness—he beheld a hundredfold more than we are telling of here. "And can I stay here always?" he asked.

"That depends on yourself," said the Fairy. "If you do not, like Adam, let yourself be tempted to do the forbidden thing, you can stay here always."

"I shall not touch the apples on the Tree of Knowledge," said the Prince, "there are thousands of fruits here as fair as they."

"Test yourself, and if you are not strong enough, then go with East Wind who brought you: he is to fly back now, and will not come again for a hundred years. That time will pass by you in this place as if it were only a hundred hours, but even that is a long time for temptation and for sin. Every evening when I part from you I must call to you, 'Come with me'. I must beckon with this hand to you; but stay where you are, do not come with me, for at every step your longing will become stronger: you will come to the hall where the Tree of Knowledge grows: I shall sleep beneath its fragrant hanging boughs: you will bend over me, and I must smile: but if you imprint a kiss on my mouth, Eden will sink deep into the earth, and be lost to you. The keen wind of the desert will howl around you, the cold rain will drip from your hair. Sorrow and trouble will be your lot."

"I shall stay here," said the Prince: and East Wind kissed his brow and said, "Be strong, and we shall meet here again in a hundred years. Farewell! Farewell!" So East Wind spread his mighty wings: they shone like ripe corn in harvest or the northern lights in

the depth of winter. Farewell! Farewell! rang out from the flowers
and trees. Storks and pelicans flew in long rows like a fluttering
ribbon, and followed him to the boundaries of the garden.

"Now our dances begin," said the Fairy. "At the end of them,
when I shall dance with you, you will see, as the sun sinks, that I
beckon to you: you will hear me call to you, 'Come with me', but
do it not. For a hundred years I must repeat it every evening, and
every time that moment passes by, you will gain more strength,
and at last you will heed it no more. To-night is the first time; now
I have warned you."

So the Fairy led him into a great hall of transparent white lilies,
in each of which the yellow pistil was a pure gold harp that rang
with the note of strings and flute. Beautiful girls, lissom and slim,
clad in billowy silk, that showed their lovely limbs, swayed in the
dance and sang how sweet was life, how they would never die, and
the Garden of Eden would ever bloom.

The sun went down; all heaven was pure gold, that gave the
lilies the hue of the fairest roses, and the Prince drank of the foaming wine that the maidens brought, and felt such happiness as never
before. He saw the further wall of the hall opened, and how the
Tree of Knowledge stood forth in a brightness that blinded his
eyes. The song that came from it was soft and lovely as his mother's
voice, as if she were singing, "My child, my darling child!"

Then the Fairy beckoned and called lovingly, "Follow me! Follow me!" and he rushed towards her, forgetting his promise, forgetting it all on that first evening, as she beckoned and smiled. The
perfume, the spicy perfume about him grew stronger, the harps
rang yet more beautifully, and it seemed as if the millions of smiling
heads in the hall where the tree grew nodded and sang: "Man
should know all things. Mankind is the lord of the world." It was
no longer tears of blood that were falling from the leaves of the
Tree of Knowledge, he thought—they were red sparkling stars.
"Follow me! Follow me!" said the thrilling notes, and at every step
the Prince's cheeks burned hotter and his blood coursed quicker.
"I must," he said, "it is no sin, it cannot be! Why not follow beauty
and joy? I will see her asleep; nothing is lost, if only I do not kiss
her, and I will not, I am strong, I have a firm will."

The Fairy let fall her radiant robe, thrust the branches aside, and
the next moment was hidden among them.

"Not yet have I transgressed," said the Prince, "nor will I," and he too pushed the branches aside. There she was, asleep already, beautiful, as only the Fairy of the Garden of Eden can be. She smiled in her dreams, and he bent over her and saw tears trickling between her eyelashes.

"Dost thou weep for me?" he whispered. "Weep not, thou love-liest of women. Now at last I feel the happiness of Paradise, stream-ing through my blood and through my thoughts. I feel in my mor-tal limbs the might of a cherub, and immortal life. Let eternal night come on! One moment like this is wealth enough." He kissed the tear from her eye, his mouth touched hers.

A clap of thunder sounded out, deep and terrible, such as none had ever heard. All about him fell in ruin. The beautiful Fairy, the flowering Eden sank, sank deep, deep—the Prince saw it sink into black night; far, far away it sparkled like a little shining star. A deathly chill ran through his limbs: he closed his eyes and long he lay as dead.

The cold rain fell on his face, the keen wind blew about his head, and consciousness came to him again. "What have I done?" he sigh-ed. "I have sinned like Adam, sinned so that Eden is sunk deep down below." He opened his eyes: far off he still saw the star that sparkled like the sunken Eden. It was the morning star in the heaven.

He rose. There he was in the great forest, hard by the cave of the winds, and the mother of the winds was sitting beside him. Wrath-ful she looked, and raised her arm on high.

"Already, the first evening!" said she. "Well, I expected it. If you were my boy, you should go into the bag at once."

"He must go there," said Death: a mighty ancient he was, with a scythe in his hand, and great black wings. "He must be laid in the coffin, but not now. I shall but mark him and let him wander yet about the world for a season and atone for his sin, and grow good and yet better. One day I shall come, when he least looks for it; I shall put him into the black coffin and set it on my head and fly up towards the star. There also does the Garden of Eden bloom, and if he is good and dutiful he can enter it then: but if his thoughts are evil and his heart still full of sin, he will sink with the coffin, deeper than Eden sank, and only each thousandth year shall I bring him back again, either to sink deeper yet, or to dwell in the Star, the Star that sparkles overhead."

The Flying Trunk

There was once upon a time a merchant so rich that he could have paved the whole street, and almost all of a little alley besides, with silver money. But he didn't do that, for he knew of another use for his money: if he paid a penny out, he got a dollar back: that's the sort of merchant he was, and then he died.

His son got all this money, and he lived a merry life: he went to the fancy ball every night, he made paper kites out of banknotes, and played ducks and drakes in the lake with sovereigns instead of stones. That was the way to make the money go, and go it did. At last he had nothing left but fourpence, and no clothes but a pair of slippers and an old dressing-gown. His friends didn't care about him any more, for they couldn't walk about the streets with him; but one of them, who was good-natured, sent him an old trunk and said, "Pack up". Well, that was all very well, but he hadn't got anything to pack up; so he got into the trunk himself.

It was a funny trunk, that. The moment you pressed on the lock of it, it could fly. And so it did: whizz! It flew up with him through the chimney, and high up above the clouds, far and far away. The bottom of it gave a crack every now and then, and he was very much afraid it would go to pieces, for then he would have made a pretty jump, preserve us all! And at last he got to Turkey. He hid the trunk in a wood under dead leaves and went into the town, which he could perfectly well do, for all the Turks went about in dressing-gowns and slippers like him. He met a nurse with a baby. "Look here, you Turkey nurse," said he, "what's that great big palace close by the town with the windows set so high up?"

"That's the King's daughter's," she said. "It's been foretold of her that she will be unlucky in a lover, and therefore nobody is allowed to visit her without the King and Queen are there."

"Thanks," said the merchant's son: and he went into the wood, got into his trunk, and flew up on to the roof and crept in at the window to the Princess.

She was lying on the sofa asleep, and she was so pretty that the merchant's son couldn't help kissing her. She woke up and was terribly startled; but he explained that he was the Turkish God who had come down to her through the sky; and that pleased her very much. So they sat side by side, and he told her stories about her eyes. They were the most lovely dark lakes, and her thoughts floated in them like mermaids: and he told her about her forehead: it was a snow mountain with the most splendid halls and images in it; and he told about the Stork, how it brings the dear little babies. Ah, those were beautiful stories! And thereupon he proposed to the Princess, and she said yes at once.

"But you must come here on Saturday," she said, "the King and Queen are coming to tea with me then. They will be very proud that I am marrying the Turkish God: but be sure you have a really beautiful story ready, for my parents are particularly fond of stories. My mother likes them to be moral and genteel, and my father likes them amusing, so that he can laugh."

"Yes, I shall bring no wedding gift but a story," said he, and they parted; but the Princess gave him a sword set with gold coins, and for these he had plenty of use.

He flew off and bought a new dressing-gown and then stayed out in the wood and made up a story. It had to be ready by Saturday, which is not so easy, I can tell you. At last he was ready, and it was Saturday.

The King, the Queen, and all the court were waiting at tea at the Princess's. He was most kindly received.

"Now will you tell us a story?" said the Queen. "One that has a deep meaning and is instructive?"

"But let there be something one can laugh at," said the King.

"Very well," said he and began; and now we must listen carefully.

"Once upon a time there was a bundle of matches which were extremely proud of being of high degree. Their family tree, that is, the great pine tree of which each of them was a chip, had been a large old tree in the forest. The matches now lay on the dresser between a fire-box and an old iron pot, and to them they told the story of their youth. 'Yes,' they said, 'when we were on the green bough we did indeed flourish like the green bay tree. Every morning and evening we had diamond tea (that was the dew), all day we had the sunshine (if the sun shone) and all the little birds were obliged to tell us stories. We could easily see, too, that we were rich, for the trees with leaves were clad only in summer, while our family could afford green clothes both in summer and winter. But then came the woodcutters; in other words, the great Revolution—and our family was split in pieces. The head of the house obtained a situation as mainmast on a magnificent vessel which could sail the whole world round if it pleased, the other branches went elsewhere, and we are now commissioned to kindle light for the common people: that's why we distinguished folk are come here to the kitchen.'

" 'Yes, it has been otherwise with me,' said the iron pot beside which the matches lay. 'From the moment I came out into the world I have been scoured and set to boil many a time. I minister to solid needs, and properly speaking am the first person in the house. My one pleasure is, as it might be after dinner, to lie cleansed and neat on the dresser, and carry on a reasonable conversation with my colleagues: but with the exception of the water bucket, which every now and then goes down to the yard, we live entirely indoors; our only news bringer is the market basket, but it talks very unrestfully about the government and the people; lately indeed, there was an elderly pot which in its alarm at this fell down and broke itself to pieces. That basket is of a turbulent disposition, I must say.'

" 'Now you're talking too much,' said the fire-box, and the steel knocked on the flint till the sparks came: 'Ought we not to have a gay evening?' 'Yes, let us speak of who is most distinguished,' said the matches. 'No, I don't care for talking about myself,' said the cooking pot, 'let us have an evening conversazione. I will begin. I will tell of things that everyone has experienced; there is opportunity for all to imagine it, and that is pleasant.'

" Near the eastern sea, among the beech woods of Denmark.'— 'That is a delightful commencement,' said all the plates; 'it will, I am sure, be a story I shall enjoy.' 'Yes, there it was that I passed my early years in a quiet family. The furniture was polished, the floor was washed, clean curtains were put up once a fortnight.'

'Now, how interesting you make your story,' said the broom. 'One can tell at once that it is a lady speaking: something so maidenly runs through it all.'

" 'Indeed, yes, one does feel that,' said the water bucket, and out of pure pleasure it gave a little hop, and "plop" sounded on the floor.

"The pot went on with its story, and the end was every bit as good as the beginning. All the plates rattled with pleasure, and the broom got some green parsley out of the dust-hole and crowned the pot with it, for it knew this would annoy the rest, and, it reflected, 'if I crown her to-day, she will crown me to-morrow'.

" 'I shall now dance,' said the tongs, and dance it did. Yes, heaven be good to us, how it did kick up in the air with its leg! The old chair cushion away in the corner split with looking at it. 'Can I be crowned?' said the tongs, and crowned it was.

" 'Mere rabble, after all, these people,' thought the matches.

"The tea urn was now asked to sing; but it had a cold, it said; it could only sing when on the boil. But this was merely standoffishness; it wouldn't sing unless it was set on the table and the family were there.

"Over in the window lay an old quill pen which the maid used to write with; there was nothing remarkable about it except that it had been dipped too deep in the inkstand, but of this it was quite proud. 'If the tea urn won't sing,' it said, 'it can let it alone. Outside, there's a nightingale hung up in a cage; it can sing. It hasn't to be sure been trained at all, but we won't say anything unkind about that to-night.'

" 'I think it extremely improper', said the tea kettle, which was the kitchen singer-in-chief and half-sister to the tea urn, 'that a foreign bird like that should be listened to. Is it patriotic? I leave it to the market basket.'

" 'I', said the market basket, 'am merely annoyed. I am more intensely annoyed than can be imagined. Is this a fitting manner of spending the evening? Would it not be far better to set the house to rights? Everyone would then fall into his right place, and I should lead the whole dance. We should then have a very different state of things.' 'Yes, let's make a real row,' they all cried out together. At that moment the door opened. It was the maid. They all stopped; no one made a sound; but there wasn't a single pot that wasn't conscious of what it could do and how distinguished it was. 'If only I had chosen,' they thought, 'it would have been a gay evening indeed.'

'The maid picked up the matches and struck them. Gracious! How they did sputter and burst into flame! 'Now,' thought they, 'everybody can see we are the quality: what a flash we make! What a light!' And with that they burnt out."

"That was a beautiful story," said the Queen. "I seemed to be really in the kitchen with the matches. Yes, now thou shalt have our daughter."

"Certainly," said the King, "thou shalt marry our daughter on Monday." (They said "thou" to him now, since he was to be one of the family.)

So the wedding was fixed, and on the evening before the whole town was illuminated. Buns and tarts were thrown to be scrambled for. The street-boys stood on tiptoe and shouted "Hurrah!" and whistled on their fingers. It was a most brilliant affair.

"Well, I must see about doing something too," thought the merchant's son: so he bought rockets and throw-downs and every imaginable kind of firework, and put it all in his trunk and flew up in the air with it.

Whizz, how they all went off and how they popped! It made all the Turks jump in the air till their slippers flew about their ears; never before had they seen such sights in the heavens. They could see now that it really was the Turkish God who was to marry the Princess.

As soon as the merchant's son was back in the wood with his trunk he thought: "I'll go into the town and try to hear how the thing went," and very natural too that he should want to hear.

Well, well, what stories the people did tell! Every single one he asked had seen it his own way, but all of them had found it charming.

"I saw the Turkish God himself," said one. "He had eyes like bright stars and a beard like foaming water." "He was flying in a mantle of fire," said another, "and lovely little angels were peeping out from the folds of it." Indeed, he heard a number of charming things said, and the next day he was to be married.

He went back to the wood to get into his trunk—but where was it? The trunk was burnt. A spark from the fireworks had remained in it, had set it alight, and the trunk was in ashes. Never again could he fly, never again visit his bride. She stayed on the roof the whole day, waiting. She's waiting still. He is wandering the world over, telling stories. But they aren't so gay now as the one he told about the matches.

The Storks

On the last house of a small town there was a stork's nest. The stork-mother was in it with her four little young ones, who stuck their heads out, with their little black beaks, which hadn't yet turned red. A little way off on the ridge of the roof stood the father stork, very stiff and upright; he had drawn up one leg so as to give himself some little occupation while he stood on guard. You would have thought he was carved out of wood, he stood so still. "It must look very distinguished, I'm sure, my wife having a sentry by her nest," he thought, "people can't possibly know I'm the husband, they're bound to think I'm under orders to stand here. That looks very well." So he continued to stand on one leg.

A pack of children were playing down below in the street, and when they saw the storks, one of the cheekiest of the boys, and then all the rest of them, began to sing the old rhyme about the storks—that is, they sang what they could remember of it:

> *Stork, Stork, Stone,*
> *Fly home to your own,*
> *Your wife's on her nest*

With four fat young 'uns,
The first'll be hanged by the neck,
The second'll be struck,
The third'll be burned,
The fourth'll be overturned.

"Oh, listen to what those boys are singing," said the little storks, "they're saying we shall be hung and burnt."

"Don't you worry yourselves about that," said the mother stork, "don't listen to it, and then it can't matter."

But the boys went on singing and pointing at the storks: only one boy, whose name was Peter, said it was wrong to make game of animals, and wouldn't join in. The mother stork, too, tried to comfort her young ones. "Don't you worry about it," she said. "Just look how quiet your father's standing there, on one leg too." "But we're so frightened!" said the young ones, and they drew their heads right back into the nest. Next day when the children came out again to play and saw the storks, they began their song. "The first'll be hanged by the neck, the second'll be stuck!" "Shall we really be hanged and stuck?" said the little storks.

"No, certainly not," said their mother, "you'll have to learn how to fly; I shall practise you all right—and then we shall go out into the meadow and pay a visit to the frogs. They'll make us a bow and sing 'ko-aks, ko-aks', and then we'll eat them up. That'll be a real treat."

"And what then?" the little storks asked.

"Why, then all the storks in the whole country will gather together, and then the autumn manœuvres will begin. You'll have to fly very well—that's of the greatest importance; for anyone that can't fly, the General runs him through with his beak and kills him. So you must mind and learn when the drilling begins."

"Then we shall be stuck all the same, as the boys said—and just listen, they're singing it again!"

"Listen to me and not to them," said the mother stork. "After the big manœuvres we shall fly away to the hot countries—oh, ever so far from here, over forest and mountains. Then to Egypt we shall fly, where there are some three cornered stone houses that rise up in a peak above the clouds and are called pyramids and are older than any stork can imagine. There's a river there that overflows, so that all the country turns into mud, and you can walk about in the mud and eat frogs."

"Oo!" said all the young ones.

"Yes, indeed, that is beautiful. You don't do anything but eat all day long, and while we're enjoying ourselves so, there isn't a single green leaf on the trees in this country; it's so cold here that the clouds freeze to bits and come tumbling down in little white rags." (It was the snow she meant, but she couldn't explain it any better.)

"And do the naughty boys freeze to bits too?" asked the young ones. "No, they don't freeze to bits, but they come very near it, and they have to sit indoors in a dark room and mope. Whereas you can fly about in a foreign land where there's flowers and hot sunshine."

Some time had passed by, and the young ones were grown so big that they could stand up in the nest and look a long way all round, and the father stork came flying to them every day with nice frogs and little snakes and every kind of stork dainty he could find; and oh, he was amusing when he did tricks for them. He would turn his head right round to his tail and clatter with his beak as if it was a little rattle; and then he would tell them stories, which were all about the marsh.

"Now attend to me! You must be learning to fly," said the mother stork one day: so then all the four young ones had to come out on to the roof ridge. Oh! how they did sway about! How they did balance with their wings and nearly tumble down!

"Look at me, do!" said their mother. "This is how you must hold your heads; this is the way you must place your feet, one, two! one, two! That's what'll help you on in the world." Then she flew a little way and the young ones made a little clumsy jump, and bump! There they lay, they were too heavy in the body.

"I don't want to fly," said one of them, creeping back into the nest, "I don't care about going to the hot countries."

"Do you want to freeze to death here, then, when winter comes? Do you want the boys to come and hang you and burn you and roast you? I'll just go and call them."

"Oh, no!" said the little stork, and he hopped out again on to the roof with the others. On the third day they were able to fly properly for a little, and then they thought they could stay hovering in the air, and they tried to, but bump! Down they came, and they had to ply their wings again. Then the boys came out in the street below and sang their song: "Stork, Stork, Stone."

"Shall we fly down and peck out their eyes?" said the young ones.

"No, let them be," said the mother, "just listen to me, it's much more important. One, two, three! Now fly to the right. One, two, three! Now to the left, round the chimney. That last flap of the wings was so pretty and correct that you shall be allowed to come to the marsh with me to-morrow. There will be several very nice families of storks there with their children. Let me see that mine are the prettiest; and mind you strut, it looks well and makes you respected."

"But aren't we to take revenge on those naughty boys?" asked the little storks. "Let them squall what they please, you'll be flying up in the clouds, and will be in the pyramid country when they'll be freezing, without so much as a green leaf or a sweet apple."

"We will be revenged on them all the same," they whispered to each other. And then there was more drilling.

Of all the boys in the street there was none so naughty at singing rude songs as the very one who had begun it, and he was quite little, not more than six years old; the storks to be sure thought he must be a hundred, he was so much bigger than their father and mother, and what did they know about the age of children and grown-up people? All their revenge must be spent on this one boy, for he had begun, and he kept on at it. The young storks were quite exasperated by him, and the bigger they grew the less could they bear it. At last their mother was obliged to promise them that they should have a revenge, but she wasn't going to take it before the last day they were in that country.

"We must see first how you behave at the great manœuvres. If you fail there, the General will stab you in the breast with his beak, and then the boys will have been right in one way at any rate. So let us see."

"Yes, you shall," they said, and they *did* bestir themselves. Every day they practised, and they flew so charmingly it was a pleasure to see them.

Then autumn came on; all the storks began to gather before they should fly to the hot countries, while we have winter here. Those *were* manœuvres. They were made to fly right over forests and towns, just to see how well they could fly, for indeed it was a long journey they had before them. The young storks did their affair so nicely that they got: "Excellent, with frogs and snakes." This was the highest possible mark, and they were at liberty to eat the frogs and snakes; and so they did.

"Now for our revenge," they said.

"To be sure," said the mother stork. "I have thought of something that will do beautifully. I know where the pond is where all the human children lie till the stork comes and fetches them to their parents. The pretty little children sleep and dream such lovely dreams as never come to them afterwards. All fathers and mothers want a little child like that, and all children want a sister or a brother. Now then, we'll fly to that pond and fetch one for each of the children who didn't sing that naughty song and make fun of storks: the other children shan't have any."

"But the one that began the song, that horrid beastly boy," screamed the young storks, "what are we going to do to him?"

"Why, in the pond there lies a little dead child that has dreamt itself to death; we'll take that to him, and he'll cry because we've brought him a little dead brother. But that good boy—you haven't forgotten him—the one that said 'it's wrong to make game of animals'. We'll bring him a brother and a sister as well; and because that boy's name is Peter, you shall all be called Peter too."

And as she said, so it came about: and therefore all the storks were called Peter, and they are called so to this very day.

The Elf of the Rose

In the middle of a garden there grew a rose tree which was quite full of blossoms, and in one of these, the prettiest of them all, lived an Elf: he was such a little tiny thing that no human eye could see him. Behind every petal in the rose he had a bedroom. He was as well shaped and as handsome as any child could be, and had wings reaching from his shoulders right down to his feet. Oh! what a sweet smell there was in his room! And how bright and pretty were the walls of it! They were the pale pink, delicate rose leaves.

All day he enjoyed himself in the hot sunshine, flying from flower to flower, dancing on the wings of the butterfly as it flew, and measuring how many steps it took to go over all the roads and paths on a single lime-leaf. It was what we call the veins of the leaf that he reckoned as roads and paths: an enormous distance he had to go, and before he had finished, the sun set. He had begun very late for another thing.

It got very cold, the dew fell, the wind blew. It would be best to go home. He made all the haste he could, but the rose was shut, and he could not get in, not a single rose was open. The poor little Elf was terribly frightened: he had never spent the night out of doors before, but had always slept sweetly, snug among the rose leaves. Oh dear! It would be the death of him for certain!

At the other end of the garden, he knew, there was a summer-house with beautiful honeysuckle on it, whose flowers looked like large coloured horns: he would get into one of them and sleep till morning. Thither he flew. Hush! There were two people inside, a handsome young man and the prettiest of girls. Side by side they sat, and wished they might never be parted, so fond they were of each other, far fonder than the best of children can be of its father and mother.

149

"Yet we must part," said the young man; "your brother wishes us no good: that is why he is sending me on a mission far away beyond mountains and lakes. Farewell, my sweetest bride, for my bride you are!"

They kissed one another: the young girl wept and gave him a rose, but before she put it in his hand she printed a kiss on it so fond and tender that the flower opened, and into it the little Elf flew and nestled his head against the delicate fragrant walls. But he could plainly hear "Farewell, farewell!" said, and feel that the rose was placed in the young man's bosom. Oh how the heart in it beat! The little Elf could not get to sleep, so fast it beat. Not long did the rose lie quiet on his heart: the young man drew it out, and as he went alone through the dark wood he kissed it so often and so hard that the little Elf was in danger of being squeezed to death. Through the leaf he could feel how the man's lips burned: the very rose had opened itself as under the hottest sun of noonday.

There came another man, gloomy and passionate, the fair girl's evil brother. He drew a long sharp knife, and while the other kissed his rose the wicked man stabbed him to death, cut off his head, and buried it, with the body, in the soft earth under a lime tree.

"He's gone and forgotten now," said the wicked brother; "he will come back no more. A long journey he was to go, over mountains and lakes, where a man can easily lose his life; and he's lost his. He won't come back, and my sister will never dare ask me about him." With that he spread the dead leaves over the disturbed earth with his foot, and went home in the dark night, but not alone, as he supposed. The little Elf kept him company, sitting in a withered rolled-up lime-leaf that had fallen on the bad man's hair as he dug the grave. His hat was over it now, and very dark it was in there, and the Elf quivered with horror and wrath at the foul deed.

The bad man got home at dawn. He took off his hat and went into his sister's bedroom. There she lay, the pretty young maid, dreaming of him whom she held so dear, who now, she thought, was travelling over hills and through forests: and the wicked brother stooped over her and laughed horribly, as a devil might laugh. The withered leaf fell from his hair upon the counterpane, but he did not notice it; he went out to sleep—he too—for a little in the early morning. But the Elf stole out of the withered leaf, crept into the ear of the sleeping girl, and told her, as in a dream, of the frightful murder; described to her the place where her brother had killed him and laid his body, told of the flowering lime tree hard by, and said: "That you may see this is no dream that I have told you, you will find a withered leaf on your bed." And so she did when she awoke.

Oh what bitter tears she wept! Yet to no one dared she confide her trouble. The window stood open all day, and the little Elf might easily have gone out into the garden to the roses and all the other flowers, but he cared not to leave her in her sorrow. In the window stood a tree of monthly roses, and in one of these he sat and watched the poor girl. Several times her brother came into the room: he was in high spirits, and unkind—but she dared not say a word of her great sorrow. As soon as night came she stole out of the house and into the wood to the place where the lime tree stood: she cleared the leaves away from the soil, dug down into it and found the murdered man. Oh, how she wept and prayed God that she might die soon! She longed to bear the body home with her, but that she could not. So she took the pale head with the closed eyes, kissed the cold mouth and shook the earth from the fair hair. "This shall be mine!" said she. So when she had laid earth and leaves over the dead body she took the head home with her, and a little branch of jessamine which was flowering in the wood where he was killed. As soon as she was in her room again, she fetched the largest flower-pot she could find, and in it she laid the dead man's head, put earth over it, and planted the sprig of jessamine.

"Farewell! farewell!" whispered the little Elf; he could not bear to look on all this sorrow any longer, and flew out into the garden, to his rose. But it had faded; only a few pale petals hung to the green fruit. "Ah, how quickly passes all that is fair and good!" sighed he. At last he found another rose, which became his house; among its delicate scented leaves he could live and make his home.

Every morning he would fly to the poor girl's window, where she would always be standing by her flower-pot, weeping. The salt tears fell on the sprig of jessamine, but day by day as she grew paler and paler, the sprig grew yet more fresh and green; one twig after another was put forth, and little white buds came and turned to flowers, and she would kiss them. But her wicked brother reviled her and asked if she were going crazy: he could not bear it, and could not understand why she was always weeping over the flower-pot. He little knew what closed eyes, what red lips, had turned to earth there: and she would bow her head over the flower-pot, and there the little Elf found her slumbering. Into her ear he crept, and told her of the evening in the summer-house, and of the sweet smell of the roses and the loving kindness of the Elves, and she slept sweetly, and while she slept her life faded: a quiet death was hers, and now she was in heaven with him whom she loved.

The jessamine flowers opened their great white bells and gave forth a perfume of wonderful sweetness: it was the only way they had to mourn over the dead.

But the wicked brother looked at the beautiful flowering shrub and took it for himself as a legacy, and put it in his room, near the bed, for it was pleasant to look at, and the smell was sweet and fresh. The little Elf went there too, and flew from one flower to another—in each of them dwelt a little soul—and to them he told the story of the murdered youth whose head was now earth in earth, and of the wicked brother and the wretched sister. "We know it!" said each of the souls in the flowers. "We know it! Did we not grow out of the slain man's eyes and lips? We know! We know!" and they nodded their heads in a strange fashion. The Rose Elf could not understand how they could be so calm, and he flew out to the bees, who were gathering honey, and told them the story of the wicked brother; and the bees told their Queen, who gave orders that next morning they should join and kill the murderer.

But the night before—that is, the first night after the death of his sister, as the wicked brother slept in his bed close by the sweet-smelling jessamine—every flower cup opened, and, unseen, but each one bearing a poisoned spear, the flower souls came forth: and first they settled at his ear and told him dreadful dreams, and then they flew to his lips and pricked his tongue with the poisoned spears. "Now we have avenged the dead!" they said, and home they went into the white bells of the jessamine. When morning came and the window was all at once thrown open, the Rose Elf hastened in with the Queen Bee and all the swarm to kill him. But he was dead already, and people were standing about him saying: "The smell of the jessamine has killed him." Then the Rose Elf understood the vengeance of the flowers and told it to the Queen of the Bees, and she hummed about the flower-pot with all her swarm. And as the bees could not be driven away, a man took the flower-pot, and one of the bees stung him on the hand, and he let the pot fall and it broke.

Then they saw the white skull; and they knew that he who lay dead in the bed was a murderer.

And the Queen Bee hummed in the fresh air and sang of the vengeance of the flowers and the Elf of the Rose, and how behind every least petal dwells one who can tell of evil deeds and avenge them.

The Pig Boy

There was once a poor Prince who had quite a small kingdom: but it was big enough for him to marry on and married he would be.

Now it was really rather bold of him to up and say to the Emperor's daughter: "Will you have me?" But he up and did it all the same, for his name was famous far and wide. There were a hundred princesses who would have said yes and thank you, too— but did she? Now we are to hear all about it.

In the Prince's garden there grew a rose tree. Oh, such a lovely rose tree! It only blossomed once in five years, and then had only a single flower; but that was a rose that smelt so sweet that anyone who only sniffed it forgot all his cares and troubles: and besides, he had a Nightingale which could sing as if all the beautiful tunes in the world were in its little windpipe. The Rose and the Nightingale the Princess should have, and accordingly both of them were put into large silver cases and sent to her.

The Emperor had them brought in before him, into the great
hall where the Princess was playing at visitors with her ladies (they
never did anything else) and when she saw the big cases with the
presents, she clapped her hands with joy.

"Oh, if only it's a little pussy cat!" she said; but out came the
beautiful rose.

"Why, how prettily it is made!" said all the ladies.

"It's more than pretty," said the Emperor, "it's nice." But the
Princess felt it, and almost burst into tears. "Ugh, papa," she said,
"it isn't made, it's real."

"Ugh!" said all the court people. "It's real!"

"Well, let's first see what is in the other case before we lose our
tempers," said the Emperor: and out came the Nightingale. It sang
so beautifully that for the moment nobody could say anything
nasty about it.

"Superbe! Charmant!" said the court ladies (for they all spoke
French, every one worse than the last).

"How that bird does remind me of our blessed Empress's musi-
cal box!" said an old nobleman. "Ah, dear me! The same tone, the
same style, precisely!"

"Ah, yes!" said the Emperor, and wept like a little child.

"I don't suppose it can be real?" said the Princess.

"Yes, it is a real bird," said the people who had brought it.
"Then you can let the bird fly," said the Princess, and wouldn't on
any account allow the Prince to visit her. But he didn't let himself
be put off: he stained his face brown and black, pulled his cap down
over his ears, and knocked at the door.

"Good morning, Emperor," said he. "Could I get a situation
here at the palace?"

"Well, there's a lot of people come asking for 'em," said the
Emperor; "but let me see, I do want someone to look after the pigs,
we've got such a lot of them." So the Prince was appointed Pig Boy
to His Majesty. He had a wretched little room given him down by
the pigsty, where he was to live; but all day he sat and worked, and
by the evening he had made a pretty little pot with bells hung all
round it, and as soon as the pot boiled, they rang out beautifully
and played the old tune:

O my blessed Augustine!
Everything's gone.

But the most ingenious part of it all was that when you held your finger in the steam of the pot you could smell at once what dish was being cooked in every fire-place in the town, and that, mark you, was quite a different thing from a rose.

Now the Princess came walking out with all her ladies, and when she heard the tune she stopped and looked quite delighted, for she too could play "O my blessed Augustine." It was the only tune she could play, and she did it with one finger.

"Why, that's the tune I know," she said; "this must be an educated Pig Boy. Look here! Go in and ask him the price of that instrument." So one of the ladies had to run in there (but she put pattens on first).

"What do you want for that pot?" said the lady.

"I want ten kisses from the Princess," said the Pig Boy.

"Preserve us!" said the lady.

"I can't take less," said the Pig Boy.

"Well, what does he say?" asked the Princess.

"I really can't repeat it," said the lady, "it's too dreadful."

"Well, you can whisper it." So she whispered it.

"He's very rude indeed," said the Princess, and walked off alone, but when she had gone a little way the bells rang out so deliciously:

> O my blessed Augustine!
> Everything's gone.

"Look here!" said the Princess. "Ask him if he'll take ten kisses from my ladies."

"No, thanks," said the Pig Boy; "ten kisses from the Princess, or I keep my pot."

"How very tiresome!" said the Princess. "Well, then, you must stand in front of me so that nobody can see." And the court ladies placed themselves in front of her and spread out their skirts, and the Pig Boy took the ten kisses and she took the pot.

Well, that was a treat! The pot had to boil all that evening and all next day. There wasn't a single fireplace in all the town but what they knew what was being cooked there, from the Lord Chamberlain's to the Shoemaker's. The court ladies danced about and clapped their hands.

"We know who's going to have sweet soup and pancakes. We know who is going to have porridge and hash! How interesting!"

"Interesting in the highest degree," said the chief lady in waiting.

"Yes, but keep a tight mouth, for I'm the Emperor's daughter."

"Preserve us!" they all said.

The Pig Boy, in other words the Prince (but they knew no better than that he was a real Pig Boy), didn't let the day pass without doing something, and this time he made a rattle; when he whirled it round it played all the waltzes, galops and polkas that had been made since the creation.

"But this is superb," said the Princess, when she passed that way. "Never have I heard a more beautiful composition. Look here! Go in and ask him the price of that instrument: but no more kissing."

"He wants a hundred kisses from the Princess," said the lady who had been in to inquire.

"I think he must be mad," said the Princess, and off she went, but when she had got a little way she stopped. "One must encourage art," she said. "I am the Emperor's daughter. Tell him he can have ten kisses, as he had yesterday, and the rest he can take from my ladies."

"Yes, but we don't like that," said the ladies.

"Rubbish!" said the Princess. "If I can kiss him, you can too. Please remember that I give you your board and wages." So the lady had to go to him again.

"One hundred kisses from the Princess," said he, "or each of us keeps his own."

"Stand in front of me," said she. So all the ladies got in front of her and he began kissing.

"Now, what can all that running about mean down there by the pigsty?" said the Emperor, who had come out on the balcony. He rubbed his eyes and put his spectacles on. "It's the ladies in waiting at their tricks. I must go down to 'em." With that he pulled his slippers up—they were shoes which he had trodden down at heel. Bless him! How he did hurry!

As soon as he got down into the yard he walked very quietly, and the ladies in waiting were so busy counting the kisses (to see fair play and that he shouldn't get too many kisses nor yet too few) that they didn't notice the Emperor. He stood up on tiptoe.

"What's the meaning of this!" he cried, when he saw them kissing; and he smacked them on the head with his slipper just as the

Pig Boy was taking his eighty-sixth kiss. "Out you go!" said the Emperor, in a passion. And both the Princess and the Pig Boy were turned out of his Empire.

There she stood crying, while the Pig Boy scolded her, and the rain came pouring down.

"Alas and alack a day," said the Princess; "if only I'd taken that handsome Prince! Oh dear, how wretched I am!" The Pig Boy went behind a tree, wiped the brown and black stains off his face, threw off his shabby clothes, and came out in his princely dress; so handsome was he that the Princess bowed down in wonder. "I have learnt to despise you," he said; "you would not have an honourable Prince. You could not appreciate the Rose or the Nightingale, but you could kiss a Pig Boy to get a plaything. I wish you joy of it." And with that he went into his Kingdom and shut the door and bolted it, and she might just stand outside and sing:

> *O my blessed Augustine!*
> *Everything's gone.*

The Nightingale

In China, as you know, the Emperor is a Chinaman, and all the folk he has about him are Chinamen too. It's many years ago now, but that is exactly the reason why it is worth while to listen to the story, before it's forgotten. The Emperor's palace was the most splendid in the world, wholly and entirely made of fine porcelain, very costly, but so brittle and risky to touch that one had to take very great care. In the garden the most extra-ordinary flowers were to be seen, and to the most magnificent of all little silver bells were tied, so that nobody might pass by without noticing the flower. Yes, everything was most carefully thought out in the Emperor's garden, and it extended so far that the gar-dener himself did not know the end of it. If you went on walking you came into a beautiful forest with tall trees and deep lakes. The forest went right down to the sea, which was blue and deep. Large ships could sail right in beneath the branches, and in the branches there lived a Nightingale, which sang so divinely that even the poor fisherman, who had so much else to think about, stopped and listened when he was out at night pulling up his fishing nets and happened to hear the Nightingale. "Lord, how pretty it is!" he said; but then he had to attend to his business, and forgot the bird. Still, the next night when it sang again, and the fisherman came out here, he said once more: "Lord, how pretty it is!"

From all the countries in the world travellers came to the Em-peror's city and were amazed at the palace and the garden; but when they came to hear the Nightingale, they all said: "After all, this is the best thing." And the travellers told of it when they got home, and clever people wrote many a book about the City, the Palace and the Garden, but they did not overlook the Nightingale: it was put at the head of everything, and those who could make poetry wrote the loveliest poems all about the Nightingale in the forest by the deep lake.

The books went all over the world, and some of them came, once upon a time, to the Emperor, too. He was sitting in his golden chair reading and reading, and every minute he nodded his head, for it pleased him to hear the splendid description of the City and the Palace and the Garden. "Yet, the Nightingale is the best thing of all," was written there.

"What's this?" said the Emperor. "The Nightingale? Why, I know nothing whatever about it! Is there such a bird in my Em-pire—not to say in my garden? I never heard of it! This is what one can get by reading."

So he called his Marshal, who was of such high rank that when anyone inferior to him made bold to address him or ask him a ques-tion, he never made any reply but "P", which means nothing at all. "It appears that there is a most remarkable bird here, called a

Nightingale," said the Emperor. "It is stated to be the very best thing in my vast realm! Why has no one ever told me anything about it?"

"I have never before heard it spoken of," said the Marshal; "it has never been presented at Court."

"I desire that it shall come here to-night and sing before me," said the Emperor. "Here is the whole world aware of what I possess, and I know nothing of it!"

"I have never before heard it spoken of," said the Marshal; "I must search for it, I must find it."

But where was it to be found? The Marshal ran up and down all the staircases, and through the halls and passages, but no one of all the people he met had heard tell of the Nightingale, and the Marshal ran back to the Emperor and said that it certainly must be an invention of the people who wrote books. "Your Imperial Majesty could never imagine the things people write; all manner of inventions, and something which is called the Black Art."

"But the book in which I read this", said the Emperor, "was sent to me by the high and mighty Emperor of Japan, so it cannot be an untruth. I *will* hear the Nightingale! It must be here to-night. It has my most exalted favour, and if it does not come, the whole court shall have its stomachs stamped upon, when it has dined!"

"Tsing-pe!" said the Marshal; and ran again up and down all the staircases and through all the halls and passages; and half the court ran with him, for they did not at all wish to have their stomachs stamped upon. There was ever such a hue and cry after this remarkable Nightingale, which was known to the whole world, but to nobody at the court.

At last they came on a poor little girl in the kitchen. She said: "O Lord, the Nightingale? I know it well; yes, indeed, how it can sing! Every evening I have leave to carry home leavings from the table to my poor sick mother. She lives down by the shore, and when I'm coming back and am tired and take a rest in the wood, I hear the Nightingale sing. The tears come in my eyes with it: it feels as if my mother was kissing me."

"Little kitchen girl," said the Marshal, "I will promise you a permanent position in the kitchen and leave to see the Emperor dine, if you can guide us to the Nightingale, for it is invited for this evening." So they all set out together for the wood where the

Nightingale used to sing. Half the court was there. As they were making the best of their way along a cow began to low.

"Oh!" said the court pages. "Now we can hear it; it's a really remarkable power for such a small animal! I'm quite sure I've heard it before."

"No, that's the cows lowing," said the little kitchen girl. "We're a long way off the place yet."

Then the frogs began croaking in the pond.

"Lovely," said the Chinese master of the palace. "Now I hear her! It resembles small church bells."

"No, that's the frogs," said the little kitchen girl; "but I think we shall hear it very soon now."

Then the Nightingale began to sing.

"That's it," said the little girl. "Hark! hark! And there it sits!" And she pointed to a little grey bird up among the branches. "Is it possible?" said the Marshal. "I could never have imagined it would be like that! And how very shabby it looks! It must certainly have lost its colour at the sight of so many distinguished persons in its vicinity."

"Little Nightingale," the little kitchen girl called out aloud; "our gracious Emperor very much wants you to sing to him."

"With the greatest of pleasure," said the Nightingale, and sang, so that it was a pure delight.

"It resembles glass bells," said the Marshal, "and look at its little throat, how it works it! It is most curious that we should never have heard it before! It will have a great success at court." "Shall I sing once again for the Emperor?" said the Nightingale, who thought the Emperor was there too.

"My excellent little Nightingale," said the Marshal, "I have the great pleasure of being commanded to invite you to a court festival this evening, where you will enchant his exalted Imperial Grace with your charming song."

"It sounds best out in the green wood," said the Nightingale. But it gladly accompanied them when it heard that the Emperor asked for it.

At the palace there was a tremendous smartening up. The walls and floors, which were of porcelain, shone with the light of many thousands of golden lamps. The most beautiful flowers, which really could ring, were set about the windows. There was a running to and fro, and a draught of air, but that made all the bells ring till one couldn't hear one's own voice.

In the middle of the great hall where the Emperor sat, a golden perch was set up, and on it the Nightingale was to sit. The whole court was there, and the little kitchen girl had got permission to stand behind the door, seeing now she had the title of Actual Kitchenmaid. Everybody was in their best state attire, and everybody was looking at the little grey bird. The Emperor nodded to it.

And the Nightingale sang so beautifully that tears came into the Emperor's eyes; the tears ran down his cheeks, and then the Nightingale sang yet more delightfully, so that it went straight to his heart; and the Emperor was greatly pleased, and said that the Nightingale should have his golden slipper to wear on its neck. But the Nightingale thanked him and said it had already had reward enough.

"I have seen tears in the Emperor's eyes; that is to me the richest of treasures. An Emperor's tears have a marvellous power. God knows I am well paid." And it sang again with that sweet divine voice.

"It is the most lovable coquetterie one can conceive," said the whole suite of ladies, and they put water in their mouths so as to gurgle when anyone spoke to them; they thought that they too were Nightingales. Yes, and the lackeys and chambermaids let it be understood that they also were satisfied, and that means a lot, for they are the most difficult people to suit. In fact, the Nightingale really did make a great success.

It was now to remain at court and have its own cage, and liberty to take exercise out of doors twice in the day time and once at night. It had twelve attendants, each of whom had a silken thread attached to its leg, which they held tight. There really was no satisfaction in these expeditions. The whole City talked of the remarkable bird, and when two people met, one of them would say nothing but "night", and the other said "gale". Whereupon they heaved a sigh and understood each other. Nay, more than eleven pork butchers' children were named after it, but not one of them had a note of music in its body.

One day there arrived a large parcel for the Emperor; on it was written, "Nightingale".

"Here now we have another book about our celebrated bird," said the Emperor; but it was not a book, it was a little machine, that lay in a box—an artificial Nightingale made to resemble the live one, but all set with diamonds, rubies and sapphires. As soon as ever the artificial bird was wound up, it could sing one of the strains the real one sang, and its tail moved up and down and glistened with silver and gold. Round its neck hung a little ribbon, and on it was written: "The Emperor of Japan's Nightingale is poor beside that of the Emperor of China."

"That is charming!" said everybody. And the man who had brought the artificial bird immediately received the title of Chief Imperial Bringer of Nightingales.

Now they must sing together; what a duet it will be!

So they had to sing together; but it wouldn't go right, for the real Nightingale sang in its own style, and the artificial bird went off into waltz-tunes.

"No blame attaches to it," said the bandmaster; "it keeps excellent time, and is entirely of my school." So the artificial bird was to sing alone. It made as great a success as the real one, and was, besides, far prettier to look at; it glittered like a bracelet or a brooch.

Three-and-thirty times over did it sing the self-same melody, and yet it was not tired. The people would have liked to hear it over again, but the Emperor said that now the live Nightingale should sing a little—but where was it? Nobody had noticed that it had flown out of the open window, away to its own green wood.

"But what is the meaning of this?" said the Emperor. And all the court people scolded, and said the Nightingale was a most ungrateful creature. "Still, we have the best bird, after all," they said; and the artificial bird had to sing again. It was the thirty-fourth time they had heard the same piece, but they didn't quite know it yet, for it was very difficult, and the bandmaster praised the bird in the highest terms, and assured them that it was superior to the real Nightingale, not only as regards the plumage and the many beautiful diamonds, but also internally.

"For observe, your lordships, and the Emperor above all, with the real Nightingale one can never calculate what will come next, but with the artificial bird all is definite; it is thus, and no otherwise. It can be accounted for; one can open it up and show the human contrivance, how the waltzes are set, how they go, and how one follows on another."

"Exactly what I think," said everybody; and the bandmaster got permission on the following Sunday to exhibit the bird to the people. They too should hear it sing, said the Emperor. And they did hear it, and were as delighted as if they had got drunk on tea (which is the genuine Chinese fashion), and everyone said "oh" and pointed the finger we call lick-pot up in the air and then nodded. But the poor fisherman, who had heard the real Nightingale, said: "It sings pretty enough, and it's like it too; but there's something wanting, I don't know what!"

The real Nightingale was exiled from the land and realm. The artificial bird had a place assigned it on a silk cushion close to the Emperor's bed. All the presents that had been made to it, gold and jewels, lay round it, and it had risen to the title of "High Imperial Nightingale Songster" and in precedence was Number One on the Left Hand Side; for the Emperor accounted that side to be the most distinguished on which the heart lay, and even an Emperor's heart is on the left side. And the bandmaster wrote five-and-twenty volumes on the subject of the artificial bird. The work was very learned and very long, full of the most difficult words in the Chinese language, and everyone said they had read it and understood it; for otherwise they would have been accounted stupid and would have had their stomachs stamped upon.

So things went on for a whole year. The Emperor, the court, and all the rest of the Chinese knew by heart every little cluck in the artificial bird's song, but precisely for that reason they liked it all the better: they could sing with it themselves, and so they did. The street-boys would sing "Zizizi! kluk, kluk, kluk!" and the Emperor sang too: in fact, it was admittedly exquisite.

But one evening, when the bird was singing its best and the Emperor was lying in bed listening to it, something went "snap" inside the bird. Whirr-rr! All the wheels whizzed round, and the music stopped. The Emperor jumped straight out of bed, and had his body physician summoned, but what use was that? They fetched the watchmaker, and after much talk and much examination, he got the bird into order after a fashion. But he said it must be most sparingly used, for it was very much worn in the bearings, and it was impossible to replace them so that you could be sure of the music. That was a sad affliction! Only once a year durst they let the bird sing, and even that was a severe strain. But thereupon the bandmaster made a short oration with plenty of difficult words, and said that it was just as good as before, and accordingly it was just as good as before.

Five years had now passed by, and a really great sorrow came upon the whole country, for at bottom they were very fond of their Emperor, and now he was ill, and, it was said, could not recover. A new Emperor was already chosen, and people stood outside in the streets and asked the Marshal how it went with their Emperor.

"P," said he, and shook his head.

Cold and pale lay the Emperor in his great stately bed; the whole court believed him dead, and every one of them ran off to pay their respects to the new Emperor. The servants of the bedchamber ran out to gossip about it, and the palace maids had a large coffee party. Everywhere, in all the halls and corridors, cloth was laid down so that footsteps should not be heard, and so everything was very, very quiet. But the Emperor was not yet dead; stiff and pale he lay there in the stately bed with the long velvet curtains and the heavy gold tassels: high up a window stood open, and the moon shone in upon the Emperor and the artificial bird.

The poor Emperor was hardly able to draw his breath; it seemed as if something was sitting on his chest. He opened his eyes, and then he saw that it was Death, who was sitting on his breast, and had put on his golden crown, and was holding in one hand the gold sword of the Emperor, and in the other his splendid banner: and round about, in the folds of the great velvet bed curtains, strange faces pushed themselves out, some quite horrible, others divinely kind. There were all the Emperor's good and evil deeds, looking at him now that Death was seated upon his breast.

"Do you remember that?" whispered one after another. "Do you remember this?" And they told him of many things, so that the sweat broke out on his forehead. "I never knew of that," said the Emperor. "Music! Music! The great drum of China!" he called out, "that I may not hear all they are saying."

They went on, and Death nodded like a Chinaman at everything that was said.

"Music! Let me have music!" cried the Emperor. "You blessed little bird of gold, sing, do sing! I have given you gold and precious things; I myself hung my golden slipper about your neck! Sing, do sing!"

But the bird was silent: there was no one to wind it up, and without that it did not sing. But Death went on looking at the Emperor out of his great empty eye-holes, and everything was still, fearfully still.

At that instant there was heard, close by the window, the most lovely song. It was the little live Nightingale that was sitting on the branch outside. It had heard of its Emperor's need, and so had come to sing to him of comfort and hope: and as it sang, the forms became more and more shadowy. The blood coursed quicker and quicker through the Emperor's weak body, and Death himself listened and said: "Go on, little Nightingale! Go on."

"Yes, if you will give me the splendid gold sword! Yes, if you will give me the rich banner, and give me the Emperor's crown." And Death gave each of the treasures for a song, and the Nightingale still went on singing; and it sang of the quiet churchyard where the white roses grow, where the elder tree smells sweet, and where the fresh grass is moistened with the tears of those who are left. Then a yearning for his garden came upon Death, and he floated out of the window like a cold white mist.

"Thanks, thanks," said the Emperor, "you heavenly little bird, I know you now. I drove you out of my land and realm, and yet you have sung the foul sins away from my bed, and rid my heart of Death. How shall I repay you?"

"You have repaid me," said the Nightingale. "I drew tears from your eyes the first time I sang, and I shall never forget it to you. Those are the jewels that do the heart of the singer good. But sleep now, and become well and strong. I will sing to you."

And it sang, and the Emperor fell into a sweet sleep, a sleep that was kind and healing.

The sun was shining in at the windows on him when he awoke, strengthened and whole. None of his attendants had come back yet, for they believed he was dead, but the Nightingale still sat there singing.

"You must always stay with me," said the Emperor. "You shall only sing when you like, and as for the artificial bird, I'll break it into a thousand bits."

"Don't do that," said the Nightingale; "it has done what good it could, keep it as before. I can't make any home at the palace, but do you let me come here when I like. Then I will sit at evening time on the branch there by this window and sing to you, to make you happy, and thoughtful too. I will sing about the happy and about those who suffer. I will sing of the evil and the good that is about you and is hidden from you. The little singing bird flies far and wide, to the poor fisherman, to the labourers' cottages, to everyone who is far removed from you and your court. I love your heart better than your crown; and yet the crown has about it a perfume of something holy. I will come, I will sing to you; but one thing you must promise me."

"Anything," said the Emperor, as he stood there in his imperial robes, which he had put on himself, and held the sword, heavy with gold, up against his heart.

"One thing I beg of you. Tell no one that you have a little bird that tells you everything. It will be better." And with that the Nightingale flew away.

The attendants came in to see their dead Emperor, and—well, there stood they, and the Emperor said: "Good morning."

The Lovers

The Top and the Ball lay in a drawer along with the other toys, and the Top said to the Ball: "Mightn't we be engaged? We lie in the same drawer." But the Ball, who was covered with morocco and thought as much of herself as any fine young lady, wouldn't reply to any such question as that.

Next day the little boy to whom the toys belonged came and painted the Top red and yellow, and drove a copper nail into it, which made a splendid appearance when the Top spun humming round.

"Look at me," said he to the Ball, "what do you say now? Mightn't we be an engaged couple—we suit each other so well. You jump and I dance; nobody could be happier than we two together."

"Oh, indeed, do you think so?" said the Ball. "You don't realize that my father and mother were morocco slippers, and that I have a cork in my body." "Well, but I'm made of mahogany," said the Top. "The Mayor himself turned me; he's got his own lathe, and he enjoyed doing it very much."

"Can I rely upon that statement?" said the Ball.

"May I never be whipped again if it's not true," answered the Top.

"You give a very good account of yourself," said the Ball; "still, I can't consent. I'm as good as half engaged to a swallow. Whenever I go up in the air he puts his head out of his nest and says 'Will you? Will you?' and recently I said 'Yes' to myself, and that's as good as a half engagement, but I promise never to forget you."

"A lot of good that is," said the Top; after which they had no further conversation.

Next day the Ball was taken out. The Top saw it flying high up in the air like a bird till at last it went right out of sight. Eight times it came down again, but always bounded high when it touched the ground; and this was due either to its aspirations or to its having a cork in its body. The ninth time the Ball disappeared and didn't come back. The boy looked and looked for it, but it was gone.

"I know well enough where it is," sighed the Top. "It's in the swallow's nest, married to the swallow."

The more the Top thought about it, the more absorbed he became in the Ball: for the very reason that he couldn't get at it, his affection for it increased. That it should have accepted another—that was the strange thing.

The Top danced round and hummed, but went on thinking of the Ball, which in his fancy grew more and more beautiful.

Thus several years went by—and the attachment was a thing of the past. The Top was now no longer young, but one fine day he was gilded all over. Never had he looked so splendid; he was now a Top of gold, and jumped about till his hum re-echoed again. That was indeed a triumph: but all at once he gave too high a jump and was gone. They searched and searched, even down in the cellar, but he couldn't be found.

Where was he? Why, he had jumped into the dustbin where there lay all manner of things; cabbage stalks, sweepings and rubbish that had fallen down from the gutter.

"Here's a nice place to be lying! The gilding will very soon come off me! And what sort of shabby creatures are these that I've got among?" he said, looking askance at a long cabbage stalk that had been stripped of its last leaf, and at an odd round object that looked like an old apple—but it wasn't an apple; it was an old ball which had lain for years up in the gutter, soaked through with water. "Thank heaven! At last here is someone of one's own class that one can speak to," said the Ball, looking at the gilt Top. "As a matter of fact, I am made of morocco, sewn together by a young lady's hands, and I have a cork in my body, though no one would think so to look at me. At one time I was about to be married to a swallow, but I fell into the gutter, and there I have lain for five years, soaking: a long long time, as you may imagine, for a young lady."

But the Top said nothing; he thought of his old love, and the more he heard the plainer it became to him that this must be she.

Now came the maid to empty the dustbin. "Aha!" said she. "Here's the gold Top."

So the Top got back into the house, and enjoyed great honour and attention; but nobody heard anything of the Ball, and the Top never said a word more of his old attachment. That's apt to disappear when the beloved object has lain for five years in a gutter and soaked; indeed, if one meets her in the dustbin, one doesn't attempt to recognize her.

The Ugly Duckling

It was very pleasant out in the country. It was summer time, the corn was yellow, the oats green, the hay was stacked down in the green meadows, and there the stork walked about on his long red legs and talked Egyptian. He had learnt the language from his mother. Round the fields and meadows there were large woods and within them deep lakes: indeed, it was pleasant out in the country. Full in the sunshine, an old manor house stood, surrounded by a deep moat, and from the base of the walls right down to the water great dock plants grew—so tall that a little child could stand upright under the largest of them. It was as lonely in among them as in the thickest wood; and there a Duck was sitting on her nest. She had got to hatch out her little Ducklings, but by this time she was well nigh tired out, they took so long about it, and she had very few callers. The other Ducks preferred swimming about the moat to coming up and sitting under a dock-leaf to chat with her.

At last, one egg after another cracked, and said: "Pip! pip!"

All the egg-yolks had come to life and were sticking their heads out.

"Quack, quack!" said she, and they said it too, as well as they could, and looked all round them beneath the green leaves; and their mother let them look as much as they liked, for green is good for the eyes.

"What a big place the world is," said all the young ones: for to be sure they had a great deal more room now than when they lay in the egg.

"Do you suppose this is all the world?" said their mother; "why, it stretches out far beyond the other side of the garden, right into the parson's field—but I've never been there. You're all there, I suppose?" and she got up. "No, that's not all; there lies the biggest egg still. How long *will* it take? I'm really almost sick of it," and with that she sat down again.

"Well, how goes it?" asked an elderly Duck who came to call on her. "Oh, this one egg takes a dreadful long time," said the sitting Duck; "it won't break. But just you look at the others! They are the sweetest Ducklings I've ever seen; they're all just like their wretch of a father, who never comes to see me."

"Let me look at the egg that won't hatch," said the old Duck; "you may be sure that's a turkey's egg. I was made a fool of once that way, and I had my share of trouble and anxiety with the young ones, I can tell you, for they are afraid of the water. I couldn't get them to go in! I quacked and I pecked, but it was no good. Let me see the egg. Ah, yes, that's a turkey's egg; you just let it lie and teach the rest to swim."

"Oh, I'll just sit on it a bit longer," said the Duck. "As I've sat so long, I may as well give it a Whitsun week!"[1] "Just as you please," said the old Duck, and walked off.

At last the big egg opened. "Pip! pip!" said the young one, scrambling out; he was very big and ugly. The Duck looked at him: "That's a fearfully big Duckling, that is," she said. "None of the others look like that. I suppose it can't be a turkey poult! Well, we'll soon see; into the water he shall go, if I have to kick him out myself."

---

[1] This needs a note, for the gist of which I have to thank kind friends in Denmark. 'Whitsun week' is meant to render 'Dyrehavstid', which should be 'Dyrehavsbak-ketid'. Dyrehavsbakken is a place of amusement near Klampenborg, which used to have a 'season' from Midsummer Day (June 24), to the feast of the Visitation (July 2).

Next day the weather was perfectly delicious: the sun shone all over the green docks, and the mother Duck and all her family came out, and down to the moat. Splash! Into the water went she. "Quack, quack!" she said, and one Duckling after another plumped in. The water went over their heads, but they were up again in a moment and swam beautifully. Their legs worked of themselves, and now they were all out in the water, and even the ugly grey one was swimming with them. "No, no, that's no turkey," she said. "Look how nicely he uses his legs, and how well he holds himself up. That's my own child! He's really quite handsome if you look at him properly. Quack, quack! Come along with me and I'll take you out into the world and introduce you to the duck-yard, but mind and keep close to me so that nobody can tread on you, and do look out for the cat."

So they went into the duck-yard. There was a terrible commotion there, for two families were quarrelling over an eel's head—which the cat got after all.

"Look, that's the way the world goes," said the mother Duck—her beak watering a little, for she would have liked the eel's head herself. "Now then, use your legs," she said; "mind and look alive, and stoop your necks to the old Duck over there, she's the most distinguished person here; she's of Spanish descent, so she's something special, and you see she's got a red rag round her leg. That is an extraordinarily splendid thing, the greatest distinction any duck can have; it means that people can't do without her, and she must be recognized by animals and men alike. Now then, look alive! Don't turn your toes in! A duckling that's properly brought up keeps its legs wide apart, like father and mother. Look here! Now then! Make a bow and say quack."

So they did; but the other ducks round them looked at them and said, quite loud, "Look there! Now we've got to have all this mob on the top of us, as if there weren't enough of us already; and poof! what an object that duckling is! We can't stand him"; and a duck rushed at him and bit him in the neck.

"Let him be," said his mother; "he isn't doing any harm." "Yes, but he's too big and odd altogether," said the duck who had bitten him; "so he's got to be smacked."

"Those are pretty ducklings that mother has," said the old Duck with the rag on her leg; "all quite pretty except that one. He hasn't been a success; I could wish the mother would alter him."

"That can't be done, your grace," said the mother Duck. "He's not handsome, but he has a really good disposition, and swims as nicely as any of the rest, even better, I venture to say. I believe he will grow handsome, or perhaps in time he will grow even somewhat smaller; he has lain too long in the egg, and so has not acquired a proper shape." And she picked at his neck and smoothed him down. "Besides, he's a drake," she went on, "so it doesn't matter quite so much. He has, I believe, a good constitution and will win through in the end."

"The other ducklings are charming," said the old lady. "Well, make yourselves at home, and if you happen to find an eel's head, you can bring it to me."

So they made themselves at home: but the poor Duckling who had come last out of the egg and looked so ugly, was bitten and buffeted and made to look a fool by the hens and the ducks alike. "He's too big," they all said; and the turkey cock, who was born with spurs, and considered himself an emperor on the strength of it, blew himself up like a ship under full sail and went straight at the Duckling, gobbling and getting quite red in the head. The poor Duckling didn't know where to stay or which way to go, he was so miserable at being ugly and the butt of the whole duck-yard.

That was the first day, and as time went on it got worse and worse. The wretched Duckling was chased about by everybody, and even his mother and sisters were nasty to him, and kept saying: "I wish the cat would get you, you ugly devil." And his mother said: "I wish you'd get right away"; and the ducks bit him and the hens pecked him, and the maid who had to feed the creatures kicked at him. So he ran away, and flew over the fence. The little birds in the bushes shot up in the air in a fright. "That's because I'm so ugly," the Duckling thought, and shut his eyes, but ran on all the same, till he got out into the wide marsh where the wild-duck lived; and there he lay all night, for he was very tired and very unhappy.

In the morning the wild-duck flew up and caught sight of their new comrade. "What sort of a chap are you?" they asked; and the Duckling turned to this side and that and greeted them as well as he could. "You're precious ugly," said the wild-ducks; "but that doesn't matter to us as long as you don't marry into our family."

Poor wretch! He wasn't thinking much about marrying, as long as he could be allowed to lie among the reeds, and drink a little marsh water. There he lay two whole days, and then came a pair of wild geese (or rather wild ganders, for they were both he's): they hadn't been hatched out very long, and so they were particularly lively. "Here, mate," they said, "you're so ugly I quite like you. Will you come along and be a migrant? Close by in another marsh there's some sweet pretty wild geese—all young ladies that can say Quack. You're so ugly you could make your fortune with them." At that moment there was a Bang! Bang! and both the wild geese fell dead among the reeds, and the water was stained blood red. Another bang! bang! and whole flights of geese flew up from the reeds, and there was yet another bang! a great shoot was afoot. The sportsmen were all round the marsh, some even sitting up among the branches of trees that stretched out over the reeds. The blue smoke drifted like clouds, in among the dark stems, and hung far out over the water. The dogs went splash! splash! into the mud, and the reeds and rushes swayed hither and thither; it was terrible for the wretched Duckling, who was bending his neck to get it under his wing, when all at once, close to him, there was a fearful big dog with his tongue hanging right out of his mouth and his eyes shining horribly. He thrust his muzzle right at the Duckling and showed his sharp teeth—and then—splash! Off he went without seizing him.

"Oh, thank goodness," sighed the Duckling; "I'm so ugly, even the dog doesn't like to bite me!" But there he lay perfectly still while the duck shots rattled in the reeds and gun after gun banged out. It was well on in the day before all was quiet, but the unhappy bird dared not get up even then. He waited several hours yet, before he looked about him, and then he hurried away from the marsh as fast as ever he could, running over fields and meadows, and such a wind got up that he had hard work to get along. Towards evening he was near a poor little cottage, so crazy was it that it didn't know which way to tumble down, so it remained standing. The wind howled so fiercely round the Duckling that he had to sit down on his tail to keep facing it, and it grew worse and worse. Then he noticed that one hinge of the door was gone, and it hung so crooked that he could slip indoors through the crack, and so he did.

Here lived an old woman with a cat and a hen. The cat, whom she called Sonny, could set up his fur and purr, and also throw out sparks, but for this he had to be stroked backwards. The Hen had very short little legs, and was consequently called "chicky short legs". She laid good eggs, and the woman was as fond of her as of a child of her own.

Next morning the strange Duckling was noticed at once, and the cat began to purr, and the Hen to cluck. "What's the matter?" said the old woman, looking all about her. But her sight wasn't good, so she took the Duckling for a fat duck that had strayed away. "That's a splendid catch," she said: "now I can have duck eggs, if only it isn't a drake! We must make sure of that." So the Duckling was taken in on approval for three weeks, but no eggs came.

The Cat was the gentleman of the house and the Hen the lady, and they always talked of "we and the world"; for they considered that they were half the world, and much the best half. It seemed to the Duckling that some people might think differently, but this the Hen could not tolerate.

"Can you lay eggs?" she asked. "No! Then will you kindly hold your tongue."

And the Cat said: "Can you put up your fur, or purr, or give out sparks? No! Then you've no call to have an opinion when sensible people are talking."

So the Duckling lay in a corner and was in the lowest spirits. He began to think of the fresh air and sunshine, and such a strange longing to swim in the water came on him that he could not help telling the Hen.

"What's the matter with you?" she asked. "You've nothing to do, that's why you get these fancies; you just lay some eggs, or purr, and they'll pass off." "But it is so delicious to float on the water," said the Duckling; "so lovely to get it over your head and dive right down to the bottom."

"Oh yes, most delightful, of course!" said the Hen. "Why, you're absolutely mad! Ask the Cat—he's the cleverest man I know—whether he enjoys floating on the water or diving down; I say nothing of myself. Why, ask your mistress, the old woman; there's no one in the world cleverer than her—do you suppose she wants to go swimming and getting the water over her head?"

"You don't understand me," said the Duckling.

The Ugly Duckling

"Well, if we don't understand you, who is going to understand you, pray? You'll never be cleverer than the Cat and the woman, to say nothing of me. Don't give yourself airs, child, but thank your Maker for all the kindness people have done you. Don't you live in a warm room among company you can learn something from? But there! You're a rubbishy thing, and there's little entertainment in your company. You may take it from me! I mean well by you, and I'm telling you home truths, and that's how people can see their true friends. Now just do take pains to lay eggs, or learn to purr or else give sparks."

"I think I'll go out into the wide world," said the Duckling.

"Very well, do," said the Hen.

So the Duckling went off and swam on the water and dived into it; but he was looked down upon by all the creatures because of his ugliness.

Autumn now came on: the leaves of the wood turned brown and yellow, the wind caught them and made them dance about, and above the sky looked cold, where the clouds hung heavy with hail and snow, and on the fence the raven perched and cried "Caw! Caw!" for the mere cold. Indeed, it regularly gave you the shivers to think of it. The unhappy Duckling had a very hard time.

One evening, when there was a lovely sunset, a whole flock of beautiful great birds rose out of the bushes. The Duckling had never seen any so handsome. They were brilliantly white, with long supple necks. They were swans, and they uttered a strange sound and spread their splendid long wings and flew far away from the cold region to warmer lands, and unfrozen lakes. They mounted so high, so high that the ugly little Duckling was strangely moved; he whirled himself round in the water like a wheel, he stretched his neck straight up into the air after them and uttered such a loud cry, so strange, that he was quite frightened at it himself. Oh, he could not forget those beautiful birds, those wonderful birds! And the moment they were out of sight he dived right down to the bottom of the water, and when he came up again he was almost beside himself. He didn't know what the birds were called or which way they were flying, but he loved them as he had never loved anything yet. He was not envious of them—how could it enter his mind to wish for such beauty for himself—he would have been happy if even the ducks had let him into their company—poor ugly creature.

The winter grew very very cold: the Duckling was obliged to swim about on the water to keep it from freezing quite over, but every night the hole he swam in became smaller and smaller. It froze so hard that the ice cracked again; the Duckling had always to be moving about to keep the water open, till at last he was tired out and sat still, and was frozen fast in the ice.

Early in the morning a labourer came that way, saw him, went on the ice and with his wooden shoe broke it up and carried the Duckling home to his wife, and there he was brought to life again. The children wanted to play with him, but he thought they meant to hurt him, and in his fright he dashed right into the milk-pan and made the milk splash out into the room. The woman screamed and threw up her hands. Then he flew into the butter-tub and after that into the meal-bin and out again. Goodness, what a sight he was! The woman screamed out and hit at him with the tongs, and the children tumbled over one another trying to catch him, laughing, calling out—by good luck the door stood open, and out he rushed into the bushes, on the new fallen snow, and there he lay almost in a swoon.

But it would be too sad to tell of all the hardships and miseries which he had to go through in that hard winter. When the sun began once more to shine out warm and the larks to sing, he was lying among the reeds in the marsh, and it was the beautiful spring. Then all at once he lifted his wings, and they rustled more strongly than before, and bore him swiftly away; and before he knew it he was in a spacious garden where were apple trees in blossom, and sweet-smelling lilacs hung on long green boughs right down to the winding moat. Oh, it was lovely here, and fresh with spring; and straight in front of him, out of the shadows, came three beautiful white swans with rustling plumage floating lightly on the water. The Duckling recognized the splendid creatures, and a strange sorrowfulness came over him.

"I will fly to them, these royal birds, and they will peck me to death because I, who am so ugly, dare to approach them; but it doesn't matter; it's better to be killed by them than to be snapped at by the ducks and pecked at by hens and kicked by the servant o looks after the poultry-yard, and suffer all the winter." So he out into the open water and swam towards the stately swans, ey saw him and hastened with swelling plumage to meet him. "Yes, kill me," the poor creature said, bowing his head down to the water, and waited for death. But what did he see in the clear water? He beheld his own image, but it was no longer that of a clumsy dark grey bird, ugly and repulsive. He was a swan himself.

It doesn't matter in the least whether you are born in the duckyard, if only you've lain in a swan's egg.

It really delighted him now to think of all the hardships and adversities he had suffered, now he could rightly discern his good fortune and all the beauty that greeted him. The great swans swam round him and caressed him with their bills. Some little children now came into the garden and threw bread and corn into the water, and the smallest of them cried: "There's a new one!" And the others called out in delight: "Yes, there's a new one come!" They clapped their hands and danced about and ran to their father and mother. More bread and cake was thrown into the water, and everyone said: "The new one is the handsomest of all; how young and beautiful he is!" And the elder swans bowed before him.

At that he felt quite ill at ease, and covered his head with his wings, and knew not what to do. He was more than happy, and yet not proud, for a good heart is never puffed up. He thought how persecuted and depressed he had been, yet now he heard everyone saying he was the most beautiful of all beautiful birds. And the lilacs bowed their branches down to the water, and the sun shone warm and pleasant, and his plumage ruffled, and he raised his slender neck, and from his heart he said joyfully: "Such happiness I never dreamed of when I was the Ugly Duckling."

The Fir Tree

But in the forest there grew a pretty little fir tree. It had a good place of its own; it could get sunshine, it had plenty of air, and round it grew numbers of larger comrades, both firs and pines; but the little fir was in a great hurry to grow. It didn't care about the warm sun or the cool air, it took no notice of the village children who came and chattered when they were out gathering strawberries or raspberries. They often came there with jugs full of them or with strawberries strung on a straw, and would sit down by the little tree and say: "Look how pretty and little it is," which the tree didn't at all like to hear.

Next year it was bigger by quite a length of stem, and the year after by a yet longer growth: for on a fir tree you can always see how many years old it is by the number of joints it has.

"Oh, if I were only a big tree like the others," sighed the little tree, "then I could spread my branches far out round me and look out into the wide world with my top. The birds would build nests among my branches, and when the wind blew I could make stately bows like the others there," and it took no pleasure in the sunshine or the birds or the red clouds that sailed over it, morning and evening.

When it was winter, and the snow lay sparkling white all round, a hare would often come bounding along and jump over the little tree, and oh, it was annoyed! But two winters passed, and by the third the tree was so big that the hare had to run round it. Oh, to grow, to grow, and be big and old! That was the only pleasant thing in the world, the tree thought.

Every spring the woodcutters came and felled some of the t trees. This happened every year, and the young fir, who was time well grown, shuddered at it; for the great stately trees fell with a crash and a smash, and when their branches were cut off they looked all naked and long and slender; they could hardly be recognized. Then they were loaded on to wagons, and drawn off out of the forest by horses.

Where were they going, and what awaited them?

In spring, when the swallow and the stork came, the tree asked them: "Do you know where they were taken to? Haven't you met them?" The swallows knew nothing, but the stork looked thoughtful and then nodded and said: "Yes, I think so. I met a lot of new ships when I set out from Egypt, and on those ships there were fine masts. I daresay it was them; they smelt of pine. Many's the time I salute them. They carry their heads high, that they do."

"Oh, I do wish I was big enough to fly over the sea too! What sort of thing is the sea really, and what does it look like?"

"Oh, that's a long affair to explain," said the stork, and walked off.

"You should rejoice in your youth," said the sunbeams, "rejoice in your strong growth and the young life that's in you," and the wind kissed the tree and the dew shed tears on it, but the fir didn't understand that at all.

When Christmas time drew near, some quite young trees were felled, trees many of which were not so big or so old as this fir who could have neither peace nor quiet, but was always wanting to be off. These young trees, and they were always the prettiest, always kept their branches; and they were laid on wagons and drawn off out of the forest by horses.

"Where are they going?" asked the fir. "They're no bigger than me; in fact, one of them was much smaller. Why do they all keep their branches? Where are they being driven?" "We know, we know," twittered the grey sparrows. "Down in the town we've peeped in at the window-panes, we know where they're driven to. Why, they come in for the greatest brilliance and glory you can imagine. We've peeped in at the windows and seen how they're planted in the middle of a warm room and decked out with the most lovely things, gilded apples, gingerbread cakes, toys, and hundreds and hundreds of lights."

"And then?" asked the fir, quivering through all its branches, "and then, what happens then?"

"Why, we didn't see any more, but it was marvellous." "Can I be destined to go by that radiant path?" said the tree, exulting. "That's even better than faring over the sea. I am sick with longing. If only it was Christmas! I am quite as tall, and stretch out as far now as those others that were carried off last year. Oh! to be on the wagon, to be in the warm room with all the splendour and magnificence, and then? Why, then will come something still better, still more beautiful, or else why should they deck me out like that? There must be something still greater, still nobler, but what? Oh! how I suffer and yearn! I don't know myself what's the matter with me."

"Rejoice in me," said the breeze and the sunshine, "rejoice in your fresh youth out here in the free air." But it wouldn't rejoice. It grew and grew; in winter and summer it stood there in green; in dark green there it stood, and people who saw it said: "That's a fine tree," and at Christmas time it was the first of all to be felled. The axe cut deep through its marrow, and the tree fell over on to the ground with a sigh: it felt a pang and a weakness, and couldn't think at all of coming happiness, so sorrowful was it at being parted from its home, from the spot on which it had grown up. It knew that it would never again see the dear old companions, the little bushes and flowers about it—no, not even the birds, perhaps. The journey was by no means agreeable.

The tree came to itself only when it was unloaded with the other trees in the yard and heard someone say: "That's a fine one. We don't want anything better than that."

Two servants in gay livery came out and carried the fir in, into a large handsome drawing-room. All round the walls hung portraits, and beside the large stove were Chinese vases with lions on their covers. There were rocking-chairs, silk-covered sofas, large tables covered with picture-books, and more than a hundred times a hundred rix-dollars worth of toys—at least, so said the children. And the fir was set up in a big tub filled with sand; but nobody could see that it was a tub, for green stuff was draped all about it and it stood on a large many-coloured carpet. Oh, how the tree quivered! What was going to happen?

Servants and young ladies came and decked it out. On the ... es they hung little nets cut out of coloured paper and every ... filled with sweetmeats; gilded apples and walnuts were ... it, looking as if they had grown there, and more than a hundred little tapers, red, blue, and white, were stuck upon the branches. Dolls that looked exactly like people—the tree had never seen the like of them—swung to and fro amid the green, and at the very tip-top was fastened a large star of gold leaf. It was splendid, splendid beyond compare. "To-night," they all said, "to-night it'll shine all right." "Oh," thought the tree, "if it were only night, if only the candles were lit! And what'll happen then? Will the trees come out of the forest and look at me? Will the sparrows fly to the window-panes? Shall I grow here always and be decked out in winter and summer too?"

Ah, it was full of it all, but it had a terrible backache from pure longing, and backache is every bit as painful for a tree as headache is for the rest of us.

Then the candles were lit. Oh, the brilliance and the glory! It made the tree quiver through every branch, till one of the candles set fire to a sprig, and it smoked furiously.

"Help! Help!" screamed the girls, and hastened to put it out. After this the tree durst not quiver. What a turn it had got! It was terribly afraid of losing any of its finery and quite bewildered with all the splendour. And now the folding doors were thrown open, and in rushed a crowd of children—fit to throw the tree right down. The elders followed sedately. The little ones stood dumb—for a moment only. Then they shouted for joy till the room rang again, and danced round the tree while one present after another was pulled off it.

"What's this they're doing!" thought the tree. "What's going to happen?"

The candles burnt down to the branches, and as they did so they were put out, and then the children were allowed to plunder the tree. Oh, how they rushed upon it, till the branches cracked! If it hadn't been tied fast to the ceiling by the top and the gold star, it would have been tumbled right over.

The children danced round about with their beautiful toys, and nobody looked at the tree except the old nurse who went about peering among the branches; but that was only to see if a fig or an apple had been missed.

"A story! A story!" cried the children, as they dragged a stout little man towards the tree. He sat himself down beneath it. "Now we're on the green," said he, "and it'll be very good for the tree to listen too; but I'm only going to tell one story. Will you have the one about Ivede Avede,[1] or the one about Humpty Dumpty who tumbled downstairs and yet got up to the throne and married the Princess?"

"Ivede Avede," cried some of them. "Humpty Dumpty," cried others. There was a deal of shrieking and screaming, and only the fir kept quiet and thought "Aren't I to take any part or do anything at all?" Well! it had taken part; it had done what it was meant to do.

So the man told the story of Humpty Dumpty, who tumbled downstairs and after all got to the throne and married the Princess, and the children clapped their hands and cried, "Go on, go on". They wanted Ivede Avede as well, but they only got Humpty Dumpty. The fir stood there quite still and full of thought; never had the birds in the forest told such tales as this; "Humpty Dumpty tumbled downstairs and yet married the Princess. Yes, yes, that's the way things go in the world," thought the fir, and believed it was all true; the man who told the story was so nice. "Yes, yes, who can tell? Perhaps I shall tumble downstairs too and marry a Princess." So it enjoyed itself with thinking of the next day, and of being dressed out with candles and toys and gold and fruit. "To-morrow I won't shiver," it thought. "I'll enjoy myself properly with all my finery. To-morrow I shall hear the story of Humpty Dumpty over again, and perhaps the one about Ivede Avede." All night the tree stood still and thought.

Next morning in came the men and the maids. "Now the dressing will begin again," thought the tree. But they dragged it out of the room and up stairs into a loft, and there put it away in a dark corner where no daylight came. "What's the meaning of this?" thought the tree. "What am I to do here, what can I listen to here?" It leant up against the wall and stood there, thinking, thinking.

It had plenty of time for that, for days and nights passed by, and no one came up there, and when somebody did come at last, it was only to stow away some big boxes in the corner. The tree was qu̇i̇ḣidden up; you might have thought it was clean forgotten. winter outside now," thought the tree. "The ground is covered with snow. The people couldn't plant me now,

[1] Nobody knows what this story was, if it ever existed.

so I shall stay here under cover till spring. What a good plan that is! Lord, how kind the people are! I only wish it wasn't quite so dark and so frightfully lonely here. There's not even a little hare. It was very pleasant after all, out there in the forest; yes, even when he jumped over me, though I didn't like that at the time. Frightfully lonely it is up here, to be sure."

At that moment a little mouse said "Pi pi," and came stealing out, and then another little one. They sniffed at the fir and ran about among its branches. "It's horribly cold," said the little mice, "but for all that it's a delightful place, isn't it, old fir?"

"I'm not at all old," said the fir, "there are a lot who are much older than me."

"Where do you come from?" asked the mice, "and what do you know about?" (indeed they were dreadfully inquisitive). "Do tell us about the loveliest place in the world. Have you ever been there? Have you been in the storeroom, where there are cheeses lying on the shelves and bacon hanging from the ceiling, and where you can dance on tallow candles and go in thin and come out fat?" "No, I don't know that," said the tree, "but I know the place where the sun shines and the birds sing." And with that it told them all its story from its youth up, and the little mice had never heard anything of the kind before, and they listened most attentively and said, "Dear me, what a lot you've seen, and how happy you've been!"

"I?" said the fir and began thinking over what it had told them. "Yes, after all, those were merry days," and then it told them about Christmas Eve when it had been decked out with cakes and candles.

"Oh!" said the little mice. "How happy you have been, old fir!"

"I'm not old at all," said the tree, "it was only this winter that I came out of the forest. I'm in the prime of life. I've hardly begun to grow properly."

"What lovely stories you do tell!" said the little mice; and next night they came with four more little mice who wanted to hear the tree tell stories; and the more it told the more plainly it remembered it all itself, and thought, "Those were very merry days, to be sure, but they may come again: they may. Humpty Dumpty tumbled downstairs and yet married the Princess. Perhaps I too shall get a Princess." And then the fir remembered a very pretty little birch tree that grew in the forest, and to it she seemed like a real beautiful Princess.

"Who's Humpty Dumpty?" the little mice asked, and it told them the whole story, for it could recollect every single word of it; and the little mice were fit to jump to the very top of the tree with delight. Next night a great many more mice came, and on Sunday two rats besides; but the rats said the story did not amuse them; and that disappointed the little mice, for it made them too think less of it.

"So that's the only story you know?" asked the rats. "That's the only one," the tree replied. "I heard it on the happiest evening of my life; but at the time I didn't think how happy I was."

"Well, it's an extraordinarily poor story; don't you know one with bacon and tallow candles in it? Haven't you any store-room stories?"

"No," said the tree.

"Oh, well! Much obliged, I'm sure," said the rats, and went off home. At last the small mice stopped away too, and then the tree said with a sigh, "It was very nice, so it was, when they sat round me, those nimble little mice, and listened to my stories. Now that's past and gone too; but I must remember to enjoy myself when I'm taken out again."

But when did that happen? Why, it was one morning when people came and rummaged about in the loft. The boxes were shifted and the tree was pulled out. They tumbled it down on the floor pretty roughly, to be sure, but then a man dragged it over towards the stairs where the sun shone.

"Now life's beginning again," thought the tree when it felt the fresh air and the first sunbeam—and now it was out in the yard. Everything happened so quickly that the tree quite forgot to look at itself, there was so much to see all about it. The yard was next door to a garden, and there everything was in bloom. Roses hung fresh and fragrant over the low fence, the lime trees were in flower, and the swallows were flying around and saying, "Kvirre-virre-vit! my husband's come!" But it wasn't the fir that they meant.

"Now I'm going to live," said the tree, in exultation, stretching out its branches. Alas! they were all withered and yellow. It was in a corner that it lay, among weeds and nettles. The gold paper star was still fixed on its crown, and glittered in the bright sunshine.

Some of the merry children who had danced about the tree at Christmas, and been so gay, were playing in the yard. One of the littlest ran across and pulled the gold star off the tree.

"Look what's been left on the ugly old Christmas tree!" he said, and he trampled on the branches till they snapped under his boots.

The tree looked at all the beauty of blossom and freshness in the garden and then at itself, and it wished it had stayed in its dark corner in the loft. It thought of its fresh youth in the forest, and of the merry Christmas Eve, and of the little mice who had so enjoyed listening to the story of Humpty Dumpty.

"Past and gone, past and gone!" said the poor tree. "If only I'd enjoyed myself when I could! Past and gone!"

The men came and chopped the tree into little bits—a whole faggot of them—and it made a rare blaze under the big brewing kettle, and deeply it sighed, and every sigh was like a little gun-fire. So the children who were playing about ran in and sat down in front of the fire and looked at it and cried "Pop, pop!" But at every report—which was a deep sigh—the tree was thinking of some summer day in the forest, or a winter night out there, when the stars were shining; or it was thinking of Christmas Eve and Humpty Dumpty, the one and only story it had heard and knew how to tell—and with that the tree was burnt up.

The boys went on playing in the yard, and the smallest of them had on his chest the gold star which the tree had worn on the happiest evening of its life. It was past and gone now: the tree was past and gone, and the story too. Past and gone, past and gone!—it's the same with all stories.

The Snow Queen

A Tale in Seven Stories

STORY THE FIRST
Which tells of the looking-glass and the bits of it

Attention, please, we're going to begin. When we've got to the end of the story we shall know more than we do now. There was a wicked troll. He was one of the very worst sort—he was the devil. One day he was in a very temper, for he had made a looking-glass which had this property: that everything good and pretty that was reflected in it shrivelled away in it to almost nothing, but everything that was no good and looked ugly came out plain and showed even worse than it was. The most beautiful landscapes looked like boiled spinach in the glass, and the best of men grew hideous, or else stood on their heads and had no stomachs. Their faces were so distorted that they couldn't be recognized, and if anyone had a freckle, you could be sure it would spread all over his nose and mouth. It was extraordinarily funny, the devil said. If a kind pious thought passed through a man's mind, there came such a grimace in the glass that the troll-devil couldn't but laugh at his clever invention. Everyone who attended the troll school (for he kept a troll school) spread the news all about that a miracle had come to pass: you could now see, they said, what the world and mankind really looked like. They ran about everywhere with the glass, and at last there wasn't a country or a person left who hadn't been distorted in it. After that they decided to fly up to heaven itself and make fun of the angels and of God. The higher they flew with the glass, the more it grimaced, till they could scarcely keep hold of it. Up and up they flew, nearer to God and His angels, and then the glass quivered so fearfully with grimacing that it fell out of their hands and was dashed on the ground below, where it broke into hundreds of millions, billions, and even more pieces; and that very thing made matters worse than before, for some of the bits were hardly as big as a grain of sand, and these flew all about in the wide world, and when they got into peoples' eyes, they stuck there, and the people either saw everything crooked or else had only eyes for what was wrong in anything; for every little splinter of the glass had kept the same power that the whole glass had. Some people even got a little bit of the glass into their hearts, and that was horrible, for the heart became just like a lump of ice. Some of the pieces were so big that they were used for window glass, but it didn't pay to look at your friends through those window-panes. Other pieces were made into spectacles, and that was a bad business, if people put on those spectacles in order to see correctly and judge rightly. The evil one laughed till he split, it tickled him so. But out in the world little bits of glass were still flying about in the air.

Now we are to hear all about it.

STORY THE SECOND

A Little Boy and a Little Girl

In the big town, where there are so many houses and people that there isn't room enough for everybody to have a little garden, and where in consequence most people have to content themselves with flowers in pots, there were two poor children who had a garden somewhat bigger than a flower-pot. They weren't brother and sister, but they were as fond of each other as if they had been. Their parents were near neighbours, living in two attics, where the roof of the one house touched the other, and the gutter ran along the eaves: a small window in each house faced the other; you had only to step across the gutter and you could get from one window to the other.

The parents had, each of them, a large wooden box outside the window, and in it grew kitchen herbs which they used, and also a little rose tree; there was one in each box, and they flourished wonderfully. Then the parents thought of putting the boxes across the gutter in such a way that they reached almost from the one window to the other and really looked like two bunches of flowers. The pea plants hung down over the boxes, and the rose trees put out long branches and twined about the windows and bent over to meet each other, and made almost a triumphal arch of leaves and blossoms. The boxes were very high up, and the children knew they must not climb up into them, but they were often allowed to get out to meet each other and sit on their little stools beneath the roses, and there they used to play very happily.

In winter, of course, that pleasure was gone. The windows were often quite frozen over; but then they would heat copper pennies on the stove, and then put the hot pennies on the frosty pane, and there came a beautiful peep-hole, as round as round, behind which peeped out a blessed little kind eye, one out of each window; the little boy's and the little girl's. He was called Kay and she Gerda. In summer they could get to each other with a single jump, in winter they had first to go down a lot of stairs and then up a lot of stairs, while the snow came drifting down outside.

"Those are the white bees swarming," said the old grandmother.

"Have they got a queen too?" asked the little boy—for he knew that the real bees have one. "Indeed, they have," said grandmother, "she flies where they swarm thickest; she is the biggest of them all, and she never stays still on the ground, but flies up again into the black cloud. Many a winter night she flies through the streets of the town and peeps in at the windows, and then they freeze into wonderful patterns like flowers."

"Yes, I've seen that," said both the children; and they knew it was true. "Can the Snow Queen get in here?" asked the little girl.

"Let her come!" said the boy, "and I'll put her on the hot stove and she'll melt." But grandmother stroked his hair and told them stories about other things.

In the evening, when little Kay was at home, and half undressed, he climbed up on the stool by the window and peeped through the little hole. A few snowflakes were falling outside, and one of them, the biggest of them all, remained lying in a corner of one of the flower-boxes. This flake grew larger and larger, and at last turned into the complete shape of a lady, dressed in the finest white gauze, which seemed to be made out of millions of star-shaped flakes. She was very pretty and delicate, but she was of ice, blinding, dazzling ice; yet she was alive. Her eyes gazed out like two bright stars, but there was no rest or quietness in them. She nodded towards the window and beckoned with her hand. The little boy was frightened and jumped down off the stool; and then it seemed as if a large bird flew past the window.

Next day was clear and frosty, and then came a thaw, and after that came spring-time, and the sun shone and the green buds peeped forth; the swallows built their nests, the windows were open, and the children sat once more in their little garden high up in the gutter in the topmost story.

That summer the roses blossomed as never before. The little girl had learnt a hymn in which there was something about roses, and at the mention of them she thought of her own, and she sang the hymn to the little boy and he sang it too.

> *The roses grow in the valley,*
> *Where we meet the Jesus Child.*

The little ones held each other by the hand and kissed the roses and gazed into God's bright sunshine and spoke to it as if the child Jesus were there. What lovely summer days were those, and how blessed it was to be out among the fresh rose bushes, which seemed as if they would never leave off blossoming!

Kay and Gerda were sitting looking at a picture book with beasts and birds in it, and then—just as the clock in the great church tower was striking five—Kay said, "Oh! Something pricked my heart, and I've just got something in my eye!"

The little girl put her arm round his neck, and he winked his eye, but no, there was nothing to be seen. "I think it's gone," he said, but it wasn't. It was one of those tiny bits that were broken off the glass, the troll-glass—you remember about that—that horrid glass which made everything great and good that was reflected in it become mean and ugly, while the evil nasty things came out, and every blemish was plain to be seen. Poor Kay! He had got a piece of it right into his heart, which would soon be like a lump of ice. For the moment it wasn't doing any harm; still, there it was.

"What are you crying for?" he asked. "It makes you look horrid! There's nothing the matter with me. Ugh!" he called out suddenly. "That rose there's worm-eaten! And look at that other, it's all crooked. Rotten roses they are, after all, like the boxes they're in."

With that he gave the box a hard kick and pulled off the two roses. "What are you doing, Kay?" cried the little girl; and when he saw she was frightened, he pulled off a third rose, and ran in at his own window, leaving dear little Gerda. Later, when she brought him the picture book, he said, "it was only fit for babies", and when grandmother told them stories, he was always breaking in with a "But". And if he could he would follow her about with spectacles on and imitate her talking; it was exactly like, and made people laugh. Very soon he could imitate the walk and talk of everybody in their street. Everything that was odd or not nice about them Kay could mimic, and people said, "That boy's got an uncommon wit, to be sure". But it was the bit of glass he had got in his eye and the bit he had in his heart; and so it came about that he would tease even little Gerda, who loved him with all her heart. The games he played were quite different now: they were very clever. One winter day, when the snow-flakes were drifting down, he brought a big magnifying glass and held out the corner of his blue jacket and let the flakes fall on it.

"Now look through the glass, Gerda," he said; and there was every flake made much bigger, and looking like a beautiful flower or a ten-pointed star: lovely it was to see. "Look how clever it is," said Kay, "it's much more interesting than the real flowers are; and there's not a single thing wrong with them, they're perfectly accurate—if only they didn't melt."

A little later Kay came in with big mittens on, and his sledge hung on his back; he shouted to Gerda, right in her ear, "I've got leave to drive in the big square where the others are playing," and he was off.

Out there in the square the boldest of the boys often used to tie their sledges to a farmer's cart and drive a good long way with it. It was excellent fun. At the height of their sport a large sledge came by; it was painted white all over, and in it was someone wrapped in a shaggy white fur and wearing a shaggy white cap. This sledge drove twice round the square, and little Kay made haste and tied his own little sledge to it, and drove off with it. Faster and faster it went, into the next street. The driver turned his head and nodded to Kay in a friendly way; it seemed as if they knew each other. Every time Kay thought of loosing his sledge the driver nodded again, so Kay stayed where he was: and they drove right out through the town gate. Then the snow began to fall so thick that the boy couldn't see his hand before him as he drove on; and he hastily loosed the rope so as to let go of the big sledge. But it made no difference, his little trap held fast to it, and it went like the wind. He called out loudly, but no one heard, and the snow drifted down and the sledge flew onward. Sometimes it made a bound as if it were going over ditches or fences. He was in a dreadful fright; he tried to say the Lord's Prayer, but he could only remember the multiplication table.

The snow-flakes grew bigger and bigger, till at last they looked like large white hens; suddenly they parted, the big sledge pulled up, and the person who was driving in it rose. The fur and the cap were all of snow: it was a lady, tall and slender, shining white—the Snow Queen.

"We have travelled well," said she; "but you mustn't freeze. Creep into my bearskin." She put him beside her in the sledge, and he felt as if he were sinking into a snow-drift. "Are you still cold?" she asked, and kissed him on the forehead. Ugh! it was colder than ice, and struck straight to his heart—which itself was almost a lump of ice. He felt as if he was dying, but only for a moment: then all was right, he didn't notice the cold about him any more.

"My sledge! Don't leave my sledge behind!" that was the first thing he remembered: so it was tied on to one of the white hens, which flew after them with the sledge on its back. Once more the Snow Queen kissed Kay, and he had forgotten little Gerda and grandmother and everyone at home.

"No more kisses now," said she, "or I should kiss you to death." Kay looked at her; very pretty she was; a cleverer, fairer face he could not imagine. She didn't seem now to be of ice, as she was when she sat outside the window and beckoned him. In his eyes she was perfect, and he felt no fear. He told how he knew mental arithmetic, and with fractions, too, and the area of the country, and how many inhabitants, and she smiled all the time, till he thought that what he knew didn't come to much. He gazed up into the immense spaces of the air, and she flew on with him, flew high among the dark clouds, and the storm wind whistled and roared as if it were singing old ballads. Over forest and lake they flew, over sea and land: below them the cold blast whistled, the wolves howled, the snow sparkled; above them flew the black cawing crows, but over all shone the moon, large and bright; and by its light Kay watched through the long long winter night; by day he slumbered at the feet of the Snow Queen.

STORY THE THIRD

The Flower Garden of the Old Woman who knew Magic

But how fared little Gerda when Kay came back no more? Where could he be? Nobody knew, nobody could tell. The boys could only say they had seen him tie his little sledge to another fine large one which had driven down the street and out at the town gate. Nobody knew where he was. Many tears were shed; sore and long did little Gerda weep. Then they said he was dead, drowned in the river that ran past the town. Dark indeed and long were those winter days.

Then came spring with warmer sunshine.

"Kay is dead and gone," said little Gerda.

"I don't believe it," said the Sunshine.

"He's dead and gone," said she to the swallows.

"I don't believe it," they answered, and at last little Gerda didn't believe it either.

"I'll put on my new red shoes," she said one morning early, "the ones Kay has never seen, and I'll go down to the river and ask about him."

It was quite early. She kissed her old grandmother as she slept, put on the red shoes, and went out of the gate to the river, quite alone.

"Is it true that you have taken my little playfellow? I'll give my red shoes if you'll give him back to me."

The waves, she thought, nodded in a queer fashion; so she took her gay red shoes, the most precious thing she had, and threw them both into the river, but they fell close into the bank, and the little waves carried them straight back to her on shore. It seemed that the river would not take the most precious thing she had because it had not got little Kay. But she thought she hadn't thrown the shoes far enough out, so she climbed into a boat that lay in the rushes, and went out to the further end of it and threw out the shoes. But the boat was not moored fast, and with the movement she made it floated away from the shore. She noticed this and made haste to get out, but before she could get back the boat was more than a fathom away, and began to drift more quickly along. Little Gerda was very much frightened and began to cry; but nobody heard her except the sparrows, and they couldn't carry her ashore; but they flew along the bank and sang, as if to comfort her: "Here we are, here we are!" The boat was carried downstream; little Gerda sat still, in her stockinged feet; her little red shoes floated behind, but couldn't reach the boat, which was now travelling faster.

Both banks were very pretty, with beautiful flowers, old trees, and sloping fields with sheep and cows; but never a man was to be seen.

"Perhaps the river will carry me to little Kay," thought Gerda. This put her in better spirits, and she stood up and for many hours gazed at the pretty green banks. At last she came to a large cherry orchard, in which was a little house with quaint blue and red windows, and for the rest a thatched roof, and outside two wooden soldiers, who were shouldering arms for everyone who came sailing by. Gerda called to them, thinking they were alive: but very naturally they didn't answer. She came quite near them; the river carried the boat straight towards the shore. Gerda called out yet louder, and then there came out of the house an old old woman, supporting herself on a crooked stick. She had a large sun-hat on, painted with the most splendid flowers.

"Poor dear little child," said the old woman, "how ever did you get out here on this great big river, far out into the wide world?" And with that the old woman stepped into the water and hooked her stick fast to the boat and pulled it ashore and lifted little Gerda out. Gerda was glad to be on dry land again, but still she was a little afraid of the strange old woman. "Come now, and tell me who you are, and how you got here," she said. And Gerda told her everything; and the old woman shook her head and said, "Hm, hm!" And when Gerda had told her everything and asked if she had seen little Kay, the woman said he hadn't passed that way, but he would come, sure enough, and she wasn't to be worried, but must taste her cherries, and look at her flowers, that were prettier than any picture book and could each of them tell a whole story.

Then she took Gerda by the hand, and they went into the little house, and the old woman locked the door.

The windows were placed very high up, and the glass in them was red and blue and yellow. The daylight shone very oddly through them, with all their colours; but on the table were the most beautiful cherries, and Gerda ate as many as she liked, for she was allowed to; and while she was eating, the old woman combed her hair with a gold comb, and the hair curled and shone lovely and yellow about her kind little face, the round face that looked like a rose.

"I've been longing for a sweet little girl like you," said the old woman, "you'll see how well we two shall get on," and all the time she was combing little Gerda's hair Gerda was forgetting more and more her foster brother Kay: for the old woman was skilled in witchcraft, but she wasn't a wicked witch, she only used witchcraft a little, for her own pleasure, and just now she wanted very much to keep little Gerda. In order to do so, she went out into the garden and stretched out her hooked stick towards all the rose bushes: and though they were all blooming beautifully, they all sank down into the black earth and you couldn't see where they had been. The old woman was afraid that when Gerda saw the roses she would think of her own roses, and then remember little Kay and run away.

Then she took Gerda out into the flower garden. Dear me! What fragrance and beauty there was there. All the flowers one could think of, flowers belonging to every season, stood there in their full bloom; no picture book could be more gaily coloured and pretty. Gerda jumped for joy and played about till the sun set behind the tall cherry trees. Then she was given a lovely bed with red silk pillows that were stuffed with blue violets, and there she slept and dreamt as beautiful dreams as any queen on her wedding day.

Next day she played among the flowers again in the hot sunshine; and so many days went by. Gerda knew every flower, but, many as there were of them, she thought that one was missing, but she didn't know which. Then, one day she was sitting looking at the old woman's sun-hat with the flowers painted on it, and the prettiest of all that were there was a rose. The old woman had forgotten to take it away from her hat when she got rid of the others in the garden. It only shows what comes of not having your wits about you. "Why!" said Gerda, "aren't there any roses?" And she ran in among the beds and looked and looked, but there were none to be found. Then she sat down and cried; but her hot tears fell exactly on the spot where a rose tree had sunk down, and when the tears wetted the ground the tree rose up all at once, blossoming just as when it sank down, and Gerda threw her arms round it and kissed the roses, and thought of the beautiful ones at home, and with them of little Kay.

"Oh, how I have been dawdling," said the little girl. "I was to find Kay—don't know where he is?" she asked the roses, "do you think he's dead and gone?" "Dead he isn't," said the roses. "We've been down in the ground where all the dead people are, but Kay wasn't there."

"Thanks, thanks," said little Gerda, and went off to the other flowers and looked into their cups and asked: "Do you know where little Kay is?"

But every one of the flowers was standing in the sun and dreaming its own story or life and of these little Gerda heard ever so many; but none of them knew anything about Kay.

What said the tiger lily?

"Do you hear the drum! boom! boom! There are only two notes! Boom! Boom! Hark to the women's dirge! Hark to the cry of the priests! In her long red robe the Indian woman stands on the pyre, and the flames rise round her and her dead husband; but the woman is thinking of the living one who stands there in the circle, of him whose eyes burn hotter than the flames, the fire of whose eyes pierces nearer her heart than the flames which will quickly burn her body to ashes. Can the heart's flame perish in the flames of the pyre?"

"I don't understand that in the least," said little Gerda.

"That's my story," said the tiger lily.

What says the bindweed?

"High above the narrow field-path hangs an ancient castle. Thick evergreens grow about the old red walls, leaf on leaf, away up to the balcony, and there stands a fair maiden. She bends over the parapet and looks down upon the road. No rose hangs fresher on its spray than she, no apple blossom borne by the breeze from its tree floats more gracefully. How her costly silken kirtle rustles! Cometh he not?"

"Is it Kay you mean?" asked little Gerda.

"I'm only talking of my story, my dream," the bindweed answered.

What says the little snowdrop?

"Between the trees the long board hangs in the ropes. It's a swing: two pretty little girls—their frocks white as snow, and long green silk ribbons fluttering from their hats—are sitting and swinging. Their brother, who is bigger than they, is standing up in the swing, with his arm round the ropes to steady himself, for in one hand he has a little saucer and in the other a clay pipe, and he's blowing soap bubbles. To and fro goes the swing, and the bubbles float with lovely changing colours; the last one is still hanging to the pipe-stem and swaying in the breeze; on goes the swing. The little black dog, as light as the bubbles, stands on his hind legs and wants to get into the swing too; it flies past, he tumbles down, and barks, and is angry. They laugh at him—the bubbles burst. A swinging plank, a waving picture in foam! That is my song."

"I suppose it's very pretty, what you're talking about, but you say it so sadly, and you never mention Kay."

What do the hyacinths say?

"There were three fair sisters, delicate and fine; the robe of one was red, the second's was blue, and the third's all white. Hand in hand they danced by the still lake in the bright moonlight. They were no elfin maidens, but of the children of men. There came a waft of fragrance, and the maidens vanished in the forest. Stronger grew the perfume. Three coffins, wherein the three fair maidens lay, glided from the depths of the forest, glided over the lake. Fireflies flew round them like tiny evening lamps. The dancing maidens, do they slumber or are they dead? The scent of the flowers tells that they are dead. The evening bell rings out over the dead."

"You make me quite wretched!" said little Gerda. "Your scent is so strong, I can't help thinking of the dead maidens. Oh, dear! Is little Kay really dead? The roses have been down in the ground and they say 'No'."

"Ding, dong!" rang out the hyacinth bells. "We're not ringing for little Kay, we don't know him, we're only singing our own song, the only one we know."

So Gerda went to the buttercup, shining out from among its brilliant green leaves. "You're a bright little sun," said Gerda;

"tell me if you know where I can find my playfellow." The buttercup shone very prettily and looked back at Gerda. What song, now, could the buttercup sing? Not one about Kay, at any rate.

"In a little yard God's sun was shining warm on the first day of spring; its beams crept down the neighbour's white wall; close by grew the first yellow flowers, shining like gold in the hot sunbeams. The old grandmother was out of doors in her chair; her pretty grand-daughter, the poor servant maid, came home upon a short visit, and gave her grandmother a kiss. There was gold, beautiful gold in that blessed kiss, gold on the lips, gold in the heart, gold up there in the early morn. Look, that's my little story," said the buttercup.

"Oh, my poor old granny!" sighed Gerda. "Yes, she must be longing for me, and unhappy about me, as she was about little Kay. But I'll soon be home again and bring Kay with me. It's no good asking the flowers; they only know their own song and tell me nothing." So she tucked up her little frock to run the quicker. But the narcissus hit against her leg as she jumped over it, and she stopped and looked at the tall flower and asked: "Do you happen to know anything?" And she stooped down to it; and what did it say?

"I can see myself! I can see myself!" said the narcissus. "Oh, how strong my scent is! Up in the little garret stands a little ballet-girl half dressed—standing first on one leg she is, then on both, and kicking out at the whole world—she's only an illusion. She's pouring water out of a teapot on to a bit of stuff that she's holding; it's her stays. Cleanliness is a good thing. The white frock hangs on its peg, it too has been washed in the teapot and dried on the roof. She puts it on, and a saffron yellow kerchief about her neck, which makes the dress shine whiter. Legs up in the air! Look how she stands on a stalk! I can see myself, I can see myself!"

"I don't care about that in the least," said Gerda, "it's no use telling me that." So she ran to the border of the garden; the door was locked, but she twisted at the rusty staple till it came away, and the door flew open, and then out ran little Gerda barefoot into the wide world. Thrice she looked back, but there was nobody coming after her. At last she could run no further, and sat down on a big stone, and when she looked about her, why, summer was over and it was late autumn. You couldn't see that inside that beautiful garden, where there was always sunshine and flowers of all seasons bloomed.

"Good heavens! How I have dawdled!" said Gerda. "It's autumn now. I daren't rest a minute!" So she got up and went on.

Oh, how bruised and tired were her little feet, and how cold and raw it was all round! The long leaves of the willow were pale yellow, and the mist dripped off them in waterdrops; one leaf after another fell, and only the sloe bush had kept its fruit—sour fruit that dried up your mouth. Oh, how grey and dismal it was out in the wide world!

STORY THE FOURTH

A Prince and Princess

Gerda had to rest herself again. And there, hopping over the road right in front of where she sat, was a large crow. For a long time it had sat and looked at her with its head on one side, and now it said, "Kra, Kra—Goo'day, Goo'day!"—it couldn't say it any better, but it meant very kindly by the little girl, and asked where she was going all alone in the wide world. The words "all alone" Gerda understood very well, and felt how much they meant; so she told the crow all the story of her life and asked if it had seen Kay. The crow nodded very thoughtfully, and said, "Maybe, maybe." "What? Do you think you have?" the little girl cried, and almost squeezed the crow to death, she kissed it so hard.

"Gently! Gently!" said the crow. "I think it may be little Kay, but if so, he's quite forgotten you for the Princess."

"Does he live with a Princess?" asked Gerda.

"Yes, listen," said the crow, "but I find it so hard to talk your speech. If you can understand crow-talk I can tell you better."

"No, I haven't learnt it," said Gerda, "but Granny knew it, and knew P-talk too. I wish I'd learnt it."

"Doesn't matter," said the crow, "I'll tell you as well as I can, but I shall make a poor business of it." So it told what it knew.

"In the kingdom where we are now there lives a Princess who is exceedingly clever; besides, she's read all the newspapers in the world and forgotten 'em again, she's so clever. The other day she was sitting on her throne, which isn't much fun after all, people say; and she happened to hum a song which was 'Heigh-ho for a husband!' 'Why, there's something in that,' said she, and she made up her mind to marry; only she would have a husband who knew how to answer when you talked to him, one that didn't merely stand there and look distinguished; that's very dull. So she had all the court ladies drummed up, and when they heard what she wanted, they were delighted. 'I do like that,' they said. 'We were just thinking something of the sort the other day.' Now you may be sure every word I'm telling you is true," said the crow, "for I've got a sweetheart who's tame and goes everywhere about the palace, and she told me the whole thing." Of course, the sweetheart was a crow too, for crow seeks his mate, and the mate's always a crow.

"The newspapers came out immediately with a border of hearts and the Princess's monogram, and you could read there how it was open to any good-looking young man to come up to the palace and speak with the Princess, and the one that spoke so you could see he was at home there, and talked the best, the Princess would take him for husband. Yes, indeed," said the crow, "you may take it from me, as sure as I sit here, the people came streaming in: there was a crowd and a commotion, but nothing came of it, either the first day or the second. They could all of them talk well enough while they were out in the street, but when they came in by the palace gate and saw the guards in silver, and footmen in gold, all up the stairs, and the big halls all lighted up, they were flabbergasted, and when they stood in front of the throne where the Princess was sitting, they couldn't think of anything to say but the last word she had said, and she didn't care about hearing that over again. It was just as if the people in there had got snuff into their stomachs and were stupefied till they got out into the street again, and they could talk. There was a row of them reaching right away from the town gate to the palace. I went there myself to look at it," said the crow. "They got hungry and thirsty too, but they got nothing from the palace, not even so much as a glass of luke-warm water. Some of the cleverest, to be sure, had brought a bit of bread and butter with them, but they didn't give their neighbours any: they thought to themselves: 'Just let him look hungry and the Princess won't have him.'"

"But Kay, little Kay," asked Gerda. "When did he come? Was

he among all those people?" "Give me time, give me time! Now we are getting to him. It was the third day, and there came a little fellow without horse or carriage, marching quite cheerfully straight up to the palace. His eyes shone like gems and he had lovely long hair, but his clothes were shabby."

"It was Kay," Gerda cried out joyfully. "Oh, then I've found him!" And she clapped her hands.

"He had a little bundle on his back," the crow said.

"Ah, that must have been his sledge," said Gerda, "for he went off with his sledge." "It might quite well be that," said the crow. "I didn't look very close at it, but I know from my tame sweetheart that when he came in at the palace gate and saw the lifeguards in silver and the footmen in gold all up the stairs, he wasn't in the least taken aback, but nodded and said to them: 'It must be dull standing on the stairs. I'd sooner go in.' The halls were shining with lights, and privy councillors and excellencies were walking barefoot and carrying golden dishes; it was enough to make anybody feel solemn. His boots creaked dreadfully loud, but he wasn't frightened a bit." "That's certainly Kay," said Gerda. "I know he'd got some new boots, I heard them creak in Granny's room."

"Yes, creak they did," said the crow, "and as bold as could be he walked straight into the Princess, who was sitting on a pearl as big as a spinning-wheel, and all the court ladies with their maids and their maids' maids, and all the courtiers with their men and their men's men, who keep a page, were stationed all around, and the nearer they stood to the door the prouder they looked: the men's men's page, who always wears slippers, can hardly be looked at, he's so proud standing there at the door."

"That must be frightening," said little Gerda, "and yet Kay won the Princess!"

"If I hadn't been a crow I'd have taken her myself, though I am engaged. He spoke, it seems, every bit as well as I do when I speak crow-talk, so my tame sweetheart tells me. He was cheerful and nice-looking. He hadn't come courting at all, but only to hear the Princess's conversation, and he thought well of it, and she thought well of him."

"Oh, yes! Certainly it's Kay," said Gerda. "He was clever: he knew mental arithmetic with fractions. Oh, won't you take me into the palace?"

The Snow Queen

"It's easy enough to say that," said the crow, "but how are we to manage it? I must talk to my tame sweetheart about it, she's sure to be able to advise us; for I must tell you that a little girl like you will never be allowed to come right in."

"Oh, yes, I shall," said Gerda. "When Kay hears I'm here, he'll come out directly and fetch me." "Well, wait for me here at the stile," said the crow, and put his head on one side and flew off. Only when it was dark did the crow come back. "Rax! rax!" said he. "She sends you her best compliments, and here's a small loaf for you which she took from the kitchen: there's lots of bread there, and I'm sure you're hungry. It's not possible for you to get into the palace: why, you're barefoot, and the guards in silver and the footmen in gold wouldn't allow it; but don't cry, you shall get in all the same. My sweetheart knows of a little backstair that leads to the bedroom, and she knows where she can get the key."

They went into the garden, up the great avenue where one leaf after another was falling; and when the lights in the palace were put out one by one the crow led little Gerda across to a back door which stood ajar.

Oh, how Gerda's heart beat with anxiety and longing! She felt as if she was going to do something wrong, yet all she wanted was to know if it was little Kay; why, it must be he; she imagined so vividly his clever eyes and his long hair; she could actually see how he would smile when they were sitting at home beneath the roses. He would, of course, be overjoyed to see her and to hear what a long way she had come for his sake, and how everyone at home had grieved when he didn't come back. How anxious and how glad she was!

They were now at the stairs: a little lamp was burning in a stand: in the middle of the floor stood the tame crow, turning her head this way and that, and contemplating Gerda, who curtsied as her grandmother had taught her to do.

"My betrothed has spoken most charmingly of you, my little lady," said the tame crow, "and your biography, as we may call it, is also very touching. If you will take the lamp, I will lead the way. We shall go by the shortest way, where we shall meet no one."

"I think someone is coming after us," said Gerda. Something came rushing by, as it were shadows passing along the wall, horses with fluttering manes and slender legs, huntsmen and lords and ladies on horseback.

"They're only dreams," said the crow, "they come and fetch the Quality's thoughts out a-hunting, and it's a good thing; you can look at them in bed all the better. Only let me see, if you come to honour and distinction, that you bear a thankful heart."

"Oh, there's no use talking about that," said the crow from the forest.

They now entered the first chamber, which was of rose-red satin with worked flowers on the walls; here the dreams were already darting past them, but they went so quick that Gerda could not manage to see the Quality. Each chamber was handsomer than the last, it was enough to bewilder anyone; and now they were in the bedchamber. The roof of this was made like a palm tree with leaves of glass—costly glass—and in the middle of the floor there hung from a thick stem of gold two beds, each made to look like a lily; one was white, and in it lay the Princess; the other was red, and there it was that Gerda must look for little Kay. She bent aside one of the red leaves, and there she saw a brown neck—oh, it was Kay. She called his name aloud and held the lamp over him. The dreams dashed back into the room, galloping—he woke, turned his head, and—it wasn't little Kay.

The Prince was only like him in the neck, but he was young and handsome, and out of the white lily bed the Princess peeped and asked what was the matter. Then little Gerda burst into tears and told her whole story and all that the crows had done for her.

"Poor little dear!" said the Prince and the Princess, and they praised the crows and said they were not at all displeased with them, but all the same they mustn't do it again. Meanwhile they should be rewarded. "Would you like to go free?" the Princess asked, "or would you like a permanent situation as court crows, with everything that is dropped in the kitchen?"

Both crows bowed and asked for permanent situations, for they had their old age in mind, and, said they, "It's a very good thing to have something in store for the old man". That was their phrase. The Prince got up out of his bed and let Gerda sleep in it, and he couldn't do more than that! She clasped her little hands and said: "How kind people and animals are." And then she shut her eyes and slept deliciously. All the dreams came flying back, and now they looked like angels of God, and they were drawing a little sledge, and in it sat Kay, nodding to her: but it was all only dreams, and so it was gone again as soon as she woke up.

Next day she was dressed out in silk and velvet from top to toe and invited to stay at the palace and enjoy herself; but she begged only to have a little carriage and horse, and a pair of little boots, and she would drive out again into the wide world and find Kay. She was given both boots and a muff, and was dressed out very nicely, and when she was to set off a new carriage of pure gold drew up at the door. The arms of the Prince and Princess shone like a star on it. The coachmen and servants and outriders (there were outriders too) wore gold crowns. The Prince and Princess helped her into the carriage themselves and wished her the best of luck. The forest crow, who was now married, went with her for the first twelve miles, sitting beside her, for he couldn't stand being driven backwards. The other crow stood in the doorway and flapped her wings; she couldn't come with them, for she was suffering from a headache since she had obtained a permanent situation and too much to eat. Inside, the coach had a provision of sugar twists, and inside the seat was fruit and gingerbread nuts. "Good-bye, good-bye!" shouted the Prince and Princess. Little Gerda cried, and the crow cried, and so it went for the first few miles. Then the crow said, "Good-bye" and that was the hardest parting. He flew up into a tree and flapped his black wings as long as he could see the carriage, that shone as bright as the sunshine.

STORY THE FIFTH

The Little Robber Girl

They were driving through the dark forest, but the coach shone like a blaze, and dazzled the eyes of the robbers and they couldn't stand it. "It's gold, it's gold!" they shouted, and dashed out and seized the horses, killed the little postilions and the coachman, and the servants, and dragged little Gerda out of the carriage.

"She's fat, she's dainty, she's been fed up with nut kernels," said the old robber woman, who had a long coarse beard and eyebrows that hung down over her eyes; "she's as good as a little house-lamb; aha, how good she'll taste!" With that she drew her bright knife, and it shone frightfully.

"Ow!" said the old hag all at once. She'd been bitten in the ear by her own little daughter, who was hanging on her back, and was so wild and rough as never was. "Nasty brat!" said her mother, and had no time to kill Gerda.

"She shall play with me," said the little robber girl, "she will give me her muff and her nice frock and sleep with me in my bed." She gave her mother another bite, so that the old hag jumped in the air and twisted right round, and all the robbers laughed and said: "Look at her dancing with her young 'un."

"I'm going to go in the coach," said the little robber girl, and she must and would have her way, so spoilt and obstinate she was. She and Gerda sat in it and drove over stumps and thorn-bushes, deep into the forest. The little robber girl was as big as Gerda, but stronger, broader in the shoulders and dark-skinned. Her eyes were quite black and had a rather sorrowful expression. She put her arm about little Gerda and said: "They shan't kill you as long as I don't get cross with you: of course, you're a Princess?"

"No," said little Gerda, and told her everything that had happened to her, and how fond she was of little Kay. The robber girl looked at her very gravely and nodded her head and said: "They shan't kill you even if I do get cross with you; I'll do it myself." And she dried Gerda's eyes and put both her hands into the pretty muff that was so soft and warm.

The coach stopped. They were in the court of a robber's castle. It had split from top to bottom. Ravens and crows flew out of the holes in the wall, and the big bulldogs, each of which looked as if he could swallow a man, leapt high in the air but didn't bark, for they weren't allowed to. In the great old sooty hall a large fire was burning in the middle of the stone floor; the smoke mounted to the vault and had to find its own way out. A large copper was on the boil, with soup, and hares and rabbits were turning on the spit.

"You shall sleep to-night with me and all my pets," said the robber girl. They had something to eat and drink, and then went off into a corner where straw and blankets were lying: up above, about a hundred pigeons were perched on laths and poles. They seemed to be all asleep, but they stirred a little when the girls came there.

"Those are all mine," said the little robber girl. She seized one of the nearest and held it by the legs and shook it till it flapped its wings. "Kiss it," she cried, buffeting Gerda in the face with it. "There sit the wood rubbish," she went on, pointing behind a number of slats nailed in front of a hole higher up. "Wood rubbish they are, those two. They'd fly off at once if they hadn't been locked up safe; and there's my own old sweetheart Bae." She pulled out a reindeer by the horn: he had a bright ring of copper on his neck and was tethered up. "We have to keep him tight too, else he'd go bounding away from us. Every blessed night I tickle him in the neck with my sharp knife, and it frightens him awfully," and the little girl pulled a long knife out of a crack in the wall and slid it along the reindeer's neck. The poor beast kicked out with his legs and the robber girl laughed, and then pulled Gerda into bed with her.

"Do you want the knife with you when you go to sleep?" Gerda asked, looking at it rather nervously.

"I always sleep with my knife by me," said the little robber girl, "you never know what may happen. But now tell me again what you told me about little Kay, and why you've come out into the wide world." So Gerda told it again from the beginning, and the wood-pigeons cooed up in their cage, and the other pigeons slept. The little robber girl put her arms round Gerda's neck, holding her knife in her other hand, and slept—you could hear her—but Gerda couldn't even shut her eyes; she didn't know whether she was to live or die. The robbers sat round the fire and sang and drank, and the old hag turned head over heels. It was a frightful sight for the little girl to see.

Then the wood-pigeons said: "Coo, Coo! We have seen little Kay. A white hen was carrying his sledge, and he was sitting in the Snow Queen's carriage which was flying low above the forest where we lay in the nest. She breathed on us young ones and all of them died but us two. Coo! Coo!" "What are you saying up there?" cried Gerda. "Where did the Snow Queen drive to? Do you know anything about it?"

"She drove to Lapland for sure, for there's always snow and ice there. Just ask the reindeer that's tied by the rope there."

"There is ice and snow, it's lovely and pleasant there," said the reindeer. "There you can run about free in the great shining valleys. The Snow Queen has her summer pavilion there, but her strong castle is up by the North Pole, on the island that's called Spitzbergen."

"Oh, Kay, dear little Kay!" sighed Gerda.

"Now just you lie still," said the robber girl, "else you'll get a knife in your belly." In the morning Gerda told her everything the wood-pigeons had said, and the little robber girl looked very grave, but nodded and said: "It's all one, it's all one. Do you know where Lapland is?" she asked the reindeer.

"Who should know better than I?" said the beast, his eyes dancing in his head. "I was bred and born there, and it's there I used to bound over the snowfields."

"Look here," said the robber girl to Gerda, "all our menfolk are out, you see, but mother's here still and here she'll be; but later in the morning she'll drink out of the big bottle and have a little nap after; and then I'll do something for you." She jumped out of bed, ran across to her mother and pulled her by the beard, and said, "Good morning to my own dear nanny goat". And her mother flipped her under the nose till it turned red and blue, but it was all done out of pure affection.

Well, when her mother had had a drink out of the bottle and was taking a little nap, the robber girl went to the reindeer and said: "I should awfully like to give you a lot more ticklings with my sharp knife, for you're very funny when I do; but no matter for that, I'm going to loose your tether and help you off, so that you can run to Lapland. But you must put your best foot foremost and take the little girl for me to the Snow Queen's palace where her playfellow is. You've heard what she told me, for she talked quite loud enough, and you were eavesdropping."

The reindeer jumped for joy. The robber girl lifted little Gerda up and had the forethought to tie her fast, and even give her a little pad to sit on. "It don't matter," said she. "Here are your fur boots, for it'll be cold, but your muff I shall keep, it's much too pretty. All the same, you shan't be frozen. Here's my mother's big mittens that reach up to your elbow, shove 'em on. Now your hands look just like my ugly old mother's."

Gerda cried for joy.

"I hate your whimpering," said the little robber girl. "Why, you ought to look really happy; and there's two loaves for you, and a ham, so you shan't starve." Both these were tied to the reindeer's back. The little robber girl opened the door, and called in all the big dogs, and then she cut the rope with her knife and said to the reindeer: "Off you go, but take good care of the little girl." Gerda stretched out her hands in the big mittens to the robber girl, and said "Good-bye", and then the reindeer bounded off over bushes and stumps through the great forest, over marsh and moor, as fast as ever he could. The wolves howled and the ravens screamed. In the sky there was a noise, "Fut, fut!" It seemed as if someone were sneezing red. "Those are my dear Northern Lights," said the reindeer, "look how they shine." Faster and faster he ran, through day and night alike. The loaves were eaten up and the ham too, and then—they were in Lapland.

STORY THE SIXTH

The Lapp Woman and the Finn Woman

They stopped at a small house, a wretched place it was. The roof reached down to the ground, and the door was so low that the family had to crawl on their stomachs when they wanted to get in or out. There was nobody at home but an old Lapp woman who stood roasting fish at an oil lamp, and the reindeer told her Gerda's story; but first his own story, for he considered that was much more important; and Gerda was so exhausted with the cold that she couldn't speak.

"Dear me, you poor dear creature!" said the Lapp woman. "You've got a long way to run yet! You must travel more than four hundred miles, into Finmark, for there it is that the Snow Queen has her country-house and burns blue lights every blessed night. I'll write a word or two on a dry cod, for I haven't any paper, and give it you to take to the Finn woman up there: she can tell you more than I can." So as soon as Gerda had got warm and had had something to eat and drink, the Lapp woman wrote a few words on a split cod and told Gerda to take great care of it, and then she tied her fast on the reindeer again, and off he bounded. "Fut, fut!" the noise went on in the sky, and all night the loveliest blue Northern Lights burned there. And then they got to Finmark and knocked at the Finn woman's chimney, for she hadn't a door.

There was such a heat inside that the Finn woman herself went almost naked. She was stout and very thick made; she made haste to undo little Gerda's clothes and took off her mittens and boots, otherwise she would have been too hot. She laid a piece of ice on the reindeer's head, and then read what was written on the codfish. Three times over she read it, and then knew it backwards, and she put the fish into the cooking pot, for it might just as well be eaten, and she never wasted anything.

Then the reindeer told, first, his own story, and then little Gerda's; and the Finn woman blinked her wise eyes, but said not a word.

"You are so clever," said the reindeer, "I know you can bind all the winds of the world in a single thread, and when the skipper looses the first knot he gets a good wind, and if he looses the second it blows strong, and if he looses the third and the fourth there's a storm that blows the forests down. Won't you give the little girl a drink, so she can get the strength of twelve men and get the better of the Snow Queen?"

"Strength of twelve men!" said the Finn woman. "That would be just the thing, to be sure!" She went over to a shelf and took out a large rolled-up skin which she unrolled; strange letters were written on it, and the Finn woman read in it till the water trickled down her brow. But the reindeer pleaded again so hard for little Gerda, and Gerda gazed at the Finn woman with such beseeching eyes full of tears that she began to blink her own eyes again, and drew the reindeer apart into a corner, where she whispered to him, at the same time laying fresh ice on his head.

"Little Kay is with the Snow Queen, sure enough, and finds everything after his own wish and thought, and believes that it is the best place in the world: but that comes of his having a splinter of glass in his heart and a little grain of glass in his eye. They must come out, or he will never become human again, and the Snow Queen will keep her power over him."

"But can't you give little Gerda something to take, so that she can get the better of it all?"

"I can give her no greater power than she has already! Don't you see how great it is, how men and beasts alike are bound to serve her, and how she has made her way so wonderfully in the world on her bare feet? She must not learn of her power from us; it lies in her heart, it lies in her being a dear innocent child. If she cannot win through to the Snow Queen and rid little Kay of the glass, we cannot be of any help. Ten miles from here begins the Snow Queen's garden, and you can carry the little girl as far as that. Put her down by the large bush that stands there in the snow with red berries on it. Don't make a long jabber of it, and make haste back." Then the Finn woman lifted little Gerda up on to the reindeer, and he ran off as fast as he could.

"Oh, I haven't got my boots, I haven't got my mittens!" cried little Gerda. She noticed it at once in the scorching cold. But the reindeer dared not stop, and he ran till he came to the large bush with the red berries, and then he put little Gerda down, kissed her on the mouth, and large limpid tears ran down over the beast's cheeks. Then he ran off back again as hard as he could. There stood poor Gerda shoeless, without gloves, in the middle of fearful ice-cold Finmark.

She ran on as quick as she could, and then there appeared a whole regiment of snowflakes. They had not fallen from the sky, for that was quite clear and shining with the Northern Lights. These snowflakes ran along the ground, and the nearer they came the larger they grew. Gerda remembered how big and how wonderfully wrought they had looked, that time when she looked at some snowflakes through the magnifying glass; but here they were quite of another sort in size and dreadfulness; they were alive, they were the Snow Queen's sentinels. They were of the strangest shapes. Some looked like great ugly hedgehogs, others like knots of snakes sticking their heads out and others again like little fat bears with bristling hair. All of them were glittering white, and all were living snowflakes.

Then little Gerda began to say the Lord's Prayer, and so fierce was the cold that she could see her own breath coming out of her mouth like a cloud of smoke. Thicker and thicker it grew, and shaped itself into little bright angels who grew larger and larger when they touched the ground. They all had helmets on their heads and spears and shields in their hands, and more and more of them came. By the time Gerda had finished saying her prayer there was a whole legion of them about her. They struck at the ugly snowflakes with their spears and broke them into hundreds of bits, and little Gerda went safely and boldly onwards. The angels chafed her hands and feet, and she felt the cold less, and on she went quickly towards the Snow Queen's palace.

But now we must see how little Kay's getting on. He certainly wasn't thinking about little Gerda, and least of all that she was just outside the palace.

STORY THE SEVENTH

What happened in the Snow Queen's Palace, and what happened after that

The walls of the palace were of drifted snow, and the windows and doors of cutting wind. More than a hundred halls there were, all just as the snow had drifted. The largest was many miles long; all were lit up with the bright Northern Lights, and they were vast, empty, ice-cold and shining. There was never any merrymaking there, never so much as a little dance for the bears, when the storms could play for them and the polar bears walk about on their hind legs and show their pretty manners: never a nice little party to play slap-in-the-mouth, and rap-your-paws: never the least bit of a coffee party for the white fox misses: empty, vast, cold it was in the halls of the Snow Queen. The Northern Lights sent up their flames with such accuracy that you could mark exactly where they were at their highest point and when at their lowest. In the midst of the endless, empty hall there was a frozen lake: it had cracked into thousands of pieces, but each piece was so exactly similar to the next that it was like a conjuring trick. In the centre of this the Snow Queen would sit when she was at home, and say that she was seated in the mirror of intellect, and that it was the only one and the best in the whole world.

Little Kay was quite blue with the cold, nay, almost black, but he didn't notice it, for the Snow Queen had kissed the shivers out of him, and his heart was practically a lump of ice. He went about dragging a number of sharp-edged flat pieces of ice which he was arranging in every possible pattern and trying to make something out of them: just as you and I have little flat bits of wood and arrange them in patterns—a Chinese puzzle it's called. Kay too, went on making patterns of the most elaborate kind—the Intellectual Ice Puzzle. To his thinking, these patterns were most remarkable and of the very greatest importance: this was the effect of the grain of glass that was stuck in his eye. He put together patterns to form a written word; but he never could succeed in putting out the exact word that he wanted, which was the word "Eternity". The Snow Queen had said: "If you can find me that pattern, you shall be your own master, and I'll make you a present of the whole world, and a new pair of skates." But he couldn't manage it. "Now I'm going to whisk off to the hot countries," said the Snow Queen. "I shall go and peep into the black pots (those were the fiery mountains, Etna and Vesuvius they're called). I must whiten them a bit: that's my job, and, besides, it'll be good for the lemons and vines. So off flew the Snow Queen, and Kay sat there all alone in the mile-long empty hall of ice, and gazed at the bits of ice and thought and thought till he crackled; all stiff and still he sat, you would have thought he was frozen to death.

It was at that moment that little Gerda walked into the palace through the great gate that was made of the cutting wind: but she said her evening prayer, and at that the winds laid themselves down as it were to sleep, and she entered the vast empty cold hall. And there she saw Kay and knew him, and flew and caught him by the neck, and clasped him close and cried: "Kay! Darling little Kay! So I've found you at last!"

But there he sat quite still and stiff and cold. Then little Gerda wept hot tears, which fell on his bosom and pierced through to his heart and thawed that lump of ice and consumed the little bit of glass that was there. He looked at her, and she sang the hymn:

The roses grow in the valley,
Where we meet the Jesus Child.

Then Kay burst into weeping: he wept so that the grain of glass ran down out of his eyes, and then he knew her and cried out in joy: "Gerda! Darling little Gerda! Wherever have you been all this time, and where have I been?" He looked about him. "How cold it is here, how empty it is and how big!" And he held fast to Gerda, and she laughed and cried with joy. It was all so happy that the very bits of ice danced about for joy; and when they were tired and lay down again, there they lay exactly in those letters which the

Snow Queen had said Kay must make up, and if he did he should be his own master and she would give him the whole world and a new pair of skates.

And Gerda kissed his cheeks and they became rosy; she kissed his eyes and they shone like hers; she kissed his hands and feet and he was well and sound. The Snow Queen might come back as soon as she liked; his release was there, written in shining bits of ice.

They took each other by the hand and walked out of the great palace. They talked of grandmother and of the roses on the roof, and wherever they went the winds lay still and the sun broke out; and when they reached the bush with the red berries, there stood the reindeer waiting for them, and he had another young doe with him, whose udder was full, and it gave the little ones its warm milk and kissed them on the mouth. Then the two carried Kay and Gerda, first to the Finn woman, where they warmed themselves in the hot room and got directions for their journey home, and then to the Lapp woman, who had made new clothes for them and repaired Kay's sledge.

The reindeer and the doe bounded along beside them, and accompanied them to the boundary of the country. There the first green leaves were peeping out, and there they took leave of the reindeer and the Lapp woman. "Good-bye!" said everybody: and now the first little birds began to twitter, the forest had green buds on it—and out of it came riding on a fine horse (which Gerda recognized, for it had been harnessed to the gold coach) a young girl with a flaming red cap on her head and pistols at her side. It was the little robber girl, who had got tired of staying at home and meant to go, first northwards and then some other way if she didn't like it. She knew Gerda at once and Gerda knew her, and they were delighted. "You're a cheerful sort of chap to traipse about after!" said she to little Kay. "I'd like to know if you're worth anyone's running to the other end of the world on your account!" But Gerda stroked her cheeks and asked after the Prince and Princess.

"They've gone travelling abroad," said the robber girl. "And the crow?" little Gerda asked.

"Oh, the crow's dead," she answered. "The tame sweetheart's a widow, and goes about with a bit of black worsted on her leg. She keeps up a fearful whining about it, but it's all my eye. But now, tell me how you got on, and how you managed to get hold of him." So Gerda and Kay both told her all the story. "And Snip-Snap-snurre-basselurre!" said the robber girl, shook hands with them both, and promised that if ever she passed through their town she'd come up and pay them a visit; and then she rode off, out into the wide world.

But Kay and Gerda went on, hand in hand: and as they went, beautiful spring was all about them with blossom and greenery. The church bells rang out, and they saw the tall towers and the big town—the very one where they lived—and into it they came and away to their grandmother's door, and up the stairs and into the room, where everything stood where it did before, and the clock was saying "Tick, tick", and the hands turning round. But, just as they passed through the door they were aware that they were grown people. The roses in the gutter were flowering in at the open windows, and there were the little stools, and Kay and Gerda sat down each on their own, and held each other by the hand. They had forgotten the cold empty splendour of the Snow Queen's palace as if it were a dismal dream. Grandmother was sitting there in God's bright sunshine and reading aloud from the Bible. "Except ye become as little children, ye shall in no wise enter the Kingdom of Heaven."

And Kay and Gerda looked into each other's eyes, and all at once they understood the old hymn:

> *The roses grow in the valley*
> *Where we meet the Jesus Child.*

There they both sat, grown up and yet children, children at heart; and it was summer, warm delightful summer.

The Darning Needle

There was once a Darning Needle who was such a fine lady that she imagined she was a sewing needle. "Mind you take care what you're holding," said the Darning Needle to the Fingers, when they picked her up. "Don't drop me! If I fall on the floor, I should very likely never be found again, I'm so fine." "Moderately so," said the Fingers, taking her firmly round the waist.

"Look, here I come with my train," said the Darning Needle, as she drew a long thread after her; but it had no knot on it.

The Fingers pointed the needle straight at the kitchenmaid's slipper, where there was a tear in the upper leather that had to be sewn up.

"This is menial work," said the Darning Needle. "I shall never get through it! I shall break! I shall break!" And break she did. "Didn't I say so?" she said; "I'm so fine."

"Now, she's good for nothing," said the Fingers. However, they had to keep hold of her, for the kitchenmaid dropped some sealing-wax on her, and stuck her in the front of her neckerchief. "Look, now I'm a breast-pin," said the Darning Needle. "I knew I should come to the front. Be something and you'll become something." And she laughed, to herself, for you can't see on the face of it when a darning needle is laughing. Now she sat there as proud as if she was driving in her own carriage, and looked all about her.

"May I have the honour of inquiring whether you are made of gold?" she asked a pin who was beside her. "You make a handsome appearance, and have a head of your own, though a small one. You should take pains to make it grow, for we can't all have sealing-wax on the end of us." With these words the Darning Needle drew herself up so proudly that she fell out of the neckerchief into the waste-tub, just as the kitchenmaid emptied it out. "So I'm going on my

travels," said the Darning Needle; "I only hope I don't get lost."
But she was lost. "I'm too fine for this world," said she, as she lay
in the drain. "Well, I have a good conscience, and that's always
some little comfort"; and she held herself stiff and didn't lose her
temper.

Every sort of thing went sailing along over her; sticks and straws
and bits of newspaper. "Look at them sailing along," said the
Darning Needle; "they don't know what's sticking fast just beneath them. It's I! Here I sit. Look! There goes a stick, thinking of
nothing in the world but 'stick', that's himself. There goes a straw!
Just look how it zig-zags about and turns round and round. Don't
think quite so much about yourself! You may run up against the
culvert! There's a newspaper; everything that's on it is forgotten,
but it's spreading itself out all the same. I sit here patient and calm;
I know what I am, and what I am I remain."

One day there came something close by that shone very finely,
and the Darning Needle thought it must be a diamond, but it was
really a bit of bottle. And as it shone the Darning Needle addressed
it, introducing herself as a Breast Pin. "You are no doubt a diamond?" "Yes, I am something of the kind." So each believed that
the other was something really valuable, and they talked about
how conceited the world was.

"Ah, yes! I used to live in a casket owned by a young lady,"
said the Darning Needle; "and the young lady was a kitchenmaid.
She had five fingers on each hand, but anything so self-centred as
those five fingers I never knew, and yet they were only there to
hold me and take me out of the casket and put me back again."

"Had they any brilliance about them?" asked the bit of glass.
"Brilliance!" said the Darning Needle. "No, it was all conceit.
They were five brothers, all born fingers; they held themselves
close up to each other, though they were of different lengths. The
outermost, Tom Thumb, was short and stout, and was outside the
rank. He had only one joint in his back, and could only bow in one
place, but he said that if he was cut off a man, that man was entirely
unfitted for war service. Lick Pot was dipped in sweet and sour,
and would point at the sun and moon, and he it was who held
tight when they wrote. Longman looked over the heads of the
rest. Gold Band wore a gold ring round his stomach, and little
Peter Playman had nothing to do and was proud of it. The whole

thing was brag, and brag it remained. So I went into the tub."

"And now here we sit and glitter," said the bit of glass. Just then some more water was poured into the drain and overflowed all the edges, and washed away the bit of glass with it.

"Ah! Now he is gone abroad," said the Darning Needle, "and I stay here! I'm too fine! Still, that's my pride, and it's an honourable one." So there she sat stiffly, and thought many thoughts.

"I could almost believe I was born of a sunbeam, I'm so fine; doesn't it seem, too, as if the sun were always looking for me under the water? Ah me! I'm so fine that my mother can't find me. If I had my old eye that broke I really think I should cry, and yet no, I wouldn't—crying isn't refined."

One day there were some street boys lying and poking about in the gutter, where they found old nails, coppers and such things; it was messy work, but they enjoyed it.

"Ow!" said one of them, who had pricked himself with the Darning Needle. "Here's another chap!"

"I'm not a chap, I'm a young lady!" said the Darning Needle, but nobody heard her. The sealing-wax had come off her, and she had turned black, but being black makes you look thinner, so she thought she was even finer than before.

"There comes an eggshell sailing along," said the boys. Whereupon they stuck the Darning Needle into the shell.

"White walls, and myself black," said the Darning Needle; "that suits well! People can see me, anyhow. I only hope I shan't be sea-sick; if I am I shall break." But she wasn't sea-sick and didn't break: it's good for sea-sickness to have a steel stomach, and always to remember that one is somewhat more than ordinary. "My illness is over now. Yes, the finer one is the more one can bear."

Crack! went the eggshell; a loaded wagon had gone over it. "Ugh, what a squeeze!" said the Darning Needle. "I shall be seasick! I shall break! I shall break!" But she didn't, though the loaded wagon did go over her. She lay there at full length—and there let her lie!

The Bell

Towards evening, in the narrow streets of the big town, when the sun was setting, and the clouds shone like gold high up among the chimneys, there was often heard, sometimes by one person, sometimes by another, a wonderful sound like the toll of a church bell. But it was only for an instant that it was heard, for there was such a rumbling of carts and such a clamour of voices—and that distracts one. People would say: "There's the evening bell ringing! The sun's setting now."

Those who went out of the town, where the houses stand farther apart, with gardens and little fields about them, saw the evening sky in yet greater beauty and heard the sound of the bell far louder. It seemed to come from a church hidden deep in the still, fragrant wood; and people looked that way and became quite serious.

Well, a long time went by, and one would say to another: "Can there be a church out there in the wood? That Bell has a strange beautiful sound; hadn't we better go out there and look into the thing?" So the rich folk set off, driving, and the poor folk, walking; but they found the way uncommonly long, and when they got as far as a clump of willows that grew on the outskirts of the wood, they sat down there and gazed up into the tall boughs, and thought they had got right into the good green wood. A confectioner came out there from the town and put up a booth, and then another confectioner came too; and he hung up a bell, right over his booth; and a bell, moreover, that was tarred outside so as to stand the rain, and had no clapper. And when the people got home again they said how romantic it had all been—and that has a meaning of its own—quite apart from tea. Three people there were who insisted that they had forced their way through the wood, to the very end of it, and all the while they had heard the strange sound of the bell; but to them it seemed as if it came from within the town. One of them wrote a whole poem about it, and told how the bell rang like the voice of a mother singing to the dearest and best of children: no music was more lovely than the sound of the bell.

The Emperor of the country, too, had his attention drawn to the matter, and promised that the man who could really find out where the sound came from should have the title of "World's Bellman" given to him, even if it proved not to be a bell at all.

A great many people now took to going to the wood for the sake of the excellent victuals they got there, but there was only one who came back with any sort of explanation. No one had been far enough into the wood; neither had he for that matter, but still he said that the bell-sound came from a very large owl in a hollow tree. It was a real bird of wisdom, and it kept on beating its head against the tree, but whether the sound came from its head or from the tree he could not say even now with certainty. So he was appointed "World's Bellman", and every year he wrote a little book about the owl, but the world was no wiser than before.

Now there chanced to be a confirmation day. The priest had spoken beautiful and moving words. The confirmands had been deeply touched; it was a momentous day for them; from being children they were all at once become grown people; their child-soul must now pass over, so to say, into a being of more discretion. It was a day of the loveliest sunshine; the confirmands went out of the town, and out from the wood there rang with marvellous clearness the great unknown bell. Instantly a great desire came upon them to go thither—all of them except three. One of these had to go home and try on her ball-dress, for the dress and the ball were the whole occasion of her being confirmed this time, otherwise she wouldn't have come with the rest. The second was a poor boy, who had borrowed a coat and boots, to be confirmed in, from the innkeeper's son, and he had to return them by a certain time. The third said that he never went to any strange place without his parents, and that he had always been a good boy, and so he would continue to be, even when he was confirmed; and that isn't a thing to make game of. But they did make game of him all the same.

So three of them didn't go with the rest; the others trotted off. The sun shone and the birds sang, and the young people sang too, and held each others hands—for why? They hadn't yet got situations and were all confirmands in the sight of God.

But, soon, two of the smallest got tired, and they turned back to the town. Two little girls sat themselves down and began making wreaths, so they got no farther; and when the rest came to the willow trees, where the confectioner lived, they said: "Look here, we've got to the place; there isn't really any bell, it's just a sort of thing people fancy to themselves."

At that moment, in the depth of the wood, the bell sounded out, so sweet and solemn that four or five made up their minds that they would after all go a little farther into the wood. It was so thick and leafy that it was really hard work to get through it; the woodruff and the anemones were almost too tall, flowering convolvulus and brambles hung in long festoons from tree to tree, where the nightingale sang and the sunlight played. Oh, it was beautiful!— but it was no place for the girls to make their way through, they would soon have their frocks torn to rags. There stood great masses of rock grown all over with moss of all colours, and the fresh spring water came babbling out and talked in a strange fashion. "Cluck! Cluck!" it said.

"That can't be the bell, can it?" said one of the young people; and he lay down and listened to it. "This must be looked into properly." So there he stayed and let the rest go on.

They came to a hut of bark and branches; a big crab apple tree leant down over it as if it would shake all its wealth of blossom over the roof, which was gay with roses; the long boughs stretched straight towards the gable, and on it hung a little bell. Could that be the one they had heard? Yes! They were all agreed about it, except one. He said that the bell was far too small and shrill to be heard so far off as they had heard the other, and that those were quite different sounds that so moved people's hearts. The one who said this was a king's son, so the others said: "That sort, of course, must always be cleverer than anybody else!"

So they let him go on alone, and as he went his heart filled more and more with the forest loneliness; but still he heard the little bell with which the others had been so delighted, and now and again, when the breeze came from the confectioner's way, he could hear as well how the people sang at their tea. But the deep stroke of the bell still sounded louder: it was as if an organ was playing, too, and the sound came from the left, from the side where the heart is set.

Suddenly there was a rustling in the bushes, and there before the king's son stood a little boy, a boy in wooden shoes and a jacket so short that you could see exactly how long his wrists were. They recognized one another. The boy was that very one who hadn't been able to come with the rest because he had had to go home and give back the coat and boots to the innkeeper's son. He had done that, and then, in his wooden shoes and his shabby clothes, he had started off alone, for the bell rang so loud and so deep that out he must go.

"Ah, now we can go on together," said the King's son; but the poor boy with the wooden shoes was quite embarrassed. He pulled at his short sleeves and said he was afraid he couldn't get along so fast, and besides he thought the bell ought to be looked for on the right, for everything that is great and noble is on that side.

"Well, at that rate we shan't meet again," said the King's son; and he nodded to the poor boy, who plunged into the darkest and thickest part of the wood, where the thorns tore his shabby clothes to bits, and scratched his face and hands and feet till the blood came.

The King's son, too, got a good few scratches; but the sun shone on his path, and he is the one we will follow, for a brisk lad was he.

"I must and will find the bell," said he, "if I have to go to the world's end for it."

The ugly baboons, sitting in the trees, grinned at him with every tooth in their heads. "Shall we smash him?" said they. "Shall we smash him? He's a king's son!"

But on he went, undaunted, deeper and deeper into the wood, where grew the strangest flowers. There stood white star lilies with blood-red stamens, sky-blue tulips that glistened in the breezes, and apple trees whose apples, one and all, looked like great shining soap bubbles—just think how those trees must have shone in the sunlight! Round the most beautiful green glades, where hart and hind played on the turf, grew splendid oaks and beeches, and whenever one of the trees had had its bark split, grass and long tendrils had grown in the cleft. There, too, were great glens with calm lakes, on which white swans swam and flapped their wings. Often did the King's son stop and listen; often he thought that it was from one of those deep lakes that the bell rang upward to him; but then he was aware that it was not there, but from a further depth of the forest, that the bell sounded.

And now the sun was sinking and the sky shone red as fire, and a great stillness was over all the forest. He sank on his knees and sang his evening hymn, and said: "Never shall I find that which I seek! Now the sun is sinking. Now night, dark night is coming on; yet once again, perhaps, I may see the round red sun before it sinks wholly behind the earth. I will climb this cliff that stands there, with the great trees on the top."

And he clutched at creepers and roots and clambered up towards the wet rocks, where the water snakes twined into knots, and the toads seemed really to bark at him—yet up he got before the sun, seen from that height, was quite down. Oh, what splendour! The sea, the great majestic sea, that rolled its long billows toward the coast, stretched out before him, and the sun stood like a huge shining altar, far out, where sea and sky met, all fused together in glowing colours. The forest sang, and the sea sang, and his heart sang with them. All nature was a vast solemn cathedral, wherein the trees and floating clouds were the columns, the flowers and grass the woven hangings of silk, the heaven itself the mighty dome. Up there the red hues were dying as the sun disappeared. But millions of stars were being lit, millions of diamond lamps shone there, and the King's son stretched out his arms towards the heavens, the sea, the forest—and just then there came from the path on the right the poor boy with the scanty coat-sleeves and the wooden shoes. He had come there just as soon, come by his own way; and they ran to meet each other, and caught each other by the hand in the great cathedral of Nature and of song.

And above them rang out the unseen solemn bell, and about it happy spirits hovered, circling in a joyful song of praise to God.

The Elf Hill

Several lizards were running about, very quick, in the clefts of an old tree trunk. They could understand one another very well, for they all spoke the lizard language.

"Dear, what a rumbling and bumbling there is in the old Elf Hill," said one of the lizards. "I haven't been able to close an eye the last two nights for the noise. I might just as well have had the toothache all the time, for I don't get any sleep then."

"There's something up there," said the second lizard, "they stood the hill up on four red stakes right up to cockcrow. It's had a real good airing, and the Elf girls have learnt some new dances, with stamping in 'em." "There's something up. I've been talking to a lob-worm I know," said the third lizard. "He came straight up out of the hill where he'd been burrowing in the ground for nights and days; he'd heard a lot. He can't see, poor beast, but he can feel about in front of him and listen, that he can do. They're expecting visitors to-day in the Elf Hill, visitors of distinction, but whom, the lob-worm wouldn't say, or else he didn't know. All the will-o'-the-wisps have been summoned to make a torchlight procession—that's what they call it—and the silver and gold, which there's a lot of in the hill, is to be polished and set out in the moonlight."

"Now, who can the visitors be?" said all the lizards. "What can be afoot? Listen! What a bustle, what a hustle!"

At that very moment the Elf Hill opened, and an old Elf maid (she had no back but was otherwise very well got up) came tripping out. She was the old Elf King's housekeeper, distantly related to the family, and had an amber heart on her forehead. Her legs went twinkling along. Trip! trip! Bless her heart, how she did trip it—right away down into the marsh, to the night-raven.

"You are invited to the Elf Hill, yes, and for to-night," said she, "but first you'll do us a very great service, won't you? Undertake

222

invitations? You can easily manage it, for you've no house to look after. We have some very distinguished guests, Troll folk, who are of great importance, and so the old King is going to show himself off."

"Who are to be invited?" asked the night-raven.

"Why, to the big ball everybody can come, even humans, if they can talk in their sleep or do any little thing of the kind that belongs to our race; but for the high table there has to be a very strict selection: we want only the most distinguished people. I had quite a quarrel with the King, for I insist that we can't even have ghosts. The Merman and his daughter must be invited first. They don't much like coming on the land, but they shall every one of them have a wet stone to sit on, or something better, and in that case I don't think they'll refuse this time. All old Trolls of the first class, with tails, the riverman and the nixies, we must have, and I think we can't pass over the grave-pig, the death-horse and the church brownie. They do belong, properly speaking, to the clergy, who are not of our sort, but that is after all merely official; they are nearly related to us and call on us quite regularly."

"Bra!" said the night-raven, and flew off to invite the guests. The Elf girls were already dancing on the Elf Hill—dancing with long scarves woven of mist and moonshine, which looked exceedingly pretty—to people who like that sort of thing. Inside the Hill the great hall was thoroughly smartened up, the floor washed with moonshine, the walls rubbed down with witches-butter, so that they shone like petals of tulips held up to the light. In the kitchens were quantities of frogs on the spit, snake skins with little children's fingers in them, salads of toadstool spawn, wet mouse-noses and hemlock, ale of the Marshwoman's brewing, shining wine of salt-petre from the vault cellars—all this very substantial; rusty nails and church-window glass for cracking at dessert.

The old King had his crown polished with powdered slate pencil—sixth form slate pencil—and it is extremely difficult for the Elf King to procure sixth-form slate pencil. In the bedroom they hung the curtains up and made them fast with snail slime. There was a bustle and a hustle, and no mistake.

"Now we must fumigate with horse-hair and pigs' bristles," said the old Elf maid; "and then I think I shall have done my share."

"Father, darling," said the youngest of the daughters, "do please tell me who the grand visitors are."

"Well, well," said he, "I may as well tell you. Two of my daughters must hold themselves in readiness to be married. Two will certainly be. The old Troll gentleman from up in Norway—he, I mean, who lives in the old Dovrefell and owns all the great cliff castles built of boulders, and a gold-mine which is better than folk think—he's coming down here with his two lads; they're to look out a wife apiece. The old fellow is a regular honest old Norseman, merry and bright. I know him of old when we drank brotherhood. He was down here then to fetch his wife. She's dead now; she was a daughter of the cliff King of Moen. He took his wife off the chalk (*really* on tick), as the saying is. Oh, how I do want to see that old Norse Troll fellow again! The boys they say are rather unmannerly youngsters—fit for the stick—but that may be doing them an injustice, and no doubt they will be good enough when they're a bit seasoned. Let me see that you can teach them how to behave."

"And when do they get here?" asked one of the daughters. "That depends on wind and weather," said the King; "they are travelling cheap: they're coming here by a chance ship. I wanted them to come overland by Sweden, but the old man doesn't cotton to that side even now. He doesn't keep up with the times, and I don't like that."

At that moment two will-o'-the-wisps came skipping in, one faster than the other, so he arrived first.

"They're coming, they're coming!" they cried.

"Give me my crown and let me stand in the moonlight," said the King. The daughters gathered up their trains and curtsied down to the ground.

There stood the old Troll from the Dovrefell, with a crown of hardened icicles and polished fir cones, and for the rest he had on a bearskin and fur boots. His sons, on the other hand, went bareheaded and without braces, for they were hardy fellows.

"That a hill?" asked the youngest boy; and pointed at the Elf Hill. "Up in Norway we should call that a hole."

"Lads," said the old man, "a hole goes in, a hill sticks out; have you no eyes in your heads?"

The only thing that surprised them down here, they said, was that they could understand the talk straight off.

"Don't make an exhibition of yourselves," said the old man. "Anyone would think you were no more than half baked."

The Elf Hill

With that they went into the Elf Hill, where a smart company indeed was gathered—in such a hurry one would think they had been blown together—and all the arrangements for everyone were charming and choice. The sea folk sat at table in large tubs of water; they said it was just like being in their own home. Every-

body's table manners were correct except those of the two young Norse Trolls. They put their legs up on the table; but then they imagined that everything they did became them.

"Feet out of the food!" said the old Troll, and they obeyed, though not quite promptly. They tickled the ladies next them with fir cones that they'd brought in their pockets, and then took off their boots to be more comfortable, and gave them to the ladies to hold. But their father, the old Troll from Dovrefell, his manners were totally different. He described most delightfully the great Norse fells, and the forces that leapt down them, foaming white, with a booming like the crash of thunder or the peal of an organ. He told of the salmon that leapt up against the rushing water, while the nixie played on his harp of gold. He told of the glistening winter nights when the sleigh bells tinkled and the boys skimmed, with flaming torches, over the bright ice that was so transparent you could see the fish start beneath your feet. Ah, he could tell of it all so that one could see and hear what he described. There were the saw-mills at work, there were the lads and lassies singing ballads and dancing the "Hallinge". Hurrah! And with that the Troll gave the old Elf maid a smacking uncle's kiss, a regular buss—and yet they weren't related—not a bit.

Next the Elf girls had to dance—plain dances and stamping dances, too, and did it well. Then came the figure dances—"treading a measure" as they call it. Bless their hearts! How they did work their legs! You couldn't tell which was top and which was tail, couldn't see which was arms and which was legs; they went in and out of each other like wood shavings at the saw-mills, and then they whirled round and round till the death-horse felt sick and had to leave the table.

"Prrr," said the old Troll; "that's leg-work if you like. But what can they do besides dance and stretch their legs and turn themselves into whirlwinds?" "That you shall see," said the Elf King; and called up his youngest daughter. She was as slim and clear as moonshine, the most delicate of all the sisters. She took a white chip in her mouth, and there!—she was clean gone! That was her accomplishment. But the old Troll said that was a trick he didn't care about in a wife, and he didn't think his boys would like it either.

The second could walk by the side of her own self and look as if she had a shadow, which Troll people don't have.

The third was of quite another sort. She had taken lessons in the Marshwoman's brewery, and it was she who knew how to lard alder stumps with glow-worms. "She'll make a good housewife," said the Troll, and winked his eye at her, for he didn't care to drink many toasts.

Then came the fourth Elf girl. She had a great gold harp to play on, and when she struck the first string everybody lifted up their left leg (Troll folk are left-legged), and when she struck the second string, they all had to do what she wanted.

"That's a dangerous woman," said the Troll; but the two sons went off outside the Hill, for they were bored with the proceedings.

"And what can the next daughter do?" inquired the Troll.

"I have learnt to love all that is Norse," said she; "and I shall never marry unless I can go to Norway."

But the littlest of the sisters whispered to the old Troll: "That's only because she's heard, in a Norse ballad, that when the world comes to an end the Norse cliffs will still stand, for gravestones, and so she wants to go there; she's so frightened of being destroyed."

"Oh ho!" said the Troll; "that cat's out of the bag. But what can the seventh and last do?"

"The sixth comes before the seventh," said the Elf King, for he could count. But the sixth wouldn't come forward properly. "I can only tell people the truth," she said. "Nobody cares about me, and I've quite enough to do to make my own grave-clothes."

Then came the seventh and last; and what could she do? Why! She could tell stories, as many as ever she liked.

"Here are all my five fingers," said the old Troll; "tell me one for each of 'em."

And the Elf Maid took him by the wrist, and he laughed till he choked, and when she came to Gold Band, that had a gold ring about his waist, as if he knew there was to be a betrothal, the Troll said: "Stick to what you've got, the hand is yours: I'll take you for a wife myself."

The Elf Maid said there were still stories to tell about Gold Band and little Peter Playman. "We'll hear them in the winter time," said the Troll; "and we'll hear about the fir and the birch and the fairy gifts and the ringing frost. You'll have lots to tell, for there's no one up there that can do it properly, and we'll sit in the stone hall where the fir chips blaze, and drink mead out of the golden horns of the old Norse Kings—the Nixie's given me a couple of them; and while we sit there the Garbo will come and pay us a visit. He'll sing you all the herd-girls' songs; it will be jolly. The salmon will leap in the force and dash against the stone walls, but they won't get in. Ah, you may take it from me, there are good times in dear old Norway. But where are the boys?"

Ah! Where were the boys? They were running about in the marsh, blowing out the will-o'-the-wisps, who had come so obligingly, and were to make a torchlight procession.

"Gadding about like that!" said the old Troll. "I've got a mother for you, and now you may take an aunt for yourselves."

But the boys said they had rather make speeches and drink brotherhood. Marrying? No, they didn't care about that. So they did make speeches and drank brotherhood, and hung the glasses on their fingertips to show they'd drunk them out; and then took off their coats and lay down on the table to sleep, for they had no false modesty. But the old Troll danced round the room with his young bride, and exchanged boots with her, which is more distinguished than exchanging rings.

"There's the cock crowing," said the old Elf maid, who was housekeeper. "We must shut the shutters now, to keep the sun from burning us alive."

So the Hill shut.

But outside, the lizards still ran up and down the old split tree, and one said to the other: "Oh, how I do like that old Norse Troll, to be sure!"

"I like the boys better," said the lob-worm: but then of course he couldn't see, poor beast.

The Shepherdess and the Chimney Sweep

Have you ever seen a real old-fashioned cupboard, quite black with age, carved with flourishes and foliage? Just such a one stood in a sitting-room; it had been inherited from a grandmother, and was all carved with roses and tulips from top to bottom: there were most elaborate flourishes on it, and among them little deer stuck out their heads with lots of antlers. But in the very middle of the cupboard was carved a whole figure of a man. He made you smile to look at him, and he did grin—you couldn't call it laughing—and he had goats' legs, little horns in his forehead, and a long beard. The children of the house called him "Top-and-bottom-general-commander-in-chief-sergeant-billy-goats'-legs"; a difficult name to pronounce, and a title earned by very few: but, after all, it was no light job to have carved him out. Anyhow, there he was, and he was always looking across at the table under the mirror, for there stood a pretty little Shepherdess of china. Her shoes were gilt, her skirt charmingly looped up with a red rose, and besides she had a gold hat and a shepherd's crook: she was beautiful. Close by her stood a little Chimney Sweep as black as coal, but, like her, made of China. He was as neat and clean as anyone could be; it was only pretence that he was a Chimney Sweep, the china-maker could just as easily have made a Prince of him; it was all one. There he stood with his ladder, looking very pretty, and with a face as pink and white as a girl's—which really was a mistake, for he had better have had a little black on it. He stood quite close to the Shepherdess; both of them had been put where they were, and because they had been put there, they became engaged. They suited each other very well; both of them were young, both of the same china, and both equally brittle. Beside them was yet another figure, three times as big: it was an old Chinese man, who could nod his head. He too was made of china, and he asserted that he was the little Shepherdess's grandfather. But this he could not prove. He insisted that he had authority over her, and therefore he had nodded his consent to "Top-and-bottom-general-commander-in-chief-sergeant-billy-goats'-legs" when he proposed for the little Shepherdess. "In him", said the old Chinaman, "you will have a husband, a husband who I almost think is made of mahogany, and who can make you 'Lady-Top-and-bottom-general-commander-in-chief-sergeant-billy-goats'-legs'. He owns that whole cupboard full of silver plate, in addition to what he has in secret hiding-places."

"I don't want to go into that dark cupboard," said the little Shepherdess. "I've heard tell that he's got eleven china wives in there."

"Then you can be the twelfth," said the Chinaman. "To-night, as soon as the old cupboard cracks, your wedding shall take place, as sure as I'm a Chinaman." And with that he nodded his head and went to sleep.

But the little Shepherdess began to cry and looked at her heart's dearest—the china Chimney Sweep.

"I think I must ask you", she said, "to come out into the wide world with me, for we can't stay here."

"Your will is mine," said the little Chimney Sweep. "Let us set off at once; I feel sure I can support you by the exercise of my profession."

"I wish we were safely down off the table," said she; "I shan't be happy before we are out in the wide world."

Then he encouraged her and showed her where to set her little feet on the carved corner, and gilt foliage down the legs of the table. He took his ladder, too, to help her, and so they got down to the floor. But when they looked at the old cupboard—such a commotion was going on! All the carved deer stuck their heads further out and pointed their antlers and turned their necks about. Top-and-bottom-general-commander-in-chief-sergeant-billy-goats'-legs leapt high in the air and shouted across to the old Chinaman: "They're running away! They're running away!"

This alarmed them somewhat, and they jumped quickly up into the drawer of the window seat. Here lay three or four imperfect packs of cards, and a little toy theatre that had been set up as well as it could be. A comedy was being acted, and all the Queens—diamonds and hearts, clubs and spades—were seated in the front row fanning themselves with their tulips, and behind them stood all the Knaves, and you could see they had one head at top and another below (as cards do). The comedy was about two people who couldn't marry, and it made the Shepherdess cry, because it resembled her own story. "I can't bear it," she said; "I must get out of the drawer." But when they reached the floor and looked up at the table, the old Chinaman had waked up and was rocking with the whole of his body—the lower part of him was all in one piece.

"The old Chinaman's coming!" screamed the little Shepherdess, and in her terror she fell on her china knees.

"An idea occurs to me," said the Chimney Sweep. "Let's creep into the big pot-pourri jar that stands in the corner; we can lie there among the roses and lavender and throw salt in his eyes if he comes." "That'll never do," said she; "besides, I know that the old Chinaman and the pot-pourri jar were engaged at one time, and there's always some kind feeling left when people have been in that situation. No, there's nothing for it but to go out into the wide world."

"Have you really the courage to go out into the wide world with me?" asked the Chimney Sweep. "Have you considered how large it is, and that we never can come back here?"

"I have," she said.

The Chimney Sweep looked at her quite sternly and then said: "My way lies through the chimney. Have you really the courage to crawl with me through the stove, through tunnel and pipe as well? We shall then be in the chimney, and there I know how to manage. We shall climb so high that they cannot follow us, and right up at the top there is a hole which goes out into the wide world."

He led her across to the stove door.

"It looks very black," she said. Still, she went with him, both through the tunnel and through the pipe, and there it was night, as dark as pitch.

"Now we are in the chimney," said he. "And look! Look! The loveliest star is shining right over us."

There was indeed a star in the sky, shining right down to them, as if it would show them the way. They clambered and they crawled

—it was a terrible way—up and up; but he lifted her, eased her, held her and showed her the best places to set her little china feet on, and at last they got right up to the edge of the chimney-top, and there they sat down, for they were tired out; as they had every right to be.

The sky, with all its stars, was over their heads, and the roofs of the town below; they could see far around, far out into the world.

The little Shepherdess had never imagined it was like that, and she laid her head on her Chimney Sweep's shoulder and cried till the gold came off her sash.

"It's too much," she said. "I can't bear it! The world's much too big! Oh, I wish I was back on the little table under the mirror. I shall never be happy till I'm there again. I've come out with you into the wide world, and now do please come back home with me, if you have any love for me."

The Chimney Sweep reasoned with her, and spoke of the old Chinaman and Top-and-bottom-general-commander-in-chief-sergeant-billy-goats'-legs, but she sobbed so violently and kissed her little Chimney Sweep so that he couldn't but yield to her, foolish as it was.

So they crawled back down the chimney, with infinite trouble, and crept through the tunnel and the pipe, which was most unpleasant, and at last there they were in the dark stove. There they listened behind the door to find out what was going on in the room. Everything was quiet. They peeped out, and goodness! There in the middle of the floor lay the old Chinaman. In his efforts to follow them he had fallen off the table and lay there in three pieces. The whole of his back was broken off in one piece, and his head had rolled into a corner, and lay there. Top-and-bottom-general-commander-in-chief-sergeant-billy-goats'-legs stood where he always had stood, thinking about it all.

"This is awful," said the little Shepherdess. "Poor old grandfather is broken to bits, and it's our fault; I shall never get over it." And she wrung her little hands.

"He can be riveted all right," said the Chimney Sweep. "He can perfectly well be riveted; don't be so hasty. If they glue his back and put a good rivet in his neck he'll be as good as new again, and be able to say all sorts of nasty things to us."

"Do you really think so?" said she; and then they climbed up on to the table again, where they used to stand before.

"Well, what a way we've been!" said the Chimney Sweep. "And we might just as well have spared ourselves all that trouble."

"Oh, if only old grandfather were riveted!" said the little Shepherdess. "Will it be very expensive?"

Well, he was riveted: the family glued up his back, and a good rivet was put into his neck, and he as was good as new; only he couldn't nod his head.

"You've got proud since you were broken to bits," said Top-and bottom-general-commander-in-chief-sergeant-billy-goats'-legs. "I don't see that that's anything to boast of. Am I to have her, or am I not?"

The Chimney Sweep and the little Shepherdess looked pleadingly at the old Chinaman, and were dreadfully afraid he would nod, but he couldn't, and it was disagreeable to him to have to tell a stranger that he had a permanent rivet in his neck. So the china people remained together, and blessed the grandfather's rivet, and continued to love each other until they were broken to bits.

The Shadow

I n the hot countries the sun can burn properly. People become as brown as mahogany all over; in the very hottest countries they are even burnt into negroes—but it was only to the hot countries that a learned man from the cold ones had come. He imagined he would be able to run about as he did at home, but he soon got out of the habit of doing that. He and all sensible people had to stop indoors. The window-shutters and the doors were kept shut all day, and it looked as if the whole house were asleep or else nobody was at home. The narrow street with the tall houses, where he lived, was so built that from morning to night the sunshine lay on it; really it was unbearable. This learned man from the cold countries—he was a young man and a clever one—he felt as if he was living in a fiery furnace. It exhausted him, and he grew quite thin, and even his shadow contracted and got much smaller than it was at home; the sun exhausted it, too. Not until evening, when the sun was down, did they begin to revive.

That, now, was really a pleasure to see. As soon as lights were brought into the room the Shadow stretched itself all up the wall—

yes, up to the ceiling, too, so long did it make itself, for it had to stretch itself to get its strength back. The learned man went out on the balcony, to stretch himself there, and as the stars came out in the lovely clear sky he seemed to himself to be coming to life again.

On all the balconies in the street—and in the hot countries every window has a balcony—people came out, for air one must have, even if one's accustomed to be the colour of mahogany. Very lively it became—upstairs and downstairs. Shoemakers and tailors and everybody else moved out into the street; tables and chairs were brought out and lamps lit—thousands of them—and some talked and others sang; and the people took walks, and the carriages drove out, and the donkeys with bells on them went by—"Kling-a-ling-a-ling!" There were funerals, with singing of psalms; the street-boys fired off throw-downs; the church bells rang out, and altogether it was very lively down in the street. Only in one house, straight opposite to that in which the foreign learned man lived, was there complete stillness. And yet somebody lived in it, for there were flowers on the balcony, that grew splendidly in the hot sun, which they couldn't have done without being watered, and there must be somebody to water them; so there must be people there. The door of it, too, was opened at night, but inside it was quite dark; at any rate in the front room. But from further in there was a sound of music. To the foreign scholar it seemed incomparably beautiful, but it might easily be that he fancied it so, for in the hot countries everything seemed to him matchless, but for the heat. The landlord said he didn't know who had taken the house opposite, for you couldn't see any people, and as for the music, he thought it horribly tiresome. "It's like someone sitting practising a piece he can't get on with—always the same piece. No doubt he's saying, 'I shall get it right in time', but he won't get it right, however long he goes on playing."

One night the foreign scholar woke up. The door to the balcony stood open where he slept and the curtain before it was lifted by the breeze, and he thought there was a marvellous light coming from the balcony opposite. All the flowers were shining like flames of the most lovely colours, and among the flowers stood a slender, graceful maiden; herself, too, shining, as it seemed. It positively dazzled his eyes, and he shut them as tight as ever he could, and woke up completely. With a single jump he was on the floor, and very quietly he stole behind the curtain, but the maiden was gone, the light was gone, the flowers shone no longer, though they stood there as fair as ever. The door was ajar, and from far within the music was sounding, soft and beautiful; such as would entrance one into delicious thought. It really was like magic—and who was it that lived there? Where was the proper entrance? The whole ground floor was a succession of shops, and people couldn't always be passing through them.

One evening the foreign scholar was sitting out on his balcony, and a lamp was hung in the room behind him, and so it very naturally happened that his shadow passed across to the wall opposite, and there it stayed, right opposite among the flowers on the balcony, and when the learned man moved the shadow moved, too—it always does.

"I think my Shadow is the only living thing to be seen over there," said the learned man. "Look how snug it's sitting among the flowers, and the door's standing ajar. Now if only the Shadow was sharp enough to go in and look about and then come and tell me what it saw! Yes, you'd be some use then," he said in joke. "Do, please, go in there! Do! Are you going?" With that he nodded to the Shadow, and the Shadow nodded back. "Well, go then, but don't stay away!" The learned man got up and his Shadow, on the balcony opposite, got up too. The learned man turned, and the Shadow turned too, and if anyone had been observing carefully, they would have seen, quite plain, that the Shadow went in by the half-open door of the balcony over the way, at the moment when the learned man went into his own room and let fall the long curtain behind him.

Next morning the learned man went out to take his coffee and read the papers. "What's this?" he said, when he came out into the sunshine. "I haven't got any shadow! Why, then it really did go away last night and has not come back; that's rather tiresome, that is."

It did annoy him, but not so much because his shadow was gone, as because he knew that there was a story about a man without a shadow which everyone at home in the cold countries knew; and if the learned man went there and told them his own story they would say he was merely imitating the other, and that he had no business to do. So he determined to say nothing at all about it, which was very sensible of him.

In the evening he went out on to his balcony again; he had put the lamp behind him, very properly, for he knew that a shadow always needs its master for a screen, but he couldn't entice it back. He made himself little and he made himself big, but no shadow came, nobody came. He coughed loudly, but it was no good.

It was amazing, to be sure; but in those hot countries everything grows very fast, and after a week had passed he saw, to his great delight, that a new shadow was growing out of his feet when he went into the sunlight: the root must have been left behind. In three weeks' time he had a very tolerable shadow, which, when he betook himself home to the northern country, grew more and more on the way, so that at last it was so long and so big that he would have been contented with half as much.

So the learned man came home and wrote books about what there was of truth and goodness and beauty in the world; and days passed by, and years—many years.

He was sitting in his room one evening, and there came a very gentle knock at the door. "Come in!" said he; but nobody came in, so he opened the door, and there standing before him was an extraordinarily thin man, so thin as to be quite remarkable. This person was, for the rest, extremely well dressed, and evidently a man of distinction.

"Whom have I the honour of addressing?" asked the learned man.

"Ah, I thought very likely you wouldn't recognize me," said the well-dressed man. "I've become so much of a body that I've actually got flesh and clothes; you never expected to see me in such fine condition. Don't you recognize your old shadow? To be sure, you certainly never thought I should ever come back. Things have gone wonderfully well with me since I was with you last, and I have become very well-to-do in every respect. If I wish to buy myself out of service, I have the means." And he rattled a large bunch of valuable seals that hung to his watch, and put his hand to the heavy gold chain that was round his neck: and how his fingers did glitter with diamond rings, and all real too!

"Well, well! I can't get over it," said the learned man. "What does it all mean?"

"I admit, it's by no means an ordinary affair," said the Shadow. "But, then, you yourself are not an ordinary man; and I, as you very well know, have trod in your footsteps from a child. As soon as you found that I was ripe to go out into the world by myself, I went my own way. I am now in the most brilliant circumstances, but there came a sort of longing over me to see you once more before you die, as die you must. I wanted, too, to see this part of the world again, for one has always a fondness for one's Fatherland. I am aware that you have got another shadow in my place; if I have anything to pay, either to it or to you, I hope you will be so good as to let me know."

"Well, and is it really you?" said the scholar. "It is indeed most remarkable! I could never have believed that my old shadow could come back to me as a man."

"Do tell me what I have to pay," said the Shadow; "I don't at all like to be in debt of any kind."

"How can you talk so?" said the learned man. "What debt is there to talk of? Be as free as the next man; I am extraordinarily pleased at your good fortune. Do sit down, old friend, and just tell me a little about how it all came about, and what you saw at the house over the way, out there in the hot country."

"I will tell you," said the Shadow, seating himself; "but you must promise me that you won't tell anyone here in the town, wherever you may meet me, that I was once your Shadow. I have some thoughts of becoming engaged. I could support more families than one."

"Be quite easy," said the scholar; "I won't tell anyone who you really are. Here's my hand on it. I promise it, and one man, one word, you know." "One word, one shadow," said the Shadow; he was obliged to phrase it so.

It was indeed most remarkable to see how much of a man the Shadow was: all dressed out in the finest possible black broadcloth, with varnished boots and a hat that would shut up so that it was only crown and brim, not to speak of what we know already, the seals, the gold chain, and the diamond rings. The Shadow was, in fact, extraordinarily well dressed, and this was just what made him a complete man.

"Now I'll tell you my story," said the Shadow, planting his feet, in the varnished boots, as firmly as he could on the arm of the learned man's new shadow, which lay at his feet like a poodle dog: and this was either out of pride or perhaps in hopes of getting it to stick to him; while the prostrate shadow kept very quiet in order to listen, for it wanted to know how a shadow could get free as this one had done, and work up to be its own master.

"Do you know who it was that lived in the house over the way?" said the Shadow. "It was the most beautiful thing there is: it was Poetry. I was there for three weeks, and the effect was the same as if one had spent three thousand years in reading everything that has been sung and written. I say it, and it is the truth. I have seen everything, and I know everything."

"Poetry!" cried the learned man. "Yes! Yes! She often dwells, a hermit, in great cities. Poetry! I saw her for one single brief moment, but my eyes were full of sleep. She was standing on the balcony and shining as the Northern Lights shine. Tell me, tell me of her. Thou wast on the balcony, thou wentest through the door, then——" "Then I was in the ante-room," said the Shadow. "You were always sitting looking across at the ante-room. There was no light there at all; there was a sort of twilight, but one door stood open, leading straight to a second, and into a long row of rooms and halls. There was light there. I should have been killed outright by the light, had I gone in to where the maiden was, but I was careful, I gave myself time—as indeed one must."

"And what sawest thou then?" asked the scholar.

"I saw everything, and I will tell you about it. But—it isn't that I'm in the least proud—but considering I'm a free man, and what accomplishments I possess, not to mention my good position and my very easy circumstances—I should very much prefer you to address me as 'you'."

"I beg your pardon," said the scholar; "it's merely old habit which sticks by me. You're perfectly right, and I shall keep it in mind. But now, do tell me everything you saw."

"Everything!" said the Shadow. "For I saw everything and I know everything."

"What was it like in the innermost hall?" asked the scholar. "Was it like being in the green wood? Was it like a solemn temple? Were the halls like the starlit sky seen from the top of the high mountains?" "Everything was there," said the Shadow; "I didn't go absolutely in, I stayed in the room next to it in the twilight, but I was admirably placed, and saw everything and know everything. I have been in the court of Poetry, in the ante-chamber."

"But what did you see? Did all the gods of ancient days pass through the vast halls? Did the heroes of old times fight their battles there? Were there lovely children playing and telling of their dreams?"

"I tell you I was there, and you may imagine I saw everything there was to be seen. Had you been over there you would not have turned into a man, but I did; and, moreover, I learned to know my innermost nature, all that was inborn in me, the kinship I had with Poetry. When I was with you I never thought about it, but, as you know, every time the sun rose or set I used to become amazingly large. In the moonlight, indeed, I was almost plainer to be seen than you yourself. At that time I did not comprehend my own nature, but in that ante-room it became clear to me; I became a man. When I came out I was matured, but you were no longer in the hot countries. I was ashamed, as a man, to go about as I was. I needed boots and clothes and all the human paraphernalia that make a man recognizable. I made my way (I tell you this, you won't put it in a book), I made my way to the cake-woman's skirt, and hid myself under it. Little did the woman think how great a thing she had in hiding, and not till the evening did I come out. I ran along the street in the moonlight. I stretched myself right up the wall (it tickles one in the back deliciously). I ran up, I ran down; I peeped through the topmost windows, into the rooms, on to the roof. I peeped where no one else could, and saw what nobody else saw, and what nobody was meant to see. Take it all round, the world's a mean place. I wouldn't have become a man if it hadn't been generally assumed that it's a good thing to be one. I saw the most incredible things, among wives, among husbands, among parents and among those darling admirable children. I saw", said the Shadow, "what no human being was allowed to know, but what everybody very much wants to know, that is their neighbours' wrongdoings. If I'd written a newspaper it would have been read, I tell you! But I wrote direct to the people concerned, and there was a panic in every town I visited. They were terribly afraid of me, and they became amazingly fond of me. The professors made me a professor, the tailors gave me new clothes. I'm admirably fitted out. The master of the mint coined money for me, and the women said I was very good-looking. In this way I became the man I am. And now I must bid you good-bye. Here's my card; I live on the sunny

side, and I'm always at home when it rains." And off went the
Shadow.

"That is a most remarkable affair," said the learned man.

A year and a day passed, and the Shadow came again. "How goes
it?" he asked.

"Alas!" said the learned man. "I write about the true and the
good and the beautiful. But nobody cares to hear about such things,
and I'm quite in despair. I feel it very keenly."

"But I don't," said the Shadow; "I'm getting fat and that's what
everybody ought to try to be. You don't understand the way of the
world, you know; you'll get quite ill like this, you ought to travel.
I'm going to travel this summer; will you come with me? I should
like to have a companion; will you go with me as my shadow? It'll
be a real pleasure to have you with me, and I'll pay expenses."

"That's going a bit too far," said the learned man.

"Why, that's as you take it," said the Shadow. "It'll do you all
the good in the world to travel. If you'll be my shadow you shan't
have a penny to pay for the trip."

"That's absolute madness!" said the learned man.

"But after all, the world's like that," said the Shadow, "and so it
always will be." And off he went.

The learned man was in a bad way: sorrow and trouble were on
him, and as for his talk about the true and the beautiful and the
good, most people appreciated it as a cow does roses. At last he
became quite ill. "You really look like a shadow," people said to
him; and the learned man shivered, for it was exactly what he was
thinking.

"You ought to take some baths," said the Shadow, who paid
him a visit. "There's nothing else for it. I'll take you with me for
old acquaintance sake. I'll pay expenses, and you shall write a
description and amuse me with it on the journey. I'm going to the
baths, for my beard won't grow as it should, and that is an ailment;
one must have a beard. Now do be reasonable and accept my in-
vitation; we'll travel as friends."

So they set off. The Shadow was the master and the master was
the shadow. They drove together, they rode and walked together
side by side or in front or behind, according as the sun shone. The
Shadow was always careful to keep in the master's place, and the
learned man didn't really think much about that; he was a very

good soul, extremely kind and friendly. And so one day said he to the Shadow: "As we've become travelling companions (as we are) and as we've grown up together from childhood, wouldn't it be nice to drink brotherhood, and call each other 'thou'. It's more sociable, isn't it?"

"Now you're talking," said the Shadow (who was in fact the master). "What you say is very frank and very well meant. I'll be equally frank and well meaning. You as a scholar know very well what an odd thing Nature is. Some people can't bear to touch brown paper, it makes them sick; others feel it all over their body when someone scratches a pane of glass with a nail. Now I get just that sensation when I hear you say 'thou' to me. I feel absolutely as if I were crushed down on the ground, as I was in my first situation with you. You understand, it's merely a sensation, not pride at all. I can't bear you saying 'thou' to me, but I'll gladly say 'thou' to you; and that's meeting you halfway."

So the Shadow addressed his former master as "thou".

"Upon my word, it's rather much," thought the learned man, "that I should have to say 'you' and he should say 'thou'." But he had to put up with it.

Eventually they came to a watering-place where there were a number of visitors, and among them a beautiful Princess, who was suffering from the complaint of seeing too well; which is, of course, very distressing.

She noticed at once that the newcomer was a very different sort of person from all the rest. "People say he has come here to get his beard to grow, but I can see the real reason. He can't cast a shadow."

Her curiosity was roused, and very soon she got into conversation with the strange gentleman, on the promenade. Being a Princess, she did not need to beat about the bush, so she said: "What's the matter with you is that you can't cast a shadow."

"Your Royal Highness must be considerably better," said the Shadow. "I am aware that your complaint is that you see too well; but it has yielded, and you are cured. I have, in fact, a quite unusual shadow. Do you see the person who always goes about with me? Other people have an ordinary shadow, but I don't care about what is ordinary. You give your servant finer clothes for his livery than you wear yourself, and just so I have had my shadow smartened up into a man. What's more, you can see that I have even given him a shadow. It costs money, but I do like to have something peculiar to myself."

"What!" thought the Princess. "Can I really have recovered? These baths are the best that exist! Waters certainly have an amazing power in these days. Still, I shan't go away; it's becoming lively here. I have an extraordinary liking for that stranger. I only hope his beard won't grow, for he'll go away if it does."

In the evening the Princess and the Shadow danced together in the great ball-room. She was light, but he was lighter, and such a partner she had never had. She told him what country she came from, and he knew it; he had been there, but at a time when she was not at home. He had peeped in at windows, upstairs and downstairs, and seen one thing and another, and so he could answer the Princess's questions and give her information that quite astounded her. He must be the wisest man on earth, she thought, and she conceived the greatest respect for his knowledge; and when they danced together a second time she fell in love with him. Of this the Shadow was well aware, for she gazed at him as if she would see through him. Yet once again they danced together, and she was on the point of speaking out. But she was careful. She thought of her country and realm and the many people she had to govern. "Wise he is," she thought to herself; "and that is a good point. He dances beautifully, and that's another. But is his knowledge thorough? That's equally important; that must be sifted." So she began very gradually to put to him some of the very most difficult questions, things she couldn't have answered herself, and the Shadow pulled a very odd face.

"Can't you answer me that?" asked the Princess.

"That was part of my nursery lessons," said the Shadow. "I really believe my shadow there behind the door can answer that."

"Your shadow?" said the Princess. "That would be most remarkable."

"Well, I don't say for certain that he can," said the Shadow, "but I think it, seeing he has been following me and listening to me all these years—I do think it. But your Royal Highness will permit me to call your attention to the fact that he takes such pride in passing for a man, that if he's to be in the right temper (as he must be to answer properly), he must be treated exactly like a man." "I'm perfectly agreeable to that," said the Princess. So she went across to the learned man at the door and talked to him about the sun and the moon, and about human nature, both outward and inward, and he answered her most wisely and well.

"What a man must he be who has so wise a shadow!" thought she. "It would be a real blessing for my people and my realm if I chose him for my consort. I will!"

And very soon they were agreed, the Princess and the Shadow, but no one was to know of it till she got back to her own kingdom.

"No one, not even my shadow," said the Shadow, who had his own thoughts about the matter.

And now they were in the country over which the Princess ruled when she was at home.

"Listen, my good friend," said the Shadow to the learned man. "I am now become as fortunate and as powerful as anyone can be, and now I will do something special for you. You shall always live with me in the palace, and drive out with me in my royal coach, and you shall have a hundred thousand rix-dollars a year. But you must allow yourself to be called a shadow by everyone, you must never say that you were at one time a man, and once a year, when I sit on the balcony in the sunshine and allow myself to be looked at, you must lie at my feet as a shadow ought to do. I may as well tell you that I am going to marry the Princess. The wedding is to take place this evening."

"No, no! That is really too much," said the learned man. "I won't allow it. I won't do it! It's deceiving the whole country and the Princess too. I shall tell the whole story—that I am the man and you are the shadow; you're only dressed up."

"Nobody will believe it," said the Shadow. "Do be reasonable, or I shall call the guard."

"I shall go straight to the Princess," said the learned man. "But I shall go first," said the Shadow, "and you'll go to prison." And there he had to go, for the sentries obeyed the one whom they knew the Princess was to marry.

"You are all in a tremble," said the Princess, when the Shadow came into her room. "Has anything happened? You mustn't be ill to-night; we're going to be married."

"I have had the most terrible experience that can occur to any-one," said the Shadow. "Only think of it—to be sure, a poor shadow's brain isn't equal to the strain—only think, my shadow has gone mad! He believes that he is the man and that I—just think of it—am his shadow!"

"That is awful," said the Princess; "I hope he is shut up?"

"Indeed he is. I'm afraid he'll never get the better of it."

"Poor shadow," said the Princess; "it's most unfortunate for him. It would really be a kindness to rid him of his little bit of life: indeed, when I come to think of it, I do believe it is essential that he should be quite quietly put out of the way."

"It's really very hard!" said the Shadow. "He was a faithful servant to me," and with that he seemed to sigh.

"You are a noble character," said the Princess.

That evening the whole town was illuminated, and the cannons went off "Boom!" And the soldiers presented arms. It *was* a wedding, to be sure! The Princess and the Shadow went out on the balcony to show themselves and receive one last "Hurrah!"

The learned man heard nothing of all this, for he had already been executed.

The Old House

Somewhere in the street there stood an old, old house. Almost three hundred years old it was, as you could read for yourself on the beam, where the date was carved out with tulips and hop vines round it. There stood a whole verse spelt out in the old fashion, and over every window a face was carved on the lintel, pulling a grimace. Each story stuck out a long way over the one below, and immediately under the roof there was a lead gutter with a dragon's head. The rain-water ought to have run out of its mouth, but it ran out of its stomach instead, for there was a hole in the gutter.

All the other houses in the street were very new and neat, with large window-panes and smooth walls. You could see, well enough, that they didn't want to have anything to do with the old house. You could see they were thinking: "How long is this old rubbish-heap going to stand there, making an exhibition of itself, in our street? The bay-window sticks out so that nobody can see, out of our windows, what's going on at the corner. The front doorsteps are as broad as if they led up to a palace, and as steep as if they were in a church-tower. The iron railings look like the gate on an old family vault, and they've got copper knobs, too. Vulgar, I call it."

Facing it, in the street, were more new neat houses, and they thought just the same as the rest. But at the window of one sat a little boy with fresh rosy cheeks and bright shining eyes, and he liked the old house far best, whether in sunshine or moonlight. When he stared at the place on the wall where the plaster had fallen off, he could sit and keep on finding out the most wonderful pictures. He could see exactly how the street used to look in old times, with steps and oriels and pointed gables; he could see soldiers with halberds, and gutters twisting about like dragons and serpents. It was a splendid house to look at. And over there lived an old man who went about in corduroy breeches, and had a coat with big copper buttons, and a wig that you could see really was a wig. Every morning an old servant used to come to him, who cleaned up and did errands, but except for that the old man in the corduroy breeches was quite alone in the old house. Sometimes he would come to the window and look out, and then the little boy would nod to him, and the old man would nod back; and so they became, first acquaintances and then friends, though they had never spoken to each other—but that didn't matter.

The little boy heard his father and mother say: "The old man, over there, is very comfortably off, but he is so dreadfully lonely."

Next Sunday the little boy took something and wrapped it up in a bit of paper, and went down to the front door, and when the man who went on errands came past he said to him: "I say! Will you take the old man opposite this from me; I've got two tin soldiers and this is one of them. I want him to have it, because I know he's so dreadfully lonely."

And the old servant looked quite pleased, and nodded and took the tin soldier across to the old house. After that there came a message—would the little boy like to come over himself, and pay a visit? And he got leave from his parents and went across to the old house.

And the copper knobs on the stair railing shone much brighter than usual—you'd think they had been polished up specially for this visit, and it seemed as if the carved trumpeters (for there were trumpeters carved on the door, standing in tulips) were blowing with all their might, for their cheeks looked much fatter than before. Of course, they were blowing "Tratteratra! The little boy's come! Tratteratra!" And the door opened. The whole of the front hall was hung with old portraits—knights in armour and ladies in silk gowns, and the armour rattled and the silk dresses rustled. Then there was a staircase which led a long way up and a little way down, and then you were in a balcony, which certainly was very rickety, with big holes and long cracks in it; but grass and plants grew out of them all, for the balcony, not to mention the court and the walls, was overgrown with such a lot of greenstuff that it looked like a garden. Still, it was only a balcony. Here stood old flower-pots that had faces with donkeys' ears; the flowers in them grew just as they liked. In one of them a mass of pinks hung over all the edges—that is to say, the green part did—in a multitude of shoots, and it was saying, quite plainly: "The air has stroked me, the sun has kissed me, and promised me a little flower for Sunday! A little flower for Sunday!"

Then they came into a room where the walls were covered with stamped pigskin and gold flowers printed on it.

"Gilding's soon past; Pigskin will last," said the walls. And there stood arm-chairs, ever so high-backed, and carved, and with arms on both sides. "Sit down! Sit down!" they said. "Ugh! How I do creak! I shall get the gout, I know, like that old cupboard! Gout in the back, ugh!"

And then the little boy came into the room where the bay-window was, and where the old man was sitting.

"Thank you for the tin soldier, my little friend," said the old man, "and thank you for coming over to see me."

"Thanks! Thanks!" or "Crack! Crack!" sounded from all the furniture. There was such a lot of it the pieces got in each other's way to see the little boy.

And in the middle of the wall there hung a portrait of a beautiful lady, young and gay, but dressed all in the old fashion, with powder in her hair and a dress that would stand up by itself. She didn't say either thanks or crack, but looked with her kind eyes on the little boy, who forthwith asked the old man: "Where did you get her from?"

"Round at the dealer's," said the old man. "There are a lot of pictures hanging up there; nobody knows them or cares about them, for the people are in their graves, every one of them. But in the old days I used to know her, and now she's dead and gone these fifty years."

Beneath the portrait was hung up, under glass, a withered bunch of flowers: they, too, must have been fifty years old, by the look of them; and the pendulum of the big clock went to and fro and the hands turned round, and everything in the room went on getting older—but they didn't notice.

"They say, at home," said the little boy, "that you are so dreadfully lonely." "Oh," said he; "but old memories and all they can bring with them come and pay me visits, and now you are come, too. I'm really very well off." And with that he took from a shelf a book with pictures, a whole long procession of the most marvellous coaches, such as you don't see nowadays; soldiers like the knave of clubs and guild-men with waving banners. The tailors had on theirs a pair of scissors, held by two horns, and the cordwainers had on theirs, not a boot, but an eagle that had two heads, because shoemakers must always have things so arranged that they can say: "There's a pair." Ah, that was a picture book!

Then the old man went into another room to fetch sweetmeats and apples and nuts. It really was delightful over in that old house.

"I can't bear it," said the tin soldier, who stood on the chest of drawers. "It's so lonely and so dismal; no, really, when one's lived in a family one can't accustom oneself to the life here. I can't bear it! The whole day is dreary and the evening drearier; it isn't like being over at your house, where your father and mother talked cheerfully, and you and all the rest of the nice children made such a jolly row. Dear, what a lonely time the old man has of it! Do you suppose he ever gets a kiss? Do you suppose he ever has a kind look from anybody, or a Christmas tree? Not he; he never will get anything but a funeral. I can't bear it."

"You mustn't take such a dismal view," said the little boy. "I think it's perfectly delightful here; and then, all the old memories, and all that they can bring with them, come and pay him visits."

"Yes, but I don't see them, and I know nothing about them," said the tin soldier; "I can *not* bear it."

"You've got to," said the little boy.

And now the old man came back, looking as cheerful as possible, and brought the most delicious sweetmeats and apples and nuts, and the little boy thought no more about the tin soldier.

Very happy and gay, the little boy went home, and days passed and weeks passed, and there was nodding to the old house and nodding from the old house, and then the little boy went across again; and the carved trumpeters blew: "Tratteratra! Here's the little boy! Tratteratra!" And the swords and harness on the knight's pictures rattled and the silken dresses rustled, the pigskin said its say, and the old chairs had gout in their backs. Ow! It was exactly like the first time, for over there one day and hour were just like the next.

"I can't bear it," said the tin soldier. "I have cried tears of tin! It is really too dismal here. I'd sooner go to the war, and lose my arms and legs. That would be a change, anyhow. I can *not* bear it! Now I know what it is to have visits from your old memories, and all that they can bring with them. I've had visits from mine, and you may take it from me there's no pleasure to be got out of them in the long run. By the end of it I was nearly jumping down off the drawers. I saw all you at the house over there as plain as if you were really here. It was that Sunday morning, you remember quite well, all you children were standing before the table singing your hymn as you do every morning. You were very serious, with your hands clasped, and your father and mother were just as solemn; and then the door opened and your little sister Mary, who isn't yet two years old and who always dances when she hears music or singing of any kind, was put in—she oughtn't to have been—and she began to dance, but she couldn't keep time, the notes were too long. So first she stood on one leg and bent her head this way, and then on the other leg and bent her head that way, but even so it wouldn't come right. You all kept grave, every one of you, though it was hard enough; but I laughed to myself, and so I fell off the table and got a bump which I still have, for it wasn't right of me to laugh. But all that, now, goes on in my head, and everything else that has happened to me, and that, I suppose, is the old memories and all they can bring with them. Tell me, do you still sing on Sunday? Tell me, do, something about little Mary, and how my comrade is, the other tin soldier? Ah, he's the lucky one! I cannot bear it!"

"You've been given away," said the little boy. "You've got to stay here, can't you see that?"

The old man came in with a drawer in which there were a lot of things to look at; pen-cases and scent boxes, and old cards so big and so begilded as one never sees now. Then there was opening of large drawers, and the piano was opened; it had a landscape painted inside the lid; and how husky it was when the old man played on it! Then he hummed a song: "Ah, she could sing that," said he, and nodded at the portrait he had bought at the dealer's—and the old man's eyes shone very bright.

"I'll go to the wars! I will! I will!" shrieked the tin soldier as loud as he could, and dashed himself down on the floor. Why, what had become of him? The old man searched and the little boy searched, but gone he was, and gone he remained. "I shall find him all right," said the old man, but he never did; the floor was too full of gaps and holes. The tin soldier had fallen through a crevice, and there he lay, in an open grave.

So that day passed, and the little boy went home; and the weeks went by, and several more weeks. The windows were quite frozen over. The little boy had to sit and breathe on them to make a peep-hole to look across at the old house, and there the snow was drifted into all the curly-wurlies and lettering, and lay all over the steps, as if there was nobody at home. The old man was dead.

Late in the evening a carriage drew up outside, and he was carried down to it, in his coffin, for he was to be driven out into the country to lie there in his family burial-place. So thither he drove off, but nobody followed; all his friends were dead. But the little boy kissed his hand to the coffin as it drove away.

The Old House

Some days after there was a sale at the old house, and the little boy saw from his window how the old knights and the old ladies, the flower-pots with long ears, the old chairs and the old chests, were carried off, some one way, some another. The portrait of the lady that had been found at the dealer's went back to the dealer's again, for nobody knew her any more, and nobody cared about the old picture.

In the spring the house itself was pulled down, for it was an old rubbish-heap, people said. From the street you could look right into the room and see the pigskin hanging, which was stripped off and torn to bits; and the greenstuff from the balcony hung all in disorder about the fallen beams—and then it was all cleared away.

"That's a good job," said the houses next door.

And a beautiful house was built, with large windows and smooth white walls. But in front of it, in the place where the old house had actually stood, a small garden was planted, and wild creepers grew up against the neighbour's walls. In front of the garden a large iron fence, with an iron gate, was put up, and it looked so imposing that people stopped and peeped through. The sparrows perched by scores in the creepers and talked into each others' beaks as hard as they could: but it wasn't about the old house that they talked; they couldn't remember that. So many years had gone by that the little boy had grown into a real man, and a good man, too, who was a great comfort to his parents, and now he had just married and moved with his little wife into this house where the garden was. And there he was, standing by her, while she planted a wild meadow flower which she thought very pretty. She planted it with her own little hands, and was patting the earth with her fingers. "Ow!" What was that? She had pricked herself; something sharp was sticking up out of the earth.

It was—only think! It was the tin soldier; the very one that had been lost up in the old man's room and had been tumbled hither and thither among the beams and rubbish, and had ended by lying in the earth this many a year.

The young wife wiped the soldier clean, first with a green leaf and then with her pocket handkerchief, which had a delightful smell—and the tin soldier felt as if he had been waked out of a trance.

"Let me look at him," said the young man; and he laughed and shook his head. "Why, of course it can't be the same, but he does remind me of an affair of a tin soldier I had when I was a little boy." And he went on to tell his wife about the old house and the old man, and the tin soldier he sent across to him because he was so dreadfully lonely. And he told it all exactly as it had really happened, and the young wife's eyes filled with tears at the thought of the old house and the old man.

"It's quite possible it may be the same tin soldier," said she. "I'll keep him and remember all that you've told me—but you must show me the old man's grave."

"Ah, I don't know it," he said; "and nobody knows it. All his friends were dead; nobody looked after it, and I was only a little boy."

"How dreadfully lonely he must have been!" said she.

"Dreadfully lonely," said the tin soldier; "but it is delightful not to be forgotten."

"Delightful indeed!" something called out, near by; but no one except the tin soldier saw that it was a rag of the pigskin hanging. It had no gilding left and looked like damp earth, but it had an opinion of its own, and spoke it out.

"Gilding's soon past. Pigskin will last."

However, the tin soldier did not agree.

The Happy Family

The biggest green leaf we have in this country is certainly
the burdock leaf. If you hold it in front of your little
stomach it makes a regular apron, and if you put it on
your head in rainy weather it is as good as an umbrella,
it's so monstrous big. No dock ever grows single—no, where one
grows, more grow. They make a beautiful show, and all that beauty
is food for snails. The big white snails (which gentlefolk used in
old times to have made into a fricassee, and they ate it and said,
"Ha! How good that is"; for they thought it tasted delicious), they
lived on the burdock leaves, and for that reason the burdocks used
to be sown.

Well, there was an old manor house where people no longer ate
snails. The snails had died out, but the docks hadn't died out. They
grew and grew, over all the paths and all the beds, so that you could
no longer get the upper hand of them, and it was a regular forest of
docks. Here and there stood an apple tree, or a plum; otherwise
you would never have guessed it was a garden; everywhere it was
burdocks, and among them lived the two last snails, who were very,
very old. They didn't know themselves how old they were, but
they could quite well remember that there had been many more of
them, and that they came of a family from foreign lands, and that
the whole forest had been planted for them and theirs. They had
never been outside it, but they knew that there was something in
the world besides it, which was called the manor house, and that
there you were boiled and you turned black and then you were laid
on a silver dish; but what happened after that nobody knew. For
the rest, what it felt like to be boiled and put on a silver dish they
couldn't imagine, but it was bound to be delightful, and was extremely distinguished. Neither the cockchafer, nor the toad, nor
the earthworm, whom they questioned about it, could give them

any information, for none of them had ever been boiled or put on a silver dish.

The old white snails were the most distinguished people in the world—that they knew. And the forest existed for them, and the manor house existed in order that they might be boiled and put on a silver dish.

Well, they lived a very solitary and happy life, and since they had no children they had adopted a small common snail whom they brought up as their own. But the little one would not grow, for he was a common snail. However, the old people, and especially the mother, thought she could see he was getting on, and she asked father, if he couldn't see it himself, to feel the little snail's shell; and he felt it and agreed that mother was right.

One day there was a heavy shower.

"Hark how it drum-rum-rums on the docks," said the father snail.

"There's drops coming, too," said the mother. "Look, they're trickling right down the stalk! You'll see, it will be wet here. I'm glad we have our good houses, and the little one has his, too. Really, more has been done for us than for all the rest of creation; anyone can see we are the gentry of the world. We have houses from our birth, and the dock forest has been planted for us. I should like to know how far it extends and what there is outside it."

"There's nothing outside it," said the father. "No one can be better off anywhere than here, and I have nothing to wish for."

"Well," said the mother, "I *should* like to go to the manor house and be boiled and put on a silver dish. That's what happened to all our ancestors, and you may be sure there's something special about it."

"The manor house has very probably fallen down," said father, "or else the dock forest has grown over it so that the people can't get out. There's no sort of hurry about it, but you are always so terribly impetuous, and the little one is beginning to take after you. Hasn't he taken only three days to crawl up that stalk? It makes me giddy to look up at him."

"You mustn't be hard on him," said mother; "he creeps very carefully. He's a great joy to us, and we old people have nothing else to live for. But now, have you thought about this: where we can get a wife for him? Don't you think that somewhere, deep in the forest, there must be someone of our family?"

"Black snails enough, I'm sure there are," said the old man. "Black snails without houses—but that's very poor work, and they have silly notions—still, we could commission the ants; they run to and fro as if they'd got something to do, and surely they would know of a wife for our little snail."

"I know the fairest of all, for certain," said the ants; "but I'm afraid it won't do, for she's a Queen."

"That makes no difference," said the old man. "Has she a house?"

"She has a palace," said the ants; "the most splendid ant palace, with seven hundred passages."

"Much obliged," said the mother; "our son shan't go into an ant heap! If you don't know of anything better we will commission the white midges; they fly far and wide in rain and sunshine, and they know the dock forest inside and out."

"We've got a wife for him," said the midges. "A hundred man-steps from here, on a gooseberry bush, there sits a little snail with a house. She's quite alone and old enough to be married; it's hardly a hundred man-steps."

"Well, let her come to him," said the old couple; "he owns a dock forest, and she has but a bush."

So they fetched the little lady snail. It was eight days before she arrived, but that was just the prettiest thing about it; it was plain to be seen she was of the right sort.

The wedding took place accordingly. Six glow-worms supplied the lighting, as best they could. Otherwise the affair was very quiet, for the old snails could not bear carousing and merriment. But a beautiful speech was made by the mother snail (father couldn't speak, he was too much moved) and they bequeathed the young people the whole dock forest, and said, as they always had said, that it was the best thing in the world, and that if they lived uprightly and honestly, and multiplied, they and their children would some day go to the manor house and be boiled black and laid on a silver dish.

When the speech was finished the old people retired into their houses and came out no more. They slept. The young snail couple ruled the forest and had a numerous progeny, but were never boiled and never attained the silver dish. So they concluded that the manor house had fallen down and that all the people in the world had died out, and as nobody contradicted them, it must have been true.

And the rain beat on the dock leaves and played the drum for them, and the sun shone to colour the forest for them, and they were very happy, and the whole family was happy; and that's a fact.

The Shirt Collar

There was once a fine gentleman, the whole of whose equipment consisted of a boot-jack and a comb, but he had the finest shirt Collar in the world, and it is about this Collar that we are to hear the history. He was now of an age to think of marrying, and it so happened that at the wash he met with garter.

"Dear me," said the Collar; "never have I seen any one so slender, so refined, so soft or so charming. Might I ask your name?"

"That I shall not tell you," said the Garter.

"Where do you reside?" asked the Collar.

But the Garter was very shy, and thought the question an awkward one to answer.

"You must be a girdle," said the Collar; "a sort of inner girdle! I see, I see; you serve both for use and ornament, little lady."

"You must not address me," said the Garter. "I do not think I have given you any encouragement to do so."

"Oh, if anyone is as beautiful as you," said the Collar, "that is encouragement enough."

"Do not come too near me," said the Garter; "you look so much like a man."

"Well, yes, I am a fine gentleman," said the Collar. "I own a boot-jack and a comb." Now this was really not the truth; it was his master who owned them, but he was boasting.

"Don't come near me!" said the Garter. "I'm not accustomed to it."

"Miss Prim!" said the Collar. They were then taken out of the tub, starched, and hung on a chair in the sun, and afterwards laid on the ironing board. Then came the hot iron.

"Lady!" said the Collar. "Little widow lady, I'm getting quite hot, a change is coming over me! All my folds are being flattened out. You'll burn a hole in me. Will you be mine?" "Rag!" said the iron, passing proudly over the collar; she fancied herself a steam engine travelling along the rails and dragging a train. "Rag!" said she. The Collar had become ravelled at the corners, so now came the paper-scissors, to cut the ravelling off.

"Oh!" said the Collar. "You are, of course, the Première Danseuse. How you do stretch your legs; the most charming thing I ever saw. No human being can do the like."

"I know that," said the Scissors.

"You deserve to be a countess," said the Collar. "My whole property consists of a fine gentleman, a boot-jack and a comb. Oh, were I but a count!"

"Are you proposing to me?" said the Scissors, much annoyed, and gave him a smart cut; so he was dismissed from service.

"I suppose I must try the comb," said the Collar. "It's very remarkable how you keep all your teeth, little lady! Have you never thought of becoming engaged?"

"Yes, to be sure I have," said the comb. "I'm engaged to the boot-jack."

"Engaged?" said the Collar. There was nobody left to propose to, so he took to despising the whole business.

A long time passed by, and the Collar found himself in a box, at the paper mill, with a vast collection of rags, the fine ones by themselves and the coarse by themselves, as is right and proper. All of them had a great deal to tell, but the Collar most of all, for he was regular prating Jack.

"I've had a terrible lot of sweethearts," he said; "I hadn't a moment's peace. In my time I was a fine gentleman—starched, too. I had a boot-jack and a comb, which I never used. You ought to have seen me then; seen me when I was laid aside. I shall never forget my first love! A girdle she was, most delicate and soft and charming. She threw herself into a washing-tub for love of me. Yes, and there was a widow, who was burning hot, but I let her alone and she turned black. And there was a première danseuse; she gave me the scar I carry now—she was so jealous. My own comb, too, fell in love with me, and lost all her teeth from unrequited affection. Yes, I've had many such experiences; but what caused me most pain is the Garter—I should say the girdle—who went into the washing-tub. I've a great deal on my conscience, and I'm really desirous of being made into white paper."

And so they were; all the rags were made into white paper, but the Collar was made into precisely this bit of white paper you see here, on which this story is printed; and that's because he boasted so fearfully in his later days of what never happened. And we must take care not to behave like that, for we really can never be sure that we shan't get into the rag box, one of these days, and be turned into white paper and the whole of our story printed on us, even the most private bits, and be obliged to run about telling it, like the Collar.

The Story of the Year

It was late in January, and a fearful snowstorm. The snow came flying in a drifting whirl through streets and lanes. The outside of the window-panes was fairly plastered over with it, and it plumped down from the roofs in masses, and caused a stampede among the people. They rushed, they flew into each other's arms, clasped each other tight for a moment, and for just so long got a firm foothold. Carriages and horses were powdered all over; the servants turned their backs to the carriages and rode backwards against the wind, foot passengers took care to keep in the lee of some cart which could only move slowly along in the deep snow; and when at last the storm sank to rest, and a narrow path had been cleared along the house-fronts, people when they met face to face stood still in it. Neither liked to take the first step and walk into the deep snow, so that the other could step by. Silent they stood, till finally by a sort of tacit agreement, each of them sacrificed one leg and let that plunge into the snowdrift.

Towards evening it became dead calm. The sky looked as if it had been swept and made more lofty and transparent: the stars looked brand new, and some of them were ever so blue and bright —and there was a cracking frost—anyhow, the top layer of snow managed to become so hard that by the morning it could bear the sparrows. They hopped about, up here and down there, wherever any shovelling had been done, but little enough could they find to eat, and how they did freeze!

"Twit!" said one of them to another. "This is what people call the New Year. Why, it's worse than the old one; we might just as well have stuck to that. I'm dissatisfied with the whole thing, and I've every reason to be."

"Yes, just now the humans were running about, shooting in the New Year," said a little small frost-nipped sparrow; "they smashed pots against the doors and were clean out of their wits with delight at the old year having gone; and I was glad too, for I expected we should get some warm weather. But nothing's come of it all; it's freezing a deal harder than before. The humans have got wrong in their reckoning."

"That they have," said a third. He was old, and white on the top of his head. "They've got hold of something they call the Almanack. It's some of their own invention, I suppose, and everything's to go according to that; only it doesn't. When the Spring comes, then the year will begin. That's Nature's order, and that's what I go by."

"But when will the Spring come?" asked the others.

"It'll come when the stork comes: but there's a good deal of uncertainty about him, and here in the town there's nobody that knows anything about it. They understand that better out in the country. Shall we fly out there and wait? One'll be nearer the Spring there."

"Yes, that may be all very well," said one of them who had gone about chirping for some time without really saying anything. "I've got some advantages here in the town which I'm afraid I might miss out there. Round here is a house with a family of humans who've had the very sensible notion of building three or four flower-pots into the wall with the big mouth inside and the bottom out, and in the bottom there's been cut a hole big enough for me to

fly in and out of. I and my husband have got a nest there, and all our young ones have flown out of that. The human family have, of course, arranged it all so as to have the pleasure of looking at us, else they'd never have done it. They throw out breadcrumbs, too —for their own satisfaction—and so we get our food: one is provided for in a kind of way—and so I think I shall stop, and my husband too—though we're very much dissatisfied—still, we shall stop."

"And we shall fly out into the country to see whether the Spring isn't coming." And off they flew.

And out in the country it was proper winter: freezing several degrees harder than in the town. The keen wind blew far over the snow-covered fields. The farmer with his great mittens on sat in his sledge and beat himself with his arms to get the cold out of them. His whip lay across his lap; the skinny horses galloped till they smoked again: the snow crackled, and the sparrows hopped in the ruts and froze. "Twit, when's the Spring coming? It stays so long."

"So long!" rang a voice far over the fields from the high slope covered with snow. And it might have been an echo that one heard; or, again, it might have been the voice of the strange old man who sat there on the top of the snowdrift in the wind and weather. He was quite white—like a farmer in a white frieze coat—with long white hair, white beard, very pale, with large bright eyes.

"Who's that chap over there?" asked the sparrows.

"I know that," said an old Raven who was sitting on the gate-post, and who was condescending enough to recognize that we are all little birds in God's sight, and so entered into talk with the sparrows and explained matters. "I know who that old chap is. That's Winter, the old man from last year. He's not dead, as the Almanack says; no, he's more like a regent for the little Prince Spring, who's coming. Yes, Winter holds the reins. Ugh, it makes you crackle, don't it, little ones?"

"Yes, now, isn't that just what I was saying?" said the littlest sparrow. "That Almanack's nothing but a make-up of the humans: it isn't arranged according to Nature. They ought to leave that to us—us that's organized more delicate!"

And a week went by—almost two weeks. The wood was black, the frozen lake lay heavily still and looked like lead that has cooled. The clouds—no, they were not clouds, they were wet ice-cold mists —hung over all the land. The big black crows went in flights without a caw. It seemed as if all things slept. . . . There shot a sunbeam out over the lake, and it shone like molten tin. The snow on the fields and on the slopes did not glisten as it used—but the white shape, Winter himself, still sat there with his gaze turned steadily towards the South. He took no note of how the snow carpet sank, as it were, into the earth, how here and there a little grass-green space emerged, and in a moment was alive with sparrows.

"Tweet, tweet, is it coming, the Spring?"

"Spring!" It rang out over field and meadow and through the dark brown woodlands where the moss shone fresh and green on the tree-trunks And through the air came flying from the South the first two storks. On the back of each sat a fair little child—a boy and a girl; and they kissed the earth in greeting; and where they set foot, white blossoms grew up from beneath the snow. Hand in hand they went up to the old ice-man, Winter, and laid themselves on his breast for yet another greeting. And in that instant all three were hidden from sight, and the whole landscape with them: a thick mist, close and heavy, veiled all things. A little after it cleared a wind sprang up. Onward it came, with mighty gusts, and cleared the fog away. The sun shone out warm. Winter himself had vanished. The fair children of the Spring sat on the throne of the Year.

"That's what I call New Year," said the sparrow. "Now, no doubt, we shall get our rights again, and some compensation for the hard winter."

Whichever way the two children turned, green buds shot out from bush and tree, the grass grew taller, the sown fields showed brighter and brighter green, and all about her the little girl scattered flowers. She had multitudes of them in her lap, they seemed to teem forth of it, it was always full, however lavishly she strewed them; in her haste she shook a whole snow-fall of blossom out over the apple and peach trees, so that they stood clad in full beauty before they had properly got their green leaves. And she clapped her hands and the boy clapped his, and out came birds, one could not tell whence, and all of them twittered and sang: "Spring is come!"

It was a lovely sight, and many an old granny came out of her house door into the sunshine and straightened herself up and looked out over the yellow blossoms that decked all the meadows just exactly as they had in her young days. The world had turned young again. "Blessed weather it is out here to-day!" said she.

The forest was still brown-green, bud beside bud, but the woodruff was out, fresh and fragrant, the violets stood there in crowds, and there were anemones, cowslips and oxslips; nay, in every blade of grass was there sap and strength; it was just a broidered carpet to sit upon, and there sat the bride and bridegroom of the Spring and held each other by the hand and sang and smiled and grew.

A gentle rain from heaven fell on them, but they marked it not.

The raindrops and the tears of joy were all one. The bride and bridegroom kissed, and in a moment the forest sprang to life. When next the sun rose, all the woods were green.

Hand in hand went the bridal pair beneath the fresh waving roof of leaves, where only the rays of sunlight and the flecking shadows varied the tints of green. A virginal purity and a refreshing fragrance were in the delicate leaves; clear and living babbled river and brook in and out of the velvet-green reeds and over the dappled stones. "Full for ever and always it is and it shall be," said all Nature. And the cuckoo called and the lark sang, and it was pleasant Spring. All the same, the willows kept woolly mittens over their flowers: they were so horribly cautious, and that is most tiresome.

And so days passed by and weeks passed by, and the heat came sweltering down. Hot waves of air passed through the corn, which grew yellower and yellower. The white lotus of the North on the woodland lakes spread out its great green leaves over the watery mirror, and the fish took shelter beneath them; and on the lee-side of the wood, where the sun blazed on the farmhouse wall and warmed the new-sprung roses through and through—where the cherry-tree boughs hung full of juicy black, almost sun-hot fruit, the beautiful Queen of Summer sat and sang—even she whom we have seen a child and a bride; and she gazed at the dark climbing clouds which in great billows like mountains, blue-black and heavy, were rising higher and higher. From three sides they gathered: then downward and down, like a sea enchanted and turned to stone, they lowered themselves toward the forest, where everything was hushed as under a spell. Every breeze was laid, every bird was still: there was a gravity, an expectation, over all Nature. But on road and path everyone was hurrying—driving, riding or on foot—to get under shelter. All at once it lightened as if the sun had burst forth, dazzling, blinding, consuming, and there was darkness again, with a rolling crash. The rain poured down in torrents—it was night—then day—stillness—then a roar. The young brown-plumaged reeds in the marsh swayed in long billows, the boughs of the forest were veiled in sheets of rain—darkness came—then light—silence—and then a crash. Grass and corn lay beaten down, deluged, as if they could never rise again. Quickly the rain dwindled to single drops, the sun shone out, and from blade and leaf the water drops glistened like pearls; birds sang, fishes leapt up from the stream, midges danced: and out on a rock in the salt, rain-whipped sea-water sat Summer himself, the strong man with the vigorous limbs, his hair drenched—revived by the cool bath he sat in the hot sunshine. All Nature about him was revived, everything was gay, strong and beautiful. It was Summer, warm lovely Summer.

Fresh and sweet was the scent that came from the thick-grown clover fields. The bees hummed there about the ancient moot-place. The brambles twined upward around the altar stone which, washed by the rain, glistened in the sunshine; and from it out flew the queen bee with her swarm, and made wax and honey. No one saw them but the Summer and his mighty spouse; it was for them that the altar-table stood covered with the thank-offerings of Nature.

And the evening sky gleamed like pure gold—no cathedral dome so nobly decked—and the moon shone betwixt the glow of evening and the glow of dawn. It was summer-time.

And days passed and weeks passed. The bright sickles of the harvesters shone in the cornfields. The branches of the apple trees bent low beneath their red and yellow fruit, the hops smelt delicious, hanging in great clusters, and under the hazel bushes, where the nuts grew in heavy bunches, rested the husband and the wife, Summer and his spouse, grown grave.

"What wealth!" said she. "All round us is blessing, homely and good: and yet I cannot tell why, I long for rest—quiet—I know no word for it. They are ploughing the fields all afresh; more and yet more mankind is after gaining. Look, the storks are gathering in groups and following the plough at a distance—the bird of Egypt, that brought us through the air. You remember the time we two came here as children into the land of the North? We brought flowers, fair sunshine and green leafage. The wind has dealt roughly with them now. They are growing brown and dark like the trees of the South; but they do not, like those, bear golden fruit."

"Is that what you would see?" said Summer. "Then have your pleasure." And he raised his arm, and the leaves of the forest were tinted with red and with gold, a blaze of colour came over all the woodland: the rose bushes shone with fiery hips, the elder-trees were hung with masses of heavy dark berries, the wild chestnuts fell ripened out of the dark-green husks, and within the wood the violets blossomed a second time.

But the Queen of the Year grew yet more quiet and pale. "It blows cold," she said, "the night brings damp mists. I long for the land of my childhood."

And she saw the storks take their flight—every one of them—and she stretched her hands out after them. She looked up at the nests that stood empty; in one the tall cornflower had grown up, in another the yellow charlock, as if the nest were only meant for a shelter and fence for them, and up came the sparrows.

"Twit, what's gone with the gentlefolk? Why, they can't bear the wind blowing on 'em, so they've left the country! A pleasant journey to 'em." Yellower and yellower grew the leaves in the wood: one after another they fell. The storms of Autumn were sounding; it was late in harvest-time. And on the yellow fallen leaves lay the Queen of the Year, gazing with gentle eyes toward the shining stars, and her husband stood by her. A gust of wind whirled up the leaves—they fell to earth again, and she was gone. Only a butterfly, the last of the year, was fluttering through the chilly air. And the wet mists came and the icy blast, and the long dark nights. The King of the Year stood there with snow-white hair, but he knew it not, he thought it was the snowflakes that fell from the clouds. A thin covering of snow lay far and wide over the green fields.

And the church bells rang out for Christmas.

"The birthday bells are ringing," said the King of the Year. Soon will the new King and Queen be born, and I shall have won my rest like her—rest in the shining star."

And in the fresh green fir-wood, where the snow lay, the Angel of Christmas stood, blessing the young trees that were to deck his feast.

"Joy in the house and beneath the green boughs," said the old King of the Year—a few weeks had aged him into a snow-white veteran. "The time hastens on towards my rest, and the young couple of the year will soon take the sceptre and crown."

"Still the power is yours," said the Angel of Christmas, "the power and not the rest. Let the snow lie and keep the young seed warm all about you. Learn to endure that homage should be paid to another while yet you are the Prince: learn to be forgotten and yet go on living. The time of your freedom will come when the Spring comes."

"When will the Spring come?" Winter asked.

"It will come when the stork comes."

And with white locks and snow-white hair, Winter sat, cold as ice, old and bent, yet strong as the winter wind and the hardness of ice, high up on the snowdrift of the upland, gazing southward ever, just as the Winter before had sat and gazed. The ice cracked, the snow creaked, the skaters circled on the bright lakes, and ravens and crows stood sharply out against the white background. There was no stir of wind, and in the still air Winter clenched his fists, and the ice grew fathoms thick between shore and shore.

Then out came the sparrows from the town again and asked: "Who's that old man over there?" And the raven sat there again— or a son of his, which comes to the same—and told them: "That's Winter, the old man from last year. He's not dead, as the Almanacks say, but regent for the Spring who's coming."

"When is the Spring coming?" said the sparrows. "When it does, we shall have a good time, and better management. The old one is no good at all."

And in silent thought Winter beckoned to the black leafless wood, where every tree showed clear the beautiful form and curve of its branches; and in their winter slumber the icy mists of the clouds lowered themselves. The Ruler was dreaming of the days of his youth and of his manhood; and towards dawn the whole forest stood fair with hoar frost. It was Winter's dream of Summer. The sunshine melted the snow from the branches.

"When is the Spring coming?" asked the sparrows.

"Spring!" It came sounding like an echo from the upland where the snow lay. The sun shone out, warmer and warmer, the snow shrank, the birds twittered: "Spring is coming!"

And aloft through the air the first stork came flying; a second followed; a fair child sat on the back of each, and they lighted down upon the green field, and they kissed the earth, and they kissed the old silent man, and like Moses on the Mount he vanished, borne away by the misty cloud.

The Story of the Year was finished.

"That's all very fine and large," said the sparrows, "and it's also extremely pretty; but it doesn't agree with the Almanack, so it must be wrong."

It's Perfectly Certain

"That's a terrible story," said a hen—it was in a part of the town where the affair had not taken place—"that's a terrible story about the hen-house! I shouldn't dare to sleep alone at night! It's a good thing there are so many of us on the perch." She proceeded to tell it, so that the feathers of the other hens stood on end, and the cock let his comb droop. "It's perfectly certain!"

But we will begin at the beginning, and this took place in a hen-house in another quarter of the town. The sun had set, and the hens had flown up to roost. One of them—she had white feathers and short legs—laid her regulation egg, and was a respectable hen in every way. Just as she got on the perch, she pecked at herself with her beak, and a little feather fell off her.

"There it goes," said she; "the more I peck myself the prettier I get!" It was said, to be sure, in fun, for she was the merry one among the hens, being for the rest, as I said, highly respectable, and thereupon she went to sleep.

It was dark all round; hen sat by hen, and the one that sat next to her did not go to sleep. She heard and she didn't hear, as indeed one must in this world if one is to live in peace and quiet, but she couldn't help saying to her neighbour: "Did you hear what was said just then? I name no names, but there is a hen who plucks herself to improve her looks. If I were a cock I should despise her."

Now just above the hens sat Mrs. Owl with her owl husband and owl children. They had sharp ears in that family; they heard every word the neighbour hen said, and they rolled their eyes, and the mother owl fanned herself with her wings. "Pray don't listen—but you must have heard what was said just then. I heard it with my own ears, and one's bound to hear a lot before they fall off! There's one of the hens who has so totally forgotten what is becoming for

267

a hen that she sits there pecking off all her feathers and allowing the cock to look on."

"*Prenez garde aux enfants,*" said the father owl. "That's not a thing for the children to hear."

"But I must tell just the owl over the way; she is such a very well conducted bird." And off flew the mother.

"Hoo hoo! Oo hoo!" they both hooted down to the pigeons in the pigeon-house, over the way: "Have you heard? Have you heard? There's a hen who has plucked off all her feathers for love of the cock! She'll freeze to death, if she's not dead already. Oo hoo!"

"Where, where?" cooed the pigeons.

"In the yard over the way. I as good as saw it myself. It's almost too improper a story to tell; but it's perfectly certain."

"I'm sure, I'm sure of it; every single word," said the pigeons, and cooed down to their own hen-house: "There's a hen—some say there are two—who have plucked off all their feathers so as not to look like the rest, and attract the cock's notice that way. It's a risky game! One can easily catch a chill and die of fever, and they *are* dead, both of them."

"Wake up! Wake up!" crowed the cock, flying up on to the board fence. He was still a bit drowsy, but he crowed for all that. "There are three hens who have died of unrequited affection for a cock; they've plucked all their feathers off. It's an ugly story. I won't keep it to myself. Pass it on!" "Pass it on!" squeaked the bats. And the hens clucked and the cocks crowed: "Pass it on! Pass it on!" And so the story went from one hen-house to another, and finally back to the place from which it had really started.

"There are five hens", it ran, "who have all plucked their feathers off to show which of them has got thinnest from affection for the cock! And after that they pecked each one another till the blood came and all fell down dead, to the shame and scandal of their family and the grave damage of their owners." And the hen who had dropped the little loose feather naturally did not recognize her own story, and as she was a respectable hen, she said: "I despise those hens. But, alas, there are many of that class! A thing like this ought not to be hushed up, and I shall do what I can to let this story get into the papers, and be known through the whole country. That is what these hens and their families deserve!"

It did get into the papers, and was printed, and it is perfectly certain: one little feather can turn into five hens.

Soup from a Sausage-Peg

"That was a first-class dinner we had yesterday," said an old lady Mouse to another, who had not been at the party. "I sat twenty-first from the old Mouse King, and that's not so bad either. Let me tell you the bill of fare, now; it was extremely well arranged. Mouldy bread, bacon-rind, tallow candle and sausage, and then the same all over again; just as good as having two dinners. The whole tone was comfortable, and the talk as lively as at a family party. Nothing whatever was left over but the sausage-pegs. So we talked about them, and the old saying came up about 'making soup out of a sausage-peg'. Everyone, of course, had heard of it, but nobody had ever tasted the soup, let alone knowing how to make it. A very neat toast was proposed—the health of the inventor—he deserved to be made President of the Board of Guardians. Wasn't that clever? And then the old Mouse King got up and promised that the young Mouse who should make the soup most savoury should be his Queen, and a year and a day was allowed for thinking it out."

"That wasn't bad either," said the second Mouse. "But how do you make this soup?"

"Ah, how *do* you make it?" They were all asking that, all the lady mice, young and old alike. Everyone would like well enough to become Queen, but they didn't fancy the trouble of going out into the wide world and learning the process; and, of course, that was necessary: and then again it isn't given to everybody to leave their family and the old chimney corner. You don't run across cheese-rind or smell bacon-rind every day abroad; no, no, one may end by being starved, or even perhaps eaten up alive by a cat."

It was considerations of that sort which deterred most of them from setting out in search of knowledge, and only four mice presented themselves for this expedition; they were young and lively, but poor. They meant to go each of them to one of the four quarters of the world, and it would depend on which of them fortune favoured. Each took a sausage-peg with her to remind her of the object of the journey; it would serve them for a pilgrim's staff. They set out early in May, and early in May the next year they returned, but only three of them. The fourth neither sent any message nor was any news of her heard, and now was the day of decision.

"Somewhat of sorrow is ever mingled with one's brightest joys," said the Mouse King. Nevertheless, he issued orders to invite all the mice for many miles around to meet in the kitchen. The three travelled mice stood in a row by themselves; for the fourth, who was missing, a sausage-peg hung with black crape was set up. No one dared to give their opinion before the three had spoken, and the Mouse King had said whatever more was necessary.

Now we shall hear all about it.

II

What the first little Mouse had seen and learned on her travels

"When I set out into the wide world", said the first little Mouse, "I thought, as many do at my time of life, that I had absorbed all the wisdom of the world, but one has not done that. A year and a day must pass before that happens. I went to sea at once: I went aboard a ship that was to sail for the North. I had heard that at sea the cook must understand how to get along, but it's easy enough to get along when you have unlimited sides of bacon, tubs of salt meat and musty flour. You live in luxury, but you learn nothing that will help to get soup out of a sausage-peg. Many days and nights we sailed; we had pitching and tossing, and we had wet. When we got to our destination I left the vessel. It was far up in the North."

"It's a strange experience to leave one's own chimney corner at home and go on board a ship where there is also some sort of a chimney corner, and suddenly find yourself more than a hundred miles away in a strange country. There were lonely forests of fir and birch; how strong the scent of them was! I don't like it. The wild plants, too, smelt so spicy that I sneezed and thought of sausage. There were great woodland lakes, whose water was clear when you were near it, but seen from a distance was as black as ink. On them floated white swans. I took them for foam, they lay so still, but later I saw them fly and I saw them walk, and then I knew them; they belong to the goose tribe, you can see it by their gait; nobody can get away from his descent. I kept to my own sort, and joined the wood and field mice, who by the way know terribly little, especially about cookery, which, of course, was what I was travelling abroad to look into. It was such an extraordinary idea to them that anyone could imagine making soup from a sausage-peg that it went at once through the whole forest; but that this problem could be solved they reckoned an impossibility, and least of all did I think that there on that very night I should be initiated into the matter. It was midsummer, and that, they said, was why the forest was so fragrant, the herbs so spicy, the lakes so clear and yet so dark, with the white swans upon them. On the outskirts of the forest, among three or four houses, a pole had been raised, tall as a mainmast, and at the top of it hung a wreath and a ribbon; it was the Maypole: girls and lads danced round it and sang, vying with the fiddler's music. It went merrily on till near sunset, and in the moonlight, but I didn't join them: what has a little Mouse to do at a forest dance? No, I sat in the soft moss, holding my sausage-peg. The moon was shining brightest on one spot where there was a tree covered with moss so delicate—why, I could almost venture to say as delicate as the fur of our Mouse King, but its colour was green, such that it did one's eyes good to look at it. Thither all at once there came marching up a number of the smartest little beings, no bigger than the height of my knee. They looked like human beings, but they were better proportioned. They called themselves Elves, and their clothes were of flower petals set with the wings of flies and midges—really very pretty. At first it seemed as if they were looking for something—I didn't know what—and then a few of them came up to me, and the leader of them pointed to my sausage-peg and said: 'That's just the sort of thing we want. It's cut out for it, it's admirable!' and he became more and more lost in admiration as he looked at my pilgrim staff. 'Lend, yes, but not keep,' I said. 'No, not keep,' they all said. They took hold of the peg, which I let go, and danced off with it to the plot of delicate moss, where they planted the peg right in the middle of the green. They too wanted a Maypole, and the one they had now got suited as well as if it had been cut out for the purpose. Next it was dressed out. Ah, it was a sight, I can tell you!

"Tiny spiders spun gold thread about it, and hung up fluttering scarves and flags of the finest weaving, and bleached to such snowy whiteness in the moonshine that it dazzled my eyes. Then the Elves took colours from butterfly wings and dropped them upon the white threads, and flowers and diamonds shone out, so that I could no longer recognize my sausage-peg. The like of such a Maypole as it made, I am sure, was nowhere to be found. Then there came, first the noblest company of the Elves, who were quite unclad. Nothing more delicate was ever seen. I was invited to look on at the show, but from a distance, since I was too big for them. Then the music struck up. It sounded as if a thousand glass bells were ringing, full and strong. I thought it must be the swans that were singing; I thought too that I could hear the cuckoo and the thrush, and at last it seemed that the whole forest was chiming in—voices of children, ringing of bells, song of birds, the sweetest melodies: and all this loveliness was ringing out from the Elves' Maypole. It was a whole peal of bells, and it came from my sausage-peg. Never could I have believed that this could come out of it, but that depends, of course, on whose hands it is in. Really, I was so moved that I wept such tears as a little Mouse can shed, out of pure delight.

"The night was all too short, but up there at that season it is but brief. With the dawn there came a breath of air; the mirror of the forest lake was ruffled, all the delicate waving scarves and banners flew off into the air, the swaying arbours of cobweb, the suspension bridges and balustrades, or whatever they were, that had been thrown across from leaf to leaf vanished into nothing. Six Elves came and brought me my sausage-peg, and asked if I had any wish that they could grant me. So I begged them to tell me how one can make soup from a sausage-peg.

" 'How do we manage it?' said the leader, and he laughed. 'Why, you've just seen! You hardly recognized your sausage-peg, did you?' 'Oh, you mean in that way?' said I, and then told them straight out the object of my travels, and what was expected from them by those at home. 'What pleasure', said I, 'can the Mouse King and the whole realm derive from my having seen all this beauty? I can't shake it out of my sausage-peg and say: "Look, here's the peg, now the soup will come." That, to be sure, would be a sort of dessert when people had eaten their fill.' Then the Elf dipped his tiny finger into a blue violet, and said to me: 'Attend now! I will anoint your staff, and when you get home to the Mouse King's palace, do you touch with the staff your King's warm breast. At once violets will blossom out all over the staff, even in the depth of winter. There! You've got something to take home, and a little more into the bargain.' " But before the little Mouse told what this little more was, she pointed her staff towards the breast of the King, and there did actually burst out the most delicious bouquet of flowers, smelling so strong that the King ordered the mice who stood nearest the fireplace to stick their tails into the fire so that one could get a little scent of burning, for the smell of the violets was too strong to be borne, and indeed was not generally liked.

"But what was the 'little more' that you spoke of?" asked the Mouse King.

"Ah!" said the little Mouse. "That is what people call an effect." She turned the sausage-peg round, and no flowers were to be seen. She now held the bare peg, which she raised in the fashion of a conductor's baton. "The violets are for sight, smell and touch (the Elf told me). Something yet remains for hearing and for taste." She began beating time, and music was heard, not such as rang out in the forest at the Elves' festival; no, rather such as is heard in the kitchen. Upon my word, there was a Cooking! All at once it came, as if the wind were roaring down every chimney. Kettles and pots boiled over, the shovel thundered against the copper—and then in an instant all was still, you heard only the subdued song of the tea-kettle—a strange song, of which you could not tell in the least whether it was the end or the beginning that you heard. Then the little pot boiled and the big pot boiled—one taking no notice of the other—it really seemed as if the pots had no sense at all. The little Mouse brandished her baton more and more wildly: the pots foamed, bubbled, boiled over, the wind roared, the chimney screamed—whew! It was so alarming that the little Mouse herself dropped her stick.

"A very odd soup!" said the Mouse King. "Will it not be served up now?"

"That is all," said the little Mouse, and made a curtsey.

"That all? Very well, then, let us hear what the next one has to say," said the Mouse King.

III

What the second little Mouse had to tell

"I was born in the palace library," said the second Mouse. "Neither I nor most of my family have ever known the privilege of getting into the dining-room, let alone the larder; it was only on my travels and here to-day that I have ever seen a kitchen. It is true that we often suffered from hunger in the library, but we acquired a great deal of information. The rumour reached us up there of the royal offer of a prize for making soup out of a sausage-peg, whereupon my old grandmother brought out a manuscript. She couldn't read it, but she had heard it read, and in it was written: 'If one is a poet, one can make soup out of a sausage-peg.' She asked me if I was a poet. I said I was not, and she said that in that case I ought to go and take steps to become one. I asked what the requirements were, for it was just as difficult for me to discover as to make the soup. But Granny had heard people read books, and she said that there were three principal things necessary: 'Intelligence, Imagination, and Sensibility.' 'You go and get these into you, and you will be a poet, and you will win through safe enough with the sausage-peg.' So I set forth westward into the wide world to become a poet.

"Intelligence, I knew, is, in every affair, the most important. The other two qualities are not in such estimation; so I made for intelligence in the first place; now where does it reside? 'Go to the ant and become wise,' so said a great king in Jewry—I knew that from the library, and I did not stop till I got to the nearest large ant-hill and lay in wait, to become wise.

"They are very respectable folk, the ants; they are pure intelligence, and with them everything is like a sum that is added up right. To work and to lay eggs, they say, is to live in the present and provide for the future, and that is what they do. They divide themselves into clean and dirty ants; rank is denoted by a number. The Ant Queen is number one, and her opinion is the only correct one, for she has absorbed all wisdom, an important thing for me to know. She said a great deal that was so clever that it appeared to me to have no sense. She said that their ant hill was the highest thing in the world; yet close by the hill stood a tree that was higher, much higher, the fact couldn't be denied, so nobody mentioned it. One evening an ant had lost its way in that direction and crawled up the trunk—not even right up to the top, but yet higher than any ant had been before, and when it turned back and got home, it spoke in the ant hill of something much higher, that was outside. This seemed to the other ants an insult to the whole community, so this ant was condemned to wear a muzzle and remain in perpetual solitary confinement. But a short time after another ant went to this tree and made the same exploration and discovery and told of it too, as was said, with caution and vaguely; and since it was also a respected ant and one of the clean, it was believed; and when it died an egg-shell was set up as a monument to it, for the ants honoured knowledge. I saw", said the little Mouse, "how the ants continually ran about with their eggs on their backs. One of them dropped hers, and had great difficulty in getting it up again, in fact could not. Two others came and helped with all their might, so that they were dropping their own eggs, whereupon they instantly left off helping —for charity begins at home: and the Ant Queen said of the incident, that it certainly showed feeling and intelligence. 'These two things serve to place us ants at the head of rational beings. Intelligence must and should outweigh all else, and the greatest intelligence is mine.' With that she stood upon her hind legs, and was so conspicuous I could not be mistaken; and I swallowed her. 'Go to the ant and become wise.' I had got the Queen.

"I then approached the large tree I have mentioned: it was an oak, very old, with a tall stem and mighty crown. I knew that in it dwelt a living being, for a woman called a Dryad is born with the tree and dies with it. I had heard about this in the library; now I saw such a tree and such an oak-maid. She gave a dreadful shriek when she saw me so close, for she was, like all women, very much afraid of mice. Still, she had more reason to be so than others, for I could gnaw through her tree, and on it her life depended. I talked to her in a friendly and affectionate way, and she regained courage and took me on her delicate hand, and when she heard why I had come out into the wide world she promised that very likely that same evening I might get hold of one of the two treasures I was still looking for. She told me that Fantasus was a dear friend of hers, that he was as beautiful as the God of Love, and that he very often came to rest himself under the leafy branches of her tree, which then rustled above the two of them with more life than ever. He would call her his own Dryad, and her tree his own tree. Indeed, the beautiful stately gnarled oak was just after his own heart, with its roots set deep and fast in the earth, its trunk and crown rising high into the fresh air, and feeling the driving keen-aired snow and the hot sun as they should be felt. 'Yes,' she said, 'up there, the birds sing and tell of foreign lands, and on that single dead bough the stork has built a nest, which is an ornament to the tree, and one hears something about the land of the pyramids. All this Fantasus enjoys, but he isn't satisfied with that; I have to tell him myself about my life in the forest, ever since I was little and my tree was so tiny that a nettle could hide it, up till now, when it is so large and stately. Sit down now under the woodruff and take good heed; when Fantasus comes I shall be sure to find an opportunity to twitch his wing and pull a little feather out. Take that: no poet ever had a better, and that will suffice you.'

"Fantasus came, the feather was pulled out, and I seized it," said the little Mouse. "I kept it in water till it grew soft—it was still extremely hard to digest, but I got through it. It's by no means easy to eat yourself into a poet, such a quantity of stuff one has to absorb. Well, now I had two things, Intelligence and Imagination, and by their help I knew that the third thing was to be found in the library; for a great man has said and has written that there are novels whose only object is to relieve people of their superfluous tears—they are in fact a sort of sponge, soaking up Sensibility. I recollected some of these books, which had always looked to me very appetizing: they had been so much read and were so greasy, they must have soaked up an infinite quantity of force. So I returned to the library and forthwith ate practically a whole novel, that is to say the soft part, the real novel, for the rind, the binding, I left alone. After digesting this and another, I could already perceive how they were working within me. I then ate a small portion of a third, and I was a poet. So at least I told myself and told others. I had headache, stomach-ache—I don't know what aches I didn't have. Then I pondered over the stories that might be brought into connection with a sausage-peg, and my whole mind became full of pegs (the Ant Queen was possessed of no common intelligence). I thought of the man who put a white peg in his mouth and became invisible, and so did the peg. I thought of old ale with a peg in the tankard, of the saying about standing on a peg,[1] putting a peg in,[2] driving a peg into one's coffin. All my thoughts ran on pegs: a poem could be written about them if one were a poet, and a poet I am—I have worn myself out to become one. I am ready every day in the week to serve Your Majesty with a peg—a story. Very well, that is my soup."

"We will now hear the third," said the Mouse King.

There was a cry of "Pi, Pi!" at the kitchen door, and a little Mouse—it was the fourth, the one they thought was dead—rushed in and knocked down the sausage-peg with the black crape on it. She had been running night and day, had travelled by rail in goods trains when she got a chance, and yet had almost come too late. She thrust herself forward, sadly out of breath; she had lost her sausage-peg, but not her voice, and began speaking at once as if everyone was only waiting for her and only wanted to hear her, and everything else in the world was of no concern to anyone. She began talking at once, and talked herself out. So unexpected was she that nobody had a moment to make any remark about her or her speech all the time she was talking. Now we must listen.

IV

What the fourth Mouse, who spoke before the third had spoken, had to tell

"I went directly to the capital city," said she; "I don't remember the name of it, I haven't a good memory for names. I went from the

[1] Dancing attendance.   [2] Putting a spoke in anyone's wheel.

railway along with some confiscated goods, to the law courts, and there I took up with the jailer. He was talking about his prisoners, and particularly about one of them, who had made rash speeches, about which there had been endless talking and reading and writing. 'The whole thing is soup from a sausage-peg,' said he, 'but that same soup may easily cost him his knob.'

"This gave me an interest in the prisoner," said the little Mouse; "and I watched for an opportunity and slipped into his cell—there's always a hole for a mouse, even with locked doors. He looked very pale; he had a great beard and big shining eyes. His lamp smoked, but the walls were accustomed to it, it didn't make them any blacker. The prisoner had scratched pictures and verses on them— white on black—but I didn't read them. I think he found it very dull, and I was a welcome visitor. He enticed me to him with breadcrumbs and whistling, and gentle words, and was delighted with me. I trusted him, and we became friends. He shared his bread and water with me, and gave me cheese and sausage, so I lived in luxury; but it was more than anything the pleasant companionship, I may say, that attracted me. He let me run up his hand and arm right up his sleeve; let me creep into his beard; called me his little friend. I got really fond of him; an attachment like that is mutual. I forgot my mission in this wide world, and left my sausage-peg in a crack in the floor—it's there now. I decided to stay where I was, for if I went away, the poor prisoner would have nothing at all left, and that really is too little in the world. Well, I stayed, but he did not. On the last day he talked to me very sorrowfully, and gave me twice as much bread and cheese-rind as usual, and kissed his fingers to me. Then he went, and never came back. I don't know his story. 'Soup from a sausage-peg,' said the jailer, and to him I went, but I ought not to have trusted him. He took me on his hand, to be sure, but it was to put me in a cage, a treadmill. It's awful! You run and run and get no further, and they only laugh at you.

"The jailer's grand-daughter was a pretty little thing with golden-yellow curly hair and merry eyes and a laughing mouth. 'Poor little mouse,' she said, peeping into my horrid cage. She pulled out the iron pin, and I jumped down on the window-sill and out into the gutter. Free! Free! That was all I thought of, not the object of my journey. It was getting on for night when I took refuge in an old tower. There lived a watchman and an owl; I trusted neither of them, but the owl least. They're like cats, and they commit the grave error of eating mice. Still, one can be mistaken, and I was mistaken: this was a very respectable, extremely well educated old owl, who knew more than the watchman and as much as myself. The young owls tried to make a great to-do about everything, and she would say: 'Don't make soup out of a sausage-peg.' It was the severest thing she could bring herself to say, such was her affection for her family. I felt such confidence in her that I called out 'Pip!' from the crack I was sitting in. This trustfulness pleased her, and she assured me that I should be under her protection, and no creature should be allowed to hurt me; she meant to see about that herself, in winter when food got scarce. She was clever in all ways; she informed me that the watchman could not hoot without a horn, which hung on him, separate. He is inordinately proud of it, and believes he is the owl in the tower. Great cry and little wool! Soup from a sausage-peg! I begged her to give me the recipe, and she explained it to me thus. 'Soup from a sausage-peg is merely a human saying, and is understood in different ways, and everyone thinks his own way is the most correct. But the whole thing is, as a matter of fact, nothing at all.'

" 'Nothing at all,' said I, and it struck me. 'Truth is not always agreeable, but truth is above all else.' That also the owl said. I thought it over, and perceived that if I brought you that which is above all else, I should be bringing something far better than soup from a sausage-peg."

"So I hurried off to get home in time, and bring that which is highest and best, namely, the truth. The race of mice is an enlightened one, and the King is at the head of them all. He is capable of making me his queen, for the sake of the truth."

"Your truth is a lie," said the Mouse who, as yet, had had no chance of speaking. "I can make the soup, and I shall now do so."

v

How the soup was made

"I have not travelled," said the third Mouse. "I stayed in my own country, which is the right thing to do. Nobody need travel, everything can be got just as good here. I stayed. I have not taken lessons from supernatural beings, or eaten myself into knowledge, or conversed with owls. What I have comes from my own meditations. Kindly put the kettle on, full of water—to the brim—light the fire. Let it burn till the water boils. It must boil over. Now throw in the peg. Will the King be pleased to plunge his tail into the boiling water and stir it round? The longer he stirs, the stronger will the soup become. It costs nothing: there is no need for any flavouring—only stirring."

"Can no one else do this?" asked the Mouse King.

"No," said the Mouse; "the virtue resides in the King's tail alone." The water boiled up, and the Mouse King took his place close by—it was almost dangerous. He stuck out his tail, as mice do in a dairy when they skim the cream off a pan and lick their tails afterwards. But he only just stuck his tail into the hot steam and immediately jumped down.

"Of course, you are my Queen," he said. "We will reserve the soup till our golden wedding. My poorer subjects will then have something to enjoy in prospect—in a long prospect."

So the wedding took place. But many of the mice, when they got home, said: "It's all very well to call it soup from a sausage-peg, but really it was soup from a mouse's tail." A point here and there in the stories, they considered, was well made, but the whole might well have been different. "Now *I* should have told it in this way. . . ."

That was criticism, and criticism is always very clever—afterwards.

The story went all over the world, and people's opinions on it were divided, but the story itself remained. And this is the right result in affairs great and small, even in soup from a sausage-peg. Only you mustn't expect to be thanked for it.

Something

"I will become something," said the eldest of five brothers. "I mean to be of some use in the world; let it be ever so humble a position, so long as what I produce is good, that's something. I'll make bricks: they are things people can't do without. Then I shall have done something."

"But something not nearly big enough," said the second brother. "What you'll do is as good as nothing: it's mere manual work, it can be done with a machine. No! Better be a bricklayer, that's something. That's what I'll be, it's a craft: you enter into a corporation, you become a citizen, you have your guild-banner, and your own special inn. Why, if things go right, I can employ labourers and be called Master, and my wife Mistress. That's something."

"It's nothing at all," said the third. "It's not within the classes, and there are lots of classes in a town, above the masters. You may be a respectable man, but even as a master you're only what is called 'Lower Class'. No, no. I know something better than that. I shall be an architect, and go in for the artistic side, the thinking side, and get up to the higher levels in the realm of the mind. Of course, I shall have to begin at the bottom. Yes, I don't mind putting it into plain language—I shall have to begin as a builder's boy, and wear a cap—though I'm accustomed to a silk hat—and run about and fetch beer and brandy for the ordinary journeymen, and they will say 'thou' to me, which is annoying, but I shall pretend to myself that it is all a masquerade, and these are the liberties that belong to it. To-morrow, I mean, when I've got to being a journeyman, I shall go my own way, and the rest of them won't concern me. I shall go to the college, and learn to draw and be called an architect. That's something, nay, that's a great deal. I may become 'Your Excellency' and 'well-born'—may have a tail to my name as well as a title in front—and build and build like the rest of them

281

before me: that's always something to reckon on. The whole thing is something."

"Something I don't care a rap about," said the fourth. "I won't sail in the wake, I won't be a copy of someone else; I shall be a genius, and become better than all the lot of you. I shall create a new style, and frame the conception of a building that shall be in accord with the climate and materials of the country, with our nationality, with the evolution of this age of ours; yes, and pile an extra story on by my own genius."

"But suppose the climate and the materials are no good?" said the fifth. "That'll be a bad job: it will affect the whole. Besides, nationality may easily become so diluted that it becomes an affectation; and the evolution of the age may make you run off the rails, as often happens in youth. No, I see none of you will really attain to being something, whatever you may think. However, do as you please, I won't be like you. I shall take up a detached position. I shall criticize what you produce. There's always something wrong in everything, and I shall pick it out and discuss it: that's something."

And so he did, and people said of that fifth brother: "There's something to him, he's a good head of his own. But he doesn't do anything!" Which of itself made him something.

Well now, that's only a bit of a story, and yet it never will come to an end so long as the world stands.

But, did nothing more happen to these five brothers? That wouldn't have been something. You must go on listening, for there is a whole tale to come.

The eldest brother, who took to brick-making, found that out of every brick when it was finished there rolled a little coin—only a copper, to be sure, but a great many little copper coins when they are put together turn into a bright dollar, and whenever you knock on the door with that, at the baker's, the butcher's, the tailor's, or all of them together, the door flies open and you get what you want. So you see that was what the bricks gave him. Some of them, to be sure, fell to bits or broke in the middle, but a use was found for them too.

Up on the dyke old mother Margaret, the poor woman, wanted very much to build herself a little house, and she was given all the broken bricks, and some whole ones into the bargain; for the eldest brother had a good heart, even though in practice he only used it to make bricks. The poor woman built her house herself. It was very little, and the only window was put in crooked. The door was much too low, and the thatched roof might have been much better. But there was shelter and dwelling there, and a wide view from it over the sea, which when it was high broke against the dyke. The salt spray spurted all over the house. It was still standing when the man who had made the bricks of it was dead and gone.

The second brother—ah, he could lay bricks after another fashion, and he was trained up to it. When his labourer's time was up, he buckled his knapsack and struck up the prentice's song

I travel can whilst I am young

and the rest of it, and so he did. In the town, when he came back and became a master, he built house after house, a whole street of them. And when they were up, and looked well, and made an ornament for the town, why, the houses built him a little house, for his very own. But how could the houses build? Well, you may ask them and they won't say anything, but the people will answer and tell you: "Why, certainly the street built his house for him." It was small, and it had a clay floor, but when he and his bride danced over it, the floor grew bright and polished, and out of every brick in the wall there burst a blossom, and that was every bit as good as an expensive paper. It was a pretty little house, and they were a happy couple. The guild-flag fluttered outside it, and the prentice boys and the men shouted "Hurrah!" That was something. And then he died, and that too was something.

Next came the architect, the third brother, who had begun as a carpenter's prentice, worn a cap and run errands in the town, and now from the college had risen to be Director of Buildings, "illustrious" and well-born. Indeed, if the houses in the street had built a house for the brother who was a master bricklayer, the street itself was named after this brother, and the prettiest house in the street was his. That was something, and he was something—yes, and with a long title before his name and after it. His children were called gentry, and when he died his widow was a widow of Position. That's something, and his name stood permanently at the corner of the street, and was in people's mouths, being the name of the street, and I say that is something.

Then came the genius, the fourth brother, who meant to hit on something new, something original, with an extra story on top. But it broke down with him, and he tumbled down and broke his neck. Still, he had a beautiful funeral with guild banners and a band and flowers on the posters and in the street, right across the pavement: and there were three funeral orations spoken over him, every one of them longer than the one before it, and that would have pleased him, for he enjoyed being talked about. There was a monument, too, put upon his grave; only one story to it, but still that's always something.

So now he was dead like the three other brothers; but the last, the one who criticized, outlived them all, which was very proper, for in that way he got the last word, and it was of great importance to him to have the last word. He was the one with the good head to him, people said, and now his hour struck too, and he died and arrived at the gate of heaven. People always come there in pairs, and here stood he with another soul who also wanted to enter in: and who should it be but old mother Margaret of the house on the dyke!

"No doubt it is for the sake of the contrast that I and this poor creature are made to come here together," said the critic. "Well, and who are you, my good woman? Are you by way of coming in here too?" he asked.

The old woman curtsied as well as she knew how, for she thought it was St. Peter himself who was speaking. "I'm a poor old body, without any belongings, Old Margaret, from the house on the dyke."

"Well, and what did you do or produce down there?"

"Really, I didn't do nothing at all in the world, nothing as can open the door for me here. It 'ud be a real mercy if I could get leave to come inside of the door."

"And in what sort of way did you leave that world?" he asked—just in order to be saying something, for it bored him to stand there waiting.

"How did I leave it? Well, I'm sure I don't know. Very sick and poorly I was in the last few years, and really I hadn't the strength to creep out of my bed and go into the frost and cold outside. It's a hard winter—but I've won through it now. For a couple of days it was dead still, but bitter cold, as your reverence knows well

284

enough. The ice was along the shore and as far out as eye could see. All the people in the town were gone out on the ice, there was what they call skating and dancing. I believe there was a big band and refreshments out there. I could hear it indoors where I lay in my poor little room, and it had got towards evening time: and the moon was risen though twasn't yet full, and from my bed I could look from the window right out over the shore: and there, right in the corner betwixt the sky and the sea, there came a strange white cloud. I lay and looked at it, and I looked at the black spot in the middle of it, and it grew bigger and bigger, and then I knew what that meant. I'm old and weatherwise: though it's not often one sees that sign, I knew it, and it gave me a turn. Twice afore in my lifetime I've seen that same thing, and I knew there'd be a terrible tempest with a spring tide, as would come right over those poor people out there that was drinking and dancing and making merry.

Young and old, the whole town was out there, and who was to warn 'em if nobody that was there saw and knowed what I did? I was that frightened that I got more strength than I'd had in a long time. Out of my bed I got and over to the window, I couldn't manage no further. However, I got the window open, and I could see the people running and jumping out there on the ice, and all the gay flags, and hear the boys shouting out 'Hurrah!' and the girls and the lads singing, all as merry as could be, and still that white cloud with the black bag in it climbed up higher and higher. I screamed out as loud as I could, but nobody heard me, I was too far away. Very soon the tempest would break loose and the ice go to pieces, and everybody that was on it go down through it, and no one to save 'em! Hear me they could not, and get out to them I could not: how could I manage to get 'em to shore? Just then our good God put it in my mind to set fire to my bed and let the house burn down, sooner than all them people should die in that dreadful way. I got a light and I see the red flames—yes, and I managed to get outside the door; but there I lay, I couldn't do no more. The fire come after me out of the window, and up over the roof. Then they saw it from out there, and all of 'em ran as hard as they could to help me, the poor old body they thought was burning to death inside. There wasn't one but what ran. I heard 'em coming, and I heard besides how all at once there came a rushing in the air. I heard it thundering like great guns fired off, and the spring tide heaved up the ice and it broke in two. But they got to the dyke where the sparks was flying all about me. I got 'em every one into safety. But I couldn't get over the cold and the fright, and so I came up here to the gate of heaven. They say that's opened for poor bodies like me, and now I haven't got my house on the dyke no more, though to be sure that don't give me the right to get in here."

At that moment the gate of heaven opened, and the angel led the old woman in. She let fall a straw outside, one of the straws that had been in her bed, the bed she had set on fire to save all those people, and it had turned into pure gold, a sort of gold that grew and twined itself into the loveliest tendrils.

"Look, that is what the poor woman has brought," said the angel. "What are you bringing? Yes, I know. You have produced nothing, not even made a brick: if you could only go back again and bring back at least so much as that! It wouldn't have been much of a one if you had made it. Still, if made with a good intent, it would always have been something. But you cannot go back, and I can do nothing for you."

Then the poor soul, the woman from the house on the dyke, pleaded for him: "It was his brother who made and gave me all the bricks and bits I built my poor little house with. That was a great thing for a poor body like me. Now can't all them bits and pieces count as one brick for him? That 'ud be an act of mercy, and he wants one now, and this is the place of mercy."

"Your brother, the one whom you called the least of you," said the angel, "he whose calling with all its honesty seemed lowest of all to you, he is now giving you his heavenly mite. You shall not be turned away, you shall be permitted to stand out here and think over your life on earth, and try somehow to raise it up. But in you shall not come till by some act of good you have achieved something."

"I could have expressed that better," said the critic, but he did not say it aloud, and that was something to begin with.

The Old Oak Tree's Last Dream

A Christmas Tale

There stood in the wood, high up on the slope, by the open shore, a good old Oak tree that was just exactly three hundred and sixty-five years old; that long time was for the tree no more than the same number of days would be for us human beings. We are awake in the daytime and sleep at night, and then it is that we have our dreams; but with the tree it is different. The tree is awake for three of the seasons, and it is only towards winter that it gets its sleep. Winter is its sleeping-time, its night, after the long day that we call Spring, Summer and Autumn.

For many a warm summer day had the Day-fly danced about the tree's top; it had lived and hovered about and enjoyed itself, and when for an instant the little creature rested itself, in quiet happiness, on one of the big green oak leaves, the tree would always say: "Poor little thing, a single day is the whole of your life! How short that is! It is very sad."

"Sad!" the Day-fly would answer. "What do you mean by that? Everything is bright and warm and lovely as it can be, and I am very happy."

"But think, only one day and it is all over."

"Over?" said the Day-fly. "What's over? Are you 'over', too?"

"No, I shall live for perhaps thousands of your days, and my day lasts for three whole seasons. That means a time so long that you can't reckon it up."

"No, I can't, for I don't understand you. You have thousands of my days, perhaps, but I have thousands of moments to be glad and happy in. Will all the beauty of the world come to an end when you die?"

"Ah, no!" said the tree. "It will certainly last longer, infinitely longer than I can imagine."

"Why, then, we both have the same amount, only we reckon it differently."

And the Day-fly danced and played in the air and rejoiced in its delicate fine-wrought wings with their silk and velvet, and in the warm air that was spiced with the scent of the clover fields and the wild roses in the hedge, of elder and honeysuckle, not to speak of woodruff and cowslips and wild mint. So strong was the perfume that the Day-fly thought it must have made him a little drunk. Long and lovely was the day, full of happiness, and the little fly always felt comfortably tired of all the pleasure. His wings wouldn't carry him any longer, and quite gently he settled down on a soft swaying blade of grass, nodded his head after his own fashion, and fell happily to sleep; and the sleep was death.

"Poor little Day-fly," said the Oak, "that really was a short life!"

And every summer day the same dance went on again. There was the same question and answer and the same sleeping away to death. It repeated itself through whole generations of Day-flies, and they were all equally gay and happy. The Oak stood there awake through the morning of spring, the noon of summer, and the evening of autumn, and now its hour of sleep, its night, was at hand: winter was coming.

Already the great winds were singing: "Good night! Good night! Here falls a leaf! There falls a leaf! We are plucking, plucking! Look out for your sleep! We are singing you to sleep, rustling you to sleep, but it's good for the old branches, eh? They creak with the pure pleasure of it. Sleep well, sleep well! This is your three hundred and sixty-fifth night: you're really only a yearling now. Sleep well. The clouds will drop snow, and there'll be a whole blanket of it, a snug coverlet about your feet. Sleep well, and pleasant dreams to you!"

And the Oak stood stripped of all his leaves, ready to go to bed for the whole winter long and to dream many a dream: and his dreams, like ours, were always of something he had experienced.

Once he too had been little; yes, an acorn had been his cradle. Now, according to our counting, he was in his fourth century. He was the largest and most vigorous tree in the wood: his crown soared high over all the other trees and was seen far out at sea—a landmark for ships: little thought he how many eyes there were that looked only for him. High up in his green crown the wood-pigeons built, and the cuckoo called there, and in autumn, when his leaves shone like plates of beaten copper, the migrant birds came and rested there before they flew away over the sea: but now it was winter, and the tree stood leafless. It was plain to be seen how bent and gnarled his branches spread. Crows and jackdaws came and sat there by turns and talked about the hard times that were setting in and how difficult it was to get food in winter.

It was just the holy Christmas time when the tree had his most beautiful dream: and that is what we are to hear.

The tree had a clear perception that it was a holiday time. He seemed to hear all the church bells of the countryside ringing: and besides it was mild and warm as on a beautiful day. He spread out his mighty crown all fresh and green. The sunbeams played between leaf and branch, the air was full of the scent of plants and bushes: spangled butterflies played hide-and-seek, and the Day-flies danced as if everything were only arranged for them to dance and enjoy themselves. All that the tree had lived through and seen round him in all the years passed by as in one great pageant. He saw knights and ladies of the olden time ride through the wood with plumed hats and hawk on hand. The hunting-horn sounded and the hounds bayed. He saw the enemy's troops, with bright weapons and gay clothing, with spear and halberd, pitch their tents and strike them; the watch fires blazed up and there was singing and sleeping under the tree's spreading branches. He saw lovers meet in the moonlight in quiet happiness and cut their names, or the first letters of them, on his grey-green bark. Once—years ago, it was—lutes and Aeolian harps had been hung up on the boughs of the Oak by merry prentices off on their journeys: now again they hung there, and rang out once more to delight him. The wood-pigeons cooed as if they wanted to express all that the tree felt, and the cuckoo cuckooed to tell how many a summer day he was to live.

Then it seemed as if a new current of life was thrilling through the tree, down into his tiniest root, up into his topmost twig, and out into all his leaves. The tree felt that he was stretching himself. He was conscious in his roots how even down in the earth below there was life and warmth: conscious that his strength was increasing, that he was growing higher and higher. Up rose his trunk, there was no pause: more and more he grew—his crown waxed fuller, spread out, spread upward—and as the tree grew his vigour grew too—his exhilarating desire to reach even higher, right up to the bright warm sun.

Already he had grown far up above the clouds which sailed away below him like dark skeins of migrant birds or great white flights of swans. And every one of his leaves could see, as if it had eyes. The stars became visible in the daylight, all large and bright; each of them shone like a pair of eyes, so kind, so clear, they reminded him of eyes he had known, loving eyes, eyes of children, of lovers, when they met beneath the tree.

A pleasant sight it was and a joyful, and yet with all the joy he felt a longing, a yearning. If only all the other trees of the wood down below, all the bushes, the weeds, the flowers, could rise along with him and feel and drink in all this light and gladness! The mighty Oak in the midst of his dream of glory was yet not completely happy unless he had them all with him, small and great; and this feeling penetrated through every branch and leaf as deeply and as strongly as in a human breast.

The tree moved his crown as if seeking something he could not find. He looked downward, and then—then there came to him a scent of woodruff, and upon that, stronger still, a scent of honeysuckle and violet: he thought he could hear the cuckoo call and answer itself. Yes, through the clouds the green top of the wood was peeping up. The tree saw beneath him the other trees growing and rising like himself: bushes and weeds shot high into the air—some tore themselves loose, root and all, and flew up more quickly. Swiftest of all was the birch; like a white flash of lightning its slender trunk flickered upward, its branches waving like green pennants and flags. The whole growth of the wood, down to the brown-plumaged reeds, was springing together, and the birds kept it company and sang, and in the grass, which flew and floated wide like a long green silken thread, sat the grasshopper playing on his shinbone with his wing: cockchafers boomed and bees hummed, every bird sang full-throated, everything was music and gladness right up into the heaven.

"But the little red flower by the waterside, that should be here too," said the Oak, "and the blue cuckoo-flower and the little daisy" —for the Oak would have them all together with him.

"We are here! We are here!" Voices rang and sang in answer. "But the pretty woodruff of last summer—and the year before there was a bed of lilies of the valley—and the wild apple tree, how pretty it was! And all the beauty of the wood for years past, many years— had it but lived and lasted till now, it could have been with me too."

"We are with you," rang the voices from yet higher up; it seemed as if they had flown on before.

"No, but this is too beautiful to be believed!" the old Oak cried joyfully. "I have them all together, big and small! Not one is forgotten! How can such happiness be possible or thinkable?" "In God's heaven it is possible and thinkable," rang the voices.

Then the tree, which was still growing, felt that his roots were tearing themselves from the earth.

"Now this is best of all," said he. "Now no bond holds me. I can soar up to the brightest of all in light and brightness, and I have all my dear ones with me, great and small—all together! All!"

That was the dream of the Oak tree: and while he dreamt, there passed a mighty storm far over land and sea on the holy eve of Christmas. The sea rolled heavy billows against the beach, the tree creaked, cracked, was torn up by the roots. Just as it was dreaming that its roots were loosening themselves, it fell. Its three hundred and sixty-five years were now as the single day of the Day-fly.

On Christmas morning, when the sun rose, the storm had laid itself to rest. All the church bells were chiming for the holy day, and from every chimney, even the least, on the cottager's roof, the smoke rose blue, as from the altar at the Druid's feast—the smoke of the thank-offering. Calmer and calmer grew the sea, and on a great ship that stood off the land and had bravely fought out the hard weather of last night, every flag was being run up, in gay Christmas fashion.

"The tree is gone, the old Oak that was our landmark!" said the sailormen. "It's fallen in last night's storm! Who'll find us such another? Why, nobody!"

That was the funeral sermon that the tree got—(short it was, but well meant) as it lay stretched on the carpet of snow on the shore—and far over it rang the sound of a hymn from the ship—a song of the joy of Christmas and of the redemption of man's soul by Christ, and of the life everlasting.

> *Unto the clouds, O flock of God*
> *Your voices raise. Hallelujah!*
> *So all mankind contenting*
> *This joy hath no repenting.*
> *Hallelujah!*

So ran the old hymn, and everyone on the ship out there was up-lifted after his own fashion by it, and by the prayer, just as the old tree had risen upward in its last and fairest dream on Christmas Eve.

The Racers

A prize—in fact, two prizes—were offered, a large and a small one, for the greatest speed attained, not in a single race, but for running during the whole year.

"I got the first prize," said the Hare. "Justice is sure to be done if one's own family and good friends are the judges; but that the Snail should have got the second prize I consider almost a personal insult."

"No", insisted the Gatepost, who had been a witness of the award, "account must also be taken of hard work and good intentions. That was what several respectable persons said, and I took the same view. The Snail, it is true, took half a year to get over the doorstep, but he fractured his thigh in his hurry, and that was in his favour. He has lived wholly and solely for this race, and he ran with his house on his back. All this is most creditable to him, and therefore he got the second prize."

"I might well have been considered too," said the Swallow. "No one, I believe, showed himself swifter in flight and in turning than I did; and then where haven't I been? Far! Far! Far!"

"Yes, that's just your misfortune," said the Gatepost. "You gad about too much. You're always off out of the country the moment the frost begins here. You have no love for your native land; you can't be considered."

"But if I was to lie out in the marsh the whole winter," said the Swallow, "if I was to sleep the whole time, should I be considered then?"

"Well, get a certificate from the Marshwoman that you slept half the time in your own country, and you will be."

"I did really deserve the first prize, not the second," said the Snail. "I know for a fact that the Hare ran purely out of cowardice, whenever he thought there was danger in the offing. I, on the other hand, made my race the task of my life, and have become a cripple in the service. If anyone ought to have the first prize, it is I: but I don't make a fuss about it, I'd scorn to do so," with which he spat.

"I can affirm in the plainest manner that each prize—or at least my vote for it—was given with honest intention," said the old Boundary-post in the wood, who was a member of the deciding body of judges. "I always proceed with method, consideration, and calculation. Seven times I have enjoyed the privilege of taking part in the award, but never before to-day have I managed to get my view accepted: at every prize-giving I have started with a definite principle. I have always gone through the alphabet from the beginning for the first prize and from the end for the second, and will you now be good enough to observe that reckoning from the beginning the eighth letter from A is H—there we have the Hare, so I voted for the Hare for the first prize—and the eighth letter from the end (I don't reckon the modified A, it's an ugly sound, and ugly things I always pass over) is S. I therefore voted for the Snail for the second premium. On the next occasion I will be the first and R the second. There must be order in everything; one must have something to hold fast to."

"I should really have voted for myself had I not been one of the awarders," said the Donkey, who was also on the committee. "Account ought to be taken, not only of the rate of speed in progressing, but of what other qualities the candidate may possess; for instance, what weight he can pull. For my part, however, I should not have raised the point on this occasion—nor again the cleverness of the Hare in his flight—his trick of suddenly leaping to one side to lead people on a wrong track away from his hiding-place: no, there is yet another quality to which many pay attention and which, in fact, deserves not to be neglected. It is what is called the Beautiful. To this I paid heed in this case, and looked at the beautiful, well-grown ears of the Hare—it is a pleasure to see how long they are. I really thought I was looking at myself when I was little, and so I voted for him."

"Buzz," said the Fly, "no—I don't want to talk, I merely want to say a word. I know this, that I have overrun more than one Hare. The other day I broke the hind legs of a young one. I was seated on the locomotive at the head of a train. I often do: it's the best position for observing one's own pace. A young Hare was running in front, not guessing that I was there. At last he was obliged to turn aside—but the engine broke his hind legs, for I was sitting on it. There lay the Hare; I went rushing on. That, I imagine, is beating him? But I don't press for the prize."

"It does seem to me," thought the Wild Rose (but didn't say it; it isn't her nature to speak out, though it would have been a good thing if she had), "it does seem to me that the Sunbeam ought to have had the first prize and the second too. It flies in an instant all that immense way from the Sun down to us, and comes with such a power in it that all Nature wakens up at it. It has such beauty that all we roses blush and give out sweetness. But the supreme authorities, the judges, don't seem to have noticed it at all. If I were the Sunbeam I should give every one of them a sunstroke—but that would only make them mad, and they're perfectly mad as it is. I shan't say anything," thought the Wild Rose. "Let's have peace in the forest: it's very pleasant to bloom and smell sweet and refresh everyone, and to live in story and song. The Sunbeam will last us all out."

"What is the first prize?" asked the Lob-worm, who had over-slept himself, and only now came up.

"A free pass to a cabbage garden," said the Donkey. "It was I who proposed the prize. The Hare was bound to win it, and therefore I, as a thoughtful and practical member, took into careful consideration the best interests of the person who was to have the prize. The Hare is now provided for. The Snail has the privilege of sitting on the stone wall and licking up moss and sunshine, and also is appointed one of the principal judges for the next award for speed. It is a very good thing to have an expert as a member of what mankind call a committee. I must say I hope great things from the future, now that we have made such an excellent begin-ning."

The Girl who Trod on the Loaf

I'm sure you have heard about the girl who trod on the loaf so as not to dirty her shoes, and what a dreadful thing happened to her for it. The story has been written, and printed too.

She was a poor child, but proud and haughty; there was a bad drop in her, as the saying is. When she was quite a little girl she took a pleasure in catching flies and pulling off their wings and turning them into creeping things. She would take cockchafers and beetles and stick each of them on a pin and put a green leaf or a little bit of paper to their feet; and the wretched creature caught at it and turned it round and round, trying to get off the pin.

"Now the cockchafer's reading," said little Inger. "Look how he's turning the page!"

And as she grew up she became rather worse than better; but she was pretty, and that was her misfortune, for otherwise she would have been handled very differently to what she was.

"That head of yours wants a sharp snub," said her own mother. "Often enough, when you were a baby, you trampled on my apron; I'm afraid when you grow older you'll often come to trample on my heart."

And so she did indeed.

She went into the country to take service with people of quality, and they treated her as if she had been their own child, and dressed her as such, and she was good to look at, and her pride grew. When she had been there a year her mistress said to her: "You ought for once to go and see your parents, Inger, dear."

So she went, but only to show herself off; they must see how fine she had become. But when she got to the side road, and saw girls and young lads gossiping by the street gutter, and just then her own mother sat down on a stone to rest, with a bundle of sticks she had picked up in the wood, Inger turned back. She was ashamed that she who was dressed out so fine should have such a ragged creature, that picked up sticks, for a mother. She didn't in the least repent of turning back, she was only angry.

Another half-year went by.

"You really ought to go home one day and see your old parents, Inger, dear," said her mistress. "Here's a large wheaten loaf for you; you can take it to them, they will be glad to see you."

Inger put on her best finery and her new shoes, and she held up her skirts and walked most carefully so as to keep neat and clean about the feet—and there was nothing to scold her about in that—but when she came to a place where the path went over marshy ground, and there was water and mud over a long piece of the way, she threw the bread down into the mud to step on it and get across dryshod. But as she stood with one foot on the loaf and lifted the other, the loaf sank down with her deeper and deeper, and she disappeared wholly, and nothing was to be seen but a black bubbling pool.

That's the story.

Where did she go to? Why, she went down to the Marshwoman who brews. The Marshwoman is aunt to the Elf girls—they are well enough known, there are ballads about them and they have had their pictures taken—but about the Marshwoman people only know that when the meadows steam in summer time it is because the Marshwoman is brewing. It was down into her brewery that Inger sank, and that's not a place you can stand for long. The dustbin is a brilliant drawing-room compared with the Marshwoman's brewery. Every vat stinks enough to make you faint away, and the vats stand thick together, and if there is anywhere a tiny opening between them where you could squeeze through, you can't, because of all the damp toads and fat snakes that cluster together there. Down there sank little Inger. All that horrible live mess was so icy cold that she shuddered through all her limbs and stiffened with it more and more. The loaf stuck fast to her and drew her as an amber button draws a bit of straw.

The Marshwoman was at home, and that day the brewery was being visited by the Devil and his great-grandmother; and she is an ancient and very venomous lady who is never idle. She never goes out without taking her work with her, and she had it with her now. She sewed biting-leather for people's shoes, and they could never be at rest. She embroidered lies and knitted up thoughtless words that had fallen on the ground—all to make mischief and sow trouble. Ah, that old grandmother! She could sew and broider and knit with a vengeance!

She caught sight of Inger and put up her spy-glass to her eye and looked her over again. "That's a girl with something to her," said she. "I must beg her of you for a souvenir of my visit here. She might make a very proper decoration for my great-grandson's front hall."

And she got her: and so it was that little Inger went to Hell. People don't always go there straight off. They may get round by a side way if they have quality.

That front hall was infinitude. You turned giddy with looking before you, and giddy with looking behind you: and there stood a host of the despised, waiting for the door of mercy to be opened; and long might they wait.

Huge fat crawling spiders spun webs of a thousand years about their feet, and these threads cut like thumbscrews and held like chains of copper, and besides that, there was an eternal unrest in every soul, an anguishing unrest. The miser who stood there had forgotten the key of his money box—he knew it was there in the lock. Oh, it would be too much to reckon up all the sorts of torments and pains that were felt there.

Inger felt it horribly, standing as a statue there: she was as it were pinned to the loaf by her foot.

"This comes of trying to keep one's feet clean," said she to herself. "Look how they glare at me!" Yes, they were all looking at her. Their evil desires shone out of their eyes and spoke without sound from their twisted mouths; they were awful to look upon.

"It must be a pleasure to look at me," thought little Inger. "I have a pretty face and nice clothes." And she turned her eyes about —her neck was too stiff to turn. Oh, dear, how muddy she had got in the Marshwoman's brew-house! She had not thought of that. Her clothes were coated over with one great clot of slime. A snake had hung itself in her hair and trailed down her neck, and out of every fold in her dress a toad peeped out and croaked like an asthmatic poodle. It was very uncomfortable. "But everyone else down here looks just as horrible." She comforted herself with that.

Worst of all for her was the dreadful hunger she suffered.

Couldn't she manage to stoop and break a bit off the loaf she stood upon? No, her back was perfectly stiff, her arms and hands were stiff, her whole body was like a stone pillar. She could only turn her eyes in her head, turn them right round so that they looked out backwards, and that was a horrid sight. Then came the flies; they crawled to and fro over her eyes. She winked her eyes, but the flies did not fly off, they couldn't, the wings had been pulled off them, they were become creeping things. That was a torture, and the hunger besides—till at last she felt as if her inside had eaten itself up, and she became perfectly empty—excruciatingly empty. "If this goes on much longer, I shan't be able to bear it," said she. But she had to bear it, and it went on.

Then upon her head fell a burning tear. It trickled over her face and bosom, right down to the loaf. Yet another fell: many fell. Who was weeping for little Inger? Why, had she not up there on earth a mother? Tears of grief, such as a mother sheds for her child, always reach it; but they do not set it free, they burn, they make the torment worse. And then, that intolerable hunger, and the being unable to get at the bread she trod on with her foot! At last she had the feeling that everything within her must have eaten itself up, and she was like a thin hollow pipe that drew every sound into itself. She heard plainly everything up there on earth that concerned her, and all she heard was hard and unkind. True, her mother wept sore and sadly, but, besides, she said: "Pride goes before a fall. That was your misfortune, Inger. How you have brought sorrow on your mother!"

Her mother and everyone else up there knew about her sin, how she had trodden on the loaf and had sunk down and disappeared. The cowherd had told of it; he had seen it himself from the hillside.

"How have you brought sorrow on your mother, Inger," said her mother. "Aye. I thought it would be so."

"I wish I had never been born," was Inger's thought at that. "It would have been far better for me. It's no good now, my mother whimpering."

She heard how the gentlefolk, the kind people who had been like father and mother to her, talked about her. "She was a wicked child," they said. "She did not respect God's gifts, but trod them under foot: the gate of mercy will be slow to open to her."

"Well, they ought to have brought me up better," thought Inger.

"Rubbed the corners off me, if I had any." She heard how a whole ballad had been published about her. "The proud girl who stood on the loaf to keep her shoes clean." And it was sung all over the country.

"To think that one should have to bear all that for such a thing, and suffer so much for it," thought Inger. "The rest of them ought to be punished for what they've done. There'd be a nice lot of them to punish. Ugh, how I do suffer!"

And her heart became even more hardened, harder even than herself. "Down here one's not likely to get much better in this company; and I don't want to be better. Look how they glare."

And her heart was angry and savage against all mankind. "They've got something to talk about up there, anyhow. Oh, how I do suffer!"

And she heard them telling her story to children, and how the children called her wicked Inger, she was so horrid, they said, so nasty, she deserved to be punished properly.

There were always hard words about her in the children's mouths. Yet, one day, when anguish and hunger were gnawing deep in her hollow shell, and she heard her name mentioned and her story told to an innocent child, a little girl, she was aware that this little one burst into tears at the story of the proud Inger that loved her finery.

"But won't she ever come up again?" the little girl asked, and the answer was: "No, she'll never come up again."

"But if she begs pardon and never does it again?"

"But she won't beg pardon," they said.

"I do wish she would," said the little girl; and she was quite inconsolable. "I'd give my doll's house if only she might come up. It is so dreadful for poor Inger."

And these words came straight into Inger's heart, and seemed as if they did her good. It was the first time that anybody had said "Poor Inger" and not added a word about her wrongdoing. Here was a little innocent child that prayed and wept for her, and she felt so strange that she would fain have wept herself; but weep she could not, and that too was a torment.

As the years went by up there, there was no change down below. She heard voices from above less often, there was less talk about her. Then one day she was aware of a sigh: "Inger! Inger! What sorrow you have brought me! I said you would." It was her mother dying.

From time to time she heard her name mentioned by her old masters, and the kindest word was when the mistress said: "Shall I ever see you again, Inger, I wonder? One does not know whither one may go."

But Inger knew well enough that her kindly mistress could never come to that place where she was.

Again a length of time passed by, slow and bitter.

Then Inger heard her name spoken again, and saw above her as it were two bright stars shining. They were two gentle eyes that were closing on earth. So many years had rolled by since the time when the little girl had cried for poor Inger and could not be comforted, that that child was become an old woman, whom God was now calling to Himself; and just at that hour when the thoughts of a whole life were rising before her, she remembered too how as a little child she had cried bitterly at hearing the story of Inger. That moment and that impression stood in living light before the old woman at her death-hour, and she broke out, quite aloud: "Lord, my God, have not I, like Inger, often trampled on Thy blessed gifts, and thought nothing of them? Have not I too often borne about pride in my heart? But in Thy mercy Thou hast not let me sink down, but hast held me up: loose not Thine hold in my last hour."

And the old eyes closed, and the eyes of the soul opened to that which is hidden: and since Inger was so vividly present to her last thoughts, she beheld her, saw to what a depth she had been dragged down; and at the sight the saintly soul burst into tears. She stood, a child, in the kingdom of heaven and wept for poor Inger. The tears and the prayers rang like an echo down into the hollow, empty shell that shut in the imprisoned tortured soul—and it was overwhelmed by all that undreamt of love that came from above. An Angel of God was weeping for her! How had that been vouchsafed to her? The tortured soul gathered up as it were in its thought every deed it had wrought in its earth life, and shook with weeping such as had never come to Inger there. She was filled full with sorrow for herself; she thought that never for her could the gate of mercy be opened; and as, in deepest contrition, she acknowledged it, in that instant a ray shone down into the heart of the abyss. The ray came with a force stronger than the sunbeam that thaws the snow-man which the boys have raised in the yard; and then, far more swiftly than the snowflake that falls on a child's warm mouth melts and drops, the stiffened shape of Inger dissolved in vapour—and a little bird shot with the zig-zag of a lightning flash up into the world of men. But it was fearful, and shy of all around it; it was shamefaced in its own sight and in the sight of all living things, and in all haste it sought shelter in a dark hole that it found in a ruined wall. Here it sat crouching down and quivering over all its body. No sound of voice could it utter, for it had none; long it sat there before it could look about quietly and perceive all the beauty that was outside. Beauty indeed there was; the air was fresh and mild, the moon shone clear, the trees and bushes sent forth fragrance, and it was so comfortable where it sat—its kirtle of feathers so clean and delicate. Ah, how all created things stood forth, born in love and beauty! All the thoughts that stirred within the bird's breast would have sung themselves forth, but the bird had no power for that; it would fain have sung like the cuckoo and the nightingale in spring. Yet God, who hears even the soundless praise of the worm, was aware of the song of praise here, which rose in chords of thanksgiving, as the psalm rang in the heart of David before it was clothed in words and music.

For days and weeks these voiceless songs grew and swelled; burst forth they must at the first flap of the wing towards a deed of good; and that must be achieved.

Now came round the holy feast of Christmas. The farmer set up a pole close by the wall, and tied on it an unthreshed sheaf of oats, that the birds of heaven too might have a merry Christmas and a cheerful meal at this the Saviour's own season.

The sun rose on Christmas morning and shone on the oat-sheaf, and all the twittering birds flew about the dinner-pole; and from the wall too there sounded a "twit-twit". The swelling thoughts were turned into sound, and the faint twitter was a whole hymn of joy. The thought of a good deed was awakened, and the bird flew out of its shelter. In heaven they knew well enough what bird that was.

The winter took fast hold. The waters were frozen thick: birds and wood-beasts had a hard time for food. The little bird flew off to the high road, and there in the wake of the sledges it sought and found every here and there a grain; at the baiting-places it would find a few crumbs of bread. It would eat only one of these itself, and call to all the other hungry sparrows that here they could find food. It flew to the towns and spied round about, and wherever a kindly hand had strewn bread by the window for the birds, it would eat but a single crumb, and give all else to the others.

In the course of the winter the bird had gathered and given away so many breadcrumbs that, weighed together, they made up as much as the whole loaf that little Inger had trodden on so as not to dirty her shoes. And when the last crumb had been found and given away, the grey wings of the bird whitened and spread out.

"There's a tern flying away over the lake!" said the children who saw the white bird. Now it dipped down into the lake, now it rose into the bright sunshine which shone so that it was not possible to see what became of it. They said that it flew straight into the sun.

Anne Lisbeth

Anne Lisbeth was like milk and blood, young and merry, and fair to see; her teeth gleamed white, her eyes were bright, her foot was light in the dance; and her mind was lighter yet, and what came of it? Why, the ugly whelp!—*he* was no beauty. He was put out with the ditcher's wife, and Anne Lisbeth went to the Count's mansion, and there she sat in a lovely room, clad in silks and velvets. Not a breeze durst blow on her, no one durst say her a hard word; it might be bad for her, and she dared not run the risk, for she was nursing the Count's boy, fine as a prince, fair as an angel. How she loved that child! As for her own, why, it had a roof over it, the ditcher's roof. No pot boiled over there, but the mouth might, and mostly there was no one at home: the boy might cry, but what the eye don't see the heart don't grieve. He cried himself to sleep, and when you are asleep you don't feel hunger or thirst. Sleep is an excellent invention.

Years went on—time goes and weeds grow, as the saying is—and Anne Lisbeth's boy shot up, though they said he was stunted in his growth. But he had quite grown into the household there, they had been paid for it; Anne Lisbeth was wholly rid of him. She was a town lady now; she had a cosy home of it there, and a hat on her head when she went out; but she never went to the ditcher's house, it was such a way off from the town: and, besides, she had nothing to do there. The boy was theirs, and they said he could eat his food. But he must do something for it, and so he looked after Mads Jensen's red cow; he could herd it and help himself a bit.

The watchdog at the hall drying ground sits in the sunshine on the top of his kennel very proud, and barks at everyone that goes by; when it rains he creeps inside and lies there dry and snug. Anne Lisbeth's boy sat on the dyke in the sunshine and whittled a tether-peg; spring came, and he knew of three strawberry plants in blossom; they would have berries right enough, that was the happiest thought he had, but no berries came. He sat there in the rain and mist and got wet to the skin, and then the keen wind dried his jacket on him. When he went to the farm he was hit and pushed about; he was nasty and ugly, the girls and lads said, but he was used to that—never loved.

How did Anne Lisbeth's boy get on? How should he get on? That was his lot; never loved.

From the land he was sent to sea on a rotten craft and sat at the helm while the skipper drank. Dirty and ugly, nipped with cold and miserable, you would say he had never once had enough to eat, and no more he had.

It was late in the year, raw, wet, blowing weather. The wind cut cold through the thickest of clothes, and worse at sea, and there under one sail went a rotten craft with only two men on board—or only one and a half, you might say—the skipper and his boy. Dark it had been all day, and now it grew blacker; it was a biting cold.

The skipper took a dram to warm his inside. The bottle was got out and the glass too; the top was whole, but the foot broken off, and instead of it it had a bit of wood cut to fit and painted blue, to stand on. One dram did good, two would do more, thought the skipper. The boy sat at the tiller and held on to it with his hard tarry hands. Ugly he was, with tousled hair, stubby and shrivelled he was; the ditcher's boy; but in the church register he stood as Anne Lisbeth's.

The wind cut on in his own way, the boat in hers. The sail filled, the wind took hold, they flew along. All around was raw and wet; but something more was to come. Stop! What was that that struck, that broke, that caught on the boat? It whirled round! Was there a cloud-burst? Was it a heavy sea? The boy at the tiller screamed aloud: "Name of Jesus!" The boat had struck on a great rock in the sea-bottom, and sank like an old shoe in a street gutter. Sank with man and mouse, as they say; and mouse, no doubt, there was, but only a man and a half, the skipper and the ditcher's boy. No- body saw it but the gulls and the fish down below, and even they didn't see it properly, for they shot away in a fright when the water burst into the boat and it sank. Hardly a fathom under water it lay. Out of sight were the two of them; out of sight, out of mind. Only the glass with the blue block for a foot didn't sink, the bit of wood held it up. The glass floated off, to be broken and washed up on the beach—where and when? Yes, there was nothing more for it to do, it had served its time and been loved: not so had Anne Lisbeth's boy. But in the kingdom of heaven no soul will ever again have to say: "Never loved."

Anne Lisbeth had lived in the market town for many a year now. She was called Ma'am—and how high she carried herself when she talked of old memories of the days in the Count's family, when she drove in a carriage and could chat with countesses and baronesses! That sweet child of hers, the Count's boy, was the prettiest angel, the lovingest soul. He had been so fond of her and she of him. They used to kiss each other and pat each other on the cheek: he was her joy, he was half her life. He had grown up now, fourteen years old he was, clever and handsome; she hadn't seen him since she carried him about in her arms; not for many years had she been to the great house; it was quite a journey to get there.

'I must go across once," said Anne Lisbeth. "I must go to my treasure, my sweet boy. I'm sure he longs for me, thinks of me, and loves me just as when he used to cling with his angel arms about my neck and say, 'An-lis'. It was like the music of a violin. Yes, I must get over there and see him again."

So, driving in the cattle cart and walking, she got to the Count's mansion. It was stately and brilliant as it had always been, with the garden in front just as before, but the people of the house were all strangers, and not one of them knew anything about Anne Lisbeth, or how important she had been there once. Ah, but the Countess would tell them all about that, and her boy too. How she yearned to see him!

And now there she was: she had some time to wait, and waiting-time is long. Before the gentle-folk went into dinner she was called in to the Countess and very kindly spoken to. She was to see her sweet boy after dinner, and then she was called in again.

How big he had grown, how tall and slim! But the lovely eyes, he had them still, and the angel mouth. He looked at her, but he said never a word. For certain he did not know her: he turned and was going away again, but she caught his hand and pressed it to her lips. "All right! That'll do!" he said, and with that he went out of the room—he, the centre of her affections, he whom she had loved and still loved best of all, he who was all her pride in this world.

Anne Lisbeth went out of the great house, along the open high road, and how depressed she was! He had been so distant with her and had no thought nor word for her: he whom she had carried night and day once on a time—whom she always carried in her heart.

A big black raven flew down on to the road in front of her and croaked and croaked again. "Get away," said she, "horrid unlucky bird that you are."

She had to pass by the ditcher's house: and there was the man's wife standing in the door, and so they had a talk together.

"You're well in yourself," said the ditcher's wife, "you're big and stout. Not much wrong with you."

"To be sure!" said Anne Lisbeth.

"The boat and them's lost," said the ditcher's wife. "Skipper Lars and the boy are drowned, both of them. That's the end of it for them: all the same, I had hoped the boy might have helped me to turn a penny some time. He won't cost you no more now, Anne Lisbeth."

"Drowned! Are they really?" said Anne Lisbeth: and no more was said about that. Anne Lisbeth was very much depressed because her boy-count had not cared to talk to her, to her who loved him and had taken that long journey to get here—it had cost money, too. The satisfaction she had got was little enough, but she wouldn't say a word of that here, she wouldn't ease her mind by talking of it to the ditcher's wife; she might think that Anne wasn't thought so much of now at the Count's. Just then the raven croaked again, flying over her.

"That black horror!" said Anne Lisbeth. "He'll give me a fright before to-day's over, I'm sure."

She had brought some coffee berries and chicory with her; it would be a kindness to the ditcher's wife to give her them to make a cup of coffee with, and she herself would take a cup too. The ditcher's wife went out to boil the coffee, and Anne Lisbeth sat down on a chair, and there she fell asleep.

She dreamt about someone she had never dreamt of before. It was odd enough; she dreamt about her own child, who had starved and squalled in this very house and been left to shift for himself, and now lay in the deep sea, God knew where. She dreamt she was sitting where she now sat, and that the ditcher's wife was outside making coffee—she could smell the berries roasting—and in the doorway there stood one who was beautiful—as beautiful every bit as the Count's boy; and the little one said: "The world is passing away! Hold fast to me, for you *are* my mother. You have an angel in the kingdom of heaven. Hold fast to me."

So he caught her, but there came such a crash—it was the world falling to pieces—and the angel rose upwards, and held her fast by the sleeve, so tight, thought she, that she was lifted up from the earth. But something hung heavy on her legs and pulled at her back; it seemed as if a hundred women were clinging to her, and they cried: "If you're to be saved, we will too. Hang on, hang on!" And they did hang on, all of them. It was too much. Ritsch, ratsch! The sleeve tore, and Anne Lisbeth had a frightful fall—so that she woke with it, just on the point of tumbling off the chair she sat on. Her head was so confused that she couldn't remember in the least what she had been dreaming—only that it was something unpleasant.

The coffee was drunk, and they had a talk, and then Anne Lisbeth set out for the nearest town, where she was to meet the carrier and drive with him all that evening and night to her home. But when she found the carrier, he said that they could not start before the afternoon of next day; so she reckoned up what it would cost her to stay, thought over the distance, and decided that if she went along the shore and not by the high road it would be almost eight miles less. It was fine weather and full moon too. So she would walk; she would be at home next day.

The sun had set, and the evening bells were still ringing. No, it was not the bells, it was Peter Oxe's frogs croaking in the pools: and now they stopped, and everything was still: not a bird could be heard, they were all at rest, and the owl was not home yet. Soundless were wood and shore; as she walked on she heard her own footsteps on the sand: there was not a ripple in the sea, soundless was everything in the deep waters; dumb everything beneath them, alike the quick and the dead.

Anne Lisbeth walked on, thinking of nothing, as people say. She was far away from her thoughts, but the thoughts were not away from her; they are never away from us, they only lie in a slumber; both the thoughts that have been quickened and have laid themselves to sleep, and those that have not yet stirred. But sooner or later they come out, they can stir in our heart, stir in our head, or fall down over us.

"A good deed hath its fruit of blessing," so it is written, and "in sin is death", so is it also written. Much there is that stands written, much that is said; man knows it not, remembers it not; so was it with Anne Lisbeth. But it may rise up before you; it may come forth!

All vices, all virtues lie in our heart, in yours, in mine. They lie there like tiny invisible seeds. Then there comes from without a ray of sun, or the touch of an evil hand. You turn the corner, to right or left—aye, that may bring it about—and the little seed quivers and swells thereat, and bursts and pours its juices into all your blood, and behold you started! There are agonizing thoughts—not felt when one is in a slumber, yet stirring; Anne Lisbeth went onward in a slumber, the thoughts were stirring. From Candlemas to Candlemas the heart has a great deal written in its account-book, the whole year's reckoning. Much is forgotten—sin in word and

thought against God, against our neighbour, against our own conscience: we do not think of it, and no more did Anne Lisbeth. She
had done nothing against the law and justice of the land, she was
highly thought of, well behaved, respectable, and she knew it. And
now, as she walked along the shore, what was it that lay there? She
stopped. What was it that had been washed up? An old hat lay
there: where might that have gone overboard? She went nearer and
stood and looked at it. Ah! What was lying there? She was quite
frightened, but there was nothing to be frightened about; it was
seaweed that lay in a tangle over a big oblong stone and looked like
a man's body: only seaweed, but she had had a fright, and as she
walked on, there came into her mind a great deal that she had
heard when she was a child of the belief in the shore-crier, the ghost
of the unburied one that lay washed up on the lonely shore. The
"shorewasher", the dead corpse, did nothing, but its ghost, the
shore-crier, followed the solitary wayfarer, clung fast to him, and
demanded to be borne to the churchyard and buried in Christian
earth. "Hang on, hang on!" it would cry; and as Anne Lisbeth repeated the words to herself, all at once the whole of her dream rose
up before her in living light; how the mothers had clung to her
with the cry: "Hang on, hang on!" How the world had sunk away,
and her sleeve had torn and she had fallen from her child's grasp,
who would have held her up in the hour of doom. Her child—own
child of her body, he whom she never had loved, no, never once
thought of—that child lay now on the sea's floor, and might come
as the shore-crier and scream: "Hang on, hang on, or carry me to
Christian earth." And as she thought of it, fear pricked at her heels
so that she walked faster. The horror came like a cold clammy hand
and laid itself on her heart's core, so that she was like to swoon.
And as she looked out over the sea, all grew thicker and dimmer; a
heavy fog came up and wrapped itself about the bushes and trees,
and they took on strange forms beneath it. She turned to look at
the moon which was behind her, and it was like a pale disk, rayless;
and it seemed as if something had settled down heavily over all her
limbs. "Hang on, hang on!" thought she: and as yet again she
turned to look at the moon, it seemed to her as if its white face
were close behind her, and the mist hung like a cloak from her
shoulders. "Hang on! Carry me to Christian earth." She tried to
listen, and heard a voice, so hollow, so strange—it came not from

the frogs in the pool, and not from raven or crow, for of them she saw none. "Bury me! Bury me!" It sounded quite plain. It *was* the shore-crier of her own child, who lay at the bottom of the sea, and could have no peace till it was carried to the churchyard and its grave dug in Christian earth. Thither would she go, there would dig. She turned in the direction where the church lay, and then, she thought, the load became lighter. It disappeared, and she thought to turn again towards the shortest way home; but then it pressed on her again: "Hang on, hang on!" It sounded like the frog's croak, sounded like a whimpering bird, sounded as clear as could be: "Bury me! Bury me!"

The mist was clammy and cold, her hands and face were clammy and cold with fear; outside it wrapped her about, and within her there opened an infinite space, for thoughts she had never till now had an inkling of.

In a single night of spring here in the North the beech wood may bud forth and stand in its bright young beauty in the morning's sun. In a single instant the seed of guilt in thought, word and deed may lift and unfold itself—sown in our earlier life. It will rise and expand in a single instant when conscience wakes, and God will wake that when we least expect it. Then is there no excuse: the deed stands and bears witness, the thoughts take to themselves words, and the words ring out plain to be heard throughout the world. We are appalled at what we have borne within us and not killed, appalled at what in pride and thoughtlessness we have strewn about us. The heart has in hiding all virtues, but also all vices, and they can thrive even in the barrenest soil.

Anne Lisbeth dimly thought what we have put into words, and she was overwhelmed. She sank to the ground and crept along for a little way. "Bury me! Bury me!" said the voice, and gladly would she have buried herself if the grave were an eternal forgetfulness of all. It was with her the true time of awakening, in horror and anguish. Old beliefs ran hot and cold in her blood, much that she could not bear to speak of came into her mind. Noiselessly, like the shadow of a cloud in the clear moonlight, a phantom passed by her of which she had heard ere now. Close in front of her four snorting horses galloped past—fire gleaming from their eyes and nostrils—and they drew a red-hot coach in which sat the wicked lord who more than a hundred years before had lived hard by. Every night at midnight, it was said, he drove to his manor and turned straight back. He was not pale, as men say the dead are; no, he was black as coal, a coal that has burnt out. He nodded to Anne Lisbeth and beckoned to her. "Hang on, hang on! And then you can ride in the Count's coach again and forget your child."

She hurried on at a quicker pace, and drew near the churchyard; but the black crosses and black ravens were confused together before her eyes. The ravens croaked as the raven had croaked that day; but now she understood what it was they were saying. "I am a raven-mother, I am a raven-mother," every one of them said, and Anne Lisbeth knew that the name fitted her too, and perhaps she would be changed into a black bird like that, and have to go on crying as they cried unless she got the grave dug.

And now she flung herself on the ground and dug a grave in the hard earth with her hands, so that the blood ran from her fingers.

"Bury me! Bury me!" was still the cry, and she dreaded the cock-crow and the first streak of red in the east, for if that came before her task was ended she was lost. And the cock crowed, and there came light in the East—the grave was only half dug. An ice-cold hand passed over her head and face, down to her heart. "Only half a grave!" sighed the voice, and died away, down toward the bottom of the sea—yes, it was the shore-crier. Anne Lisbeth sank to the earth overwhelmed, stricken, without thought or sensation.

It was bright day when she came to herself, and two men were lifting her up. She was not lying in the churchyard, but down on the shore, and there she had dug in front of her a deep hole in the sand, and cut her fingers deep on a broken bit of glass, the sharp splinter of which was stuck in a wooden foot painted blue. Anne Lisbeth was very ill. Her conscience had shuffled the cards of old beliefs, and laid them out and expounded them, to the effect that now she had but half a soul. The other half her child had taken away with him to the bottom of the sea; and she could never fly upward to the mercy of heaven till she got back the other half, which was imprisoned in the deep water. Anne Lisbeth returned to her home, but she was no longer the woman she had been. Her ideas were tangled like a ravelled skein; she had but one thread clear, that she must carry the shore-crier to the churchyard and dig it a grave, and so get back the whole of her soul.

Many a night she was missed from her home, and always found

down on the shore, where she waited for the shore-crier. A whole year passed away thus, and then she disappeared again one night and could not be found; all the next day was spent in fruitless search.

Towards evening, when the sexton entered the church to ring the bell for sundown, he saw Anne Lisbeth lying before the altar. There she had been since early morning. Her strength was well nigh gone, but her eyes were shining and her face had a rosy glow. The last rays of the sun shone in upon her, and gleamed over the altar table and the bright clasps of the Bible which lay there, open at the words of the prophet Joel: "Rend your hearts and not your garments, and turn unto the Lord your God." Merely an accident, people said; so many things are merely accidents.

On the face of Anne Lisbeth, lit up by the sun, peace and pardon were to be read. It was well with her, she said, she had won the fight. That night the shore-crier, her own child, had been with her, and had said: "You dug but half a grave for me; but now for a year and a day you have buried me wholly in your heart, and that is where a mother can best bury her child." And then he had given her back the lost half of her soul, and guided her here into the church.

"Now I am in God's house," she said, "and they that dwell there are happy."

When the sun had quite sunk down, Anne Lisbeth's soul was risen quite up, where there is no more any fear, if the fight has been fought out: and it had been fought out by Anne Lisbeth.

The Beetle

The Emperor's horse was being shod with gold; a golden shoe on each foot. Why was he shod with gold?

He was the most beautiful beast, with slender legs, wise eyes, and a mane that hung over his neck like a veil of silk. He had borne his master through the clouds of powder smoke, and the rain of bullets, had heard the balls whistle and scream; had bitten, kicked, joined in the fight when the enemy pressed hard, had leapt with his Emperor over the fallen horse of the foe in a single bound, had saved his Emperor's crown of red gold, saved his Emperor's life that was more precious than the red gold, and that was why the Emperor's horse was shod with gold, a golden shoe on each foot.

The Dung Beetle crawled out.

"First the big ones, then the little ones," said he, "though it's not the size that tells." With which he stuck out his thin leg. "What do *you* want?" asked the Smith.

"Gold shoes," replied the Beetle.

"You haven't slept it off yet," said the Smith. "Do you mean you want gold shoes too?"

"Gold shoes," said the Beetle. "Aren't I as good as that big beast, who must forsooth be waited on and curry-combed and looked after and have his food and his drink? Don't I belong to the Emperor's stable just as much?"

"Yes, but *why* does the horse have gold shoes?" said the Smith. "Don't you understand that?"

"Understand? I understand that it's a piece of spite against me," said the Beetle. "It's an insult, so I shall go out at once into the wide world."

"Cut along," said the Smith.

"Coarse being!" said the Beetle, and went out. He flew a short way and found himself in a pretty little flower garden, fragrant with roses and lavender.

"Isn't it delightful here?" said one of the little Ladybirds who were flying about, with black spots on their red shield-like wing-cases. "How sweet it smells here, and how pretty everything is!"

"I am accustomed to better surroundings," said the Beetle. "Do you call this pretty? Why, there isn't even a dung-heap in the place." So he went further, into the shadow of a large stock. A Caterpillar was creeping over it.

"What a beautiful place the world is!" said the Caterpillar. "The sun is so warm! Everything so pleasant! And when I fall asleep some time, and die, as they call it, I shall wake up and be a butterfly."

"Only fancy!" said the Beetle. "We're going to fly about as butterflies, are we? I come from the Emperor's stables, but nobody there, not even the Emperor's own horse, who by the way goes about in my cast-off shoes, has such ideas. Get wings? Fly? Very well, I *shall* fly." So off he went. "I don't want to get cross, but I am getting cross all the same."

And he plumped down on a large grass plot, where he lay for a little and then went to sleep.

Mercy, what a deluge came pouring down! The Beetle was woken up by the splashing, and tried to get into the ground at once, but couldn't; he rolled about, he floated on his stomach and on his back—there was no question of flying—he was sure he would never get away from the place alive. He lay where he was and did not stir.

When it cleared a little and the Beetle had blinked the water out of his eyes, he got a glimpse of something white—it was linen being bleached. He went towards it and crept into a fold of the wet stuff; it wasn't quite the same as lying in the warm dung-heap in the stable, but there was nothing better to be had on the spot, so he stayed there a whole day and a whole night, and still it rained. In the morning the Beetle crept out; he was extremely cross with the climate.

On the linen were sitting two frogs, whose bright eyes glistened with pure pleasure. "It's divine weather," said one of them. "How it does freshen one up, and the linen holds the water together beautifully; it gives me a quivering in my hind legs as if I was going to swim."

"I should like to know", said the other, "whether the swallow, who flies so far in all directions, has found on his many journeys abroad a better climate than ours. Such drizzle as we get! Such moistness! One might be lying in a wet ditch! Anyone who does not enjoy it is no true lover of his country."

"You have, I suppose, never been in the Emperor's stable?" asked the Beetle. "There there is both moisture and fragrance. That is what I am accustomed to; that is the climate for me, but it is impossible to take it with one on a journey. Is there no dung-heap in this garden, in which persons of quality like myself could lodge and feel themselves at home?"

But the frogs either did not or would not understand him. "I never ask a question twice," said the Beetle, after he had asked this one three times and got no answer. So he went on a little to where there lay a broken pot; it had no business to lie there, but being there it offered a shelter. Here lived several families of Earwigs, who do not require much accommodation, but like society. The ladies are richly endowed with motherly affection, so here the children of each were the prettiest and cleverest that could be.

"Our son has become engaged," said one mother, "the sweet innocent. His highest aim is to be able to creep one day into a clergyman's ear. He is so deliciously childlike, and his engagement will keep him from running wild; that is a great joy for a mother."

"Our son," said the second mother, "the moment he came out of the egg was at his tricks; he bubbles over with life, he'll run his feelers off. An immense joy for a mother; is it not so, Mr. Beetle?" She knew the visitor by his figure.

"You are both perfectly right," said the Beetle, whereupon he was invited to come indoors—so far as he could get under the broken pot.

"Now you shall see my little Earwig too," said a third and a fourth of the mothers. "They are darling children, and so droll! They are never naughty except when they've got a stomach-ache, but that is a thing one so easily gets at their age." So each of the mothers talked about her young ones, and the young ones talked too, and used the little pincers on their tails to tweak the Beetle's moustache.

"Little rascals, they're always after something," said the mothers, beaming with maternal affection. But it bored the Beetle, so he inquired if it was far from there to the dung-heap.

"Oh, that is right out in the world, on the other side of the ditch," said an Earwig. "So far, I do hope, none of my children will ever go. I should die of it."

"So far, however, I shall try to get," said the Beetle, and set off without taking leave: that is the most correct fashion.

At the ditch he met with several of his own race, all dung-beetles. "Here we live," they said, "and very cosy it is; may we venture to invite you down into the best mud? You must, I am sure, be tired with your journey."

"Indeed I am," said the Beetle. "I have had to lie upon linen in the rain, and cleanliness is very bad for me. I have besides got gout in my wing-joint from standing in a draught under a broken pot. It is really refreshing to get to one's own people at last."

"You come, I presume, from the dung-heap?" the eldest Beetle asked.

"From a more elevated station," said the Beetle. "I come from the Emperor's stable where I was born, shod with gold. I am travelling on a secret mission, about which you must ask me no questions, for I shall not answer them." With this the Beetle climbed down into the rich mud. There sat three young lady beetles, who giggled, for they did not know what to say.

"They are not engaged," said their mother, and they giggled again—this time from embarrassment.

"None fairer have I ever seen in the Emperor's stable," said the travelling Beetle.

"Do not trifle with my daughters. Do not speak to them unless your intentions are serious—but that they are, I am sure, and I give you my blessing."

"Hurrah!" cried all the others, and the Beetle was betrothed: betrothal first, then wedding, there was no reason to delay. The next day passed very happily, the following one was got over some-how; but on the third the Beetle had to think about providing food for a wife, and perhaps little ones.

"I have allowed myself to be taken in," he said. "I must just take them in in return." And so he did. He was gone, gone all day, gone all night, and his wife was left a widow. The other beetles said it was a rank adventurer whom they had adopted into the family.

Now there was his wife on their hands. "Well," said her mother, "she can take her place as a girl again, take her place as my child. Shame on the loathsome wretch who has abandoned her!"

He meanwhile was on a voyage; he had set sail on a cabbage leaf to cross the ditch. Later in the morning two people came by, saw the Beetle, picked him up, turned him over and over, and both— especially one of them, a boy—were very learned about him. "Allah sees the black Beetle in the black stone in the black rock. Isn't there something like that in the Koran?" he asked, and went on to translate the Beetle's name into Latin and discourse about its species and habits. The elder scholar objected to taking the Beetle home,

for, said he, "they had every bit as good specimens". And this, the Beetle thought, was by no means a polite remark, so he flew out of his hand, flew for some distance, for his wings were now dried, and eventually came to the hot-house, where he could with the greatest ease, a window being open, slip in and bury himself in the fresh manure. "This", he said, "is luxury."

He very soon fell asleep, and dreamt that the Emperor's horse had fallen down dead, and that Lord Beetle had received its golden shoes and the promise of two more. This was gratifying, and when the Beetle woke up, he crawled out and looked about him. What splendour was here in the hot-house! Great fan-leaved palms spread out above; the sun made them transparent, and beneath them grew a profusion of green, and flowers shone there, red as fire, yellow as amber, white as new fallen snow.

"What matchless splendour of vegetation," said the Beetle. "How nice it will taste when it goes rotten! This is a capital larder: some of my family are sure to be living here. I will go and explore and see if I can find some suitable company. I *am* proud, and I am proud to be so." So on he went, thinking about his dream and the golden shoes he had won.

Suddenly a hand grasped the Beetle: he was squeezed and tumbled about.

The gardener's little boy and a friend were in the hot-house, had caught sight of the Beetle, and meant to have some fun with him. Wrapped in a vine-leaf, he was thrust down into a hot trouser-pocket. He scrabbled and scrambled, but only got a squeeze from the boy's hand, who was running to the big lake at the end of the garden. Here the Beetle was first put into an old broken wooden shoe that had lost its instep. A peg was stuck in for a mast, and to this the Beetle was tethered with a bit of worsted. So now he was a skipper, and must put out to sea.

It was a very large lake; the Beetle thought it must be an ocean, and was so bewildered that he tumbled over on his back, and waved his legs in the air. The wooden shoe sailed along, for there was a current in the water; but as soon as the vessel got a little too far out, one of the boys turned up his trousers, waded out and brought it back. However, when it began drifting a second time someone called the boys, and sharply too, and they hurried off and left the wooden shoe to its fate. It drifted further and further out from land—steadily onward. It was appalling for the Beetle; he couldn't fly, he was bound fast to the mast.

He now received a visit from a fly.

"Beautiful weather we're having," said the fly. "I can rest here, and sun myself. Very pleasant situation, this, of yours."

"A lot of sense you've got, talking like that. Don't you see I'm tethered up?"

"Well, I'm not," said the fly, and off he went.

"Now I know the world," said the Beetle, "and it's a despicable world. I am the only honourable being in it. First of all, they refuse me gold shoes, next I have to lie out on wet linen, and stand in a draught, and after that they foist a wife on me. I make a bold dash into the world, to see how people are circumstanced, and how I ought to be, and then comes a human whelp, tethers me up, and sets me sailing on the roaring ocean. Meanwhile the Emperor's horse goes about in gold shoes; that's what rankles with me most. But it's no good looking for sympathy in this world. My life-history is interesting in the highest degree; but what's the use of that if nobody knows it? Nor does the world deserve to know it, or it would have given me gold shoes in the Emperor's stable when his horse stuck out its legs and was shod. If I'd had the gold shoes, I should have been a credit to the stable. As it is, the stable has lost me, and the world has lost me, and it's all over."

But all wasn't over yet; a boat with some young girls in it came along.

"There's a wooden shoe sailing about," said one.

"There's a little creature tethered up in it," said the second. They came quite close to the wooden shoe and picked it up, and one of the girls took out a little pair of scissors and clipped the worsted without hurting the Beetle, and when they got to land, she put him down on the grass.

"Crawl off, crawl off! Fly away, fly away, if you can!" she said. "Freedom's a blessing."

And the Beetle flew straight in at the window of a large building, and sank down, tired out, upon the long soft silky mane of the Emperor's own horse, as it stood in its stall—the home of it and of the Beetle. He clung to the mane and sat there for a little and composed himself. "Here am I sitting on the Emperor's own horse—sitting like its rider. Now what's that I was saying? To be sure, now it comes back to me. A good notion, and a sound one—why did the horse have golden shoes given it? That's what the smith asked me, too. Now I've got the rights of it. It was on my account that the horse got gold shoes." And thereupon the Beetle was put in a good humour. "Travelling does clear one's ideas," he said.

The sun shone in upon him very pleasantly. "The world isn't such a bad place after all," said the Beetle, "if only you know how to take it."

So the world was beautiful because the Emperor's horse had been given gold shoes in order that the Beetle might ride on it.

"I shall now go down to the other Beetles and tell them how much has been done for me. I shall tell them of all the comforts I have enjoyed on my foreign tour, and I shall say that I now propose to remain at home until the horse has worn out his gold shoes."

What the Old Man Does is Always Right

I'm going to tell you a story now which I heard when I was little, and every time I have thought of it since it has seemed to me to become nicer; for it is with stories as with many people, they grow nicer and nicer as they grow older, and that is very pleasant.

Of course you have been out in the country. You have seen a good old cottage with a thatched roof; moss and weeds grow on it of themselves. There's a stork's nest on the roof-ridge—you can't do without a stork—the walls are crooked and the windows low; there is in fact only one of them that will open. The oven sticks out like a little fat stomach, and an elder bush hangs down over the fence to where there is a little pond with a duck or ducklings just underneath the gnarled willow tree. Yes, and there's a dog on a chain, too, that barks at everybody.

Just such a cottage there was out in the country, and in it lived two people, a countryman and his wife. Little as they possessed, they could manage to do without one article, to wit a horse, which used to go and graze in the ditch beside the high road. Father used to ride it to the town, the neighbours would borrow it, and he would get one service in exchange for another. Still, it would pay them better to sell the horse, or exchange it for something or another that would be of even more use to them. But what should that be?

"That you'll understand better than me, old man," said his wife. "It's market day in town; just you ride there and get the price of the horse or make some other good bargain. What you do is always right. Off with you to market!"

So she tied his necktie, for that at least she understood better than he did. She tied it with a double bow, which looked very smart, and then she brushed his hat with the flat of her hand, and kissed him on his warm mouth, and then off he rode on the horse that was to be sold or exchanged. Aha! The old man understood his job.

The sun was burning hot, and there were no clouds. The road was dusty; there were so many market people on it in carts or on horseback or on their own legs. It was very hot, and the road had no shade whatever.

Someone came along driving a cow, which was as nice a cow as can be. "I'm sure she'd give beautiful milk," thought the countryman, "it would be a good bargain to get her. Look here! You with the cow," he said. "Shall we have a word together? A horse, I suppose, is worth more than a cow, but that don't matter. I should make more out of the cow, shall we swop?"

"Yes, to be sure," said the man with the cow. So they swopped.

Now that was done, and the countryman might have turned back, for he'd done what he wanted, but as he'd made up his mind to go to market, to market he would go, if only to look at it. So on he went with his cow. He got along briskly, and the cow did too, so very soon he came abreast of a man who was leading a sheep: a fine sheep it was, in good condition and with a good fleece.

"I'd like to own that one," thought the countryman, "it wouldn't want for grazing on our bit of ditch, and in winter one could take it indoors. After all, it 'ud be more the thing for us to keep a sheep than a cow. Shall we swop?"

"Yes." The man who had the sheep was quite willing, so that bargain was made, and the countryman went with his sheep along the high road. By the stile he saw a man with a big goose under his arm.

"That's a heavy chap you've got there," said the countryman. "He's got fat and feathers too; he'd look well tethered out by our pond, and be something for mother to save scraps for. She's often said, 'If only we had a goose', and now she can have one, and she *shall* have it: will you swop? I'll give you the sheep for the goose and thank you too."

"Yes," the other was quite agreeable, so they swopped, and the countryman got the goose. He was by this time close to the town, and the crowd on the road grew and grew. There was a swarm of people and cattle, they were on the road and in the ditch, right up among the turnpike-man's potatoes, where his hen was tethered so that she mightn't run off in her fright and be lost. She was a short-tailed hen who winked with one eye and looked very nice. "Cluck, cluck," said she. What she was thinking about I am unable to say, but the countryman, when he saw her, thought: "She's the prettiest hen I've ever seen, prettier than parson's brood hen. I'd like to own her. A hen can always peck up a grain, she can pretty near keep herself. I think it 'ud be a good bargain if I got her instead of the goose." "Shall we swop?" he asked. "Swop?" said the other. "Yes, that's not a bad idea." So they swopped. The turnpike-man got the goose and the countryman the hen.

A lot of business he had got through on the way to the town, and it was hot, and he was tired. He sorely wanted a dram and a bit of bread, and here he was close to the inn, and there he meant to go in. But the ostler was coming out, and met him in the doorway, carrying a sack chock-full of something. "What have you got there?" asked the countryman.

"Rotten apples," said the man, "a whole sackful, for the pigs."

"There's a terrible lot there! I'd like mother to see that. Last year we hadn't but one apple on the old tree by the peat-house. That apple had to be taken care of, and it lay on the chest of drawers till it burst. 'That's property, anyhow,' says mother; but here she could see property if you like! Ah, I'd like to make her a present of that."

"Well, what'll you give me?" said the man.

"Give? I'll give you my hen for it." So he gave his hen in exchange, took the apples and went into the inn-room, straight up to the bar. His sack of apples he leaned up against the stove, not thinking about what was in it. There were a lot of strangers in the room. Horse-dealers, cattle-dealers, and also two Englishmen—and they're so rich their pockets are bursting with sovereigns, and they make bets, as now you shall hear.

"Ss-ss!" What noise was that by the stove? The apples were beginning to roast.

"What is it?" Why, they found out very quickly—the whole story of the horse that was swopped for a cow, and all the rest, right down to the rotten apples.

"Ah, you'll get a smacking from Mother when you get home!" said the Englishmen. "There'll be the devil of a row."

"I shall get a kiss and no smack," said the countryman. "Mother'll say: 'What the old man does is always right.'"

"Will you bet on it?" said they. "Coined gold by the bushel, a hundred pound to the ton?"

"A bushelful will do," said the countryman. "I can only bet a bushelful of apples, and me and mother on the top; but that's more than strike-measure, that's top measure."

"Done! Done!" said they, and the bet was made.

Out came the landlord's cart. The Englishmen got in, the countryman got in, the rotten apples got in, and off they went, to the countryman's house.

"Good evening, mother!"

"Thanks, father."

"I've made my bargain."

"Yes, you know how to do that," said his wife, giving him a hug, and forgetting all about the sack and the strangers.

"I swopped the horse for a cow."

"Thank God for the milk!" said his wife. "Now we can have milk to cook with, and butter and cheese on the table. That was a splendid swop."

"Yes, but I swopped off the cow for a sheep."

"That's even better, for certain," said his wife, "you're always so thoughtful. We've got just a plenty of grazing for a sheep. Now we can have sheep's milk and sheep-milk cheese, and woollen stockings. Yes, and wool nightgowns too: a cow wouldn't give us that; why, she only drops her hair. You really are a man to take thought."

"But I swopped off the sheep for a goose."

"Then shall we really have a Michaelmas goose this year? Dear old man, you're always thinking of something to please me; it really is a nice idea of yours. The goose can be on a tether and get ever so fat by Michaelmas."

"But I swopped off the goose for a hen," said the husband.

"A hen! That was a good swop," said his wife. "A hen'll lay eggs and hatch 'em out and we shall have chickens, and a regular poultry yard. That's just what I've been longing for with all my heart."

"Yes, but I swopped off the hen for a sack of rotten apples."

"Now I really must give you a kiss!" said his wife. "Thank you, my own dear husband. Now I'll just tell you something. When you'd gone off, I thought about getting you a real nice supper—

omelette and chives. Eggs I'd got, chives I hadn't. So I went across to Schoolmaster's; they'd got some chives there, I know, but the wife's a stingy woman, a pretty dear! I asked her to lend me—'Lend?' says she. 'Nothing whatever grows in our garden, not so much as a rotten apple. I couldn't lend you even that.' Now I can lend her ten—I can lend her a whole sackful. That's a good joke, father." And with that she kissed him right in the middle of the forehead.

"That's what I like," said the Englishmen. "Always going downhill, and always as pleased as ever. That's worth all the money, that is." So they paid over a ton of gold sovereigns to the countryman who got a kiss and not a thrashing.

Yes, it always pays for the wife to see and to tell other people that the old man is wisest and what he does is right.

So there's a story for you. I heard it when I was little, and now you've heard it too, and you know that *what the Old Man does is always right.*

The Snow Man

"I'm crackling proper, it's so lovely cold," said the Snow Man, "the wind does really bite life into one, and how she does blaze, that blazer there!" It was the sun he meant, which was just going down. "She won't get me to wink. I shall hold on to my bits fast enough."

These were two big three-cornered bits of roof-tiles which he had for eyes; his mouth was a piece of an old rake, so he had some teeth.

He had been born amid the cheering of the boys and saluted by the tinkle of bells and cracking of whips from the sledges.

The sun went down and the full moon rose, round and big, bright and beautiful, in the blue sky.

"There we have her again from another direction," said the Snow Man. He thought it was the sun showing itself again. "I've taught her to leave off blazing! Now she's at liberty to hang there and light up, so that I can look at myself. I only wish I knew how people set about moving themselves. I would like to shift myself: if I could do that I'd go down and slide on the ice as I saw the boys do, but I don't know how to run."

"Off! Off!" barked the old watchdog; he was rather hoarse, and so he had been ever since he was a housedog and lay under the stove. "The sun will teach you to run all right. I saw that happen with the one before you last year, and with the one before him. Off! Off! Yes, they're all off."

"I don't understand you, mate," said the Snow Man. "Will that one up there teach me to run?" He meant the moon. "Why, she ran away right enough before, when I looked sharp at her, and now she comes creeping up from another direction."

"You don't know nothing," said the watchdog, "but then you've only just been put together. The one you see now is called the moon, the one that went off was the sun. She'll come up again to-morrow, and she'll teach you to run, down into the moat. We shall soon get a change of weather, I can feel that in my left hind leg, there's a twinge in it. The weather's on the change."

"I don't understand him," said the Snow Man, "but I do get the impression that it's something uncomfortable he's saying. The one that blazed and went down, that he calls the sun, she isn't a friend to me either, that I can feel in myself."

"Off! Off!" barked the watchdog, and turned himself round three times and then laid himself down in his kennel to sleep.

There did, in fact, come a change in the weather. A mist, all thick and damp, spread itself in the early morning far over the whole neighbourhood. At dawn a breeze sprang up: so icy was the wind that the frost took a tight hold, but what a sight was there to see when the sun rose! Every tree and bush was covered with rime-frost; it was like a whole forest of white coral. It was as if every branch was loaded with dazzling white flowers. Those infinitely many fine twigs, which in summer you cannot see for the leaves, now came to view, every single one of them. They formed a lace-work, so brilliantly white that a white radiance seemed to flow out from every bough. The weeping birch waved in the wind; there was life in it, as there is in the trees in summer time. It was match-lessly beautiful, and when the sun came fairly out, why, how it all sparkled, as if it were powdered with diamond dust! And all about over the earth's snow coverlet big diamonds shone out! Or you might fancy that numberless little lights were kindled, whiter than the white snow itself.

"It is incomparably beautiful," said a young girl, who with a young man came out into the garden; they stopped just by the Snow Man and looked at the glistening trees. "A lovelier sight one doesn't get in summer," said she, and her eyes shone.

"And such a chap as that one isn't to be seen either," said the young man, pointing to the Snow Man. "He's prime."

The girl laughed, and nodded to the Snow Man and danced off with her friend, away over the snow, which creaked under their feet as if they were walking on starch.

"Who were those two?" the Snow Man asked the watchdog. "You've been longer on the place than I. Do you know them?"

"That I do," said the watchdog. "She's often patted me, and he's given me a bone. I don't bite them."

"But what's their business here?" the Snow Man inquired.

"Sweet-hear-r-r-ting," said the watchdog. "They're to move into another kennel and gnaw the same bone. Off! Off!"

"Do those two matter as much as you and me?" asked the Snow Man.

"Why, they belong to the quality!" said the watchdog. "On my word, it's precious little people know that were only born yester-day. I see that by you. I have age and experience. I know everybody about this place, and I have known the time when I didn't stand out here in the cold with a chain. Off! Off!"

"The cold is lovely," said the Snow Man. "Tell us, tell us all about it, but you'll please not rattle your chain, for it makes me crackle."

"Off! Off!" barked the watchdog. "I was a puppy. 'Pretty little thing,' they said, when I lay on a velvet chair in there in the house, yes, lay in the lap of the best of the quality, was kissed on the mouth and had my paws wiped with a worked pocket handkerchief. I was called 'Sweetest' and 'Little Toddlekins'. But then I got too big for them, so they gave me to the housekeeper, and I went into the basement. You can see into it from where you stand, you can look down into the room where *I* used to be the quality; for that's what I was with the housekeeper. To be sure, it was a lower situation than upstairs, but it was comfortabler. I wasn't hustled and pulled about by children as I was upstairs. I had just as good food as before and lots more of it. I had my own cushion, and then there was a stove; at this time of the year that's the loveliest thing in the world. I used to creep right in under it so that I was clean out of sight. Oh, that stove! I dream of it still. Off! Off!"

"Is a stove so very beautiful to look at?" asked the Snow Man. "Is it like me?"

"Just the opposite of you. Coal black it is: has a long neck with a tin pipe. It eats fuel, and that makes flames come out of its mouth. You can put yourself by the side of it, close up, right underneath it —there's no end to the comfort of it. You can see it in there, through the window from where you stand."

And the Snow Man looked, and he did see a black polished object with a tin pipe and fire shining out underneath. The Snow Man felt very odd, he had a sensation he couldn't explain to himself; something came over him which he knew nothing of; but all human people know it if they are not Snow men.

"And why did you forsake her?" said the Snow Man. He felt that the stove must be a female. "How could you leave such a position as that?"

"I was obliged to," said the watchdog. "They pushed me out and put me here on a chain. I'd bitten the youngest of the young ones in the leg, because he kicked away the bone I was gnawing, and I thought, 'bone for bone'. But they took it ill, and from that time I've been chained up and lost my clear voice. Listen how hoarse I am. Off! Off! That was the end of it."

The Snow Man listened to him no more; he kept gazing into the housekeeper's basement, into her room, where the stove stood on the four iron legs, and appeared to be about as big as the Snow Man himself.

"A strange crackling there is inside me," he said. "Shall I never get in there? It's an innocent wish, and our innocent wishes may surely be granted. It's my highest, my only desire, and it would be almost unjust were it not appeased. I *must* get in there, I must nestle up against her, even if I have to break the window."

"You'll never get in," said the watchdog. "And if you do get to the stove you'll be off! off!"

"I am as good as off," said the Snow Man. "I'm breaking up, I think."

All day the Snow Man stood and looked in at the window. When dark came, the room became still more attractive: from the stove there shone a light so kindly as neither the moon gives nor yet the sun, nay, such as only a stove can give when there's something in it. When anybody opened the door the glow poured forth, that was its regular habit: it blushed a bright red on the Snow Man's white face, which shone red from his breast upwards.

"I can't stand it," he said. "How pretty she looks when she puts her tongue out!"

The night was very long, but not too long for the Snow Man; he stood absorbed in his own beautiful thoughts; and they froze so that they crackled again.

In the early hours the basement windows were frozen over; they bore the loveliest ice-flowers that any Snow Man could wish for, but they hid the stove. The panes would not thaw: he could not see her. It crackled, it crunched, it was just such frosty weather as might delight a Snow Man, but he was not delighted. He might and ought to have felt exceedingly happy, but he wasn't happy—he had stove-sickness.

"That's a bad complaint for a Snow Man," said the watchdog. "I've suffered from it too, but I got over it. Off! Off! Now the weather's on the change."

There was a change of weather. It turned to a thaw.

The thaw came on, the Snow Man went off. He said nothing, he didn't complain, and that is the plainest of symptoms.

One morning he tumbled down. Something like a broomstick remained sticking up where he had stood. The boys had built him up round it.

"Now I understand about that yearning of his," said the watchdog. "The Snow Man had a stove-shovel in his body! That's what stirred itself in him, but now it's past and over. Off! Off!"

And soon the winter was past and over too.

"Off! Off!" barked the watchdog, but the little girls at the house sang:

> *Bloom, you woodruff fresh and stout!*
> *Hang, you willow, your woolly gloves out!*
> *Come, lark and cuckoo, come and sing.*
> *February's here, we must have spring.*
> *I'll sing with you, Cuckoo, twit! twit!*
> *Come, dear sun, make haste with it.*

And there's nobody thinks about the Snow Man any more.

In the Duck-Yard

Once upon a time a Duck was brought from Portugal— some said from Spain, but it's much the same thing. She was called the Portuguese—she laid eggs, she was killed and cooked; that is her life-story. All the ducklings that crept out of her eggs were called the Portuguese, and that stood for something. At last, of all that breed only one was left in the duck-yard here, a yard to which the hens also had access, and in which the cock paced about with infinite pride.

"He makes me ill with his violent crowing," said the Portuguese, "but he is handsome, there's no denying, though he isn't a drake.

He ought to control himself, but self-control is an art; it betokens a superior education. The little singing birds in the lime-tree in the garden next door have it. How deliciously they sing! There is something very touching in their song. I call it Portugal. If I had one of those little singing birds for my own, I would be a mother to him, loving and kind, it's in my blood, in my Portuguese nature."

Just as she was speaking there did come a little singing bird. He came headlong down from the roof. The cat was after him, but the bird got off with a broken wing and tumbled down into the duck-yard.

"That's just like the cat, that scum of the earth!" said the Portuguese. "I know him of old, ever since I had ducklings myself. To think that such a being should be permitted to live and go about on the roofs! I cannot think that would occur in Portugal." And she was sorry for the little bird, and the other ducks who were not Portuguese were sorry for him too.

"Poor little dear!" they said, coming up one after another. "To be sure, we're not singers ourselves, but we have got a sounding-board or something like it in our insides; we feel it, though we don't talk about it."

"But I will talk about it," said the Portuguese, "and I'll do something for him, for that is one's duty." So she got into the water-trough and splashed in the water so that she nearly drowned the little bird with the drenching he got, but it was well meant. "That's a kind action," said she. "Others can see it and take pattern by it."

"Pip!" said the little bird. One of his wings was broken, and it hurt him to shake it, but he quite understood the splashing was done out of kindness.

"You are exceedingly good, Ma'am," he said, but he didn't ask for any more.

"I never have thought much about my disposition," said the Portuguese, "I only know that I love all my fellow creatures, with the exception of the cat, whom nobody can expect me to like; he ate two of my children. But now do you make yourself at home here; it's easy enough. I myself come from a foreign land, as you can see from my bearing and my plumage. My drake is a native; he has none of my blood in him, but I'm not proud. If anyone here understands you, I can safely say I can do so."

"She's got Portulak in her crop," said a little common duck, who was witty; and the other common ducks thought this joke about Portulak excellent. It sounded so like Portugal, and they nudged one another and said: "Quack! Uncommonly witty she is." And therewith they began to talk to the little bird. "That Portuguese has a gift of speech, to be sure," they said. "We don't go about with big words in our beaks, but we have just as much sympathy as she. If we don't do much for you, we don't make a fuss about it, and that we consider is the civilest way to behave."

"You've got a charming voice," said one of the eldest. "It must be delightful to know that you give pleasure to so many people as you do. To be sure, I don't understand anything whatever about it, and so I hold my tongue, and that I'm sure is better than saying such silly things as a lot of people do say to you."

"Don't tease him," said the Portuguese. "He needs rest and nursing. Little bird, shall I give you another douche?"

"Oh, no! Do let me keep dry," he begged.

"Well, the water-cure is the only thing that does me any good," said the Portuguese. "Recreation too is of some use. Very shortly the neighbouring poultry will be calling. There are two Chinese hens who go about in feather-trousers, and are most cultured. They were imported too, which raises them in my estimation."

Accordingly the hens arrived, and the cock with them; he was on his good behaviour that day, and refrained from any vulgarity.

"You are a real singing bird," he said, "and with your little voice you do all that can be done with a little voice like that; but it wants a bit more of the steam-engine behind it, so that people can hear it's a gentleman speaking."

The two Chinese were ravished with the appearance of the little bird; he was so ruffled up with the douche he had had over him that they thought he was like a Chinese chick. "He's charming," they said, and entered into conversation with him, speaking in whispers and sounding their P's in the most distinguished Chinese manner. "We are of your kin. The ducks, even the Portuguese, belong to the swimming-birds, as you have doubtless observed. They do not even now appreciate us; but how many appreciate us, or care to do so? Not one, even among the hens, albeit we were born to sit on a higher perch than almost any of them. It matters not: we go our quiet way among the rest, whose principles are not ours; yet we look only on the good side, and speak only of the good in them—though it is hard indeed to find it where none exists. With the exception of our two selves and the cock, there is not a soul in the hen-house who is in the least gifted, but they are worthy, and that cannot be said of the inmates of the duck-yard. We warn you, little song-bird, trust not yonder one with the short tail, she is sly. That speckled one with the crooked stripe on her wings—she has a passion for wrangling and never lets anyone else have the last word —yet she is always in the wrong. That fat duck speaks ill of every-one, and that is repellent to our nature; if one cannot speak well of others, let him hold his tongue. The Portuguese is the only one who has the least pretensions to culture, and with whom one can associate, but even she is very passionate and talks too much about Portugal."

"What a lot those two Chinese have got to whisper about!" said some of the ducks. "They bore me; I've never said a word to 'em."

The drake now came up. He took the little bird for a sparrow. "Oh, well! I can't see these differences," he said, "they're much of a muchness. He's just a toy, and if you have 'em you have 'em."

"Never mind what he says," whispered the Portuguese. "He's excellent at his business, and business is the first consideration. But now I'm going to lie down and rest. One owes it to oneself, so as to be nice and fat when one comes to be embalmed with apples and prunes." So she lay down in the sun and winked with one eye. It was very nice lying there, she was very nice, and she went very nicely to sleep. The little bird pecked at his broken wing, and then nestled up to his protectress. The sun shone warm and pleasant, and it was a good place to be in. The neighbour hens went about and scratched; it was really only to look out for food that they had come there. First the two Chinese went off, and then the rest. The witty duck said of the Portuguese that she was fast getting into her second ducklinghood, and the other ducks shrieked with laughter. "Ducklinghood! She really is too funny." And then they repeated the former joke about Portulak—it was so amusing; and then they lay down too.

And there they were for a time, but suddenly someone threw down some mess into the duck-yard, which made a splash, and all the sleeping crew started up and flapped their wings. The Portuguese woke up too, rolled over, and gave the little bird a dreadful squeeze.

"Pip!" he cried. "You did tread hard on me, Ma'am."

"Well, why do you lie in my way?" she said. "You mustn't be so thin-skinned. I've got nerves too, but I never called out Pip."

"Don't be angry," said the little bird, "the Pip slipped out of my beak unawares."

The Portuguese paid no attention, but darted at the mess and made a hearty dinner. When she had finished and lain down again, the little bird came up and, meaning to make himself pleasant, he sang:

> *Tillelit*
> *Of your head and wit*
> *I'll sing a bit*
> *As I flit, flit, flit.*

"I want my after-dinner nap now," she said. "You must learn the ways of the house here. I'm going to sleep."

The little bird was quite taken aback, for he had meant to be very nice. When my lady woke up later on, he was standing in front of her with a little corn he had found. He laid it before her, but she hadn't slept well, and was consequently cross.

"You can just give that to a chicken," said she. "Don't stand there hanging about me."

"But you're angry with me," he said. "What have I done?"

"Done?" said the Portuguese. "The expression is by no means refined, I would have you observe."

"Yesterday it was sunny," said the little bird, "to-day it's dark and grey. I am very unhappy."

"You're out of your reckoning," said the Portuguese. "Why, the day isn't over yet. Don't stand there looking such a nincompoop."

"You're looking quite fierce at me, like the two horrid eyes when I tumbled down here into the yard."

"Impudence!" said the Portuguese. "Do you compare me to the cat, that beast of prey? Not a drop of bad blood have I in my body. I've taken you in hand, and I must teach you how to behave."

With that she bit off the head of the little bird, and there he lay dead.

"What now?" said she. "Couldn't he stand that? Well, then, he wasn't fit for this world. I've been a mother to him, that I know, for I have a heart."

The cock from next door stuck his head into the yard and crowed with steam-engine power.

"You'll be the death of me, crowing like that!" she said. "The whole thing is your fault. Now he's lost his head, and I feel like losing mine."

"Well, there ain't much of him lying there," said the cock.

"You'll please to speak respectfully of him," said the Portuguese. "He had tone, he had the power of song, and superior culture. He was affectionate and gentle, and that's as becoming to animals as it is to so-called humanity."

All the ducks gathered about the little dead singing-bird. Ducks have strong passions, whether of envy or of sympathy, and since there was nothing here to envy, they were sympathetic, and so were the two Chinese hens. "Such a singing bird we shall never find again! He was almost Chinese. And they wept till it made them cluck, and all the hens clucked, but the ducks were reddest in the eyes.

"We have a heart," they said. "Nobody can say we haven't."

"Heart!" said the Portuguese. "Of course we have—almost as much as you would in Portugal."

"Well, let's see about getting something into our tummies," said the Drake. "That's the first consideration. If one of our toys has come to bits, we've plenty left."

Chicken Greta's Family

Chicken Greta was the only person who lived in the handsome new house that had been built for the chickens and ducks at the Manor. It stood where the old mansion of the feudal days had stood, with its tower, its crowstepped gables, its moat and drawbridge. Close by it was a wilderness of trees and bushes. The garden had been there, and had extended down to a large lake which now was but a swamp. Rooks, crows, and jackdaws flew screaming and cawing over the old trees, a swarming multitude of birds. They didn't get any fewer if a shot was fired among them, they only flew the faster. You could hear them even in the hen-house where Chicken Greta sat and the ducklings ran about over her wooden shoes. She knew every hen and duck from the moment it crept out of the egg, and was proud of her hens and ducks, proud too of the handsome house that had been built for them. Clean and neat was her little room: the lady of the house (to whom the hen-house belonged) insisted on that. She often came there with smart genteel visitors, and showed off what she called the Hens' and Ducks' Barracks.

There was a wardrobe and an arm-chair there, and there was a chest of drawers on which stood a brightly polished plate of copper: and on it was engraved the word "Grubbe"; which was no other than the name of the ancient and noble family that had lived here at the Manor house. This copper plate had been found in digging there, and the Parish Clerk had said that it was of no value except as a monument of old times. The Parish Clerk knew a great deal about the place and about old times; he was book-learned, and a great deal of writing was laid up in his table drawer. He had to be sure a deal of information about the old days, and yet the eldest of the crows perhaps knew more, and screamed about it in his own language—however, that was crow-talk, and the Parish Clerk didn't understand that, clever as he might be.

After a hot summer day the marsh would steam with vapour, so that it spread like a great lake out beyond the old trees where the rooks and crows and jackdaws flew about. It had looked like that in the days when Squire Grubbe lived there, and the old Manor with its thick red walls was still standing. The watchdog's chain used to reach right across the gateway. Through the tower you entered the stone-paved passage to the rooms. The windows were narrow and the window-panes small, even in the great hall where the dancing went on. But in the last Grubbe's days there had been no dancing within living memory. All the same, an old kettle-drum still lay there, which had served for the band. Here too stood a richly carved cupboard in which rare bulbs were kept, for Lady Grubbe was fond of gardening and used to nurse trees and plants. Her husband liked better to ride out and shoot wolves and wild boars, and his little daughter Marie always accompanied him. When she was but five years old she sat her horse proudly and stared boldly about her with her great black eyes. She enjoyed slashing at the hounds with her whip; her father would sooner she had slashed at the peasant boys who came to look at the gentry.

The peasant in the mud hut close by the Manor had a son, Sören, of the same age as her little ladyship. He was a good climber, and always had to go up and take birds' nests for her. The birds screamed as loud as they could scream, and one of the biggest gave him a peck just over his eye, so that the blood flowed, and it was thought the eye was gone; but there was no harm done.

Marie Grubbe called him her Sören. This was a great favour, and turned out very lucky for his father, poor John. John once committed some offence and was to be punished; he was to ride the wooden horse. It stood in the court, with four stakes for legs and a single narrow plank for a back. On this John was to ride astride and have some heavy bricks tied to his legs so as not to sit too light. His face was ghastly to see, and Sören cried and implored little Marie; and she gave orders at once that Sören's father was to be taken down: and when they paid no attention to her, she stamped on the pavement and pulled at her father's coat sleeve till it tore. She would have her way, and she got it, and Sören's father was let down.

Lady Grubbe, who was by, stroked her little daughter's hair and looked kindly on her, Marie couldn't think why. She was going to the kennels and not with her mother, who walked over to the garden and down to the lake where water-lilies and water-daisies were in flower, and bulrushes and scented rushes swayed to and fro among the reeds. She gazed at all the luxuriance and freshness of it. "How pleasant it is!" said she. In the garden there stood a tree, rare in those days, which she had planted herself; a copper beech it was called—a kind of blackamoor among the other trees, so dark brown were its leaves. It needed strong sunlight, otherwise its leaves, if it stood always in shadow, would become green like the rest, and it would lose its characteristic. In the tall chestnut trees were numbers of birds' nests, and more in the bushes and the green sward. It seemed as if the birds knew they were in sanctuary, for no one could go popping their guns off here.

Little Marie came that way with Sören. He could climb, as we know, and many an egg and callow young one was brought down. The birds flew about in anxiety and fright; big and little, they all flew. The plover out on the open field, the rooks, the crows, and the jackdaws in the tall trees screamed and screamed again; just such a screaming there was as the tribe keeps up still in these days.

"Why, what are you doing, children?" cried the gentle lady. "That is the devil's work."

Sören stood abashed, and her little ladyship too looked somewhat askance, but then she said—shortly and sulkily: "Father lets me do it."

"Get away, get away!" screamed the big black birds, and off they flew, but they came back next day, for they were at home there.

The quiet gentle lady, however, did not stay at home there long. God called her to Himself; and indeed she was more at home with Him than there at the Manor, and the bells tolled solemnly when her body was taken to the church, and the poor mens' eyes were full of tears, for she had been kind to them.

When she was gone nobody took care of her plants, and the garden fell into neglect.

Herr Grubbe was a hard man, people said, but his daughter, young as she was, could stand up to him. He had to laugh it off, and she got her way. She was twelve years old by this time, and strong-built and well grown. She looked through and through people with her black eyes; she rode her horse like a man and fired off her gun like a practised sportsman.

Great visitors came to these parts, visitors of the highest degree, the young King and his half-brother and companion, Herr Ulrik Frederick Gyldenlöve. They came to shoot wild boars and spend a day at Herr Grubbe's Manor.

Gyldenlöve sat next to Marie Grubbe at table: he seized her by the neck and gave her a kiss, as if he were one of the family, but she gave him a slap in the mouth and said she couldn't abide him, and there was great laughter at this as if it had been the best of jokes. Perhaps, indeed, it was; for five years later, when Marie was full seventeen years old, there came a messenger with a letter. Herr Gyldenlöve asked for the noble maiden's hand. That was something.

"He's the noblest and gallantest lord in the realm," said Herr Grubbe. "He's not one to be turned off."

"I don't care much about him," said Marie Grubbe: all the same, she did not turn away the noblest in the land, who sat next to the King. Silver plate, woollen and linen stuffs were shipped over to Copenhagen. She made the journey by land and took ten days. The trousseau had the wind against it, or else no wind at all, for months passed before it arrived, and by the time it did Lady Gyldenlöve was gone.

"I'd sooner lie on sacking than in his silken bed," said she. "I'd rather trudge barefoot than drive in a coach with him."

Late one evening in November two women came riding into Aarhus town—Gyldenlöve's wife, Marie Grubbe, and her maid. They came from Veile and thither they had come by ship from Copenhagen. They rode up to Herr Grubbe's stone-walled Manor. He was by no means pleased with the visit. She got hard words, but a room to lie in, and her breakfast next day, but no breakfast talk. Her father's wicked temper showed itself in a way she was not wont to hear. She was of no gentle nature, and as one is called, so one answers. She had her answers ready, and spoke with malice and hate of her lawful husband; with him she would not live, she was too decent and honourable for that.

Thus a year went by, and not pleasantly. Ill words were bandied between father and daughter, such as should not be. Ill words bear ill fruit. What would be the end of it?

"We two can't live under one roof," said her father one day. "Move out of here to our old house: but bite your tongue off sooner than let lies get abroad.

So they parted! She and her maid went off to the old house where she had been born and bred, where the quiet godly lady, her mother, lay in the vault at the church. An old cowman lived at the Manor, and that was the whole population of it. Cobwebs hung in the rooms, black and heavy with dust; the garden grew as it lived; hop-vines and bryony wove nets over trees and bushes, hemlock and nettles grew rank and large. The copper beech was overgrown and hidden in shade, and its leaves were as green as those of the other common trees; its beauty was past and gone. Rooks, crows and jackdaws flew in swarming multitudes over the tall chestnut trees; there was a squalling and screaming as if they had important news to tell each other. "Here she was again, the little girl that had had their eggs and young ones stolen." The actual thief who had taken them was climbing a tree without any leaves; he was sitting on a tall mast and getting his fair share of the rope's end when he didn't behave himself.

All this story the Parish Clerk told in our own days; he had gathered it and put it together from books and notes, and along with much else it lay written and kept safe in his table drawer.

"Up and down goes the world," said he. "It's a strange thing to hear tell of." And we will hear tell how it went with Marie Grubbe; but for all that we won't forget Chicken Greta sitting in her smart hen-house in our time. Marie Grubbe sat too in her time, but her temper was not like Chicken Greta's.

Winter went by, spring and summer went by, and the windy autumn came again with its wet cold sea fogs. It was a lonely life and a wearisome life there at the Manor.

Well, Marie Grubbe took her fowling-piece and went out on the heath and shot hares and foxes, and what birds she could hit. Out there she met, more than once, the noble lord, Palle Dyre of Norrebaek. He was out too with his gun and his dogs. He was big and strong, and bragged of it when they talked together. He might have measured his strength with the late Herr Brockenhaus of Egeskov in Funen, of whom men still talked as a strong man. In imitation of him Palle Dyre had hung up at his own gate an iron chain with a hunting horn, and when he came riding home he would grasp the chain and lift himself and his horse from the ground and blow the horn.

339

"Come and see it for yourself, Lady Marie," said he. "There's a fine fresh air at Norrebaek."

When she came to his home is not recorded; but on the chandeliers of Norrebaek church you may read that they were given by Palle Dyre and Marie Grubbe of Norrebaek Manor.

Body and strength had Palle Dyre. He drank like a sponge, he was like a barrel that could never be filled, he snored like a whole sty of pigs; he was red and bloated in the face.

"He's sly and he's a bully," said Lady Palle Dyre, Grubbe's daughter. She quickly tired of living with him, but it grew no better as it went on.

One day the table was spread, and the dinner grew cold. Palle Dyre was out fox-hunting, and his lady was not to be found. Palle Dyre came home towards midnight, Lady Dyre neither at midnight nor at dawn; she had turned her back on Norrebaek and had gone off without a word of farewell.

The weather was grey and damp, and the wind blew cold, and a flock of black screaming birds flew over her; they were not so homeless as she.

First she turned southward, far on the way towards Germany. Solid gold rings set with precious stones she pledged for money, and then she went eastward, and then again turned westward. She had no goal before her, and she was angry with everyone, even with God, so miserable was she in mind; and soon her body too shared her misery, and she could hardly drag one foot after the other.

A plover flew up from its grass-tuft when she stumbled over it, and cried, as they always do: "Stop, thief! Stop, thief!" Never had she stolen her neighbours' goods, but birds' eggs and young birds she had as a little girl had brought to her from tuft and tree, and that came to her mind now.

From where she lay she could see the sandhills by the shore. Fishermen lived there, but she could not get so far, she was too ill. The great white seagulls came flying over her and screaming, as the rooks and crows and jackdaws screamed at her home in the Manor garden. The birds flew quite close to her, and at last she thought they had turned coal black; and then everything was dark before her eyes. When she opened them again she was being lifted and carried; a big tall fellow had picked her up in his arms. She looked

340

straight into his bearded face. He had a scar above his eye, cutting the eyebrow clean into two halves. He carried her, weak as she was, to his ship, where he got harsh words from the skipper for his good deed.

Next day the ship sailed. Marie Grubbe was no longer ashore, she went with it. But she came back? Yes, but when and where?

This too the Parish Clerk was able to tell, and it wasn't a tale he had made up himself. He had the whole extraordinary course of it from a trustworthy old book, a book which we can take down and read for ourselves. Ludwig Holberg, the Danish historian, who wrote so many books worth reading, and also those amusing comedies, from which we learn to know his age and the people who lived in it—he tells in his letters of Marie Grubbe and where and how he met with her. It is worth hearing, but for all that we won't forget Chicken Greta, sitting cheerful and happy in her smart hen-house.

The ship set sail with Marie Grubbe aboard; that was where we left off.

A year went by, and yet more years.

The plague was raging in Copenhagen; it was the year 1711. The Queen of Denmark moved to her German home, the King left his capital, everybody who was able hurried away. The students, even those who were lodged and boarded free, went out of the town. One of them, the last who had stayed at what was called Borch's Collegium, near the Regent's palace, was now setting off. It was two o'clock in the morning; he started with his knapsack, which was fuller of books and manuscript than merely clothes. A wet cold mist hung low over the town; not a soul was to be seen in all the street he was passing through. About him on doors and gateways crosses were drawn; either the sickness was there or the people had died. No more life was to be seen in the broader, winding Flesh-monger street, as that one was called which leads from the Round Tower down to the King's palace. Just then a great ammunition cart came rumbling by. The driver was plying his whip, and the horses were at a gallop. The wagon was full of corpses. The young student held his hand to his face and inhaled a strong spirit which he carried in a sponge in a copper vinaigrette. From a pot-house in one of the alleys came the sound of the shrieked-out song and dismal laughter of people who were drinking out the night and trying to forget that the pestilence was waiting at the door and meant to have them into the wagon with the rest of the dead. The student made for the palace bridge, where a few small craft lay. One was weighing anchor to get away from the beleaguered town.

"If God spares us, and we get a wind, we're bound for Grönsund on Falster," said the skipper; and asked the student who wanted to come with him, what his name was.

"Ludwig Holberg," said the student. The name sounded just like any other, but now we hear in it one of the proudest names of Denmark; at that time he was only a young and unknown student. The ship glided on past the palace. It was not yet full day when she got into open water. Then came a light breeze, the sail filled, and the young student lay down with his face towards the fresh wind and fell asleep; not exactly the wisest thing he could have done.

By the dawn of the third day the ship lay off Falster.

"Do you know anyone here with whom I could lodge cheaply?" Holberg asked the Captain.

"I think you'd do well to go to the ferry-woman at the Borre-hus," said he. "If you want to be very polite, her name's Mother Sören Sörensen Möller, but it may very well be she'll turn nasty if you're too finicky with her. Her husband's doing time for a crime and she works the ferry-boat herself; she's got a fist of her own."

The student took his knapsack and went to the ferry-house. The door was not locked, the latch lifted, and he entered into a room with a tiled floor, where the most important piece of furniture was a bedstead with a large leather coverlet. A white hen, with a brood of chickens, was tethered to the bedstead, and had upset the water-bowl so that the water was running over the floor. There was no-body either there or in the next room, only a cradle with a child in it, whether man or woman it wasn't easy to say. The personage had a big overcoat on and a fur cap and a hood on the head. The boat came ashore.

It was a woman who came walking into the room. She looked quite imposing when she stood up straight. Two proud eyes looked out from under black eyebrows. This was Mother Sören, the ferry-woman. The rooks and crows and jackdaws would scream out a different name, one which we know better.

She had a sullen look, and did not care to talk much, but thus much was said and settled, that the student struck a bargain for his keep for an uncertain time, as long as things were so bad at Copenhagen.

Often there came to the ferry-house, from the market town hard by, one or more worthy citizens. Frands, the Cutler, and Siverts, the Searcher, would come and drink a jug of ale in the ferry-house and have a discussion with the student. He was an able young fellow, who knew his *Practica*, as it was called, well, could read Greek and Latin, and knew about learned matters.

"Well, the less you know, the less it worries you," Mother Sören would say.

"You're hard worked," said Holberg one day when she was bucking the linen in the sharp lye, and then had to chop up wood herself for fuel.

"Let me get through it," she answered.

"Have you always had to drudge and work since you were a child?"

"You can read that for yourself in my fists," said she, and showed him her two hands—small, to be sure, but hard and strong, with the nails bitten close. "You're scholar enough to read."

Towards Christmas the big snowfalls began. The cold got a grip and the wind blew keen as if it had vitriol in it to wash people's faces with. Mother Sören wasn't daunted, she wrapped her great coat about her and pulled the hood down on her head. It got dark in the house early in the afternoon. She piled wood and peat on the fireplace, sat herself down and new-footed her stockings, there was nobody else to do it. Towards evening she talked to the student, more than she usually did; she spoke of her husband.

"He happened to kill a skipper from Dragör by accident, and for that he's got to work in irons on the Holm for three years. He's only a common sailor, so the law must take its course."

"The law's the same for the upper classes too," said Holberg. "Think so?" said Mother Sören, gazing into the fire. Then she began to speak again. "Did you ever hear of Kai Lykke, who had one of his churches pulled down, and when Parson Mads thundered at him from the pulpit he had Herr Mads laid in bolts and irons and brought an action and condemned him to lose his head himself; and it was cut off too. That wasn't an accident, yet Kai Lykke got off scot-free that time."

"Well, he was within his rights according to those days," said Holberg. "We've got past that now."

"You can tell that to the idiots," said Mother Sören, and got up and went into the room where "baby", the little child, lay. She tended it and put it to bed, and then tidied the student's bed. He had the leather coverlet, he felt the cold more than she, and yet he was born in Norway.

New Year's morning was a real bright sunny day. There had been a frost, and there was one still, so strong that the drifted snow lay frozen hard enough to be walked on. The bells in the town were ringing for church, and student Holberg wrapped his woollen cloak about him and set off to the town.

High over the Borrehus flew the rooks, the crows and the jack-daws with scream and squall; you could hardly hear the church bells for them. Mother Sören was out of doors filling a copper kettle with snow to set on the fire and get drinking water; she looked up at the swarm of birds and had thoughts of her own about it.

Student Holberg went to church. Both going and coming he passed Sivert the Searcher's house door. He was asked in to take a cup of hot beer with syrup and ginger. The talk turned on Mother Sören, but the Searcher didn't know much about her; indeed, few did. "She didn't come from Falster," he said. "At one time she must have had some little means; her husband was a common sailor, a hot-tempered man; he had killed a skipper from Dragör. The fellow beats her, but yet she takes his part."

"I wouldn't stand such usage," said the Searcher's wife. "Besides, I come of a better stock; my father was stocking-weaver to the King."

"And for that reason you have a royal official for a husband," said Holberg, making his bow to her and the Searcher.

It was Twelfth Night. Mother Sören lighted a Three-King's candle for Holberg—that is to say, three tallow dips she had made herself. "A light for each man," said Holberg.

"Each man?" said the woman, looking sharply at him.

"Each of the wise men from the East," said Holberg.

"Oh, you mean it that way," said she, and was silent for a long time. But on that Twelfth Night he got to know more than he had known before.

"You're fond of the man you're married to," said Holberg, "but people say that he keeps on ill treating you."

"That don't concern anybody but me," she answered. "The beatings would have done me good when I was young. I suppose I get them now for the wrong I've done. How good he has been to me, I know." And she stood up. "When I was lying ill on the open heath and nobody cared to touch me, except maybe rooks and crows to peck me, he carried me in his arms and got hard words for the game he brought to the ship. I wasn't the kind to lie ill, so I got better. Everyone has his own ways, and Sören has his, but one mustn't judge the horse by the bridle. On the whole, I've lived more happily with him than with the one they called the gallantest and noblest of all the King's subjects. I was married once to Governor Gyldenlöve, the King's half-brother. Then I took Palle Dyre. Six of one and half a dozen of the other. Every man to his taste and I to mine. It's a long story—but now you know all about it." And she left the room.

It was Marie Grubbe! So strange had been the ups and downs of her fortune. She didn't live out many more Twelfth Nights. Holberg has recorded that she died in June, 1716, but he has not recorded, for he did not know it, that when Mother Sören, as she was called, lay dead in the house, a swarm of great black birds flew over the place. They made no sound, they seemed to know that there must be quietness about a burial. As soon as she was laid in the grave the birds were seen no more. But the same evening there was seen in Jutland—near the old Manor house—an immense flock of rooks, crows and jackdaws, shrieking into each other's beaks, as if they had some news to tell; perhaps of the man who when he was little had taken their eggs and their callow young; the peasant's son who was wearing iron garters on the King's Holm, and of the noble maiden, who ended her life as ferry-woman at Grönsund. "Bra, Bra!" they screamed, and the whole tribe of them screamed "Bra, Bra!" when the old Manor house was pulled down. "They scream it out still, now there's nothing to scream about," said the Parish Clerk when he told the story. "The family's died out, the Manor house is pulled down, and, where it used to stand, the smart hen-house stands now with its gilded vanes and old Chicken Greta in it. She's very happy in her pretty dwelling-place; if she hadn't had that, she'd have been in the poor-house."

The pigeons cooed above her, the turkeys gobbled and the ducks quacked all round her.

"Nobody knew her," they said. "Family she has none. It's an act of charity that she's here. She's got no drake-father or hen-mother, and no young ones."

Family she had, for all that. She didn't know it, nor did the Parish Clerk, however much he had got recorded in his table drawer, but one of the old crows knew about it, and told about it. She had heard tell from her mother and her grandmother about Chicken Greta's mother and her grandmother, whom we too know about, from the days when as a child she rode over the drawbridge looking proudly about her, as if the whole world and all the birds' nests in it were hers. We saw her lying on the heath by the sandhills, and last we saw her at the Borrehus. Her grandchild, the last of all the race, was come home again to where the old Manor house had stood, where the wild black birds screamed—only she sat among the tame birds, known of them and knowing them all. Chicken Greta had nothing more to wish for. She was glad to die, and old enough to die.

"A grave, a grave!" shrieked the crows.

Chicken Greta was laid in a good grave; nobody knows it but the old crow—if she isn't dead too.

So now we know the story of the old Manor house, and the old time, and all Chicken Greta's family.

Notes
TimeTable for Home
Sat
9:00 Sleep